PRAISE FOR *A DANGEROUS FRIENDSHIP*

"Robin Merle has written a brave book about ending things and starting things—about the friends we choose and the friends who choose us. Her characters and the choices they make during a sometimes funny and sometimes heart stopping summer escape from New York City will stay with you long after you have read through to the explosive conclusion."

—Diane Cohen Schneider, author of *Andrea Hoffman Goes All In*

"With biting humor and vivid language, Merle masterfully delves into the intoxicating highs and crushing lows of obsessive friendship."

—Jeanne McWilliams Blasberg, author of *Daughter of a Promise*

"*A Dangerous Friendship* is a psychological dreamscape...The reader is left questioning what is real and what is an illusion . . ."

—Jill Di Donato, contributor-at-large for *HuffPost*, and author of *Beautiful Garbage*

". . . a thrilling twist-filled ride. With every chapter, the stakes climb higher, leaving you breathless and eager to know what happens next. And when the final page turns? You'll wish there was more."

—Michelle Renaldo Ferguson, author of *Women Mentoring Women*

A DANGEROUS FRIENDSHIP

A DANGEROUS FRIENDSHIP

A NOVEL

Robin Merle

SHE WRITES PRESS

Published in 2025 by
She Writes Press, an imprint of The Stable Book Group

32 Court Street, Suite 2109
Brooklyn, NY 11201
https://shewritespress.com
Library of Congress Control Number: 2025910776
Print ISBN: 979-8-89636-002-5
E-ISBN: 979-8-89636-003-2

Interior Design by Tabitha Lahr

Printed in the United States of America

All of these voices
Debate in my head
One thinks I'm crazy
And one thinks I'm dead
I am alive when I battle with you
You think you amaze me
I think that it's true

—"Mad Love"
The Pretty Reckless

CHAPTER ONE

I HAD TO LEAVE NEW YORK FOR A WHILE. I was at the end of a series of losses, and I needed someone to talk to me directly: "I like you. That's not nice. You're pretty."

I can't explain to you all the complications that led to this state, but I can tell you they were real enough because I proceeded to do things I'd never done before, and I did them with a woman who was politely referred to as an "interesting person" but not an "appropriate partner." I will also say this, which is the culmination of many dreams, thoughts, and nightmares about what happened and how it could have happened, and which seems obvious after hearing the story of another woman, completely unrelated to me.

This woman lost her husband and her best friend at the same time because they fell in love with each other. She moved to the northern coast of Molokai, Hawaii, where she contracted to take care of someone else's children for three years. Her town was not far from Kalaupapa, the leper colony. In all this time, she did not buy new clothes or have her hair professionally cut or apply any cosmetics to her face. Her thirty-third birthday came down to two cousins, one friend, and the friend who told me this story and knew her before her exile.

He said, "She was obsessed with a house she was building on the cliffs of the island where nobody builds because it's too damned lonely and too likely to be wiped out. The whole idea of paradise was lost on her."

That's when it became obvious to me: Once love is taken away from you, taken out of your hands, or beaten into a fearful thing, you lose the capacity to salvage yourself in the presence of another person. You lose the nuts and bolts of yourself and allow yourself to play without a safety net. Because it doesn't matter. It doesn't matter what happens to you, all the time you're traveling to the edge for an experience that will make you ask, "Does it matter yet? Have I gone far enough to save myself yet?"

I did not travel to Molokai or Istanbul or Minsk for my danger; I did not have that kind of money, nor the courage to stray very far from my home in New York City. At least my confusion seemed familiar there. The apartment I lived in alone on Twenty-Third Street had my scent and my sense of organization, though fractured in places. My sweaters, for instance, were in boxes since the bureau was gone. I also had unexpected phone calls from the man who had been married to me for eight years. And every so often a flyer came in the mail announcing that B. Edward Jones or Mickey B. or Bill Sadler—all Edward—was appearing in a Riverdale production of *King Lear*, admission five dollars. And I wondered when Edward would stop sending me these flyers as if I were still, after so much time, not supposed to notice that the company could not even afford address labels.

We are both twenty-nine now. He came from the town next to my hometown, and we moved to New York together. He fought and struggled the same as I did to feel a purpose in this city. We worked our way together for almost a decade, and when it was clear he was not successful and I could no longer hide the fact, which was his silent request, that I knew he had not gotten what he wanted, he accused me of being in his way, and I accepted the accusation.

Once, when he was looking for a new place to live, he called from an empty apartment in Brooklyn and he said, "The loss. I can't stop thinking about what I'm losing."

His voice echoed in that empty apartment. And he said maybe we should try again in Brooklyn where the apartments were larger. Maybe the problem was the smallness of where we lived.

I couldn't go back. I'd already been made sick by love and worked myself up to writing a will for the life I used to have. I spent many hours and many days sleeping, knowing I was going to have to take a new direction if I wanted to survive and not do so badly next time because selfish as it was, I did not want to feel pain in that density again.

Over time, I became less and less sleepy, and eventually I began taking my trips.

MY TRIPS WERE LOCAL, two- to three-day binges of scaring up the bizarre and becoming a witness to it. Spike, the inappropriate woman I met later, seemed to have been a witness to the bizarre for most of her life—more than a witness. It blew around her as if she were the eye of a hurricane.

The first time I saw her, I was so frightened, I actually shut the door and stepped back.

But I'm getting ahead of the story. Working up to that moment was an effort of barely contained conventional insanity. I found myself at parties I shouldn't have known about. I ended up at a beach party in Chinatown and an absinthe ball in the Meatpacking District. Then there was the time I was walking down Eighth Avenue at three in the morning with a dancer who called himself The Wizard, and I trusted him simply because he was from Ohio.

He spotted a lighted doorway and said, "Hey, let's go in here!" and we walked into a room off the back of a greasy restaurant and surprised two Latino boys pumping iron.

They were stripped to their boxer shorts, their biceps large and brown as coconuts. The Wizard slapped them five, and the boys, smiling and laughing, insisted on showing us their home-made chest expansion gizmo, explaining it all in Spanish. I didn't speak the language, but I understood that to them it made sense for us to be there, which stunned me.

Soon after, I ended up at a salon for people who wanted to receive messages from spirits from the other world. It was one o'clock in the afternoon, and what struck me as subtly strange (the rest was obvious) was that the acquaintance who took me there didn't seem surprised to find we were the only guests.

In the apartment, a snack table had been set up next to a large suburban-style kitchen gleaming with appliances, and a sign informed us donations would be happily accepted for herb tea and boxed cookies. After a few perfunctory bits of conversation and a donation of fifty cents, which I dropped into the cup for one Oreo, we shuffled into the living room and took our seats. I had the uncomfortable feeling of being back in high school and sneaking into the den of my girlfriend's parents' house to talk about twittery, sexy things in the middle of the afternoon.

The apartment was painted lavender from floor to ceiling, as if it had been dipped in a tub of paint, leaving no room for the walls to breathe or for the light to pick up any flaws. The effect was like having too much cream, and I felt suddenly nauseated. I had a vision of us all smothering to death in a sea of bland, creamy lavender and a voice, probably mine, screaming, "Why didn't I guess!"

The hostess, whose eyelids were also painted lavender, inquired if we were ready to make a presentation about our essence and our substance. We had been asked to bring objects that best represented each. Of course, I thought this was incredibly silly. I also thought that maybe something would come of it.

That is the lost seeker's thought—against all odds, maybe something here will tell me something I need to know.

I was asked to present first. For my essence, I held out a gold heart on a chain around my neck, a gift of jewelry I'd always been embarrassed about because it was so sweet. And to represent my substance, I held up my bitten fingernails. That should've told them something right there.

I waited. There was no discussion. I became annoyed. I wanted to hear their feedback: "I liked that. I didn't like that. That was good. That was dumb. You've got it backward." All opinions would be considered.

The hostess was stroking an amethyst crystal and smiling to herself. My acquaintance began a deep search in her handbag for where she *thought* she'd put her essence but couldn't find it. I surmised this was supposed to be only a way of introducing ourselves like the campfire circle where you said your name and who you were and nobody challenged you.

My acquaintance slid to the floor opposite the hostess. They crossed their legs in the lotus position so that their ankles kissed their kneecaps and leaned toward each other, murmuring. I let myself out.

I ran to the park. The sprint left me with an ache in my diaphragm, but I wasn't ready to return home yet, and I decided to run three more miles.

Oh no, it wasn't over.

WHEN YOU'RE HALF OFF the moon with your own thoughts, you find the time to dash from one bad story to the next. I ran the three miles, and when I was finished, I saw the man I'd come for.

He was in his sixties and he spoke hesitant, unadorned English, mixing it sometimes with Italian. He was deeply tanned with crinkly silver hairs on his chest, and he wore, as usual, only khaki shorts, his sneakers, and his socks. He sat at the park day after day and spoke to almost everyone, waving from his seat to the runners. A week ago, his picture was posted on the fence. He was Giacomo Salvetti, the man who had inaugurated this path as a running track forty years ago, and the mayor had given him a merit award. I wanted to see if he would tell me why running the same road for forty years had been one of his goals.

"So the mayor dedicated this track to you?" I asked.

Giacomo Salvetti nodded. "Every day at lunch I come from the factory and I run this path. I eat my lunch not like the other men. I eat no meat. I eat vegetables."

"Did the other men run with you?"

"No. I run alone. They did not know about running like they do today. Today"—he made a gesture of incredulity—"everybody runs. Back then, they work all day at the machines, they take coffee breaks, they smoke, they get fat."

"Did they wonder about you?"

He stared at me as if either he didn't understand my words or the thought of being strange had never occurred to him. "I was a runner. I ran the track every day at lunch. I eat only vegetables." He looked away and waved gaily to someone jogging behind me.

"You just finish?" he asked. "How much?"

"Twice around."

He nodded—more accurately, he hung his head to one side and shook it, all the while examining me with his eyes.

"You are thin," he said. "But you have good legs. Come." He motioned to my feet. "I give you a massage. I give all the girls massage."

Ahh, he is playing me for a sucker, I thought. For a person as gorged on lavender and wizards as I was, this represented nothing unusual. I could have said no thanks and kidded him, whether he understood or not, about his desires. Then I could have trotted home, satisfied at maintaining my distance, and eaten a nice dinner.

Instead I lay down on the metal bench and let Giacomo Salvetti slip off my sneakers. He began by working my toes, his fingers as strong as clamps. I let him grope my feet, then my ankles, then my calves, and I wondered how far I would let him go because this was too perverse to give up. He stopped of his own accord and I sat up, blinking a few times to refocus. Giacomo Salvetti was sitting with one hand on the waistband of his khaki shorts and the other draped over the back of the bench. In my dreamy state, I'd almost forgotten the picture that went with the hands; now his tanned shoulders pressed in on me, looking caramelized in the sun.

"One girl . . ." he said. "I massage her feet every time she runs and she brings me dinner on Thursdays. Another girl, she brings me shirts from her father. She comes Fridays. Another girl, she brings me a little money. I look for her at the beginning of the month."

"I see." I was standing away from him now, looking down at his nearly bald head, the silver hairs standing out from the tan as much as the crinkled hairs on his chest. "Well thanks." And I thought, *Were there so many of us that Salvetti could actually exact payment? Was there a school of women—men too—roaming in the afternoons, looking for a hit of something and falling prey to anyone who seemed to offer it, no matter who offered and what "it" was?*

SPIKE GAVE ME A HIT of something, all right.

"If only I had half her power," I wrote in my journal soon after meeting her. "What a lot of ability she has, and confidence and brains, and the careers she's been through! She's all fire and piss and vinegar, then she's generous with praises and gifts—maybe because she's had money. She's 'What the fuck, let's try it!' and I'd die to travel with someone like that, though she's much faster and wilder than me."

I felt like a thirteen-year-old. I hung on to the stories she told me, and I was thoroughly convinced that everything she told me was true. To this day, I do not know what was and what was not the truth. And it did not occur to me that someone could be honest without telling the truth. I became enthralled, almost pulled to her. Spellbound, even in that last month when everything was torn apart faster than I had ever experienced and would ever want to experience again. In the end, I remembered what I had known in the beginning and recorded in that journal I kept during my trips.

"It's tough to say whether Spike is good or evil. Or whether I imagine too much about her. But I have to admit, even without knowing, I want to be with her."

CHAPTER TWO

I MET SPIKE DURING ONE OF MY TRIPS, this time to New Hampshire. I had found in the classifieds a listing for an artists' colony that required only a down payment, no submitted material. Sight unseen, I paid for a week's stay in a bungalow, listing my art as freelance journalism. The colony, it turned out, was led by a widow named Tillie Skokel, who had written a series of romances in the fifties. A wooden sign that said Writing School in big, blue block letters was posted at the entrance to Tillie's eighteen acres, which enclosed a collection of bungalows half sunk in vines and, up the hill, Tillie's own large ancient house.

On my very first morning, before breakfast, I opened the door of my bungalow to walk onto my private porch—and there she was. Spike. There, at least, was her hair, which is what I saw first. A massive reddish curtain, a little stiff from dye, hung over her shoulder and continued hanging down over her arm, then beyond the seat of the chair. I glimpsed a pair of pink-and-gray clammers, a bright yellow shirt, poised cigarette, notebook, the raised eyebrows of her expression, and I inhaled strong perfume.

"*Ihhh!*" I stepped back. "Sorry." And I closed the door.

The odd thing was she never stood up and knocked on her side of the door to explain what she was doing on my porch. And I never went back and opened the door to explain my actions. And later, long after so much happened between us, a boy told me a story that reminded me of that morning.

"About eight months ago," he said, "an arsonist who'd been in the jail at Heugonot escaped. They found him in Leed's Socket sitting on somebody's back porch. Just sitting there. He'd been in prison thirteen years and all he kept saying was that he didn't want to hurt anybody. That's what he wanted to tell everybody. That's why he escaped."

SPIKE WASN'T AT BREAKFAST with the rest of the colonists that day, and in spite of looking for her, I didn't see her again until she reappeared for the lecture. On Tuesday nights, Tillie Skokel gathered her writers at the dining room table in her house and by the light of a tiny, bug-spattered lamp delivered a lecture on romance.

"A romance," she told us, "is a tale based on heroic love and adventure or the supernatural. It is usually involved with mysterious events." Her eyes lowered to the typewritten page of notes she had preserved in a looseleaf notebook. "It always deals with the emotions. Strong emotions," she continued, "can compel a person to take immediate action. Emotions are easily recognizable, though may appear at the same time to produce different effects."

I took a survey of the audience: a housewife from New Jersey, a former English teacher from Maine, a Lebanese restaurant owner in his fifties, Tillie's seventy-eight-year-old sister, Faye, who lived on the premises and cooked us breakfast, Spike, and me.

Tillie turned the page from which she had been reading and began to read from pages she had torn from a magazine.

"This appeared in *The Saturday Evening Post* in 1953. It is the story of a widower who undertakes a strenuous hike into the mountains—to the spot where he married his wife—every year on the anniversary of his wife's death."

She read slowly; we kept our heads bowed and at midpoint in the reading, Tillie stopped and wept. I glanced at Faye, forced to make flapjacks every morning for her sister's writerly guests, but she was cleaning her nails with a Stim-u-dent. Tillie finally calmed down.

She clicked back into the present and finished reading the story, removing her eyeglasses with an air of prissy authority, and asked, "Any comments?"

Spike, I noticed—and I had been watching her surreptitiously throughout the reading, wondering what this mysterious woman was thinking—had let her chin drop onto the table and was supporting her head with the help of the table and her hand. She appeared to want to slump her way out of the room, but suddenly she spoke, the first to unknot the silence we'd all fallen into.

I realize now that it must have taken enormous restraint for her not to rise and bludgeon Tillie Skokel with that looseleaf notebook. And I was astonished when she gently—almost gravely—told Tillie how much she enjoyed the story, particularly the description of the man's walking stick and what it meant to him.

I felt ashamed. I had looked forward to *one* of us lashing out with, "What do you take us for?" and had elected Spike to do it because she looked the part. I wanted to talk to her, explain about the morning, but as soon as the lecture was over, she swept out the door and disappeared into the woods.

On Wednesday mornings, Tillie held writers' conferences in her office by the creek. According to her rules, the conferences were to last exactly ten minutes, though we could have an extra session with her in the afternoon for an additional five dollars. During this time, she reviewed a paragraph submitted to her in advance and gave each writer the same criticism, which we learned after making comparisons: We did not understand point of view.

When it was my turn, and I had obediently plunked down some pages and taken my seat next to her desk, she began by pointing out various photographs of people tacked to the walls of her office.

"You're too young to remember," she said to me in her sing-song voice, recalling the name of the celebrity whose hand she pressed in the picture.

But I did not think youth was the divider. There was something very birdlike about Tillie, in her delicacy, her musical voice, and in the way she flitted from subject to subject.

"Do you have the remaining balance for your bungalow?"

I did.

"I like this last paragraph. Are you poking fun at the president? He is gypping us of our social security."

I nodded.

"Are you married?"

"Not anymore," I told her.

"Who did your taxes previously?"

"He's dead now," I said. "My accountant died. That's the way things happen in the city."

"Oh. That won't do. I think your time is up," she said, shaking her wrist around to look at her watch. Then she gave me a seraphic smile. "Would you like to buy one of my books?" she asked, graciously indicating the pile that had been resting conspicuously between us on the desk. "At a considerably reduced price," she added.

I figured it would make a much better memento than a post-card, so I pulled out ten dollars for *The Duchess and the Dungeon*. Her smile grew brighter.

"I'm sure you'll be married again soon."

I had to pass by Spike's cabin on my way back, and I saw her sitting next to the window, her profile framed, the rest of her hidden from view. The keys of her typewriter, which was also out of sight, sent up a clatter into the hot, humid morning. She looked incredibly serene and I tried to make as little noise as possible since her concentration seemed to extend beyond her window to the garden. I walked softly, but she must've turned to watch me.

Suddenly, I heard her ask, "So how'd you like your morning conference?"

I held still. There was a smirk in her voice, and when I finally looked up, I saw the woman who had bowed to Tillie's indulgences last night ready to burst with impatience and indignation.

"About what I expected," I said.

"I'm writing a letter to the magazine that advertised this as anything other than an outpatient facility. I paid for two weeks at this place. And this cabin costs extra! Tillie's a sweet woman. She may not know any better, but you know what, there have been too many times when I've had to pay for what someone else didn't know."

She was almost breathless, she was talking so fast. "And I'll tell you something else. She gives me the creeps. Sometimes I catch her looking at me as if she's startled to see me here." She mimicked Tillie's eyes flickering behind thick lenses. "Did you ever get the feeling that fate has a sick sense of humor and likes to throw people into the orbit of people they might become?"

"Oh, come on." I laughed and as soon as I did, realized she was deadly serious. Her tone became wincingly formal.

"My aunt"—pronounced *ont*—"told me what she dreaded most about growing old was the possibility that she would become senile and have no control over her behavior. She was sure that she would act out the impulses that had resided since infancy in the deep recesses of her mind—as if a person's compulsion to do all the horrifying things she always wanted to do never, ever went away. She said to me . . ." Spike leaned out her window, twisting her face to look conspiratorial, "'Do you know what your grandmother Cicely did when she grew senile? She liked to get on her knees and scoop her business out of the toilet.'"

Spike widened her eyes at me, then extracted a cigarette from a pack on the table I couldn't see and let the silence build as she lit up. This gave me plenty of time to gaze at her profile dramatically framed, as if by contrivance, by the window. "I worry about taking care of myself when I grow old," she said finally. "I don't envision anyone doing it for me."

"I don't think about it much," I said, and again as soon as it was out of my mouth, I knew it was the wrong thing to say. "Then again," I offered, to take the curse off my passivity, "it's obviously entertaining to think about."

"You're young," she said, as if we were ice ages apart. "I'm only five years away from forty. It makes you think differently."

Of course I wanted to argue "not that differently," but she returned abruptly to her typing, as if all the time she'd been talking to me, she'd been rehearsing what she was trying to put down on the page. I stood there awkwardly outside her window, not knowing if there was more to come and not wanting to leave in case there was. Finally I said, "I discovered a local swimming hole, and I'm going there right after I do a little work. Would you like to come?"

"Sure," she answered, not taking her eyes off the page she was typing. "Just come by when you're ready. I'll be here."

I typed letters in my bungalow until ten. Then I decided I would put together an article on this tiny village of Pentacook, starting with Abbey, a little girl I'd met at the swimming hole, and I'd talk about the village from the point of view (Tillie's influence) of a New Yorker and send it somewhere, maybe to *Yankee*. I wanted to start the article with a piece of dialogue that struck me as a profound example of human communication at its best—that is, it was straightforward and simple, exactly what I'd left the city for.

Abbey, who was ten years old, had walked over to me and asked, "Do you know a girl named Ruth Morlock?"

"No."

"You look like her. Except she's got curly hair."

"I hope she's pretty," I said.

"She is. Except sometimes she's mean." I filed away the story idea and jotted down another about an article on artists' colonies to stay away from. Having made these plans, I felt productive enough to muse about Spike and having her to myself, at least for a while. Already I was anxious, partly from caution, partly from awe. What a way she had of serving herself up.

I didn't want to appear too eager, so I puttered among Tillie's cumbersome mahogany furniture and slipcovered chairs, seeing spinsterhood in all of it, and when I couldn't take the stuffiness anymore, gathered my things and trudged the long road that cut through the woods between my bungalow and Spike's cabin. I was thinking of all the things we might talk about—Tillie and that sister of hers. And, of course, how Spike ended up here—I'd ask her that. I started thinking I might buy a field guide to North American wildflowers so that I could identify the scattered clumps of yellow and white petals I was tramping through and impress somebody.

I called to her through her window. I knocked on the door, tried the handle, and it was locked.

Of course, I thought then. *Of course she wouldn't wait. It wasn't firm, anyway.*

I took off without leaving a note, ignoring her response to my overture just as I had ignored her overture, or whatever it was, on my porch that first morning.

CHAPTER THREE

MY PORCH BECAME THE SITE OF nightly gatherings since it was the logical place to convene outside of the main house and Tillie's "program." We lit citronella candles, passed around half gallons of cheap wine, ate processed cheese and crackers, and held readings, after which we would comment, criticize, and drink more wine.

Once enough wine had sopped our senses, someone would open up with a story they swore they had never told anyone else. But now they could because artists did not condemn the extraordinary. Spike showed up for these "salons" usually wrapped in a black shawl, her extravagant hair draped over her shoulders and arms. We didn't actually speak to each other; she spoke to everyone at once, telling stories and talking rapidly without any of the ont-ish airs she'd shown to me.

"I had just arrived in New York," she began one night, heated by our laughter and the wine. "This was about six years ago, and I was working for one of the city's hottest public relations firms. Our clients were Helmsley, Koch, Paley, Rohatyn—there wasn't a power broker in town my boss didn't own. About a week into the job, I got a call from the receptionist who told me she had a friend of a friend she wanted me to meet. Handsome, never been married, a partner in one of the firms that was our major competitor, so I knew he couldn't be hurting for money."

I tried to picture a matter-of-fact Spike sitting in a plush office talking on the intercom phone to her receptionist. *How*, I wondered, *did she wear her mass of hair during office hours?*

The story continued. "I said, 'Sure, I'll be glad to do you a favor.' He called me about two nights later, and he sounded normal enough on the phone. He told me that we'd be going to Lutesce for dinner with another couple, then to the opera, and perhaps a nightcap on his boat which he kept off Glen Cove." Her voice became smug. "All the right things, you know."

Then innocently, she said, "And I didn't know this was unusual. I'd just moved from Montreal, and this was my first date in the city. He picked me up in a maroon Jaguar, shiny enough so that I could tell it was rarely used. He was wearing a Giorgio Armani suit, Ferragamo shoes, and he held a bouquet of six long-stemmed white roses. Plus he looked like a combination of David Bowie and Daryl Hall . . . or John Oates . . . I always get them confused. Meanwhile, I'm shitting in my pants. Looks, charm, money—all this from a receptionist?

"First, we went to his Park Avenue apartment for a drink with the other couple," she explained. "They turned out to be a little younger, but they had a horse farm in Lyford Cay and a house in Litchfield, Connecticut. We talked a lot about the merits of skiing at Sun Valley or Aspen, and we talked about sailing to Nantucket and how the water was always warmer there than at the Vineyard because Nantucket is closer to the Gulf Stream, and so on and so on, and somewhere in there I excused myself to use the bathroom." She smiled, remembering the moment. "The apartment, by the way, was gorgeous—Louis XIV chairs and Pissarros and Manets holding up the walls.

"I was washing my hands in the bathroom, which was marble and brass, when I heard a rustling sound coming from behind the shower curtain. It was the kind of noise that shouldn't have been there, unless he had a cat and the cat was in the litter box. But I hadn't seen any cat. As I was pulling back the curtain, repeating to myself, 'Please don't let it be anything I don't want to see!' I could just tell . . ." Her eyes widened as if she were seeing behind the curtain.

"Two snakes were writhing in the tub! I ran out screaming,

and my date stood up and asked me what was wrong. I pointed . . ." Spike stabbed the air, "and he said, 'I don't understand.' All I could do was go, '*Ssst. Ssst.*'

"'Show me,' he said. I shook my head no, and he practically dragged me back to the bathroom. 'Something in here?' I was nodding mutely, in shock, and he kept smiling like it was a big tease. Then he said, 'Hmm, where'd the other one go?'

"I ran out of there so fast I forgot my shoes and my coat, and it was twenty degrees outside. I can't tell you how I got home, but my toes were so frozen I thought they were broken. It took two Valium to get me to sleep. I told the receptionist that if that was a typical New York date, I'd rather drink mai tais by myself on Saturday nights at the Marriot and imagine I was just a tourist."

Mary Beams, the former English teacher from Maine, giggled and snapped open another beer. "A few days later," Spike went on, "I got a package in the mail at my office marked *Ssst!* I promised Lorenzo, from our mail room, I'd buy him dinner if he'd open it and kill anything inside.

"He undid the wrappings, then climbed on a chair to open the box with a pair of tongs. I was ready with a yardstick. First came my shoes, then a little gift—a snakeskin wallet.

"He sent me snakeskin gifts for a month and then he started badgering me on the phone, asking if I'd seen his gecko in the kitchen. I finally had to have my boss call *his* boss to have it stopped."

"Did it?" asked one of the listeners in the dark.

"Of course. You have to understand something. My boss is one of the most powerful men in Gotham. And I was—am—his pet."

I sat quietly in the dark, questions switching on and off like fireflies. Who was this woman who found Lutesce ordinary? Why did the snake man continue to pursue her? What about the other couple? Were they in on it? Wasn't there an easier way to meet someone?

I'd never been to Lutesce. I'd never been courted by anyone driving anything more exotic than a Toyota. *Courted*, I thought, conscious of the images of dust motes this brought to mind, or maybe the dust was in my habits. The men I'd dated since my eight years' abstinence were lightweights, or they were actors, or they were too young to have much money. And I had lost track of clothing designers. Actually, I never *kept* track even when I was married. I was satisfied with mail-order catalogs from Eddie Bauer, REI, and L.L. Bean. A shrink might ask, "Why do you live in the city of Macy's, the 'World's Largest Store,' and make your purchases in Wisconsin?"

And even now, in reporting the details of the snake man's getup, I'm not sure if I have the names right.

One thing I was sure of. I had a heady feeling I was onto something, and I took another gulp of cheap wine. The best thing for a neophyte like me was to be with someone like Spike, who could "take it or leave it," who could "play hardball." That way, going forward wouldn't be so terrifying.

I had only to get her to open up to me again, if that's what I really wanted, and I became lost in strange thoughts, bubbling over each other to float to the surface.

MY OPPORTUNITY CAME ONE evening when it was Spike's turn to read one of her short stories. She was the last one to "present," as we called it, claiming she couldn't decide on the right piece to share with us, but I thought it had more to do with her run-in with Mary Beams. Mary Beams was a stickler for plot. She tore my first effort to shreds, but since I wasn't serious about it, I said, "Okay, Mary, better luck next time." I had written a short story about two little girls whose father went to Greenland to build an airport runway. They're left behind in a small town in Georgia where the temperature never dropped below 103 degrees. My favorite part was when one of the little girls picked a half-melted Hershey bar off the school playground and ate it.

Mary Beams wanted to know what my point was. She wanted to know why I had sent the father to Greenland.

"Why hadn't the family gone too?" she asked, pointing out that it *was* a long-term assignment.

I had no answers. To me the story pivoted on that Hershey bar; it was so sad. Mary Beams wanted to know why I wrote the story in the first place. I didn't know. It probably had something to do with my life.

Her assault on Spike had the bad timing of coming right after Faye had offered her unsolicited opinion of Spike's first story earlier in the week. Spike had written about a woman who confronted her former lover in a Korean greengrocer on the Upper East Side.

"Does this take place in Korea?" Faye asked. "Then why is it a Korean fruit market? Is she friends with these people?"

Mary Beams asked Spike, "Did you know the ending before you began writing?"

"No," Spike said.

"It shows," declared Mary. "I don't think anything worthwhile can be written unless you know everything you're going to say before you write it down."

"Then why write? You write to find out what you're going to say. Otherwise, it's dull work."

"Think of your reader. Not yourself," Mary said.

"I do it differently."

"What about this part here, where you mention her remembering his budding erection. Do you mean a personal erection?"

Spike stared at her.

Mary Beams ignored the silence. "Why is he getting excited enough to have an erection?"

"It's explained," Spike said.

"At least he isn't Korean," Faye added.

Now that we knew we might never see each other again, Spike elected to read a story called "Happyland," about a little girl named Sunny Lee.

Sunny Lee came from a wealthy family and led a luxurious life among 150 head of Jerseys and 500 acres of land in a remote corner of Massachusetts. The family owned a peach orchard, an apple orchard, and a granite quarry. On Sunny's fourth birthday, her father bought her a mountain—really a foothill to a mountain—and named it SunnySide Up.

According to the story, Mr. Lee was a man who could express his feelings only by actions, and he had an unpredictable, nasty temper.

"One night, when Sunny was five years old, her father woke her up in the middle of a lovely dream," Spike read. "She had been dreaming in the lushest of colors, entranced by the vibrant pink of the organdy dress she was wearing. She was standing on SunnySide Up, but the mountain was no higher than an ant hill and it was sinking under her weight. She woke, shattered and desolate, and stared into the burning eyes of her father. Sunny knew something was wrong because her father never woke her, not even in the morning, and he was pushing her. She became more and more tangled in the bedsheets, and finally he put his hands under her arms and lifted her off the bed. He smelled of manure and whiskey. When he swung her near his face, she became frightened because he did not seem like her father. She grabbed his leg, and he pushed her away with the same hard object he'd been using to roust her from bed. She fell and he cursed, 'Damn it, get up!' He grabbed her arm and flung her ahead of him. Now she could see that the cold, hard object was his rifle. She felt it at the back of her legs as he nudged her forward down the stairs.

"Sunny did not understand. All of the lights in the living room were on and her mother and baby brother, Alex, were sitting on the sofa. Alex was rubbing his eyes and trying to lean his head against his mother's arm, but she kept bouncing him away. Lily Lee looked terrified. Sunny had never seen her mother look so terrified before.

"Her father pushed her with the nose of his rifle toward the sofa, and she ran to her mother. Lily's hand was ice-cold when she closed it over Sunny's hand, still warm from sleep.

"Without looking at them, her father told them to get up and walk in single file out to the truck. Alex started to bawl. 'Make him get up,' her father said. Lily pushed Alex and Sunny outside to the garage. He told them to get into the truck. He climbed into the driver's seat and switched on the ignition with the windows up, the garage door closed. Lily screamed and he told her to keep quiet. She started kicking and punching him. Her father slammed out of the truck, raised the rifle at the three of them, and held it steady for what seemed to be years.

"Sunny heard the shots before she felt anything. She heard her father run out the door, then she heard her mother screaming. The tires were all shot out. Alex was crying. Her mother was crying.

"Lily grabbed Sunny and ran her hands over her as if she were checking for punctures. 'Thank God,' she said. 'Thank God, you're not hurt. He didn't get you, did he?' But Sunny Lee did not respond. Sunny Lee did not, it turns out, utter another word for almost two years."

The story ended with the adult Sunny Lee swinging on a tire put up by the family that had bought the dairy farm after the Lees lost most of their fortune, and Sunny Lee inquiring if in all the time she'd been away, anyone had ever caught up with her father (he'd become a woodsman/hermit/alcoholic) and found out why he did it.

Spike looked at us shyly and affected a "Fuck-you-if-you-don't-like-it" gaze.

"The vividness!" someone said.

And Spike admitted she had rewritten the story at least eight times, but felt she had finally gotten it right.

Mary Beams snapped open a beer. "It has something of James Cain in it," she muttered. "I'm reminded of the scene where Dora and what's-his-name try to send a car down a ravine— except in that story we know why they're attempting murder. In this, the reader is left as puzzled as Sunny Lee."

Mary Beams was starting to wear on me. "Exactly," I said. "That's why it hits home. We don't know, do we? We never know."

"Know what?" Mary Beams sounded annoyed.

"Why things happen."

"Pffft!" was all she said to me, but Spike, I saw, was grinning.

Spirits and goblins danced with us that night on Tillie Skokel's bungalow porch. Spike was ecstatic that we had liked her story, and the velocity of her happiness swept us into a winey conspiracy.

No longer loyal subjects were we, placidly accepting Tillie's rules. Spike wanted to go out dancing and as soon as she said it, I realized I had momentarily forgotten about my old pained self. I thought, *Oh yes, the mating thing. Oh yes, I forgot about worrying about that.*

The closest we could find to a dance club was a bar in Portsmouth that had music but no dancing. Mary Beams didn't join us; even so, we looked very out-of-town. What were a fifty-year-old Lebanese man, a fortyish housewife from New Jersey, a fiery redhead in a clingy black T-shirt dress, and a willowy brunette in jeans doing together? Spike's dress ruled out religion. With her thick, brick-red hair falling in stiff pleats down to her waist, and her curvy full-breasted body clinging to her dress, she was a visual explosion.

We were stared at.

She plucked a cigarette from her pack and pounced into the conversation. "Boy, am I glad you showed up!"

I was taken aback. I wanted to ask, "Then why weren't you in your cabin when I came to get you for the swimming hole?" but didn't have the chance.

"I thought I was going to be stuck with Tillie. Then these two came. And then you. I really like your work."

"Thank you."

"No, I mean it. I get the feeling you don't think people mean that when they say it. You're smart."

"Thank you." I was getting embarrassed . . . embarrassed that I was so intent on adoring what she was saying to me. So this is some of what this frightening person thinks, I told myself. Unless she was testing to see how far she could go in pushing my buttons. I didn't know any powerful men. I hadn't once been engaged to a millionaire's son, as she told us she'd been in Montreal. I didn't know anyone with a boat moored off Long Island. How could I rank with all those interesting, smart, wealthy people?

She narrowed her eyes and stared at me as if sighting a large hole in my psyche—and to prove how well she could read my mind, said, "I'm sorry I didn't make it to the swimming hole with you. I just had to get away from Tillie. I drove all the way here to Portsmouth, bought pâté and cheese and sat in this very square and ate it and got very drunk on some bad wine and let some sixty-year-old try to pick me up until I told him he should be ashamed of himself."

I thought of Giacomo Salvetti fingering all the girls, fingering me. Spike leaned closer. "Let me tell you, when you're having something with a twenty-five-year-old, you don't want to touch anything that's not fresh." She took a sip of her dry Rob Roy, probably served for the first time at that bar, and I realized my face felt flushed.

If I'd been imagining her as more compelling than she was, back there on Tillie's porch, I didn't have to work at it now. Suddenly, I became aware of the many pairs of eyes staring at her, attracted to her heat, the clothes she wore, her wild hair, her full breasts—captured by her constant motion.

A semblance of supreme cunning came over her. She began shifting in her chair, alternating the direction against which she would turn her back. I thought that even in the city, she would draw men to her in an unending stream, and if nothing else, at least I could watch. At least I could see what it took to have power over a man instead of knowing what it took for a man to have power over me.

I slept fitfully that night, and when I went to the swimming hole the next day, it was overcast but I was there anyway, recovering from a light hangover and a medley of dreams from the overflow in the bar. I kept switching between feeling as if a lot was slipping away and a lot was about to be gained. Gazing up at the pines, I remembered one of the last things Spike and I had laughed about after the others had gone. She had just read in the paper that scientists found falling in love could actually make you smarter. It worked like an amphetamine.

"Getting a prescription is easier," she retorted.

Sitting at the pond, I had my own version of what the scientists meant. Out of love, I saw the world plainly. Mountains were mountains, beaches were beaches, jobs were jobs. So what was I after? How could I have the enchantment without the pain, the ambivalence, the bafflement? It was awful, this . . . messiness.

At that moment, I felt someone behind me and turned around.

She laughed and talked about how hard it had been to find me. "Isn't this beautiful!" she exclaimed when she looked around her. "Oh, Tina, why didn't you make me come here before?" She hurried on. "I was so scared last night walking down that long dark road from your porch to my cabin with my flashlight. I thought I might run into the ghost of Tillie baying to the moon."

"You were brave," I said. "I wouldn't have done it."

"Bullshit! You're not brave in the same way you're not smart. I think of you as someone who would do a lot of things. Some things even *I* wouldn't do." Her agitation startled me, and I shrank back.

"Oh come on."

"Do I have a secret reason to say these things? Do you think someone's paying me?"

"Well," I said, returning the flattery, "I meant it when I said I liked your story. Especially the part about the father and the rifle. How did you come up with that?"

"It was my dad."

"Oh." I should have kept my oath never, ever to ask a creator of any work what the source was! I should have simply enjoyed the piece and talked no more about it.

"Yeah. We lost all our money. My mother went crazy after the shooting. My brother was institutionalized once. So was I, once. I don't think anyone's worth their salt until they have a nervous breakdown."

CHAPTER FOUR

"YOU CAN TELL WITHIN THE FIRST few minutes if someone is going to be in your life," I told Spike during one of our late-night dialogues, much later during our time together. It was the reason I stepped back and closed the door when I first saw her on my porch at Tillie's. Exactly why she was sent, I didn't want to know. While I'm not a superstitious person, she did seem sent. As if the ripples in the lake finally calmed and in the limpid pool I saw the reflection of everything I denied I was or could be. The messenger sat on my porch. She had long red hair. She brought me presents. The impulses in her eyes would drive me to my knees, scooping turds out of the toilet.

The presents came later.

My memory shies from evoking too much at once. It is too painful, too obvious, too sad, too much like one long shriek overwhelming the whispers, the deep laughter, the murmurings, "Are you all right, are you all right, are you all right?" Scenes bubble up.

There is a scene in the summer right after I returned from Tillie's bungalow colony.

Spike is sitting on a warped stool in a sticky, big-screen bar on Twenty-Third Street in the city, and it is the first time I've seen her after thinking I'd never see her again. I'm shocked.

I'd remembered her all wrong. I'd muddied her features and here they were, clearly defined and not pretty but handsome in a strong, Germanic way. Any weariness was gone. I'd carried an image of her huddled in her black shawl on my bungalow porch as the night cooled, and an image of her talking too much and too fast in the bar in Portsmouth, turning her back on the attention she excited, and here she was with a sunny tan, shorts, and a white tank top, looking as breezy and relaxed as if she'd just stepped off a sailboat after a light lunch of salads and fruits.

She was laughing. Why was she laughing? A man wearing a suede cowboy hat with quail feathers in the band was fiddling with her shoe. Why was he doing that? Did she know him? Was I supposed to be friendly toward him? The shoe was in his hand, which kept rising and plunging because he kept rising and plunging with the pitch of God-knows-how-much booze. In his other hand was a nine-inch gutting knife he was using like a razor on the sole of her shoe.

"My sandal broke and this charming fellow has offered to fix it," Spike told me when I walked up to the bar. She laughed some more.

"This lovely lady requested my assistance and as I am the only true hero left in this bar who comes here promptly at four o'clock every day, I said I would oblige with my knife"—he leaned closer to Spike—"which fascinates her."

The bartender, a burly fellow whose nameplate read "Mike," said, "Okay, Len, that's enough."

And because Len went right on sputtering and swaying close to Spike's ear, Mike said it again. "That's enough, Len."

"Enough of what? Enough of wit? Enough of chivalry? Enough of tits?"

"You're outta here. Give her her shoe."

"Madam," he said to Spike, relinquishing the shoe. "And associate madam," he said to me. "Fuck you all!"

"Nice," I said.

"Oh he's harmless." She was still laughing. "Hey, it's good to see you, Tina. I missed you."

"Me?"

"Still insecure?" She was half teasing, half serious. I did not mention I had doubted I would hear from her again at all—that the person who told me she'd been institutionalized after her father had tried to kill her might elect to behave like a stranger you meet on a bus.

"It's only been a week," I said, to explain why I was surprised to be missed.

"Ha! Let me tell you what happened to *me* in a week. Tina, you're not going to believe this, except you're probably the only one who would. I feel like we're graduates of Tillie's bungalow colony for the deaf, dumb, and stupid."

"Hey—"

She waved me off, burbled on, and in a flash, the easy, light lunch of salads and fruits was gone and she was in a storm of words.

That mouth. Her mouth. It was unforgettable. Whole worlds flew out of her mouth. She had large, cream-colored teeth and sliding, smiling, puffy lips, and when she talked, her mouth took on a fever. It percolated a fantastic stream of stories and flatteries, insults, offers, and demands. When she laughed, it opened like a wide door to a furnace, and when she ate, she ate like a she-wolf, sometimes doubling over in cramps from the speed of it. Even when she slept, her teeth ground away at each other, trying to bite, chew, stop the silence from rushing in.

"All I can say is that Tillie drove me to it," she told me. "I was sick of having daddy longlegs crawl up my pillow, and my diaphragm was collecting mouse droppings. So I went out one night to a bar a guy at the swimming hole told me about.

"The bar was in Portsmouth, across the street from where we'd gone the other night. Too bad we didn't know about it then, I would've loved to have had you there with me, boy, would I have loved that. I walked in and, get this . . . *it's all men!* I almost shit in my pants. I went straight to the restroom. I stood next to the sink and I took deep breaths and I said to myself, *Okay, Spike, calm down. Okay, you can do it. Put one foot in front of the other. There you go.*

"Tina, do you know what it feels like to have twenty pairs of eyes on you at once? I'm telling you, twenty pairs of eyes watching you order a drink, sip from a glass, take out a cigarette. Four, count 'em, four cigarette lighters snapped open at once.

"I chose a stool at the end because it was the closest to the TV and that gave me something to look at. The man next to me asked if I liked the Mets since I seemed so glued to the screen. Then another man tried to join the conversation, and Tina, I hadn't seen a man built like that since I moved to this city. A fucking stanchion. Built from hard labor, not this wimp-ass Nautilus shit. His shoulders must've been forty-six inches across, I swear, and his waist was no bigger than mine." She put her hands on her own. "And I just knew he had that nice indentation in his ass.

"But before I got a chance to even open my mouth, the first man said to him, 'Can't you see I'm talking to this woman?' and the other one backed down right away as if he knew something I didn't. I found out that the man I sat down next to was Tommy Joe Johnson. And, by the way, he's the son of the richest yacht owner in Boston Harbor!"

"What?" How did she do it? How did she circle in on one of the wealthiest men in the state of Massachusetts? She laughed like a heated hyena.

"Not only that," she went on, "Tommy Joe Johnson is gorgeous. Six foot two, slim, brown hair, doe-brown eyes. And here's the best part." She rocked on her barstool, barely able to contain herself. "Guess what he likes to do best?"

"What?"

"Eat women!" she shrieked.

I looked at Mike, the bartender. Had he heard that? Had everyone heard that? "What a crime to keep the city of New York out of his range," she went on.

"Yeah," was all I had a chance to say.

"Let me tell you about his house. First of all, I had to have four bourbons to get me there, I was so nervous. Then when we got there, I had two more bourbons. And let me tell you, I am not good at drinking.

"He carried me up a long, winding staircase to his bedroom, which was a godsend because I couldn't walk by then. Everything was done in Laura Ashley print wallpaper with mahogany wainscoting."

"That's what I would do, notice the wallpaper."

"Right! Because it's odd, right? It's too feminine. I found out he was supposed to be married three weeks ago, but his fiancée who had picked out all the furnishings for the house took off to London with somebody else. That's not all. We got to his bedroom and the box spring was cracked and the bed was lying broken in the middle of the room. 'You're not that good,' I said, and he leered. He had the most awful, sexy leer. He laid me down on the bed, and Tina, it was so good I passed out!"

"What?"

"Yes!" She laughed deep in her throat, gloating. "This guy was giving me the blow job of my life, and I was out cold!

"I came to on the porch in one of those swinging lounges. I was dressed in his robe, my head was in his lap, and there was a woman standing at my feet."

"A woman? He had guests?"

"'I want to talk to you,' she said." Spike imitated a high, sweet voice. "'Not now,' he said. 'When? I tried to reach you for three days,' she said. 'Not now!' he yelled, and he threw a pillow at her.

"I closed my eyes. I couldn't believe it was real. And when I opened them, she was gone. 'Who was that?' I said. And he said, 'Nobody for you to worry about, sugar.'

"Tina, Tina—" She squeezed my arm and pulled herself closer as if she were afraid I couldn't hear her. "He didn't even see that other woman. He acted like I was the only woman around."

I shook my head. This wasn't making sense.

"Wait!" She held up her hand like a squadron leader, her palm out to my face, and tucked her chin in, half smiling, half smirking. "It gets better. In the morning he asked me if I minded cooking breakfast if he got some groceries. It took him over an hour and a half to bring back a dozen eggs, a quart of orange juice, and a loaf of whole wheat bread. I was already looking in the phone book for cabs. He told me he had swung by his parents' house and they wanted us to stop by for lunch."

"He wanted you to meet his parents already?" I squinted, trying to get clear on the picture.

"I told you it got better. But I thought, *Hey, pass up a chance to play hardball with one of the richest men in the state?* We drove off to *the house*. Picture a scaled-down Breakers. I was a little disappointed, though, only forty acres. The family was in the back having a barbecue. Tommy Joe walked over, holding my hand. He introduced me, took one look at the grill, and said, 'I don't want to eat this. I think we'll go somewhere else.'

"'Sit a while,' his dad said. And his mother came up to him as if she were pleading for her life.

"'I'll see you later,' he said, and we left. We went back to his place, he carried me up to the broken bed, and just as he was about to go down on me, the phone rang. It was his mother. I know because he said, 'Mother, you saw the woman I was with. What do you think I'm doing?' He fucked me four times. It was dark by the time we crawled out of there. I was so sore, even my feet hurt. He invited me up to the family's hunting lodge next month." She stopped to catch her breath. "Tina," she said, "there *is* a God."

I sat there wiggling my sneakers, offering congratulations. Spike laughed, sucked down the ice cubes in her glass, and asked for another round. Then she treated me to another description of Tommy Joe's body. Eventually she asked if I had any news.

"Well," I said hesitantly. "I met somebody too."

"Terrific, sweetie. Who's that?" She began playing with the lemon twists in a glass by her hand.

"His name is Frank Lucas and in some ways he looks like a Lou. He's overweight, but he's really more like someone you would know."

She raised her eyebrows but didn't ask.

"He's too old for me," I began. "He's forty-three. He's handsome, charming, and wealthy. Boy that sounds simple." I grinned at her serious face. “He has a duplex off Fifty-Fifth and First, and he drives a Mercedes with a phone in it. Oh yes, he’s sunk three hundred thousand dollars into a new business to market frozen, microwavable crepes.”

I waited for the furnace door to open and blast me with a hot laugh. I thought it exceedingly funny when I first heard about the French crepes. Ready-to-wear haute cuisine? Who knew. But the intensity with which Frank Lucas studied and talked crepes left no room for giggling or questions, and I looked at Spike, ready to collapse with her in laughter.

“Why did he use his own money?” The change in her voice caught me off guard.

I shrugged. “He’s got some investors, but he’s looking for more.”

“Is he the general partner?”

“Yes.”

“Does he know that makes him personally liable if the business fails?”

“I guess so. He’s got his money tied up in rent and equipment that’s just sitting around because he’s still looking for investors.”

She grunted. “Who is he going to distribute through?”

“Distribute? How should I know? He’s never brought it up.”

“What is this guy, a dumb blonde?”

I laughed. “Look, it doesn’t make sense to me either, but then I’m not a businessman.”

“Business is common sense,” she snapped back. “Don’t sell yourself short all the time.”

I ignored that and went on with what I thought were the important facts. “He gets calls at all hours. He gets up at five in the morning on Sundays to drive to Staten Island for business.”

“Where did you find this guy?”

“I was introduced—through distant connections.”

CHAPTER FIVE

LOOKING BACK ON THAT TIME, I realize it was an eerie coincidence to have met someone like Frank Lucas at all. It was as if I were playing with my own version of Spike's snake man. He had "all the right things, you know," but there was something not quite right. I struggled, and during this time Spike moved in and out of my life, sometimes riding only the periphery, other times sweeping in and pulling me out to a different world where, as I became more anxious and sorrowful, she would comfort me by giving me lessons on what she saw.

"You refer to him as Frank Lucas," she said to me one night. "First name, second name. Do you know why you refer to him that way? Because you are dating his distance. You are dating his image. This will be a man remembered for his dinners, his clothes, his car, his phone in the car, his wavy hair, his smile, his nail cosmetics in the bathroom cabinet. Don't blame yourself. That's who he is. And if it's too little for you, you will withdraw, then dissolve the relationship."

There is a scene I remember. Frank Lucas was giving a dinner party. He threw dinner parties every Saturday night so we were always surrounded by people. Before then, we had gone to restaurants all over the city, with Frank calling for last-minute reservations from his Mercedes. I remember a warm summer night, his silver car whisking us down the FDR Drive, the metallic smell of the East River, his silver phone pressed to his ear, his black hair waved back from his forehead. I remember a Japanese restaurant in Tribeca that pulsed with punk music, a waitress whose face was a natural pentagon, and a flaming dish of ice cream tempura that thrilled me as much as any circus trick.

Now we were in his kitchen. He wore a chef's apron and was sweating, annoyed that the beef carpaccio was not thin enough and the aioli sauce was bland. I learned a lot about food with Frank Lucas. I also gained weight and so did he. He had a weakness for double-cream cheeses, pasta with Gorgonzola sauce, French toast with hazelnut liqueur, and crème fraîche on everything. Frank was cursing the carpaccio, and I was on the phone with Spike, who sounded as if she were at the bottom of a tunnel. For two days she hadn't answered her phone and her answering machine wasn't turned on. Finally at seven-thirty that night, I reached her.

"Are you all right?"

Frank was banging the carpaccio with a hammer wrapped in cellophane, and I could barely hear her. "What? What?"

She sounded hoarse. She talked slowly as if she had taken sleeping pills. "I said I spilled coffee grounds all over the kitchen. I couldn't figure out how to clean it up. I went to make coffee, and I spilled the boiling water on my foot by accident. When I jumped back, I knocked the bag of coffee grounds over, and they poured into the sink. And into the stove. And onto the floor. I just stood there looking at all that coffee and I said, 'Fuck it,' and opened another bottle of wine and fell asleep in the living room." She sniffed as if she had a cold. "I'm not doing too good, Tina. The only reason I answered the phone is I thought it might be you."

"What happened?" Now Frank was singing in Italian and shaking a pan rapidly over a flame. I covered one ear.

"Oh nothing much." I heard her light a cigarette. "Tommy Joe Johnson hasn't called like he said he would, I can't write shit, and I found out Sam's in the hospital because he had a heart attack."

"Your father? I didn't know you knew where he was."

"We knew." She blew out some smoke and her tempo picked up. "They had to strap him into the bed because he kept pulling out his IV, trying to go home. My uncle Willis smuggled his pistol to him, and he tried to shoot one of the nurses." She coughed. "I've got coffee all over the floor here. I keep stepping on it."

The buzzer sounded. Frank's first guest was downstairs, and I buzzed back. "I'm at Frank's," I said. "I only have a few minutes to talk."

"Oh." She sounded wistful, like Sunny Lee standing on top of her shrinking mountain.

"I called to invite you to dinner here. But anyway. Is he all right now?"

"Yeah. They have him sedated. But it doesn't look good. His liver's shot. He only has one kidney. Tina, he's going to die and I'm not going to be able to ask him anything." She started crying.

"Oh, Spike, I'm so sorry."

"He asked for me."

"Good." I tried to sound enthusiastic. "That's good."

"I'm scared. What if I go up there, and he doesn't remember me?" She was talking between breaths, almost as if she were hiccupping.

"He asked for you. He'll remember you. Take deep breaths."

"I want to tell him I love him."

"You will. Take deep breaths. Think of the restroom in Portsmouth. One foot in front of the other. Twenty pairs of eyes."

"That shit. I hope his prick turns to lard."

"You mean Tommy Joe?" I encouraged.

"What kind of an asshole has a broken bed he can't manage to fix in three weeks? I'd give my left tit to talk to his old girlfriend."

"Why don't you just invite her for drinks. It's less physical."

"Ha!" She almost laughed. "Oh, Tina, I'm so glad you called."

"Well, I'm glad I called too. We have lots of food here."

"I'll bet. Crème fraîche for days?"

"Yeah."

"And those friends of his? What're you going to talk about this time? Club Med? Maybe Frank'd like to invest in one in Teaneck, New Jersey."

"Come on. I'm standing right here. They're arriving as we speak. I have to behave."

"Why? Look, Frank has the intellectual powers of a squid. I'm sure you can say plenty before he catches on that he's being insulted. I know you. I've seen you do it."

A woman named Linda bounced by, carrying a bottle of wine. "What're you going to do now?" I said.

"Sleep. I'll clean up the coffee tomorrow."

"I wish you were here."

"You'll have to go through that one by yourself."

"That's not what I meant."

"I know." She blew out more smoke. "I've got to get a new pack of cigarettes and they're in the bedroom. Give Frank my regards. On second thought, don't give him anything from me."

Frank happened to walk by at that moment, scowling. "What are you so happy about?" He bustled into the dining room with a corkscrew.

THERE'S ANOTHER SCENE FROM that night that involved what I came to call our famous dictionary talk. The dinner had gone well except I hadn't said much. The only real burst of thought I remember coming from me was when Linda reached for a first piece of pie, then humbly withdrew.

"Go ahead," I almost shouted. "Don't be so self-effacing. You deserve it." I wondered if that was Spike talking through me, and who, exactly, I was addressing.

Otherwise I was quiet. There was the usual competitiveness to the dinner conversation, which revolved around investments, travel to Europe, art acquisitions, someone's—not anyone at Frank's table—career fiasco, and whether it was better to buy pink leather gloves at Bergdorf Goodman's or Bendel's. Since I was only Frank's newest girl and at least ten years younger than his friends, I was often asked to explain what I meant when I did speak, and like the earnest new kid on the block, I did try but not that night.

After everyone left, Frank asked me for the first time what I thought of his friends. "We come from different worlds," I said.

"What does that mean?"

"Well, your friends are interested in different things than I am," I began. "I don't know anybody who can spend that kind of money on bad art. I can't talk about Bergdorf's. I've never been there."

"And you look down on that?"

"No." I did.

"But those things don't matter," he said. "Clothes, cars, trips, where you spend your vacation, what kind of store you walk into. What matters is that you and I have the same values."

"We do?" I didn't have to rush out at five on Sunday mornings to Staten Island to meet with someone about a balloon loan.

"I think so."

"Okay, here's a small example," I said. "I don't even know if this qualifies as a value, but let's say it's a standard. I have a standard that says people should call when they say they're going to call and show up when they've promised to. When you say, 'I'll call you tonight,' and I don't hear from you for three days, that's not right—according to my values or standards. I would never do that to you, to anyone."

"That's because you and I have different dictionaries," he said calmly.

"Huh?"

"When I say, 'I'll call you tonight,' it's just my way of saying goodbye. Like, 'See you soon.' It doesn't mean I'll call you that night. I can understand, though, where you get that. You're a journalist, and you're trained to write literally."

Why did I feel like I was talking to Giacomo Salvetti? "One girl, she brings me dinner on Fridays. Another girl, she brings me money."

It didn't really matter what he said. All I did was think about him, talk about him, analyze him. I told Spike he was dangerous to me. I told her I was in it only for the money and hated myself for it. I despised his "wisdom."

"Don't worry about tomorrow, it'll be worse." Or "I don't think people change. I think we get older, do the same damn things, but understand them better."

And I would say, "So my attempts not to make the same mistakes are futile?"

And he'd say, "Yes."

I was so excited, so confused, and so hopeful in the beginning. I wanted him to lift me out of my life and put me in his fancy duplex and feed me and buy me things. But I didn't know how to be the kind of woman who was helpless and shrewd enough to get those things or the kind of woman who could ignore what he believed in. I held on, like a parasite, raging to Spike and getting sick of myself.

Then one night, he asked me over for fettuccine Alfredo. As I was bulldozing my fork through the fettuccine, he said, "Something's missing between us."

I was so happy, I could've hugged him. Relief. "Thank God. Thank God, you noticed!"

"Why didn't you say something?" he shot back.

"I did."

"When?" And Frank Lucas told me, "You let me walk all over you. If you didn't like what I was doing, you should've told me to get the hell out."

"Then you would have left. You don't believe people can change."

"Maybe. The point is, I don't care if she's smart, stupid, or what, but I want a woman who says, 'I am what I am.' And I say, 'I am what I am.' And that's that."

I looked at him. I went home.

And Spike comforted me with these words: "A nervous breakdown comes from being mind-fucked."

I couldn't understand this New York City–style romance. What happened to us here that we stayed with people we didn't even like to talk to and baited them and saw dollar signs and hated them? What happened to me?

I started sleeping every two hours or so for three hours at a time. I had enough money saved up to do that, and I didn't need much . . . just milk and cereal and beer. Spike went off to see Tommy Joe Johnson in New Hampshire after he finally called.

I watered my plants, vacuumed, arranged flowers, drank beer, cleaned the bathroom, ran in the park without looking around for Salvetti, and talked to friends who said, "Weird the way some people get their points across, huh?" and "It's for the better," and blah, blah, blah.

I needed to get out of New York. I wanted someone who would say, "I'll call you at seven," and do it. My dictionary was too basic for this city.

As I was figuring out exactly how I would swing my departure, Spike came back from New Hampshire, looking as if she'd seen the ghost of death.

CHAPTER SIX

"IT USED TO BE THAT I WAS SO desperate I couldn't get anyone to talk to me at a bus stop. It's like they could smell it. Now I don't know what it is. What is it about me, Tina? Why do I attract Tommy Joe Johnsons and snake men?"

Spike sat in my living room, shivering, though a warm, lazy breeze from the valleys between the city's buildings had nearly lulled me to sleep before she arrived. Her hair, spread over her breasts like seaweed, looked wild and vampish, and with one arm she clutched her waist, her fingers working the fabric of her creased linen dress. The other arm was bent at the elbow so that her hand was ceilingward and the smoke from her cigarette hovered above our heads.

"I only want to tell this once. I don't want to have to remember it," she said. "I'm going to regurgitate it here and you take it and burn it. Can I sleep here tonight? I'm afraid to go home. I can't remember if I gave him my home number or my office number. I don't want any calls, I don't want any mail, I don't want anything from him."

I told her the couch pulled out to a bed, then offered her a beer, which she said she couldn't stomach, and while she fidgeted and smoked, I fished around until I found a dusty airplane bottle of amaretto. The old cap needed pliers. "Don't watch. We're down on supplies here." The truth was I hadn't entertained anyone in over a year. We either went out or dined in on a six-pack of beer.

"Oh, honey, I'm sorry," she said. "I didn't even buy you a present. I wish I could've been here for you. I'm glad you ended it. It took a little longer than I thought, but you did it. Dissolve and withdraw."

I shushed Frank Lucas out of the conversation; he didn't belong here with his microwavable crepes and airborne theories about the dictionary. Spike was back, bright with tales from another life—a traveler to the unbelievable. And I knew whatever she said, however disastrous her visit with Tommy Joe Johnson had been, it would be more compelling than anything I had ever experienced. That in itself would give me hope. I wanted to be lifted from the shores of predictable disappointments. If this sounds peculiar, consider how it feels to swim in a storm-whipped ocean that soars and crashes, then to swim in the afternoon at low tide. One of those times you will never forget.

"Well, it started out okay." Spike pulled her lips from the little neck of the amaretto bottle. "No, it didn't. It was fucked from the beginning. My plane was forty-five minutes late from Boston, and he was pissed. No 'Hi, how are you, I've missed you, you look good, sorry for your trouble.' Just 'Let's go.' I'm thinking, *Great, this is just great.* Meanwhile, he'd grabbed my suitcase and bolted for the parking lot, and I had to run to catch up to him. He threw my case in the back seat of a station wagon I didn't recognize and stepped on the gas before I had a chance to close my door.

"Then instead of getting on the highway, he drove to a bar. He jumped out and walked in ahead of me without saying a word. Tina, I felt like I was shot in the heart. I'd come all this way with visions of making love all night long in front of a stone fireplace, and there I was at a bar behind the interstate.

"I got out of the car, walked into the bar, where he was nowhere to be seen, and found out where the telephone was. I figured I'd call my brother in Lynn and ask him to pick me up and drive me to his house where I could stay until the next flight home. The call was just about to connect when a hand came up from behind me and hung up the receiver.

"'Who're you calling?' His eyes, Tina, were like flat stones. He had one hand around the back of my neck, and he was blocking my view to the bar so that if I wanted to wave for help, no one could see me. I got the feeling that if I yelled, he'd clap his other hand over my mouth. I told him the truth because I couldn't think of anything else.

"'My brother,' I said.

"'Why?' he asked me.

"'So he'll come and get me.'

"Then just like that he changed. The poisonous look in his eyes vanished. His voice became soft. He relaxed and dropped his hand from my neck. 'I'm sorry I made you nervous,' he said. 'Come on, have a drink with me. I've ordered you a Rob Roy, dry like you like it. Come on, sit with me a minute.' He took my hand and held onto it for three drinks. I thought whatever bug had gotten into his system, it took off. My visions of brandy by the fireplace could come out and play a little. And, of course, as soon as I began flirting with the idea of pleasure, the pressure on my hand increased and he slid his hand up my arm and said we had to leave. Tina, no warning, nothing, he just began squeezing my arm as if I'd told him I wanted to kick him in the balls.

"The instant we got on the highway, he floored it, and this was no fast car he was driving. This was a beat-up, old station wagon. I don't know what happened to his other car. He pushed it to eighty, eighty-five, ninety, and the car was shaking like an old man on ice. I waited for the exhaust to fall off or a piston to go through the engine. It was pitch-black and the lights on the car were dismal and naturally he wouldn't put on the brights. I knew we were climbing because my ears popped and my back was pressed into my seat. The road was switching from left to right. I was sure this maniac was going to plow us right into a tree. I had a brief discussion with myself about why I would end up wrapped around a tree with someone like this. I couldn't breathe, there was sweat all over me even though it was forty degrees, and finally he stopped the car, jammed on the brakes, and we skidded.

"He threw open his door, threw open the back door, took my suitcase, and stormed into the dark.

"I was at the top of a mountain. I'd never heard anything so quiet in my life, like the silence had been waiting for us and I was in a decompression chamber. My hands were trembling; I still couldn't catch my breath.

"I put my head back on the seat and closed my eyes. It felt nice. I was all alone. I thought if worse came to worse, I would sleep there and in the morning find his keys and drive back to the airport. I began picturing myself walking into the airport, boarding the plane home, maybe even taking a side trip to Bermuda as a consolation prize.

"The next thing I knew his face was right up to my cheek. 'Are you coming?' he whispered. Like a snake, he hissed again, 'Are you coming?'

"He startled me, so I banged my knee against the dashboard. I hadn't heard him coming, like he'd crawled on his belly or something. He opened my door and held out his hand to me, but I stood up without his help. 'Have it your way,' he said, and disappeared again. He hadn't, by the way, turned on any of the house lights and we were parked, it turned out, at least fifty feet away, at the end of a long, sloped driveway. So I hunted around in the glove compartment until I found a flashlight that worked and stumbled my way up to the house. By the time I got there, of course, the place was lit like a birthday cake. He was in the kitchen, fixing himself a peanut butter and jelly sandwich.

"I asked him where everybody was. It was supposed to be an annual family picnic and hunt, but the house was empty.

"'Oh they won't be here till tomorrow,' he said. Then he chewed his sandwich and watched me turn white. I thought I might be sick so I just kept swallowing until I could speak again. 'Where am I staying?'

"'I'll show you.'

"He took me upstairs.

"'I'm in here,' he said, pointing to a closed door. 'And you're in here.' He kicked open the door next to his.

"'Does it lock?' I said.

"He stopped chewing and rolled his head to the side and looked at me. 'Don't be like that,' he said. 'I can't help it if I lose my temper sometimes. I just get like that, but I come around.'

"So I told him, 'You're scaring me.'

"'I'll try to be better, honest. I don't mean to scare you,' he said, keeping his eyes on me. 'Now let's get you settled in here. Take all the time you want. I'll be downstairs.'

"My mind was going a mile a minute. I had no weapons except insect repellent. I was miles away from anyone I knew. I looked out the one window and the darkness was so dense, the glass might as well have been painted black. I stared at the huge pink roses on the bedspread—they didn't belong in the same house with that maniac. I lit a cigarette and smoked, feeling that if I burnt a hole in the bedspread that would be the natural thing to do.

"Finally I went downstairs, resolved to ask him if he was on any kind of medication, but he'd disappeared. I tiptoed from room to room. I was sure any minute he was going to sneak up on me and grab me by the neck and say in that poisonous flat voice, 'What're you looking for?' I must've been slinking around like that for close to an hour. Finally, on my third pass by the liquor cabinet, I poured myself four ounces of scotch, drank it all at once, and dragged myself up the stairs.

"Then you won't believe what happened. I thought I was dreaming, that someone was blowing in my ear, poking me with, you know, a rifle. I opened my eyes. At first all I saw was a pale blotch, then I heard him hissing.

"'Are you asleep? Hey, are you asleep?' "He was naked," Spike said.

"'Look. Look what I have for you,' he said, and grabbed my head and pulled me toward his cock. I yanked back so hard I almost gave myself whiplash. I was still trying to wake up and my coordination was off. I felt like I didn't have any strength.

"'Hey, come on,' he said. 'Hey, don't you want to be with me?'

"'No,' I said.

"'But we won't have a chance tomorrow.'

"'You're scaring me. Who are you? Why're you doing this?'

"'What do you mean?'

"'Why're you sneaking up on me?'

"'You were asleep. I didn't want to scare you.'

"'Why weren't you downstairs like you said? Where did you go?'

"'I went for a walk. I wanted to get some air. I wanted you to relax. You seemed jumpy.' He bent down and started kissing my fingers and looked up at me with that leer, that awful leer.

"'I guess you still are,' he said, and bent his head back to my fingers. Then he started kissing my hand and working his way up my arm. All of a sudden, he stood up.

"'Uh-oh. Too late. Look what you've done to me,' and he swung his limp cock in my face. 'Christ. What a lady you are.' That's exactly what he said."

Spike had stopped shivering and her face was no longer wan. Instead her eyes looked dilated and brilliant, and she spoke like an enraptured Scheherazade.

"His parents must have arrived in the dead of night because I heard his mother's voice in the kitchen the next morning as soon as I woke up.

"'When is she coming down? When is she coming down?'" Spike raised her voice to a brittle chirping.

"'Does she like eggs? How does she like her eggs? Does she eat one egg or two? Have you ever seen her eating eggs?'

"His mother was one of those high-strung, genteel women. I felt sorry for her, I really did. She had this dainty pot belly and she wanted me to call her Irma, and—I couldn't believe it—she thought she was serving breakfast to her future daughter-in-law! That's what she kept saying.

"'And when you're settled, when you move into your house, when you two decide you need these things.'

"I wanted to scream, 'Wait a minute! What did he tell you? Your son's a sick boy!' but her mind was blind as a bat. She ushered me to the oak chest in the dining room and pointed out the gravy bowl and the family crest on the bone china that would soon be mine. She patted my hair, and you know how I don't like strangers touching my hair.

"Finally, around noon his aunts and uncles began arriving for the hunt. Tommy Joe had disappeared. He just wasn't there, hadn't been since breakfast. I sat around drinking tea from one of the bone china cups I was to inherit and talked to his aunts about nothing. His mother, who was the only one who seemed to care that Tommy Joe was gone, said, 'Maybe he's practicing his shot. When he gets an idea into his head, you never know when he'll be back. When he was younger he used to adore collecting muskets. That's all he'd talk about, muskets, and he'd disappear for hours.'

"I began gulping the sherry. Then I said I didn't feel well and excused myself. They let me sleep through dinner. I woke up at three and couldn't place where I was. Finally I tiptoed out of my room and saw his door was open. I could tell he wasn't there. It felt too safe, and I didn't hear him breathing. Fine, I thought, maybe he's gone to Portsmouth. I went back to bed, thinking in the morning that I would call a cab or an airport car and get the hell out of there.

"That, of course, would've been too easy. He came into my room again. It was barely dawn. I heard the crows and then I heard him whispering, mixing me all up with talk about the sunrise and broom crowberry and rattlesnakes. He wanted to shoot rattlesnakes. And you know how I feel about snakes.

"'Come on,' he said. 'Come for a walk with me. I've missed you.'

"'Where were you all day?' I asked him.

"'I had some business to take care of in town. Didn't my mother tell you? Come on, I've packed us some cakes for breakfast and some orange juice. You haven't seen much, have you, stuck all day with the aunts and uncles? I thought you liked life a little faster than that. That's why you came here, isn't it? Don't you want to be with me?' He practically dragged me out of bed, threw my clothes at me, and stood in front of me with his arms folded across his chest. 'I'll wait here,' he said.

"'Uh-uh, you can wait outside,' I told him.

"'Right,' he said, almost snarling, 'like I haven't already seen your tits,' and he left. Then the door swung open again and he said, 'I didn't mean that.'

"We drove up an old logging road, got out, and the first thing he did was shoot a rabbit. He had a twelve-gauge shotgun and he blew the thing to pieces. He shot it once and that killed it. Then he shot it two more times at close range. My stomach started to spasm, and I wobbled away to a pine tree to get control of myself. All he had to do was leave me there, but the idiot came up behind me and I started screaming. 'You didn't have to do that! You didn't have to do that! Bury it.'

"'You bury it,' he said. I got by him and took off my shoe and started digging with my heel. That didn't work, so I broke off a branch. Finally I just covered the bloody mess with pine needles and walked off. I wasn't able to cover it entirely. In fact, I was barely able to cover any of it. I had to keep picking up my shoes and wiping the soles on the pine needles. It was disgusting. My hands felt like death; it smelled like death. Then he snuck up behind me again, and this time I didn't know he was there until I heard the click of the trigger.

"'Ever shoot one of these things?' He was holding the shotgun right over my head. Tina, it was like déjà vu. When I turned around, he lowered it to my eye. 'Did you?' he said. 'Did you?'

"I backed away and started to run. I heard him laughing. Then I heard him shouting for me. 'Hey, hey, come on! I'm only teasing you. Come on.'

"I didn't look to see if he was behind me, I just kept running. I kept going until I was at the bottom of the mountain and it was marked Johnson. I turned left onto another road and that was marked Johnson. There was Johnson Road and Johnson Lane and Old Johnson Road. Johnson Cove. Johnson Mews. Johnson Lake. I thought I was going crazy. I thought they might've come out the night before and painted over the signs. I didn't know what else to do, so I kept running. Past Johnson Meadows and Johnson

Mountain Lane. Johnson Road again. I heard a car behind me slowing down.

"'Get in!' he said.

"I screamed at him. 'You're crazy! You're a maniac! Get away from me!'

"'Get in the car. It's fourteen miles to the house!'

"'I'm not going anywhere with you. You want to kill me!'

"'Then fuck off!' And he sped away.

"I walked fourteen miles back to the house. No one was there. I called the police and asked them to come get me. The man I spoke to must have covered the receiver with his hand, but I still heard him laughing to someone at his desk that the yachtsman's son was at it again. They wouldn't come. The police suggested I call an out-of-town taxi service at one of the airport companies, since they doubted a local taxi would come either. They gave me a number and I called, then I packed my bags. Just as the service arrived, Tommy Joe screeched up to the front door. The side of the station wagon was battered. He barged right past me without even looking and slammed a door upstairs. The driver practically threw me in the van. I held onto my bags, and before I knew it, I was out of there. I was never so happy to see people and baggage and counters and newsstands in my life!

"But I kept looking over my shoulder. I'm still doing it. I can't remember if I told him where I live!" She rubbed her eyes.

"I can't believe it. I still feel like I have rabbit blood on my shoe. I feel marked. Tina, I feel like Tommy Joe was some kind of a warning! I don't understand. I don't understand. Why're these things happening to me?"

CHAPTER SEVEN

AT THE TIME, I COULDN'T BEGIN TO explain what was happening to her, but I have a theory now. It begins with the idea that lifelines are in the shape of eggs. We start out as a simple gaga, say, at three o'clock on the egg. Then we work our way back up over the top of the oval and down the other side, farther from all we know about ourselves. We skid downward through more and more confusion and times and places and people that seem fraught with déjà vu, for now we're on the dark side of our own moon and there is the distinct impression of a twisted familiarity. Then we reach the bottom of the egg. From that depth we look up and say, *What a long way to get to the same point.* And that's when we begin the trek up and back to where we started, shedding as we go, peeling off the skins we wore to make it through the confusion and the darkness, the times and places and people.

Spike and I hadn't been marked by rabbit's blood for special torture. We were just trying to get back to where we were before we became part of other people's trips.

After the Tommy Joe Johnson fiasco, Spike and I spoke every night, usually till after midnight. We talked about what we wanted. Me: to live in a place like Pentacook, New Hampshire, and write calming, naturalist essays like John McPhee—twenty pages, say, about the beech tree.

"And," I added, "to fall in love with a good person."

Spike: to finish writing at least five good short stories about anything. "Writing," she said, "it gets me higher than sex. I'm interested in motivation. The why. Why people do things."

"Hell," I said, "that's a bottomless question. And what if you find out and it still doesn't give you peace about what they did?"

"It may not. It'll probably be even more devastating. But the information itself is comforting. Name me one Perry Mason show that doesn't end with the criminal explaining why he did it so we'd feel better."

"But he still did it, didn't he? That's what I look at, that he did it."

And she'd say, "Why can't I talk like this to a man? Why can't I have as good a time on a date as I have with you?"

"Come on, they're not aliens."

"No, you don't understand. They walk away from me when I talk like this. If I were to suddenly fall to the ground and kick my feet in the air in ecstasy, they'd be embarrassed. You wouldn't. You might walk away till I got over it, but you'd come back."

"Go to sleep," I'd say after a while. "It's late," But we never hung up. She'd keep talking and I'd listen with my eyes closed, and her words in my half sleep took on the rhythm of an incantation.

"When women are with women," she'd say, "there's freedom. It's the freedom of not being told what they can't do. I don't want some guy to say, 'Here, let me do it, you shouldn't climb on the roof.' Why should he be the only one to see the world from the roof? If it were you and me, we'd both get on the roof, and there wouldn't be anyone standing with his hands on his hips, snickering, waiting for us to do something dizzy. With men, you make a mistake once, you don't get to try it again. It might take me three times to learn how to change a tire. Big deal. But to them I'm a fuck-up because I can't do something so obvious."

And she'd say, and she'd say, and she'd say. I'd fall asleep still feeling the impression of the phone against my ear but also feeling a peculiar sense of usefulness and purpose. Then again, her rush of thoughts and epiphanies was like a faucet that wouldn't shut off and once, after a long and arduous midnight call, I wondered if it were possible to drown.

I reread an essay by Ralph Waldo Emerson that I dimly remembered.

"Almost all people descend to meet. All association must be a compromise, and what is worse, the very flower and aroma of the flower of each of the beautiful natures disappears as they approach each other. . . . Our faculties do not play us true, and both parties are relieved by solitude."

Okay, I thought, *but in so many ways I felt ascendant—or was that trickery? Was it true that in some areas of my perception, reality was suspended?* There was the matter about money, for example.

There used to be days, when I was first left with the apartment to myself, where I would spend my time averaging the phone bills and the electric bills and the rent and the weekly amount spent on food, then estimate how much I could spend from then on for a week, a month, a year; then I'd check my figures the following week and the week after that.

No more. Spike showed me that money would appear whenever you wanted it. It was uncanny, and shouldn't have been, but for her, poverty and abundance were tied to her moods.

In September, she quit her job. I suspected it was because she didn't have enough time to care for her father, at least emotionally. She began working as a part-time secretary at an accounting firm that was so stingy, the partners had skimped on the width of the hallways, phonied the wood in the doors with rec-room paneling, and left the floors bare except for the thick-nap carpeting in their own offices. When I would call her at Drudge and Drudge, as we dubbed it, her voice would be atonal and she would talk of her father, who, she knew now, would probably never leave the hospital. She would have to visit him. She was terrified. She said he would "pull her down into his soul and she'd never come up again. Never. Never."

The worse her father's condition became, the more hours she put in at Drudge and Drudge until she was spending her Saturdays and some Sundays in that phony-wood office that smelled of formaldehyde. Since they paid minimum wage and no benefits for part-timers, the take-home wasn't exactly equaling her expenses, and soon her rent was overdue.

"At least the office manager isn't here," she'd say when I called on Saturdays. The office manager was a teased-hair teenager from Brooklyn who declared that coffee could not be drunk at the desk and no one could leave their desk except to go to the bathroom or the copy machine. And coffee could not be drunk at the copy machine.

"Get out of there!" I'd say.

"I can't."

She began selling her antique books for cash. She decided to sell her camera and her linen tablecloths. The camera was ancient, heavy, and cumbersome, she claimed, and the tablecloths were musty.

"Actually I wouldn't mind getting rid of everything," she confided, and went ahead and had her grandmother's diamond engagement ring appraised.

Then, right before the diamond sale date, she went to see her father. I heard from her late at night and her voice was spooky.

"Tina, it was horrible. He was lying in the bed like a gully, a human gully, and his breath was quicksand. The stench was unbelievable. He pulled me close to him, and I swear it was like he wanted to suck me inside of him and if I didn't resist, he would've done it."

"It's all right," I told her, exhausted. "You're home now."

"There was something so pitiful about him. He wanted to shoot the nurses and hop over the bed and run down the mountain to die."

He died in his bed. From acute alcoholism. Spike visited his house, which was more like a shack deep in the woods.

"Tina, his bedroom was like a shrine to me. There were pictures of me on the dresser and on the nightstand. He still had my report cards. He had all the letters I'd sent him that he never answered. And he kept journals and I read through them. He was a terrible speller, and it must've been like being constipated for him but he wrote every day. He wrote how much he missed me and wished I could forgive him."

I thought this would be like the clang of the prison doors opening for her. Her father didn't despise her; he adored her. But, curiously, when I mentioned these things to her later in the summer, she grunted, and I was left with the strong impression that she had no idea what I was talking about, no memory of a shrine or journal entries.

When she returned to the city, one of her former bosses called . . . just like that.

And the next week she left the petrifying stink of Drudge and Drudge and began working PR at a salary high enough to pay for a head of lettuce with a hundred-dollar bill. (She didn't have anything smaller, she told the cashier.) There was also an inheritance and a car, her father's car.

"Meet Sam," she said, slapping the hood of a Honda.

"You're not going to call it Sam. That's sick."

"Yep." She laughed.

"What if it breaks down?"

"Then I'll call it Spike." And she burst out laughing.

She remembered the "Wants" list she'd tacked to her bedroom wall one Friday night when she'd had only a bowl of cereal for dinner, and she started to check off and purchase each "Want." A color TV set to replace the one she wouldn't shut off or else, she claimed, it wouldn't come on again. A dishwasher to empty her sink of dishes piled near-cabinet high and scattered on the counter. A French door with drapes to disguise the closet in her entryway and create the illusion that her apartment was not in Brooklyn but in Paris. She wanted a baby grand piano and a Louis XIV chair. She wanted a Turkish rug. We spent a full day running our hands over the plush weavings, gazing at designs that to me seemed so tortured and busy, so formal and worried, they reminded me of too many families I knew. I had to sit down and look at nothing at all.

When I landed an assignment with the *New York Courier*, she sent me flowers— beautiful lilies and orchids that must've cost a fortune. She took me to dinner at Montrachet and ordered a bottle of Dom Perignon and toasted, "We did it! We did it! You might even grow up to believe you're smart."

I frowned. I didn't think it took too much to interview immigrants about their feelings for the Statue of Liberty. (This was my job—to write features about people who came to America, so the *Courier* could help raise money for the statue's renovation.) But I reveled in feeling celebrated and in feeling this constant shifting of the winds and miraculous boons. Maybe life didn't have to be so planned. Counting pennies was one way to organize against disaster. Walking a tightrope across it was another. Here, in her bare living room, stood a baby grand piano. Here, in the sad kitchen, was a spanking new dishwasher. On my desk were lilies and orchids. I had never felt as invincible, as charmed, as full of possibilities. And so following along, I began to feel immune to bad luck, which, Emerson might say, was the beginning of my descent.

IT WAS THIS DIZZY OPTIMISM THAT LED me to say, "Let's get what we want. Let's go to the mountains and write our asses off."

In early March, I drove us to the Catskills, which were bleak and wet with fog and offered a much less lush version of Pentacook. I had a headache. My eyes were swimming. A cold was taking over my nose. My body, no doubt, was trying to tell me something, but ultimately the effect was to keep me in a foggy, clogged-up daze until the contracts were signed.

Spike made all the arrangements. We drove into a town called Warrenville on the Delaware River. Here, the river was so narrow that if I had a good pitching arm, I could stand in New York, throw a rock across the Delaware, and it would land in Pennsylvania.

We met with Jamie Ann, a realtor about our age. I crawled into the front seat of Jamie Ann's Jeep, my head throbbing. Spike took up the back, smoking a cigarette and chattering about the groundwater level or some such thing.

Jamie Ann interrupted her to say, "I think you'll like the house we're headed to. It's a perfect summer rental for artists like yourselves. We have two artists living in town already. One just bought an old Victorian to renovate, and the other is a writer who lives right next door to where we're going."

I glanced at Spike. What had she told this woman about us?

Pine trees rumbled by. Jamie Ann prattled on about the local attractions and, almost willfully, my eyes were drawn to her foot on the gas pedal. It was the tiniest foot I'd ever seen. I was mesmerized. Big Jeep, big pedal, tiny foot—it was enough to keep me staring at her toes all day, like the rabbit who gets hypnotized by the fox's dance. I kept thinking, *What kind of house would be perfect for artists like ourselves?*

Abruptly the Jeep turned into a driveway just past Al and Nancy's Roadside Bar and right before a barracks-style motel that looked abandoned. Two yappy dogs dashed around garbage cans to bark at our wheels. Under Jamie Ann's miniature foot, the Jeep rocked through ruts past a wooden sign that said No Trespassing in Day-Glo orange. Beyond this was a trailer with Italianate trim and a plot of ragweed and grass. This was where the neighbors lived: Alma, the writer, and her sister, Imogene. Finally, at the tail end of the road was a leafless old oak and a cabin.

It was inarguably ugly, though it didn't have to be that way. The basic structure of a log cabin on a surface foundation was fine, but the owners, a Mr. Ely Pullet and his sons, had painted the logs a diarrhea yellow. They had let the plaster foundation crack and flake, and white dust and chunks that looked like pieces of moonscape were scattered on the lawn.

The lawn was a scruffy piece of dirt with patches of wild grass and moss, matted pine needles, and a network of ant hills at the edge that looked like blemishes on a chin. We walked past a pine tree that was bleeding sap down its trunk from the wound of a brutal pruning.

The best thing about the cabin—in fact the only thing to recommend it—was the pond at the end of the lawn. There was the cabin, the scruffy piece of dirt that was the lawn, then the water. The pond held the shape of an *S* for as long as you could see it from the cabin, then, Jamie Ann told us, it curled around, tapered a half mile farther in an area of tree stumps, and ended in a marsh. The cabin was set at the opposite end of this marsh, where the pond was deep and flowed past the property and eventually under a wooden bridge and down a ledge.

Something about the pond felt very private. There were no floating docks or buoys or moored sunfish to change its character. The bank appeared torn rather than shaped, with freshly exposed roots, brambles, and vines. The water was a deep brown.

The ragged, dark appearance of the pond no doubt had something to do with the chilly, gray March day. The beech trees, sumac, and blueberry bushes were still bare of leaves, and the arm of a skinny birch hung forlornly close to the water. Directly across, a maple that had been struck by lightning had fallen into the pond and was decomposing in the water like the long arm of a wraith.

I left the bank and began circling the cabin. There was something peculiar about its "feel." It did not have the feel of any of the houses I'd ever rented or lived in before. There was no sense of any person even remotely like me having lived there, and as soon as I thought this, I knew its effect on Spike would be the opposite. I turned to find her looking beatific, leaning on an oak canted toward the water. Beneath her feet was a worn strip of land that led to a cinder block in the water.

"Alma puts her canoe in there," Jamie Ann explained. "I'm sure she'll let you use it. Alma's the writer I mentioned to you."

"She better let us use it," Spike whispered to me as we followed Jamie Ann back up the slope of near-frozen mud and pine needles. "This is our land."

We entered the cabin through a side door, which was the only door, and waited in a vestibule decorated with a crumbling wreath of oak leaves while Jamie Ann worked the key. Spike pulled out a notepad and pastel pen. The ink was magenta.

"This window'll have to be fixed," she said, picking up and putting down the broken handle.

Inside the smell was muckish. The watery mist from the pond swelled the stale odors that had been in residence all winter: sour cushions, old cigarette ash, mothballed army blankets. The cabin was small with only one real bedroom. The other was a makeshift arrangement on the enclosed deck that fronted the house and overlooked the pond.

It struck me immediately how strong an affinity the Pullets evinced for the drabness of life. Beach houses I had rented with Edward may have had some paint-by-number fife-and-drum scenes on the walls, and tablecloths and pot holders with inane sayings about goodness, but there was almost always a cheerfulness to these secondhand trimmings.

Here, by the chill of the pond, I could imagine a man who hung his head and drank all night trying to figure out how to fix the hot water heater without paying for a repairman.

Certainly, the Pullets saved their paper goods. The kitchen shelves were stocked with three different kinds of napkins—industrial strength, as if taken from a public restroom; a single-ply generic economy pack; and a cocktail stack printed with "Texas Longhorns" over the pimply grain. The Pullets—and it was just the sons who lived here, Jamie Ann told us—had also collected an assortment of bulky glass ashtrays and even two flimsy aluminum ashtrays of the kind found in airports or hospitals. There was a pile of cracked and chipped plastic wear, an old box of cocoa that had caved in, two cans of evaporated milk, a bag of crumbling marshmallows, and a box of toothpicks spotted with bug droppings.

In the living room, a plain square table with four unmatched chairs was set in the middle and covered with oilcloth. A foul-smelling sofa bed covered with cheap, nubby fabric banked one wall. Above that a threadbare American flag had been push-pinned into the wall to cover an inset mural. This mural was obviously the pride of the original owner (and builder), given the amount of space devoted to it.

I lifted the flag and saw that over the years the painting had darkened into lugubrious shades of green. The scene was of geese arriving at a pond, but the dark, olive-colored light now bled from the sky into their feathers and into the marshy bank, so that the flock could have been arriving in the morning or at dusk, right before a storm or immediately after, or bringing the storm and the darkness with them. Though the gloom made it easy to understand the Pullets' desire to cover the picture completely, I was fascinated by the way the dense hues spilled over and changed the color of the sun and much else that once made sense.

The most interesting rooms in the cabin were the bedrooms. One of these had been constructed by cutting off part of the living room with a wall. This chamber was long and narrow with a single bed, a dresser, and a large, floral-print chair. This bedroom was dainty, with white lacy curtains and gold leaf trim on the dresser. The second bedroom was the opposite of the first since it was essentially an outdoor deck. It was, of course, more exposed to the weather with one wall made up entirely of windows overlooking the pond. A double bed was squeezed between the windows and the musty interior wall. A section from the nubby sofa was stored at one end along with a rack of dog-eared books whose titles echoed one another: *Out West*, *Sands of the Desert*, *The Wayward Wind.*

There was an odd touch to this room, which made me think that the man hanging his head over repair bills would do better just to go ahead and pay them. The Pullets had installed large, expensive Andersen windows but they opened into the deck instead of out toward the pond, so for the sake of a breeze, one-quarter of the space was obstructed. Then we noticed that in the bathroom the Pullets had shaved the top of the door so that it looked like a lopsided slice of bread. In the kitchen, lemon-colored curtains hung only five inches above the burners on the stove.

Spike continued making furious notes in magenta ink, picking up broken hinges and switches, clucking and shaking her head at the design hazards, but I knew the inventory didn't make a difference. I'd seen her face at the oak tree and 50 percent of us was already tearing down those curtains and screwing in light bulbs.

"Jamie Ann," I piped up, "aside from the cabin, is that motel at the beginning of the driveway always vacant?"

"Always," Jamie Ann said. "No one stays there anymore."

"What about Al and Nancy's Roadside Bar? What is that like?"

She misunderstood me. "Oh, you wouldn't want to go in there. Not that there's anything wrong with it. It's just there're much better places to go." She looked at my stricken face. "Don't worry, you're gonna have a good time—both of you girls!"

I asked for time to think.

Jamie Ann dropped us back at my car and said the office would be open till five that day. Fine. I took three more aspirin, sank into the familiar vinyl smell of Japanese bucket seats, and drove Spike and me to the one-truck-limit bridge that crossed the river into Pennsylvania. I wanted to see the area.

The bridge dumped us immediately into a town called Lomatia Falls, where the foothills to the mountains pressed close to the shoulder of the road. I drove to what looked like the center of town and slowed down to pass three grown men, one on a tricycle, all wearing flannel shirts as red as their ruddy faces, all bearing a family resemblance. It started in the blond hair, dirty and shaggy, went down to the brow, and broadened to a bulldog expression that said, *Who the hell are you?* Still looking for a main street, I made a left into a wide road that turned out to be a lumberyard, managed a K-turn between two walls of cut lumber, drove past the men who were still watching, and rode out of town. Spike was laughing. "Well now we know. The US is on one side of the bridge and Lomatia Falls is on the other."

I came to a halt outside Pauline's coffee shop, next to the realtor's office, feeling better that at least we were back in the same state as New York City, but then I looked up. It was a war zone. On the coffee shop roof was a sheet painted with a large black circle crossed by a black slash. Underneath in bold, black letters someone had scrawled, "NFS Get Out of Town!"

What was "NFS"?

My eyes felt as if they were covered with cling wrap and my head was full of bricks.

"Milkshake?"

"What!" I whirled on her.

"Hey, take it easy."

"What about that motel?" I said, as Spike let me follow her into Pauline's toward one of the many vacant tables. "You believe no one goes in there? It's only a few drunken steps from the door of the bar."

She looked at me as if to say, *What a disappointment.*

I tried to redeem myself. "I didn't say I was good at this. I've never rented a house with another woman before—alone in the woods, right behind a bar I don't want to go into, and a motel that nobody goes in and out of."

"Okay," she said patiently, "we'll go back and have another look."

"That's all right, I remember."

She smoked and said, "We'll go back and see if it strikes you the same way. Don't even look at the chain saw in the bedroom," which there was.

It was getting dark and the neon of Al and Nancy's Roadside Bar was beginning to glow a zesty blood-red. My car bounced through the ruts in the dirt road. Apparently, the dogs were tied up since it was quiet. The silence was soft and eerie. Suddenly I saw a shadow in the rearview mirror and braked. "Look at that!" A woman in stiletto heels was picking her way across the gravel between the motel and the bar. She wore black spandex slacks and a white sweater over breasts big as footballs.

Spike unleashed a riot of laughter. "Bambi!" she shouted. "It's Bambi!"

"I don't believe it." I was shaking my head full of bricks. "It's started already." What I meant was it seemed like a story Spike would have told me over the phone, except now I was in it. My head cold kept me in a foggy, clogged-up daze until the rental papers were signed. When I felt healthy again, back in the city, I met Spike for a drink and told her straight out, "I don't want a lot of strange men there."

She may have been hurt; she may have even been proud—it's hard to say.

"What do you think, they're going to be banging down the door as soon as I set foot in Warrenville? At the general store they're going to pass around a flyer that two girls are alone in the woods by Al and Nancy's Roadside Bar?"

"Don't say that!" I had an image of local men in rusted cars driving down the rutted road and blocking our exit. I wished I were bolder, but I would stay up late at night (after talking to my immigrants who had made voyages across the ocean) and feel the sting of tiny worries and imagined catastrophes and wonder if I would live to see the next September. In my mind, the cabin loomed as the final reckoning, the hellhole where punishments would visit like fog slipping in under the door.

Spike asked, "Why are you so afraid?"

I didn't know. It was just a feeling.

I wanted to keep Spike around me. I didn't want to be alone, because when I was alone the demons attacked and I would begin to think that I was living the last days of my life as an innocent, safe girl. I needed to keep feeling her, even if it boiled over into another zone of craziness. I proposed a scheme that would keep us together: We would help each other paint our apartments before we left. That way, we wouldn't be returning to the same landscapes.

Spike said, "That's my MO. What I usually do is move into a town, furnish my apartment, paint it, strip the floors, then move out."

I remember three things from that time. First, I remember drinking a lot of coffee in coffee shops with my fingers always curled around my keys because I felt homeless. I remember Spike organizing all of my furniture into the bedroom and painting two walls to my one. And I remember the way we met Cody, who was, Ralph Waldo Emerson, maybe the second step in my descent.

CHAPTER EIGHT

THIS WOULD NOT BE HAPPENING IF *I didn't know her. This is down, this is low, this is whore-talk*, and I held my hands up—*whoa*—and leaned back so they could talk in front of me, as if I weren't there.

Cody. I was sure she had invented him. I went to the ladies' room for a few minutes and when I came back, he was there, one barstool over, spun into existence like cotton candy. Mike, the bartender, was there. And Spike was laughing, the same sunny laugh I'd heard before as if she'd just stepped off a sailboat with fresh pineapple still on her lips. Cody was dressed in a boat-necked shirt and tight jeans and was almost unbearable to look at. He was handsome beyond polite imagination. I could see him striding through a beach club, his body engorged and tan and looking too thick for clothes, and Spike, too, could see it—she was thrusting her breasts and tossing back her hair and when I joined the conversation, Cody was talking about whores.

"They took care of me, darlin', fresh-squeezed every morning. If you want to be looked after, live in a house full of women."

We were covered in paint and had come for a margarita break. It was a humid Saturday evening, just about five o'clock, when the only people left in the city were the ones who couldn't find a way to get out. Cody was still trying, busy making telephone calls at the pay phone. He had a canvas satchel, and a huge address book lay open on the bar.

He talked rapid-fire, approaching Spike's speed, and his smile was sinister. It was impossible to see if his eyes matched his smile since they were hidden behind opaque glasses. I guessed him to be around forty trying to pass for mid-thirties. With his spectacular looks and his air of offensiveness/defensiveness, I figured he had to be involved in the image profession as a model or an actor.

"The whores fed me in bed," he continued telling us. "I was fond of all of them, but there was one in particular, Kristen, who I really liked. She came from a hot-shit family in Greenwich, Connecticut, and one day we decided to have ourselves a visit. We spent the week on her father's yacht, fucking our brains out. We knew her father's third wife liked to listen at the door, so one day we caught her and pulled her in and played extended family." He smiled until his dimples stretched so far they must've knifed his eyes under those dark glasses.

"I bet that was fun," Spike said, egging him on, her eyes like slits and her voice throaty.

"Well, Kristen's stepmother introduced me to all her friends. I went to Greece that summer. Africa, Morocco. I bought enough hash to keep me aeronautic for a year." He grinned. "I like to live well."

"I bet you do," Spike said, her mouth twitching.

"I've been around the world twice. Once as the first mate on one of Kennedy's yachts. I'd like to live in Capri for a while. Do you know Capri? The whores there are beautiful, clear like the water. You just want to suck them down and swim in them and float on top of them. Here," he said, pulling a book from his satchel. "Read this." He went to make another call. In between dialing, he shouted, "Read the back. The back! The book is intense."

"Uh-oh," I said to Spike. It was a book on numerology. "That handsome head is full of goo."

"Don't be so judgmental," she snapped at me.

"Hey, are you talking about me?" he shouted from the pay phone. "No girl talk!"

"I'm trying to get to Brigantine," he told us when he regained his barstool. Do you know Brigantine?"

"It used to be nice," I said. "Then the condos went up for the dealers who moved there to get jobs in the casinos in Atlantic City. It's like a poor, overdeveloped desert now."

"I didn't ask for a history. I just wanted you to say yes or no. My friend, anyway, has a large house with a hot tub."

"In Brigantine? That's hard to believe."

"So don't." He flashed me a nasty smile.

"Who's your friend?" Spike asked, implying that whoever she was, she was a pig compared to Spike.

"She's rich!" The dimples creased his cheeks and the edges of crow's-feet peeked out from behind the glasses. "Loads of bucks. And she likes to rub my back. She's got a bed the size of this room. A 360 SL that I get to drive and a live-in cook."

"All that for free?" Spike said.

"More or less," Cody said. "But I'm not greedy. She gets what she wants."

"I bet she does."

"Whoa," I said. "I don't want to be in this conversation."

"You're not," he said. "I'm talking to your friend. Relax. What's with you, anyway? You a schoolteacher?"

"She's an essayist," Spike said. "And I'm a writer. We're writers painting."

Cody wanted to know so much about us, he immediately went to the phone and started dialing someone else.

Spike continued undaunted. "So if we fuck up, it's okay. We're not supposed to know how to paint a house. But we're doing it anyway."

"No one home," he said. "So what're you painting?"

"Our apartments."

"Shit work, isn't it? I do carpentry to make some extra bucks."

"How often?" I asked.

He stared at me.

"Just asking."

"Mainly I make it from modeling. Here." He opened his satchel again and threw an eight-by-ten glossy across the bar. In the picture he wasn't wearing the dark-shaded glasses, and his eyes were a light blue. He had a square jaw, an aquiline nose, full lips, thick, brown hair, a rich tan, and that engorged body. He was handsome in such an overwhelmingly desirable way. I could see him advertising island vacations, expensive scotch, and exotic sports cars, as if he'd groomed himself to be a fantasy.

And that's when I knew that he wasn't just joking, and Spike knew it too. He *was* a whore. Maybe only when the modeling got slow, but still . . . And right now what he'd done was crawl onto the barstool next to Spike like a dutiful little fantasy between jobs.

He made another phone call and reached a woman in Bayhead. "Do you know Bayhead?" he asked.

I had stopped talking, trying to ignore the courtship they were bantering into existence and wondering if Spike could have summoned him in some extraterrestrial psychological way. "You look like you know about head," he said to her. I winced. She laughed.

"That's for you to hope for," she said.

"Yeah? I've got twenty minutes to catch the train. Here. Take my number. Call me." He wrote it on the back of his eight-by-ten glossy. "I didn't have it typeset because I knew I was moving. Will you call me?"

"Maybe."

"You should. We should see each other again. We have something in common, you and I. I can feel it. There's something about you that's like me. Don't you think so?" He turned to me. "Don't you think we're alike somehow?"

"How the hell do I know?"

"Well you've been talking to me and you know her." I frowned.

"Come on," Spike said, "I'll drive you to the station."

"You have a car?"

"Yeah. Sam."

"Sam?"

Apparently I had the role of interpreter because he looked at me. When I didn't answer, he tickled me in the ribs.

"Hey!" I protested, but I was laughing.

"Is someone named Sam in the car?"

"Ask her."

"She won't tell me. Look at that bitch face. She's a cockteaser, I can smell 'em a mile away. I love 'em!" he roared, grabbing her upper arm and squeezing it till Spike yelled, "Ouch!"

I shook my head. "Christ."

"Don't be so disapproving," he said to me, sounding sincere for the first time.

"She calls her car Sam after her father who just died. That's how she got the car," I explained.

"That's weird."

I shrugged. Spike, I noticed, was watching me though still-slit cat eyes, smiling off the side of her cigarette. I gathered I was performing correctly: agent-interpreter to femme fatale. The role was uncomfortable but not impossible, close I'd say to referee-voyeur.

Cody and I were alone for one profound moment that night. The three of us were on our way to Sam when Spike remembered she'd left her car keys on the bar. I wanted to run back with her. I had no training for a man like him, and frankly, I didn't know how to talk to him as if he were real. But as soon as Spike rushed away, the fast-talking giddiness disappeared. He looked bleak.

"My father died nine months ago," he said. "It's awful." He said this twice, not sure if I'd heard him.

"Yeah," he said. "I came back home after the funeral and my pickup died out on me. Then my TV went."

"Here's Spike!" I shouted, pointing to her running figure half a block away.

"She's short, isn't she?" he asked, leering.

"No." We were standing side by side watching the approaching comet. "She's all in proportion."

"Okay, let's go." Spike charged up. She whisked off her painter's cap and her hair fell down in a zingy ponytail. "Let's go, everybody in, get ready!"

He hollered all the way across Forty-Second Street and Spike laughed, that throaty, wicked, insane laugh of hers as if she were leaving a trail of flaming horseshit behind her. She ran red lights, slalomed across five lanes, and kept laughing, steering with one hand and pounding her windshield with the other to get the traffic to move.

"Slow down!" Cody yelled, crashing around in the back seat.

We skidded through a pack of cabs to Penn Station. The clock on her dash told us his train had left three minutes ago, but Spike waved him out of the back seat. "Hurry up, hurry up. You'll miss your train!" and he ran out yelling about Valium and his phone number.

She banged her head against the headrest and snorted. "What a poor schmuck. I feel sorry for him. I really do."

That same evening, sitting in her car that was double-parked outside my apartment, she lectured me on tolerance. The night air was as smooth and soft as black silk, and the lights from her dash glowed a yellow green.

The front seats of cars have always been more seductive to me than the back—with the candlelight from the dashboard and the movie screen of the stars and the aura of power from the dials.

"Drive me somewhere," I once said to Edward, who had pulled into a parking area in downtown DC. "Drive me across the water to the Jefferson Monument."

"Drive me somewhere," I wanted to say to Spike. "Let's not talk anymore." My head was resting on the back of the seat. I watched her grab her ponytail, twist it into a roll, hold it there with one hand, and with the other jam a heavy metal clip around her hair.

Almost as soon as this was done, she lit a cigarette and blew out the smoke, not gently, but as if it needed to be pushed.

"It was obvious you dismissed Cody right away," she said. "You have no compassion for people who are different from you."

"You called him a poor schmuck after you dropped him off late."

"I felt sorry for him. Listen, the guy obviously had something go wrong or he wouldn't be selling it, you know what I mean?"

"Who cares? If he weren't incredibly handsome, if he weren't into money, you wouldn't care either."

"That's not true."

"Oh, come on."

"I really feel bad for the guy. He seems like he's trying to do something for himself, but he hasn't got a clue."

"Why not warm up to men who do have a clue? Why choose men who are troubled? I couldn't stand all that crap about whores. And that phony bit about what he did to make money. Why bother with someone like that? He's almost forty years old."

"Tina," she said, and I could hear the warmth in her voice though I wasn't exactly sure who or what she was warming up to. "Listen to yourself. I'm not saying I want to change him. I'm not saying he's not struggling. All I'm saying is to have a little compassion. Did you see his face when you asked him how often he has to hammer boards together to make money? The guy was speechless. It's like he crossed some imaginary line of horror you have in your head, and as soon as he did that, you zapped him."

"I didn't zap him."

"Oh yes you did. He looked at you with his mouth open. I could see all of his bottom teeth. He crossed the line of horror for you, and you didn't want to hear anything more he had to say because you didn't want to have to stomach it."

"He annoyed me. No, I didn't want to hear he was a whore. I didn't want to sit there talking with a man his size who lets himself be used."

She threw back her head and laughed. "See. See. The line of horror. Tina," she said, putting her arm around my shoulders and pulling me so close I could smell the tar on her breath. "Just listen to what they have to say. That's all. You won't get hurt."

I pulled away. "It's not that. I get bored when people bullshit me. I'm not interested. I stop listening when I know they're giving me stock narrative. To me it's rude, so I'm rude back."

"Not everyone exists to entertain you," she said softly.

"Spike, if they're giving me stock narrative, what kind of story are they telling themselves? There's something I don't want to know about people who've been walking through the same script for twenty years and they've outgrown the age range—by a long shot."

"Well, what you don't want to know crosses that line."

"Look, this is not the time to suggest tolerance to me. I'm not interested. Those are your needs, not mine."

And she said, in a voice sweet as an angel's, "That's okay, honey. We can disagree. If we didn't there'd be something wrong. One of the reasons I like you so much is because you don't always agree with me. You exercise my mind."

"Hmmm." I sat quietly, feeling pleased with myself.

Spike smoked. A woman walking her dog let it sniff our front left tire, then changed her mind.

"Brutus," she said, glancing nervously at us. "You're disturbing the people." She yanked the leash and hurried on.

"That's the first whore I ever met in my life," I said finally. I waited two beats. "Are you going to call him?"

"You want me to, don't you?"

"Yeah."

"Why?"

"Because he crosses the line."

"Of horror?"

"That's right."

She didn't look at me and I, too, stared straight ahead. "You can handle him," I said. "I can't. Invite him up to the cabin."

"I thought you said you didn't want any men there."

"I don't. Not locals. He's just . . . such a centerfold. I've never been around a man who looks like that."

She reached across to open the car door for me. "Maybe I'll leave a message on his machine. After we leave town."

CHAPTER NINE

SPIKE AND I STOOD WITH OUR HANDS stuffed in our pockets, smiling, and bucking the wind, while a man lounged on his Harley a few feet away. He revved the engine, then pulled it back into a fast tick. He watched us, his legs straddling the bike, and yanked on one glove.

"Need directions?" he asked.

"No thanks."

"Your car okay? Need any help?"

"We're fine."

"Want to know where you are?"

We both looked at him. He was pulling on the other glove and twitching the fingers. "Want to borrow money?"

Spike laughed into the wind, then swiveled her body in his direction.

He smiled. "You can't blame a guy for trying, huh?" He shoved his helmet down tight and snapped it at his ear. "Bye-bye, girls." The engine exploded and farted, and the bike swerved out of the gravel bed onto the blacktop.

Spike was still laughing. "What do you think, Whirly, is this going to be a summer or what?"

"Whirly? Where'd you get that from?"

"That's what I call you. Didn't I ever call you that before?"

"No."

"It's because you remind me of a whirligig about to take off. Or fall over."

"Christ, that's awful." I glowered at my sneakers. "Just don't call me that in public."

"Why not?"

"It's goofy."

"I'm goofy," she said. "Hey, you!" she shouted to the mountains. "I'm goofy and this is my friend Whirly, and if Pullet shows his dickhead this weekend, we're going to yank it off."

"Pullet?" I'd forgotten about the landlord. I'd forgotten about troubles of all kinds.

They seemed attached to a different location, far from where we were now.

When Spike first spoke to him over the phone, he had agreed to meet all of her demands about repairs. She called me late that evening, pleased and excited. "He's flying in from Texas to meet me at the cabin and go over my list."

"Texas? Is this the same man who put the windows in backward?" I asked.

"I think it was one of his sons."

"The apple doesn't fall far from the tree."

"Tina."

"I know. Compassion. Tolerance. I hope he doesn't disappoint you."

When I heard from her next, she was steaming with rage. "My biggest fear now is that Pullet's sons'll breed. Then there'll be new Pullets all over the state, looking at their dicks, saying, 'Are these upside-down?'"

"What happened to the promises?" I asked wearily, holding the phone away from my ear a little.

"It wasn't so bad, even when he spent half an hour fingering the threads on the screw to the window latch explaining to me why it couldn't be fixed—I could live with that. But when he told me he wanted the hot water heater turned off every time we left the house, that each time we would physically have to relight that fucker with a match and pray the gas wouldn't build up and explode, I lost it. That was my first glass of wine. Thank God

Imogene was there—our neighbor? She took me into her trailer and poured me some Taylor Rose so I'd calm down.

"Okay, so I calmed down. I tried again. I asked him if he ever went swimming in the pond, and he said, '*Ycch!*' and curled his fingers up like a two-year-old. If Imogene hadn't come out right then, I would've decked him. He was carrying on about snapping turtles and slime, and Imogene said, 'What're you talking about? You've been swimming there since I've known you. So have your boys.'

"What a sweetheart she is. She has a voice that could maim you, though, charbroiled, heavy on the smoke, a thick Bronx accent. She took Pullet aside and talked to him while I drank another glass of wine in her trailer. He came back to tell me that he was going to do me a favor and come by next weekend—*the first weekend we're going to be there!*—to make sure the guy comes to get the rotting mattress out of the basement. I didn't tell you about *that*. The stink in the cabin is from a mattress that's been sitting in water since last summer! His sons had a whole year to do it, and he claims they called the guy but nobody ever showed up. Hell, the guy probably listened to them for five minutes and figured it was just more dumb fucks on the loose." She stopped to take a breath.

A great lethargy had swamped my legs and was seeping upward. I don't remember when she stopped talking. I only recall drifting off, unsurprised and slightly unnerved. Why did some people seem so unbearable lately? Were they truly, or were they just crawling out of the same pot we kept being drawn to with an appetite?

WHEN WE FINALLY DROVE UP to the cabin around noon, it looked as somber and undisturbed as deep forest, our hoots and hollers the only sound shooting up the calm. The dried oak wreath fluttered from the swing of the door. Then we were *in*, casting about for landings for our sacks of clothes and utensils and books.

Spike mixed a pitcher of inaugural vodka and tonics and I said, "Thanks," raising my glass. She looked at me curiously, pursing her lips to say something but changed her mind. "For getting me here,"

I continued. She cocked her head and studied me, all the while grinning with a certain light coming from her smile, then her eyes.

"When are you going to realize how much you could do if you only knew what you had?" Her voice was soft and fluffy.

"Oh, I know," I said defensively.

"No, you don't. You don't think you're smart. You don't think you're pretty. You don't think you know anything special."

I shrugged. "I think I'm pretty. But only to weird people. Big guys like Cody . . . I'm too skinny. Or talkative—in a way they don't like."

"Talk!" she whooped, and the light from her eyes charged over her features. "Anyway, I didn't get you here, we both got us here."

"No." I shook my head. "I would've run away from Death Knoll. I'm not one to face off chain saws or taunt Bambis in stiletto heels."

"So what were you doing in a Latino boy den on Eighth Avenue at three in the morning?"

I considered this while she eyed me. "Following somebody," I said.

It was midafternoon and the sky was beginning to mass over with clouds. Then sun, just clear of the clouds, threw huge swallows of the pond into darkness, leaving points of silver light.

"I love being up here, Tina. I love it."

"I know."

"This is what I wanted." We were whispering. I snuck up to the bank. Up close, the water carried miniature suns with dark centers that contracted and expanded into one another. By the leafy bank, the greens swam upside down in a reflection.

"And this," I said, taking a sip of my tonic and turning around to make a wide sweep of our setup. "These wonderful lawn items."

"Our very own!" She slammed her drink down on our newly purchased Kmart wrought iron cocktail table that we had planted between our Kmart lounges.

And I was no longer willing to think about anything else save the pond and the trees, having tossed around us sunscreen and flip-flops and towels and hardcovers, and carefully placed in the ashtray a rolled joint to ensure catatonia by dusk.

"Look at that!" Spike said just as the sun escaped through a hole in the clouds. I turned toward the overhanging birch tangled in the threads of light. "No, that!" In the thicket off by the bank was a moving patch of darkness. It jerked and I saw it was feathered with white. "See the crest, the mess of feathers on its head. I bet it's quail. My father used to hunt quail."

"Quail?" I watched it strut to the edge of the thicket. "Let me get my camera."

Just then a ferocious smashing started up and two quail broke out of the cover, their wings slapping to rush them down the pond and out of sight beyond the S curve. We turned around to see a black Cadillac bullying into the driveway.

The car rocked into "park." Its gleaming black flank opened in the middle and a man with a large, wooly black poodle stepped out. The man wore a suit and tie, all of an olive color, and his thin gray hair and clip of a mustache also had an olive tinge so that he looked like the military. He walked with a quirky rigidity, negotiating his way across our scruffy piece of lawn, noticeably chewing gum and yelling at his dog.

"How-do." He came to a standstill by our cocktail table. "Did a young fella happen by this morning?"

Spike looked up; this had to be Pullet. "We only just got here," she said grimly. "We were celebrating."

He didn't even hear her. He was waiting to be introduced to me, his second tenant, whom he'd been trying to size up. This seemed to be the real reason for his arrival—to see if his house was going to be torched by not one but two crazy women. We shook hands.

His eyes, I noticed, were small and black with tiny shots of light.

"Nobody showed up yet, that right? Well you girls won't mind if I went inside and dished out Dandy some water while I'm waiting. She's awful thirsty since she snitched some of my hot dog on the way up. Bad dog." He aimed a loving threat at Dandy's pom-pom and darted his eyes back to about our chin level. "I hate fat dogs," he said churlishly.

"Why don't you try the hose?" Spike said.

"The hose?" he asked, as if she'd suggested he drive his car into the pond.

He began following Spike, who stopped at the propane tanks on the side of the cabin where the spigot was. Suddenly I heard a squabbling in the grass, and Dandy lowered her head to check out the stream.

"Well, long as I'm standing here, why don't I move that mattress into the shed so it won't bother you girls." He jumped over the soggy patch, disconcerting the change in his pockets, and proceeded to charge down the slope.

"That, over there?" Spike pointed to a wooden curl of a building listing into the bracken. "Don't bother, I wouldn't want it rotting in the shed. We'll just take it to the dump."

"Won't be but a minute."

"No, no, we'll load it on my car and take it to the dump."

"It's no problem."

"It should be thrown out."

He glanced at me to see if he had an ally, and I looked toward the pond.

"Why don't I just use the phone and call that fella and see when he plans on coming over here. He's probably out doing a job I'm paying for somewhere else." He faked a laugh and strode back toward his car. "I have to be here anyway. I'm expecting another fella to give me an estimate on redoing that stucco!"

"When?" It was my first peep.

"This afternoon. Don't worry," he added, glancing at my face, "he probably won't show up either. I've had more trouble with these people. I've got nothing against them except they got something against keeping a schedule."

"And then what?"

"Pardon? Why, I'll get an estimate. I used to be in the estimating business myself, did I say?"

We stared at him.

"I'll just drive into town, make my call."

"What'd I tell you?" Spike said after the Cadillac raced down the dirt driveway.

"He won't be back," I said. "He just shouldn't come back."

A FEW HOURS LATER, Pullet came ambling across the lawn with another man. We'd almost forgotten about him, since we'd been trying to understand the water. The wind jostled the top water, shunting the current in a new direction every so often. It had to be the wind, even though the breeze seemed slight from our shelter behind the trees. At one point, the breeze died altogether and the water became absolutely still and a deep, earthen slumber made the afternoon heavy.

"That's no good either?" Pullet's voice was high and whiny. We turned around.

Not three yards away, Pullet and a thickset man in a black T-shirt were discussing the stucco that was turning green and cheesy.

"Now lookit here." Pullet's voice was full of disbelief. When he asked a question, the black T-shirt answered by kicking a hole in the stucco or pulling off a chunk and tossing it at Pullet's feet. The man ripped one of the screens, then walked into the basement. He walked out a few seconds later and tore another chunk off the wall.

"Do you believe this shit?" Spike said.

"He's turned us into trees," I said. "He doesn't even see us. We're not renters, we're just part of the property." I stole a look at the pond. The harder I tried to shut my ears to what was happening, the thinner the calm became until I was listening to every word, horrified.

"I couldn't get anybody to keep an appointment," Pullet complained. "Damn if I didn't have to fly in from Dallas." The black T-shirt kicked at the base of the cabin again until another chunk was dislodged. "I was here all day last week," Pullet said. He didn't seem to notice that one of the trees had moved, that I was standing next to him.

Finally I said, "When are you going to do this work?"

The black T-shirt stopped talking. Pullet smiled and looked past my stony face. "Why, we're discussing that right now. This young fella here is the one I've been waiting on."

"I know. That's why I'm here. When're you planning to do it?"

A smile again. "I have to talk to the fella to find out when he can fit it in his schedule, now don't I?" He nearly winked.

"You're not going to do it now."

A grin flitted across his face, then died. He struggled to gain some impassivity, inhaled deeply through his nose, and revived. "Why, I have to see when he's available."

I was aware of Spike suddenly standing behind me. I was also aware that my dream of a private cabin in the woods was becoming a farce. "You're not going to do it now. You rented this place, remember?"

The lights in his eyes shifted. They bounced all over the place searching for a retreat.

"We didn't come here so we could hear jackhammers," I said.

Suddenly, Spike began shouting in a thin, childish voice, "Leave us alone!"

Don't, I wanted to say. *Keep cool.*

The black T-shirt leaned back on his heels and watched. Pullet ignored her. The olive hue in his complexion had turned grainy, making his smile appear all the more useless.

"Why, the fella'd do the work during the week when you weren't here."

"And what do we do?" Spike put in, her tone more level. "Walk around the pieces of crap on the weekends?"

"Look," he said, no longer managing to hide his annoyance. "Whatever I do, I won't inconvenience you."

"You're inconveniencing me *now*," I said.

He narrowed his small eyes, his fingers working in Dandy's pom-pom, and I couldn't help thinking that if I were a man, especially a man with a family, the situation wouldn't have gotten this far. That's a way of thinking that I didn't want to hold up, but still, there it was. I became a little intoxicated with the desire to sucker-punch him and send him to the moon so it'd take him a long time to come back. I glanced at the other man who was enjoying the show but who probably needed the money. Spike was beginning to get jumpy again—any second she'd start shouting—and I could see it—huge chunks of the foundation covering the lawn all the way down to the pond. "Did you ever wonder why nobody shows up to work for you?"

Pullet shrank back. "What do you mean?"

"You complain you make appointments that no one keeps. No one, nobody in this whole town looking for work shows up." I looked again at the black T-shirt. "It's because you do things like this. Things that aren't right. You don't begin construction on a summerhouse after you've rented it. It's unprincipled."

"All right, sweetheart," he answered tightly. "I'll discuss it with the fella."

"Discuss it for September."

"Leave us alone!" Spike shouted again.

He hitched his pants and flap-walked back to the Caddy, pulling the man along with him. They talked and while Pullet was brushing off his shoes, I was trying to keep from shaking.

"We're going to start the work in September," he called to me.

"Good choice," I called back from my station at the hose.

He shouted for Dandy and whomped his sleek door shut. In another minute, he shot the Cadillac out of the driveway.

I was still shaking.

"Go, Whirly! Did you see the way he looked at you like he wanted to punch you?" Spike cried gleefully.

"Me?"

"Me?" she mimicked in a high, coy voice. "Shit, I guess the poor fart crossed the line of horror."

"I just didn't want him taking our cabin away. I couldn't stand that. Like we'd be pushovers."

She started chewing the inside of her cheek, regarding me as if I'd just enacted some lesson she'd been trying to teach me. I headed for the door and she followed me.

"That was great, Whirly," she continued, gushing the words. "That was great! While you were telling him what a joke he was, I was pointing at his head and holding my nose and the other guy was trying not to laugh."

Not remembering why I'd come in, I grabbed some fruit from the refrigerator and started washing it.

"That was great, Whirly," she repeated.

"I think I stepped over my own line," I said. Finally my breath stopped rushing and I held out two peaches. "Transference," I offered. "Or identification, that's what they call it. When two people begin to act alike?" I looked up at her, straining to see what I felt was happening. She bit into the peach and chewed noisily with her mouth a little open so I could watch the mashing. "I've never done anything like that before," I went on. "Said all the things I wanted to say to . . . protect something." I was thinking of her shouting behind me, and I was thinking of her sitting in a coffee shop with me, letting me know it was all right to let go of my house keys, and then I got too confused as to who was doing what.

"Well good for you!" She grinned, peach goo slobbering over her teeth. She ground her teeth into the peach pit, then blew it out into the sink. "C'mon," she said, and grabbed the second peach out of my hand and walked out of the cabin, letting the screen door slam behind her. She fell into her chair, reached over and picked up the joint, lit it, and waved it in the air for me to follow.

AND LATER THAT SUMMER, Imogene confided that she'd never heard Pullet in such a state when he had called her that evening on the phone, threatening to get a lawyer to break our lease.

But Imogene assured him, "They're harmless, Ely. Believe me."

CHAPTER TEN

PULLET BECAME A TARGET FOR the weekend. Almost as soon as the weed kicked in, Spike began talking about him in every room of the cabin until his presence was everywhere. “Look at this shit.” She was in the basement. “Come on, help me tie this sucker to the roof of the car so we can get it to the dump.” The sucker—the mattress—looked as if it’d been eaten by bacteria. I grabbed the other end, trying not to smell it. We hoisted it up and when it hit the roof, a dusting of disintegrated foam, like pollen, covered the rear windshield.

“*Ycch!*” I said, but Spike already had a heavy rope and was lashing it down with double knots. She got in the car, slammed the door, and floored it.

“Take it easy.”

“I hate this damned thing. It reminds me of Pullet’s fat-ass tongue.”

“He left, didn’t he?”

“Yeah, he left his remains.” And she thrust her cigarette at the roof, almost burning it. I was thinking of the picture we made with this floppy hat on our car, sending foam spores throughout the neighborhood, letting everyone know that this is what we grew in the basement.

The dump was at the top of the mountain. Spike had to downshift to second to make the climb, which wound narrowly in switches from left to right. The road was paved almost to the top, then the car climbed onto a dirt road, and we took it slowly through the pointy rocks and stones, some as big as fists. The mattress flopped like a tail providing balance. The road narrowed to a crusty path, and soon we were driving between mounds of decaying garbage. The first hand-painted sign said Do Not Dump Here!

"Great," Spike said.

The second hand-painted sign said Do Not Dump Here!

"Well, just follow the road," I suggested. "Maybe it's organized." The third hand-painted sign said Do Not Dump Here!

We passed a mound of mutilated metals. "This must be the used car parts lot," I said, then pointed. "Over there."

The fourth sign said Dump Here! with an arrow. This was painted on the back of a leatherette easy chair facing the drop off the mountain. Next to the chair was a snack table with a radio and an opened bag of pork rinds. In the "Dump Here!" district, a bulldozer was plowing garbage over the side of the mountain. It stopped and was set to idle—sounding like a beast with congested breathing—and a man jumped from the seat, waving his hands for us to drive forward. "Don't go too far," I warned. Spike bounded out of the car and I followed.

"Watcha got there?" he said, looking at the mattress. "That it?"

"Yeah," Spike said, sounding like she wanted to punish somebody. "Our landlord's been promising to get rid of it for months. He said he couldn't find this place. We just followed the road. Look at this, he left this rotting in the basement for a year."

The man shook his head. His arms and face were smudged with black, and his T-shirt and pants were smeared with what looked like grass stains. He had a pair of eyeglasses tied around his neck with a shoelace, and he had a happy, clownish expression emphasized by a fringe of hair that ran horizontally from ear to ear. "Well, all he had to do was come to the top of the mountain, except he has to pay."

"Oh, you mean you have to pay to dump here?" I asked.

"Sure do. I can't even handle what I got now. You seen that

junk you come through? But listen, just put that in front of the dozer real quick so I won't see it."

"Maybe Pullet knew he had to pay," I mumbled to Spike.

"Okay," she said to the man.

"Here, let me give you a hand."

The three of us loosened the knots Spike had tied and slid the corpse off the car. The man dragged it in front of his machine. Then he hopped back into his seat inside a glass cubicle. He pulled the throttle and the beast lurched forward, our mattress in its way. The plow lifted, and the mattress was tossed off the mountain like a sheet. We climbed back into the car as the man opened the choke and the machine clamored to a grinding racket. Spike honked the horn, and he thrust his arm out the side window of his cubicle to give us the thumbs-up sign.

"We ought to come back and visit," Spike said. "Bring him some brownies. He probably has a lousy diet."

We stayed on the road. Spike wasn't ready to return to the cabin, I could tell, because she just kept driving. Then she told me she'd seen a sign for a rummage sale in Lomatia Falls and decided we both needed to buy some new old clothes. Besides, she claimed that shopping calmed her down.

It was late afternoon and the streets were empty, asleep. Even the men with the tricycle were gone. We drove up and down the same four roads looking for the Methodist church where the sale was being held but saw no church. The center of town was one block long and one block wide, and in the middle of the block was the Broadway Gas Station. We pulled in to ask directions. Should we go up three hundred feet or back two hundred feet?

"There's St. Elizabeth's Church, but I don't know no Methodists," the attendant told us.

A heavy man in a blue T-shirt and brown slacks who was leaning against a pump waited for us to ask him the same question.

"There's St. Elizabeth's," he repeated. "Don't know no other church." Spike eyed him suspiciously.

We drove to the post office next to the tackle shop, which also had a sign out for shoe repair. The driver of a UPS truck, a Hertz rental painted brown, pulled up to the curb.

"I think there's a church on the way out of town," he said. "Right before the hill."

We followed where he pointed and there it was, set back from a large, empty parking lot, with a spray-painted sheet hung over a rope between two trees. Rummage Sale 2-Day! The only car around the side was a rusted-out Chevy Nova.

"Why do you want to do this?" I asked. "This is depressing."

"It's shopping, pal," she said in a scornful voice. "Welcome to the working class."

The front door emptied us directly into the church kitchen where we surprised a gray-haired woman who'd been sorting clothespins at a table. "I'm sorry," I started to say, but she was already rising to greet us.

"Come right this way," she offered, and hurried us into the rummage sale room.

Sparrows. That's all I could think of—sparrows roosting on a wire. Wispy, chattering gray-haired women were seated at a long cafeteria table, waiting to make change, but not one customer was in the room. "Hello," I said weakly, and nods and coos rippled down the line as I walked blindly into the racks of lumpen dresses. Everything looked to be in such poor shape, as if it'd all been beaten, put on show, beaten for not being sold, and put on show again. The table of children's clothes was the sorriest. All of the play in them was long gone and they looked overtired, ready to slip under the table where there were shoes, broken and kicked, and some "grab-bag" cartons with a sign that said for a dollar we could take as much as we could fit in a brown bag.

I found Spike filing through the dresses on the seventy-five-cent rack. "Let's get out of here," I whispered.

"Whirly!" she said. "What do you think of this? Kim Novak? 1965?" It was black, low-cut, with a short skirt and a gift-box bow at the empire line. "Jean Seberg?"

"Jean Seberg?" I said, momentarily forgetting the mildewed dresses. "What was it that happened to Jean Seberg? Something happened to her, didn't it?"

"Went nuts, who the fuck knows. I always liked Jean Seberg. I'm getting this. Whirly, don't you even want to look? You might find something. You'd look great in black!"

"No, these clothes give me the creeps."

"Don't be such a pussy."

"I look terrible in black that black."

The line of women at the cafeteria table waited for Spike to bring them the dress, and when she did they congratulated her in chorus.

"Ooh, so pretty. So pretty. Ooh, ooh."

"It reminded me of Jean Seberg," Spike explained, smiling. "Remember her?" They shook their heads and a wavelet went down the line. "Seberg? No. Hmmm."

"Hey," Spike exclaimed, "isn't that pretty? Whirly, look. Look at all those colors." One of the women smiled and held up the colored threads she was knotting. With one hand she held the knots she was finishing and with the other she pulled and kept pulling and apparently the threads ran all the way out into the kitchen. "It's beautiful," Spike said.

"Yes," I echoed. What was it?

"You girls might be interested in coming to our kaffeeklatsch Friday afternoons," a woman spoke up.

I don't think so, I thought.

"Fridays?" Spike said. "What do you do?"

"Much the same," said the woman, knotting the colored threads. "We talk. We have a grab bag. Everything you can fit in a bag for fifty cents. Today it's a dollar. Fridays it's fifty cents."

"Maybe so," Spike said. "Maybe we will. We'll come this Friday."

"See?" One of the women pointed to a plaque over the entranceway. It read Donated by Eva Leib for the Kaffeeklatsch.

What was donated?

"Look, Whirly."

"I'm looking at it."

The line of women turned to gaze with me, and in the periphery, I saw Spike pick up a ten-cent marzipan square and eat it. They all turned back.

"This Friday then," Spike said. "Bye-bye."

"Bye, girls."

"Are you crazy?" I said out in the parking lot.

"They're just nice old ladies. I'm going to be there Friday like I'm going to be in Paris Friday. Have some." She held out the marzipan. "It's too sweet."

"You took more? You stole that!"

She shrugged. "The dress was overpriced."

When we were back at the cabin, she said, "Come on, Whirly, don't be so serious. One of them offered me the cake earlier while you were still feeling the dresses."

"She did?"

"How do I look?" She sprang out of her bedroom wearing the short black dress.

"Like a combination of Ann-Margret and Martha Raye."

"Bitch. You think I should wear this for our barbecue?"

"No." I grabbed a knife and a bowl of shrimp and took both out to the pond.

The light had evened so that all of the trees on both banks showed in the water, their images hanging like bats, the leaves furred by the inexactness of the reflection. Spike joined me.

"You think fat-ass Pullet'll be back?" she asked.

"He's gone."

"Oh," she sighed. "This is incredible."

When the sun thinned, the pink in the sky changed the pine needles to black, and soon we couldn't see far at all. We lit a citronella candle and barbecued the shrimp on our Kmart grill and ate them in the dark save for the small light from the candle and the red glow from the coals. And the stars! The city ate up its stars, gummed them to death with fluorescent haze. Here it was as if the sky had thousands of tiny slivers.

We lit a fresh joint and I went inside for more food. I brought out marshmallows and bananas and cookies and corn chips and a box of chocolates that Spike had run up from the city. We spread everything out on my chaise lounge along with our plates and the heap of shrimp tails and Spike took a picture with a flash.

"This'll be our first photo. The Karen Carpenter story. Ha!" Then she located a twig and speared a marshmallow, chocolate, and hunk of banana together, leaned over the coals, and let the mess ooze into her mouth. Soon there was nothing but the sound of our chewing and licking and the crickets.

"This silence is interrupting my Fritos," I said finally.

"I think I'm going to throw up." She let out a brazen laugh. "Give me those Fritos." I tossed them at her stomach.

"How can you eat this crap?" she asked, chewing noisily.

"I'm stoned."

"They remind me of this guy who used to work at the PR firm. Gus. He used to eat Fritos, too, get them stuck in his teeth." She fluttered her gooey fingers in the candlelight. "He was a gnome. He used to come into my office and watch me work. Watch me. One day he decided he couldn't hack it so he quit to teach English literature at a private school and earn maybe eighteen thou a year. He thought teaching was going to save his soul, but guess what? It wasn't his fucking soul. He needed a hair transplant and to grow a few inches. He came back, holding his dick in his hand, asking the firm to give him a break, but they didn't care. Did not care. They had five guys hammering for his office as soon as he left—and nobody wants to watch you jerk yourself off in public."

"So what happened?"

"He's selling insurance now."

"Aaahh!"

"What he should've done," she said, "is told his boss whatever he needed to hear. That's what you have to tell people . . . what they need to hear. Once you're in, do whatever you want. But get in the door."

"Edward," I said, "used to tell me I was selling out." I thought a moment. "To what, I can't remember."

"Oh, please. Yeah, play with yourself, Edward. You'll never own a Rolex watch."

Spike paused. "You know what?" she said, her voice louder. "If you're not going to sell out, then fucking live on Velveeta cheese."

"It's sort of a young idea, anyway," I said. "Used by those who don't have a clue how to turn things their way." I reached for a piece of chocolate.

"I always feel sorry for very little men," she said sweetly. "Like Gus."

"Have we changed the subject?"

"But especially really good-looking ones. Have you ever seen devastatingly good-looking ones and they're tiny?"

I stole a glance at her but could make out only the red tip of her cigarette.

"Their heads always look too big," she said. "Why do you think people stoop?"

"Is this a new subject?"

"Like their shoulders are stuttering. Big stooping goofies."

I cut in. "Did I tell you about this stooper at the paper who's been sniffing around me? A midlife-crisis guy, tinted his car windows black?"

"Well," she said, pinching her voice like a bad little girl. "There are little mice things you could put around your desk. Those little mice triangles, they've got mice poison in them. He'd get the idea. Just put 'em on the four corners of your desk and say, 'Oh, there's some mice in here, sniffing around.'"

I started to laugh.

"Aaahh!" Spike hit her knee with her drink, spilling it. "Shit, now I'll have to lick it."

"Don't." I reached for her hair.

"I should get a towel."

"It's all the way back there." I meant the cabin. We started giggling.

Rising almost made me dizzy. I pulled her up and smelled the shampoo and perfume in her hair. It was eleven o'clock.

"Whew! We are loaded," I said, giggling again. We slugged our way to the top of our lawn and at about the same time noticed the lights. A procession of headlights, one pair after another, was sloping down the road.

"I bet they're going to the Starlite," Spike said. "That's the direction."

We didn't move.

At last, I made it inside, dumped off a plate, and shuffled back out to the pond. The moon drew me until I couldn't look away. All at once, I was startled because I was so glad not to be back in the city with violet-lidded psychics and concrete walls.

Spike came up behind me and whispered, "We created this for ourselves, Whirly. We made this for ourselves."

And suddenly I wanted to shout, "Don't leave me! I'm so happy! I'm afraid!"

CHAPTER ELEVEN

I HAD A FEVER TO GET BACK TO the mountains. When I returned to the city to make money, the days weren't even there. The days passed virtually uninhabited—much like an ocean wave you watch but don't swim in.

Then I was back. Spike on ahead of me because of her shorter workweek and me driving up alone Thursday at dusk to a cabin dark as a tomb in the rain. Not at all like before.

It continued to rain through the night. It was raining Friday when we woke up. It rained past lunch and into the evening. The rain bent the birch low over the pond, and the lawn turned to mud and bled down the banks. Spike was curled in a blanket, scribbling a pen over a pad of paper. She was making revisions to the Sunny Lee story, the story of the little girl whose father woke her up one night with a rifle and almost shot a line of bullets into her head—the tale, really of what had happened to her, or what she remembered happening, but now she was rewriting the story.

She looked ashen, almost frozen in her blanket. The welcome mat outside the door was swamped by water that had risen to the front step. The cabin felt marooned, uneasy. Suddenly she stopped writing and looked at me.

"What do you think it would be like," she said, "if everyone in a certain situation knew something about each other and they're afraid of it? They're afraid of the information?"

"What do you mean?"

"This information will make them want to hurt each other."

The lights had been on all day, burning a mustard yellow that made the flooded darkness outside appear even darker, and every bit of brightness inside stood out as if in relief. When she reached for her cigarettes, she, too, stood out pale and wild-haired. She found the pack empty and leaned across the nubby sofa for a new one.

"That doesn't necessarily mean they would strike out." I looked behind her at the dark, wet sky on the other side of the glass.

"I keep thinking," she said, frustrated, "that I don't know what happened. I keep seeing a woman's hand on the rifle—in the story."

The rain hammered the roof of the cabin.

Spike withdrew to her narrow bedroom and the uninterrupted buzz of her typewriter's electric motor. No keys clacking told me she was deep in a thought hole: turn the thought around, turn the thought around, turn the thought around until you're buried. I was trying to read one of my old psych texts from the 1970s.

"From the biological standpoint this movement toward friendship must be considered a regressive phase of civilization, for on account of it many potential wives and mothers have remained unmarried. Yet regarded from a psychological angle, it reveals itself as a drawing back to get a fresh start. This movement of society may foreshadow the development of the woman of the future . . . into a freer life in which she will find herself as a conscious and complete individual."

Spike was chain-smoking. I could tell by the fouled air. And she was drinking. Picking the glass up. Slamming it down. What the hell were we doing here anyway? I wasn't writing. She wasn't writing. My eyes were smarting from the smoke, and I went to pour myself some cognac but the bottle was in her room. And while I was thinking of what to do, the buzzing suddenly stopped. I heard her scrape back her chair. She crossed the room. A moth suddenly crashed into the lampshade next to me and I jumped. I tried to concentrate on what I'd been reading, but then I smelled her heavy perfume. It seemed to sink the air.

At last she came out of her room. Her hair, still wild, was tucked beneath the collar of a leather jacket and she looked brightly out of sorts in green-and-pink toreador pants, a white turtleneck, and black patent leather shoes.

She said, "I'm going to get ice cream." She might just as well have mumbled, "I'm going to get murdered," that's how bad she sounded.

I listened to her start her car and back up. Then the sound of the motor retreated down the dirt road, rutted by the dogs.

Women of the future, my ass, I thought. The cabin felt deathly empty. And there was something else.

I walked around the room, picked up my Golden Nature book of wildflowers, put down the book, picked up a cassette tape, put it down, picked up a pen, put it down, looked out the window. I did not want to look in a mirror. I went into her room.

She had positioned her typewriter so that it faced the window, and the moon was shining through the partially drawn white curtains. She was using the flowered Victorian chair and had placed two big pillows in its lap so she could comfortably reach the typewriter. The bottle of cognac, half empty, was next to the paper-release lever. One sheet of paper was crammed into the roller, and I saw the black markings on it. I didn't want to look. Whatever it said would unnerve me, I knew it. I knew it as soon as I made out the first word, "She," and after that, "allowed her hands to be tied behind her back . . ." I walked away and studied the moonlight. I was going to find a message since I wasn't supposed to be here. I took a hit of the cognac and filtered it to the back of my throat.

". . . and let the girl viciously snap the rifle to her forehead. She didn't move. Instead, she half hissed, half whispered, 'I always knew you were a dangerous person.' The girl lowered the rifle to her mouth and urged her, 'Kiss it, tongue it!'"

I tore back to the living room with the bottle and stood by

my book, not able to sit down. This was insane. This writing stuff could really get out of hand, the way some people thought; it was embarrassing to read what they were thinking. But . . . she didn't really think that way, did she? That was just a character she inhabited when she wrote who thought that way.

The first shot of cognac had burned the back of my throat. I poured some more. Then I was back at her typewriter, spending too much time making sure the bottle was in the exact position from where I'd lifted it and feeling a fool.

What the hell had she left in her wake? *Kiss it! Kiss it!*

And I tried to hear a calm voice that was my own, but instead I heard Spike's car pull in.

I dashed back to the living room and started reading again from my psych book. "A girl of this type will say the most provocative things and will allow herself to become involved in a compromising situation with one whom, perhaps, she really dislikes . . ."

She closed the front door, walked back into her room—I didn't look up—and the keys began clacking again. I waited. How could she just pick up where she left off? I walked over and stood just barely in her doorway. She was still wearing her leather jacket. The lamplight was burning a vicious bleach across her face, exposing the lines around her eyes and mouth. "Did you get ice cream?"

"I negotiated my way to the Starlite and back again," she said tonelessly, "so that when I finish this piece I can go to the Starlite and get shit-faced and not have to worry about finding my way home."

I nodded. It sounded sensible. The window was open and the white sheers lifted slightly with a breeze.

"So you want to go out?" I asked, meaning, *It's not okay just to stay here with me and write awful things, you want to go out?*

"I'm going out."

"But you didn't go in? To the Starlite?"

"Tina, I came back to finish this piece and then I'm going out."

I couldn't look at the paper in her typewriter.

What was it? What was it about creating a home—any home—that made it seem as if I were now, and from now on, being threatened with desertion? "I don't know why," I began, "but I got the heebie-jeebies after you left."

"I think I'm going to go nuts with this fucking rain." She pushed back from her typewriter. "I just want to look at them, you know? I just want to see how they grow them up here."

"The men?"

"Yeah," she breathed.

Twenty minutes later, we were both in her car. I'd drunk some more cognac and Spike had finished the bottle, and whatever was in the house still had a hold of me, making me jittery and speedy as a tree rat.

The night was dense. There were no streetlights on these roads and it felt as if we were driving through black glue. About a quarter mile from the club, we fell in with a line of Trans Ams, Firebirds, and Camaros. "Uh-oh." I couldn't help grinning and shaking my feet at the same time.

"You should've seen the two babes getting out of the car when I came here," Spike said. "They were all dolled up, their hair done in spades, lots of makeup, and I said to myself, *Oh no, I'm going home. I'm going to finish my piece first, and I'll come back at about eleven when it's a little more crowded.* So I drove all the way back. Got in the driveway and thought, *Whirly's gonna think I'm nuts. I think I'll tell her I went out for ice cream.*"

"That's what you said."

"I know."

"You said that before you left." She laughed.

Didn't she say it? I thought. *Did she forget or was she just telling a story?*

"I can't believe it." She nudged me. "There was nothing, nobody here when I came an hour ago."

Up ahead a tall, cavernous man with a flashlight was directing cars into the parking lot where they were already going. My feet were still shaking, but Spike cruised by him without even turning her head. He started jogging to keep up, shouting all the time and waving his flashlight.

"Spike," I said. "Don't hit him." A scream of electric guitar jolted me as the car slid past the open door of the club.

Spike pulled into a spot, and the man in a rage shouted, "Closer! Closer!" She rolled down her window. "What?"

"Closer, closer."

I could see the vein in his forehead swelling.

"Right." She got out, locked the door, and gave him the finger on her way past.

"He looks like he's going to have a stroke."

"Let him."

"This isn't a good sign."

She ignored me, and my mind was chattering away anyway: Keep moving, you don't want to miss this. Spike'll bully us through, keep moving.

I followed her across the lot into the stream headed for the door—a jumble of jeans and shirts and spiked heels—toward the pounding of skinny, white rock and roll.

"Trash! The hottest dance band on Long Island." Spike hyena-laughed at the handbill.

"Spike," I said, but she didn't hear me. She was already walking inside, moving up to the card table. Two boys were standing behind it, collecting three dollars. They barely looked at me, put my money in a cigar box, and stamped the back of my hand.

"Whirly!" Spike screamed over the music. "I haven't been stamped since I was eighteen!" She was crazy with laughs.

"Yeah!" I screamed back.

The flow carried us past the bar, a large U-turn, toward the dance floor and stage. Five bony men, plastered in black velveteen, with bare, pale chests were punching the air with their guitars. They grasped the necks of their guitars and began choking them sentimentally, climactically. I felt giddy.

Spike touched my arm. "What I tell you?" she said close to my ear. "Bumper crop!"

I looked around us. Men, boys, clumps of them were watching the band. Clusters of them were fencing in a pool table. Groups of three men, groups of five were standing around with their arms folded across their chests. *Groups of men, waiting for women.* It even sounded funny. I hadn't seen so many straight, unattached men in one place since I'd moved to New York City, and I suddenly felt drunk. I had a strong desire to gorge myself, however humanly possible—*bam, boom, let me dance till I'm exhausted. Give me sunglasses. Give me time.*

"Where have we been?" Spike yelled to me at the same time a voice said, "Wanna dance?"

"Yes!"

I didn't even look except to notice he was tall and he wore tennis shoes. Then I couldn't take my eyes off his legs. He danced as if his legs were rubberized, and from the knees down he had no bones at all. Rhythm curved up and down his spine and spun him around like he'd had a fuel injection to his heart and his cock. His neck pulsed and his eyes were absolutely lewd.

"Here, let me have that," he said, and ripped off my jean jacket. He tossed it over a chair, made a few spins, and he was back in front of me, working his cheeks and staring with horny intensity.

"How 'bout a beer?" he rasped finally.

"Okay."

"Are you from Pennsy?" he asked on the way over to the bar. What a sly young face, I finally noticed. "Pennsylvania," he explained, hitting the bar with his hips.

"No. New York City."

"All right! A city girl. I like city girls. How'd you find this place? It took me an hour to find it in my Ferrari."

What? I thought. *He didn't just say that. This sounds like a story Spike would tell.* "Maybe a Volkswagen would've been faster."

He touched my nose. "I like you. You're cute. Let's dance."

"What about the beer?"

"Later." He pulled me after him.

I looked around for Spike but couldn't find her. This was hers, I kept thinking, not mine. *I don't find guys like this; someone has us confused.* Speed-cock dancing! He wrapped one leg around the other, one arm around the other, spun, darted forward and back like an eagle pecking at flesh. He shouted his name. I thought he said Mozzarella. I don't know what he said, but from then on I called him Mozzarella, because he looked kind of stringy. Mozzarella Klein. He leaned arrogantly back, shook in sweat under the spotlights, then slithered, exhausted, back to the bar. Where was Spike? There. Standing alone near the stage, still with her leather jacket on, gazing at the band.

"Hey, do me a favor," Mozzarella said quickly. He dug into his leather jacket for bills. "Buy me a beer, I'll be right back."

What? I wasn't his date.

I bought him a beer. Then turned to a stranger in a blue blazer. "When your friend comes back, you can give him his change and his beer?"

"Huh?"

"Your friend. He's not your friend? Well here's his money in case he's looking for it." I walked to the side of the dance floor where some couples were slumped in the dark at their tables, their inertia probably some kind of foreplay.

"Hey." I put my hand on Spike's hair. She was drinking Courvoisier from a plastic cup and her eyes were glassy, her smile not as cocky as usual.

"The bass player wants me to meet him outside," she said.

"He does?"

"I'm not into musicians anymore. Besides, he's not tall enough."

"Come with me to the bar. I want to get a beer."

"I don't drink beer."

"I do. I want company." She looked at me as if she were haunted. As if she were standing there, thinking of all the lousy and failed things she'd ever done, which was why she deserved to be so monumentally alone. I put my hand on her back and steered her out of the alley of tables back through the crowd.

At the bar wedged between a post and a stool was Mozzarella Klein. He saw me as soon as I saw him and let escape a mean, spiteful look, but his comeback was swift and flashy. He kissed his fingertip and touched it to my shoulder. "Thank you for the beer."

"You're welcome. This is Spike, my housemate."

"Is that your name or what you do to punch?" He grinned.

She dug in right away. "It's what I do to balls." Her mouth opened for a bull-blast laugh and Mozzarella shimmied all over as if he'd been hit by lightning.

"What do you do for encores?" he said, laughing even louder than Spike.

"You don't want to know."

"Try me." He leaned back, baby-faced smug, and smiled. Spike cupped his ear and whispered something that made him throw his head back and roar. "Come on," he said, and they were off, both of them.

I drank my beer. I was free now. Free from what?

The club was definitely charged, hitting into the hunger hour, and the dance floor was boiling with couples out to sea. At the bar, shadows glided around each other, and I kept on drinking, watching, shaking my legs. I saw a pair of eyes twinkling like Santa Claus and I laughed, giddy again, because this was not the music for merriment.

"Can I buy you a drink?" he said.

"I already have one."

"Can I buy you another one? Heck, you got two hands. Look at Joey." Joey, who was standing next to him, raised two glasses. Even in the dark I could see that his eyes were such a strong blue, they looked dyed. Electrified. There was something wrong behind those eyes that looked permanently dilated. The rest of Joey's face was relaxed around a vacant smile.

"My name's Chuck. Joey's my cousin. We came up for my sister's wedding. This here is all the Peels family."

I nodded and laughed.

"Jimmy." He knocked someone on the back. "Turn around." Then to me, "This is Jimmy Peels."

"How ya doing," he said, and he shook my hand, a lanky, blond farm boy.

"And that's Dennis over there. My sister's out there dancing with Karl. They're the ones got married."

"Where did you come up from?"

"Virginia. But I used to live in Lomatia Falls. Most of the Peels still do. Hey—" He made a fist of triumph. "The Peels family!" Joey lifted his two glasses in salute.

I laughed again, my legs still shaking. "I'm here with a friend. We're sharing a house for the summer in Warrenville," I said, and kept on babbling, spilling over. "I've never been here before. I've never seen so much rain. How can you stand this rain? We got cabin fever. Our lawn turned into a swamp."

"What kind of a friend?"

"A woman." I giggled.

"Is she here?"

"Out there. I just want to dance. I've been cooped up all day from that *rain.*" I heard myself, like air rushing out of a tire.

"What're you waiting for?"

"Not much."

He laughed. "Hey, now, I don't believe that for you. Not you. I'll try again. You ready to dance yet?"

"Oh. Sure."

"Well, okay then."

I led him around the dancers until we were next to Spike and Mozzarella. Spike was shaking her breasts and making baseball bat swinging motions with her arms. Mozzarella was all slippery knees and wound-up spins that stopped with his two feet planted apart and a thrust to show exactly where his nerves were centered.

Spike saw me and grabbed me around the neck. "Whirly," she said, her breath boozy and her body still moving, "you've got to get me away from this guy." Then she swung back to Mozzarella.

"That's my housemate," I said to Chuck.

He laughed and cocked his head as if to say, *Shit, that woman ain't regular*, but he said nothing. He moved his hips in tight, small jerks, and he circled around me like a lasso, curling his hands in the air. Joey slid by us with a fresh drink in each hand, his eyes like blue moonbeams.

"Will you do me the honor," he shouted over Trash!, "of saving me a dance?"

"Sure!" I yelled, and he was gone.

"That's Joey." Chuck shook his head, grinning.

"Is he from Lomatia Falls too?"

"Yeah. You been there?"

"Twice." The men with the tricycle, the kaffeeklatsch at the Methodist church.

"You been to the Lomatia Falls Lodge?"

"No," I said.

"You should go."

"Why?"

"It's in Lomatia Falls, that's why!" He bucked his hips back and forth and twirled one hand above his shoulder like the Temptations used to do, and I laughed. "There's Karl. The guy who married my sister. Hey, Karl!" He waved. I turned to look and saw that Spike and Mozzarella were gone.

CHAPTER TWELVE

I CHECKED THE STARLITE'S PARKING LOT and Spike's car was still there, but no keys and no Spike. It was too dark and too far from home to walk, and the drizzle, though light, was still giving the town a good soaking. I wasn't sure if I wanted to, or could, go back into the club without her. The magic seemed shot. And as I was standing there, breathing in the watery air, the Peels emerged from the club, en masse.

"Hey," Chuck Peels called. "You disappeared. I turned around and you were gone."

"I came out to find my friend."

"So where is she?" I shrugged.

"You want to come with us? We're going to the Lomatia Falls Lodge so Karl can lose at pinball."

"Nah. Thanks anyway."

"You sure? You don't get too many chances to hang out with so many Peels at once." Joey floated in front of him and hoisted a drink to me.

I shook my head at the drink. "No. I better wait."

"Up to you."

"You sure she's coming back?" Jimmy asked. In the light from the club's sign, his farm-blond hair looked white.

"I guess so. Her car's here."

"I'll take you home if you think you need a ride," Chuck offered.

"I'll take her home," Karl said.

"Get outta here. You married my sister. Peels don't shit on Peels."

"I'll wait," I said. "She'll be back."

"You gonna be around next weekend?" Chuck asked. "I'm coming back with some friends from Virginia."

"I guess so."

"Well maybe I'll see you then."

"Okay."

"Maybe you won't disappear."

"Maybe," I said.

"Maybe?"

I wasn't concentrating, wondering instead whether or not Spike really would be back. "Yeah, sure," I said.

"Yeah, sure," he mumbled, and waved off.

"Say hi to your nutty friend when she comes back," Karl called.

"Shut up, Karl," Chuck said. "Git. Git!"

It was cold and there was nothing I could think to do but to go back into the club. I showed my stamped hand and stepped into the darkness. Then I got my bearings, and I noticed the change. The club was on its 3:00 a.m. legs, and the crowd had thinned to the hardcore. Trash! was pounding mercilessly, the lead singer hunched over the microphone, and the dance floor seemed to be loaded with men, some of them with their arms straight up in the air, their hands shaking. A revival meeting? "Shout" was the song. Trash! played it slow, then fast, then slow like a shrewd hand job, working the men into a frenzy. Men grabbed men and rocketed each other around in a sloppy Lindy; men jumped off tables and landed in squats on the floor; men shook their heads like wet dogs, rolled somersaults on the floor, thrust their hands in the air, fingers pointed, and commanded, "Shout! Shout! Everybody shout now!"

"Look at that!" I said out loud to no one.

"Yeah, they're crazy," said a morose voice next to me. "My friends. We do this every year. Except this year I busted my car up. I busted my car up, God, shit, first time."

He was leaning against a post and spilling-over drunk, watching the dancers like a slow-motion camera recording a riot. He was tall and thin with sparse, dark hair and a tough accent. His shirt said "Visit Paradise!" on the front and "Hawaii" on the back.

"Can I buy you a drink?" he said.

"Sure."

I sat down. All I wanted now was to take cover and wait until Spike showed up.

He made it back from the bar without tripping or spilling anything. "Give me your hand," he said after he put down the drinks.

"Why?"

He pumped it up and down. "Just a handshake. My name's Frank, but my friends call me F. W. Rank 'cause I rank 'em out."

"How do you do that?"

"They think I ask too many questions. Like, I'm gonna blow your head away with some serious questions."

Maybe throwing myself onto the dance floor was a better idea. I looked out. Too frenzied. Out of control. I looked back. "What's that, Frank?"

"Okay." He gulped some of his drink and closed his eyes when he swallowed. Then he fixed me with a blunt, liquored gaze. "What do you do when you got nothin' else to do?"

I stared back at him, puzzled. "I rarely have nothing else to do."

"Can't hear that!" He shook his head and took another gulp of his drink. Then he looked out at the dance floor with that slo-mo vision that surfed over the crowd and out into spaceland. When he turned back, he had another question.

"What do you do when you go over the edge? You gonna throw me a rope?"

"You mean if you go over the edge?"

"Yeah, yeah, I go over the edge, you gonna throw me a rope?"

"Well, Frank," I said honestly, "I stopped throwing ropes. No, I probably wouldn't. That's not nice, is it?"

"You're ranker than me! Why wouldn't you throw me a rope?"

"It's not you, Frank. I just don't throw ropes anymore."

"What, somebody stick ya?"

"You have any other questions?"

"You took me for a local, didn't ya?"

"Yes."

"These are my casual clothes," he said, pushing back from the table so I could better see his clean, pressed jeans and "Visit Paradise!" shirt. He pulled his chair closer and flung his arm around my shoulders so he could shoot his words directly into my eardrum.

"I'm twenty-eight," he said. "I own my own house. I own a laundromat. I own my own car. I don't owe money to nobody. What else is there?"

Without hesitating I said, "A lot."

"Like what?"

"Art and love."

He couldn't hear me. "Our love?"

"Art," I said louder, "and love."

"Yeah." He was pleased. "I know somebody who does that. He does graphics for an agency."

"My work," I said.

His eyes popped open and he let go of my shoulders, dropping his hand to the table like a cleaver. "I'm not asking you to retire."

"You asked me what else mattered."

For the third time he shook his head. "I don't like a woman that outsmarts me. And you just did. See? I'm speechless. You left me with nothin' to say."

"Hey, wanna dance? Frank won't mind." A man was peering at me from behind a post.

Frank who? Oh, Rank. "I'm waiting for my girlfriend."

"Where'd she go?" Frank asked.

"Left with a guy with a Ferrari."

"I met that dude. Friendly, eh? He didn't like me."

"Well, Frank, everybody's different."

"That dude." He pointed and there they were, Spike and Mozzarella.

"Spike!" I jumped up. "Where'd you go?"

"Hey, how you doin'?" Frank extended his hand to Mozzarella who nodded, keeping both his hands in the pockets of his leather jacket.

"Whirly!" Spike bent over me, her breath sour with cigarette smoke and dry excitement. "Turn around!"

"Shout" was over and the men who had been seething in the ring were strung out along the bar, drinking, calm, as if they'd shot their juice and could hear again. The room had returned, and there were no women at the bar, only men.

"What do you think the ratio is in here?" Spike pressed against me.

"Can we go home now?" I said.

"Just dance with me," she said. "I want to dance at least one dance with you tonight.

"Me?"

"Come on. Give them something to cream over." And as she pushed me onto the floor, I swore I caught a glimpse of blond Jimmy Peels—returned?—laughing at Spike pushing me, but when I glanced again the spot was empty.

OUR CABIN LOOKED COMPLETELY different at 4:00 a.m. The rain had finally stopped and the fresh air felt like a cool sheet; the lights we'd left on were not as brash and yellow as before, the tensions exhumed and washed away. Spike brought out a bag of store-bought popcorn and sank into the nubby sofa, crunching the popcorn and combing her hair at the same time.

"That guy, Mozzarella, he mentioned his Ferrari three times."

"I don't doubt it," I said.

"He said, 'Please come out and see it.'"

"Why?" Sleep was on my mind, but now I was overtired and I was up, awake. I sat stiffly in the hard-backed chair at the living room table and rolled a joint to smoke myself to sleep. "Did he just get it?"

She smiled benevolently, not at me, but at what she was thinking. "I said, 'Why, will that make you high?' He said, 'Yeah.' So I went for a ride with him."

"Why was that again?"

"Because he could actually admit, yeah, it would get him high."

"Boy, we really don't give men credit for admitting much, do we?"

She cut her eyes to me, nervous, then decided to take a more gentle tone. "He's young."

"Meaning he can't express himself, or he should be excused from expressing himself?"

"He just doesn't get it yet." She looked at me with an expression that was somehow both empathetic and lofty.

"Get what?"

"Life."

I glanced from the joint I was rolling not so expertly to the mural of the lugubrious geese arriving at dawn or dusk to the quiet marsh. If I could find that marsh and those geese maybe I could figure out if the sun was rising or setting, which seemed to me, right then, a serious question.

"He's got money." She smiled conspiratorially. Then suddenly, she seemed to come out of her reverie and she looked at me, happy and excited. "Where are these rich guys coming from? Where were these guys all winter when I was living on peanut butter and granola and working at the accounting firm? Where were these guys? I don't need them now. It would've been a nice benefit. Well, you had one. What am I talking about? You had one."

"One what?"

"The guy with the car and the money and the dinners and the *neh-neh-neh-neh-neh*. Where do they come from?" She had one hand in the bag of popcorn she wasn't eating. "He had the most beautiful jacket. I said to him, 'I really want to get a soft leather jacket.' He said, 'Here, try this on.' It was like liquid. Like it wasn't even dead yet. Liquid. I tried to talk him into giving it to me. But I would've had to kiss him."

She laughed. "That's how bad he was. Whirly, he's unbelievable. He's got it real bad. I'm telling you, sweetie, he will be engaged by October. It doesn't matter. He's got mating fever. And he'll do anything. Anything. You've never seen guys like this? Watch the summer. He won't be the first one you'll see. We'll see other guys up here who have mating fever. They'll do anything."

"It's like New York City in reverse," I offered.

"That's the way it is in the rural parts where I'm from. I'm very serious."

"The guys are like that? Not the women?"

"The guys are like that."

"Hey," I said, taking a toke, "it must be great to be in demand like that all the time. Think of all the money saved in therapy."

"It's unbelievable." She giggled. "You always have two or three boyfriends. Always. At least two. And when one falls away, there's a third. And relationships change and you go out with people's older brothers. I loved it. I really did. It was a big shock to me when I came to New York. I went, 'What's this?'" She sounded as if she were looking into a sewer.

Her eyes widened and she stared at me, incredulous at how things were when she'd arrived. "I'd never seen Jewish men before."

"You'd never seen Jewish men before?"

"Where would I see them? There aren't any where I'm from. And the ones that are, are totally assimilated. They get their noses done, they wear preppy clothing, they buy their shoes at The Papagallo Shop, and they have houses at the beach. They change their names. All of them. They were a fascination to me." She reached for the joint. "I thought they were really silly, trying to fit in. Then I found out they were serious. No thanks, no more."

"You mean you thought it was adorable until you found out it was true—that they really did want to fit in?"

"Have you ever been to Minnesota?" Spike asked, now at the refrigerator. She pulled out a chunk of watermelon and bit into it, leaned over the garbage, and started spitting seeds.

"No."

"Well how many Jews do you think they have there? One? And you know what else? There aren't any Italians either. They're Midwestern people. They have big, goofy-looking faces. The men are just different."

I took a hit off the joint and walked over to the mirror, something I'd managed to put off for about five hours. I looked bad, green around the mouth, and my eyes were bloodshot. My hair was lank with sweat from dancing. "You must be right," I said. "It must be mating fever."

"Whirly, look at me. I haven't looked this bad in weeks." We both started cackling. "I know it. I know it!" she screamed. "I've got adult acne and this guy is practically creaming in his pants. I'd like to think it's my charming personality, but I can't buy it right now." And she kept laughing, deep in her throat.

"My God," she went on. "I have the feeling the men'll do anything up here. Just to smell you. It's like they don't have women to talk to."

I was still staring at myself in the mirror. "I would really like to look better than this," I said seriously.

"Those guys, those guys in the bar who were looking at you when I walked in with Mozzarella . . . You were talking to a drunken slob who was half asleep on his chair and I'm thinking, *Does Whirly really want to talk to this guy?* There were guys behind you staring at you from their barstools. Just staring. And when I walked up, they moved to look around me. I heard one of them say, 'What's she doin'? The girl?' And another one, 'I dunno.' That's when I said to you, 'Turn around. Turn around, Whirly!' And when you did, your eyes got so wide, like we were *it*!"

"We were! It was awful. I hate that kind of responsibility."

"I just like to look at all the different ones. See the problem with a Mozzarella is that you have to stick by him. I would've liked to have met him at the end of the night. But I wanted to ride in a Ferrari. It was cool."

She put down the joint and looked out the window where the light of the sun was just beginning to show. "This is a strange weekend," she said softly. "Boy, we're having some weird days, I'll tell you."

"Each one is different."

"I know."

"It's only the second weekend."

"I know."

"Why do they feel like months?"

"I know!"

"I can't stand it," I said.

She slid to the floor and grabbed my leg. "I can't stand all this relaxation," she said in a fit of belly laughs. "I can't take it. Take me back to New York. Give me some scheduling. Ask me for anything, I'll do anything. Just give me a job. Give me a small space and no time to do it in, then yell at me if I don't do it on time."

"That guy," I said, catching my breath from laughing. "Chuck Peels was nice. He's only twenty-five, though. He's from Lomatia Falls."

"Great. Maybe he'll take you out on his tricycle."

"Funny."

We were flat on our backs, staring at the shadows on the ceiling. "This guy, Mozzarella, has a big party every year at his parents' house on the river," she said. "I think we should make him our friend. I'd like to go to his party. We don't have to play with him." She paused. "He knows a lot of different people."

"People like him?" I said.

"All different kinds. Who knows? I'm sure we'll have plenty of opportunity to find out, if we work it right."

CHAPTER THIRTEEN

FIVE HOURS LATER, I WAS IN THE CAR with a stunning hangover. The sun couldn't have been brighter, as if making up for its poor performance the last few days, shining gleefully on the road and flattering the rolling country hills of Route 72. I felt faintly carbonated, like chalk was percolating in my veins.

My mind was chasing its own tail. This guy, that guy—and about Mozzarella: *We don't have to play with him, we'll just make him our friend to see what he's got.* Could I be as guiltless? Was I already? I heard her laugh at me.

Whirly, you're not such an innocent. You come off as a snob sometimes, you know. Besides, guilt is less valuable than shit.

All right, all right, but when had it happened? When had I started hearing her everywhere I went?

My goal for today was to have my friend Ohara come back to the cabin for a swim in the pond. This seemed innocent enough. Ohara and her fiancé, Ben, had been friends of mine (and Edward's) for a long time, and she and Ben were always doing things for me from letting me sleep on their sofa when Edward refused to leave the apartment, to cooking me dinners and birthday cakes. I was glad for the chance to make an offer to Ohara finally, if only for a swim in the pond—it seemed I hadn't had a place worth inviting her to for such a long time.

I had blithely offered to pick her up at her house and drive her back home. On the map, the distance was only a few inches. In real time, it was two and a half hours each way. Route 72, the longest stretch, wound through acres of untended land, a few farms, a family restaurant here and there, and a host of automobile repair shops. There were few other cars in sight, and soothed by the soft breezes, my headache began to lift. If this continued, it would be almost analgesic.

As soon as I saw Ohara in her garden of cosmos, I was struck as usual by how beautiful she was. Tall, hips as narrow as a man's, full breasts, blonde, she had come to New York from Oregon with Ben to pursue modeling, but her disposition was too placid for it. And truly, sometimes her dreamy silence reminded me of the layer of cream that formed over milk, mainly because when the layer was skimmed, she wasn't dreamy at all but necessary in an abiding way. Still, with her beauty, she was shy, and with Ben around, who was the opposite, she preferred to be an audience.

"He doesn't give her a chance," Spike said after she met them. "Look, they've been together since they were in high school. You think that's conducive to personal growth? It's sick. And she's young."

That famous "young" that meant protected, not enough medals pinned on her chest from battles in the real world of bastards and insanity.

"She's like a whole other species to me," she said. "And look at Ben," she continued. "You think he needs to prove something or what?"

"No, that's just how he is."

"Come on. He's shorter than her. He's not half as good-looking. He'd like to think he's James Dean, but I'm sorry, he doesn't make it."

"I don't think so."

"Whirly," she said, impatient. "The guy's an actor, painter, makes furniture, runs around with an axe in his hand chopping wood, talks nonstop about himself—you don't think that's overcompensating?"

"I don't really care. I like the stuff he does. At least he does it and doesn't just talk about it. I know a lot of people think it's The

Ben Show—that's their problem. I'm sure he can be overwhelming if you're in a contest."

"Would you like to live with him?"

"No, but that's not the point."

"I rest my case."

"Bullshit."

"Would you like to live in that house?"

Their house was bought cheap on a windfall from a grainy French film Ben starred in, and since they didn't mind their heat supplied by only a woodburning stove and fireplace, didn't mind cutting their own wood or using a compost toilet, living without water when the well went dry, existing on vegetables for most of the summer, and sitting on chairs and benches that Ben made from the trees on their property, they did all right. Their stylishness disguised their poverty. An odd stone from a farmer's wall was placed under a spotlight so that it took on the shape of a woman's body. A twisted old hoe was braced to the wall. A basket of purple loosestrife was positioned in the vestibule. And Ben's wild, violent art was tacked to the wall, sometimes the paper still curling at the ends.

"I like their house."

"Try living in it. It may look like a magazine spread, but can you find a comfortable chair to sit in?"

"They're going to get married there this summer."

"They're not even married, and they've been together since high school."

"Lay off, will you?"

"Why's your face so red?" Ohara asked, as soon as she got in the car for our drive to the cabin.

"Hangover." I didn't want to say I was anticipating what might happen if Spike joined us for dinner tonight. Why couldn't people just get along?

"Covetousness," I imagined Spike's answer. "You're covetous of her. I'm covetous of you. You're covetous of me. That's why."

Spike had set out a chair for herself and was reading and drinking a peach daiquiri when we arrived. She let Ohara stand around, holding her rolled towel, while I fetched two lawn chairs, then asked if anyone wanted a fresh drink or a new drink.

"Boy, this is nice," Ohara said of the pond, settling her long limbs on the chaise.

My very own bramble-edged version of a swim club, I thought. Now the trick was to make everything as friendly as tea and cookies. Spike preempted me.

"Did Whirly tell you about our night?"

"Whirly?"

"That's what she calls me," I explained wryly.

In a voice girlish with intimate secrets, Spike explained, "Because I picture her with a little beanie on her head with a propeller ready to take off like a whirlybird."

Ohara laughed. She looked quizzically from me to Spike. "What about last night?"

"We met this guy," Spike began. She proceeded to tell the rest of the story on her feet, her mouth a wide grin between sentences, tossing her hair, waving her hands. She was wearing a men's oversized white shirt and a purple bikini that was too small for her, making her appear overripe. Her eyes, which I knew had to be dilated, were hidden behind sunglasses with peppermint-striped frames. "So I said to him, 'Will it get you high?' And he said, 'Yeah.' So that's why I went to see it."

Ohara looked puzzled. "So what's why?"

"Why I went to see it, because he said it would get him high."

"Oh." She glanced at me. "Sounds like"—she paused—"I don't know. The kind of guy I don't like."

"An asshole," I said. It came out more surly than I intended.

"I feel sorry for him," Spike said. "He's a baby, that's all."

I knew Ohara well enough to be sure that she found this explanation thin. I had just turned to look at her when I heard that voice.

"Hey there, gorgeous!"

"Christ," I muttered.

"Is that him?" Ohara was incredulous.

"Yep. Do you believe it?" I said.

Mozzarella was wearing tiny shorts and a T-shirt cut in half to show his midriff. A gold chain adorned his neck. He helped himself to a lawn chair from the basement. It was a low, surfside chair for sitting at the beach, and he crashed into it and sat with his cocky legs out in front, his bent knees high in the air. "Hey, so, what's up, ladies?"

Spike remained standing. "How'd you find me?" He gazed up at her.

"Is that your car in our driveway?" I asked.

"You gave me the address," he said, gloating.

There was a high-hormonal-level breakout on his chin and around his eyebrows, and his hair was short, dark, and intensely curly. He looked like he'd always been tall for his age, and started to move, a twist to the right, to the left. Spike agitated herself into a pantomime of a hostess, dipping down to pick up empty glasses and jerking up to ask if anyone would like a peach daiquiri.

"Sure, babe."

Mozzarella swiveled his baby-egg face without moving his torso to watch her walk up the steps at the door of the cabin. Then he turned his head back and stared straight ahead at the pond, his palms flat on top of his thighs.

"This is my friend Ohara," I said grudgingly.

"Hi. How are you?" His aura of ownership faded slightly, but I didn't take this as a sign of hidden timidity.

I said, "We were talking about something on our drive over here that maybe you have an opinion on."

He glanced at me for a split second, then focused back on the pond.

"Ohara knows two couples who have just broken up," I went on. "In both cases, Ohara says it was out of the blue. I don't think anything like that can be a complete surprise. What do you think?"

Without much rumination, he said, "People are into deception. They don't always tell you what they're really feeling or they make you think they're feeling something that they're not. It happens all the time. They misrepresent themselves. When somebody's deceived somebody else, that's when it seems like it's out of the blue."

"I don't think deception's that easy," I said. "It's only easy if somebody isn't paying attention."

"She never said anything to him," Ohara insisted. "She never let him know how she felt. She just left."

"She must've said something," I argued. "We always say something. You can tell when people are unhappy. The thing is, sometimes you don't pay attention because there isn't much you can do—or want to do. But then you stop listening, and when you stop listening it becomes a mess."

Ohara looked sulky. "I think it's more complicated than that."

"You told me this morning that the woman's husband hadn't slept with her in over a year. You call that out of the blue?"

"He was always like that. Not very sexual."

"Why?"

"Shit," Mozzarella said, wiggling his knees.

Ohara fidgeted with her towel, annoyed. "I don't know. Ask her."

"People don't just get up and leave," I said, trying to reassure us both.

"Not if they're trustworthy," Mozzarella said. "But how do you know that?"

He jerked his head up as Spike touched a cold daiquiri glass to his back. "Hey, beautiful." His knees were still wiggling. His feet were jiggling too. "You ladies going to the club tonight?"

"The Starlite?" I said, and thought, *Again?* "I'm going to Ohara's for dinner."

His feet were bouncing out a rock beat. "What about you?" he asked Spike.

She answered shyly. "I'm going with them."

She is?

"What about later?" he pressed her.

Again, she sounded coy. "I'll probably stop by."

"Good. I'll look for you."

He popped out of his chair and was off, cutting across long swaths of lawn on his way to his Ferrari.

"Oooh boy," Ohara said. "He's pleased with himself, isn't he?"

"I find him interesting," Spike said, sipping his daiquiri.

"Why?" I frowned at her.

"What makes a guy like that have an attitude like that?" she answered.

"Who cares!" Ohara shouted.

"I do."

"I'd rather find out about people I like," I said arrogantly. Spike saluted me with her drink, then gave up talking to us.

"WE'LL TAKE MY CAR," Spike informed me, "because you don't like to drive at night."

"I'll be all right."

"No, you won't, and I don't want to drive your car back. We'll take mine and you can drive up."

"Ohara wants to drive."

"You drive," she said, not liking strangers to drive her car.

"I can drive," Ohara volunteered, as Spike opened the rear door for her. I slid behind the steering wheel and felt as if my body still hadn't unfurled from the morning's alcohol-vaporizing road trip.

"Ugh," I said, slamming the door, and Ohara piped up from the back seat, "I'd be glad to drive."

Ben was in the yard, splitting wood, when we pulled up.

"Hi there!" he shouted, the axe still in his hand. "Hi, Ohara. Hi, girls. Three. Three girls just for me."

Spike snorted.

"We were going to bring Mozzarella Klein," Ohara said gamely, "but he decided to go to the club instead. He drives a Ferrari and wears gold chains."

Ben suddenly grabbed me from behind and squeezed me in a tight, undulating hug. This was definitely not going to go well.

"You like men in gold chains?" Squeeze. "Huh?"

"Not me." I winced, peeling away his grip.

He let go and whipped around. "How about you?" he said to Spike as if nothing had happened.

She looked at him wearily and took out a cigarette.

DINNER WAS GRILLED CHICKEN, fresh trout—caught by Ben—and corn. We grilled the chicken in a barbecue pit Ben had constructed from stones he'd salvaged. Spike groused about the distance of the pit from the kitchen. She complained about the amateur setup of the grill. She pointed out the uneven stonework in the kitchen floor.

She muttered about the hardness of the hand-hewn furniture and said, "This place is not designed for convenience. It's pretty to look at, but so what? Our place is ten times better. Plus we have a pond."

Over dinner, Spike carried a monologue, disconnected and rapid-fire, and I grew uncomfortable, knowing these were the symptoms of frazzled nerves and pain—ideas floating in her mind that compelled her to unravel on a public stage. Finally, she said it was time to leave. It was a little past midnight.

"You're not going to the club, are you?" Ohara was grinning. "You wouldn't get there till after two."

"Probably," Spike threw off.

"Not me," I declared flatly.

I fell asleep in the car almost immediately and was jolted awake every now and then by a wide turn or fast swing around a curve. Spike was in a hurry. I walked in the door of the cabin and sacked right out. Spike backed the car around and left me.

CHAPTER FOURTEEN

WHISPERING. THE CHILLY, GRAY MORNING mist rolled a phrase, a "*shhh*," a rustle into my bedroom. Someone was at the outer door. Two voices. Dawn, barely a day yet. Spike and Mozzarella. "Wait here—" A loud whisper.

I drifted off to sleep again.

Ten o'clock. Shouting by the pond. "Where's the hose?"

"There!"

"Is it on?"

"Go look."

I peeked out the window. Mozzarella, bare-chested, in a pair of Spike's shorts, and Spike in a white, flouncy, low-cut dress I'd never seen before. There were laces, undone, across her breasts. She ran—out of my line of vision—and returned lugging something black. "Just hold it the way you're doing," she ordered. "Turn toward me." It was her old clunky Nikon, the one she hadn't had to sell after all.

He posed: A skinny Tarzan with his shoulder turned into the morning light, hips thrust, hose extended at cock level spraying into the red canoe. Spike snapped the picture and skipped toward him. "Great, great hose."

I had a mug of coffee before I went outside with my second.

"Hey, beautiful," he said when he spotted me stumbling along the lawn with my coffee.

"Whirly!" Spike skipped toward me. "We're going fishing." Her mouth was bubbling, *goo goo ga ga.*

I looked at her breasts, half exposed.

"Good." My voice sounded bass and congested. My God, was this the same weekend?

"I told you," she said, whispering smoke into my ear, "we don't have to play with him. I just want him to teach us fishing."

"Right."

"Hey, S," called Mozzarella. "These won't hold up."

The khaki shorts, already rolled to his groin, looked like a bunched-up grocery bag, and they were slipping down his hips.

"You want a belt?"

"How about your teeth?"

"Keep dreaming, Klein."

"I will."

Oh boy. I turned to walk back inside, but Spike said, "Look, look at what he brought with him so we'll know."

There was a Shakespeare spinning rod, minnows for bait, a rope to pass through the gills of the fish once they were caught, and a Swiss Army knife. Spike grabbed the filthy glove we used when we barbecued.

"A fish glove," she said. "I don't want to touch them with my hands."

Mozzarella put Alma's canoe in the water. He spread a towel over the front plank. "My lady," he said, sitting in the back of the canoe and offering his hand.

"Bye-bye," Spike said to me, and stepped in. With the paddle he pushed the canoe away from the bank and off they went toward deeper water and the marsh.

I gulped down my coffee and decided to use the caffeine for running. I ran to the corner of Blind Pond Road, then down the road itself, which followed along a trout stream. I stopped at the one-lane bridge that crossed the stream. Beyond was an abandoned fruit tree orchard. I skidded down the rocks on the bank next to the bridge and sat, stirring the brown water with my fingers. I waited until I could extract a thought that made sense. After all, I'd hardly had time to wake up, and there I was running and feeling like I was running away.

I sat and looked at the swollen water and what I came up with was that I was jealous, no matter how detestable I found Mozzarella. I was sickeningly jealous that Spike was with a man and I wasn't, and that he was with her and I wasn't. And I wanted to know *how* it happened—how they actually spent the night together. Talking? With Mozzarella creaming in his pants while she said, "No, no, no, you don't get it yet"?

What's happening to me? I thought then. *Why do I feel so coiled up and choked?* I stared at the water for a long time until I was able to remind myself that I had a history, separate from how I was with her. And how could I be so impressionable anyway? Wasn't I too old for this sort of thing? And why, to Ohara, was Mozzarella simply "the kind of guy I don't like," but to me an omen about Spike?

Oh, stop it, I reprimanded myself. *You've always exaggerated. Open your eyes. Look around you.*

The beauty was mesmerizing. The air was still wet from last night's rains, and the leaves looked polished. The brook with its belly full of rain was churning tawny beneath the surface and foaming white above. There was something about the sound of water and the breeze off the water that slowed everything down. Then a Jeep hit the wooden bridge and exploded the quiet. I suddenly felt listless and didn't want to go back. I leaned against the face of a rock until I figured out there was nowhere else to go and driving to the city was out of proportion.

By the time I returned to the cabin, looking, I thought, like any calm, unquestioning person, Mozzarella had lavished himself face down on a chaise, looking very much like a paid boy at Miami Beach. Spike, next to him, was sitting up in her lounge chair, smoking and reading, the top of her dress completely undone. The book, which I'd seen around her things in the cabin, was a collection of short stories about suicides and other fatal acts, written in a deadpan style by a woman about Spike's age.

I headed directly for the cabin.

"Whirly!" she called. "I caught a fish. Come see it."

"I will," I promised, and let the door slam on her entreaty. I pulled on my one-piece and started to march into the basement for my inner tube.

"Whirly! Whirly! Come see." She ran after me and tugged me with her across the lawn.

There, half dead in the muck by our bank, was her fish. "It's a pickerel," she announced proudly.

"What's a pickerel?" I asked.

"A fish." She laughed. "Mozz says they're like freshwater barracuda. They've got teeth. Look." She picked up the rope that had been threaded through its gills, and the fish opened its mouth, gasping, so I could see its teeth.

"Can't you just kill it? Does it have to stay there like that?"

"How am I gonna kill it?"

"I don't know. Ask him."

She raised then lowered the fish into the water as if she were dipping laundry in and out of a basin. She was crouching beside me so close, I could smell the pond in her hair. "Guess who fell in the water?" she said, her mouth working, an awful bitterness in her delight.

"You?"

"No! Klein." She jerked her head to where he was basking under the sun. "He got so excited when I caught my fish, he stood up. You never stand up in a canoe. He lost his balance and dove in. The jerk was wearing his glasses."

"Prescription?"

"Yep. Three hundred and fifty bucks."

"What an idiot."

"Yep."

So why was she half dressed? Why was she with him at all? And what was the point of whispering all this to me twenty feet from where he was sunbathing?

I couldn't think anymore. "Whoops, I forgot my towel," I said, and ran back to the house, calling, to cover up my lack of grace, "Does anybody want anything?"

"Your body," Mozzarella said, awake after all.

"You're an asshole," I heard Spike say.

She barely glanced at me as I strode by this time. The inner tube was dusty with grit, and it was easy to imagine the dust as powdered sugar on a big, black rubber donut. I rolled my toy across our bumpy lawn until it wobbled out of control and fell flat, like a clumsy pudge. I picked it up and rolled it into the water at the launch site where the muck huddled around two cinder blocks used to buttress the canoe and where the rope dangled that was holding her dying fish. Stepping over the cinder blocks, I delicately lowered my bottom into the donut hole and pushed off.

Feet kicking, hands paddling, I was finally a self-contained demon, and I charged ahead trying to make progress against the current. The undersides of my arms were becoming chafed from the rubber, so I had to alter my technique a little, sit higher up in the donut hole, turn on my belly even, and use a breaststroke. Whichever way I propelled it, the big, black rubber tube was such an ungainly beast on the water and so stupid-looking, it made me laugh. Even when I realized that as soon as I got to where I wanted to be, the current floated me back, and I had to paddle like mad to go forward again. *Give me a drink or a joint, and I can spend an entire afternoon like this*, I thought. And, looser now, I grabbed a Patsy Cline song out of the air and began to sing, "If you loved me half as much as I loved you, you wouldn't worry me half as much as you do."

Suddenly, I heard a disturbance in the bushes by our bank. Two tanned, skinny legs were blocking the light.

"What's that song?" Mozzarella asked.

I felt like a sitting duck in my black donut, flapping in the water. He could see me, but I could see only his legs. I yelled the title into the bushes.

"It's pretty!" he yelled back. "Keep singing."

So I stopped. I paddled my way to the middle of the pond, where I rested. The current bobbed me back to shore.

They were both sitting up in their chaises, smoking a joint, when I climbed out of the donut onto the bank. "Good stuff?" I asked, sure of the answer.

"The best," Spike piped up, the smoke from her toke streaming out the sides of her clenched teeth. She started to cough.

"Take it easy," Mozzarella said, patting her shoulder, too lazily stoned to reach her back.

"That good?" I snickered.

"Yeah." She choked. "If I die you know it's grade A."

I took a hit. "Straight from the glove compartment of the Ferrari, huh?"

"That's it, babe."

"Whirly." Spike had downed part of a club soda and was still catching her breath. "Get Mozzarella to take you fishing."

"He's right here. What kind of ploy is that?"

"Well ask him."

"I'm not interested in fishing."

"How do you know?"

"I can just tell."

He tapped my knee. My turn for the joint. "You might catch something," Spike persisted.

Mozzarella said, "Come on, Whirly."

"Don't call me that."

He shrugged, overdoing his indifference.

Spike said, "I thought you didn't like people who wouldn't try new things." I frowned. Why was she pushing me into this?

"Come on." Mozzarella passed me the joint again. "I'll show you how to fish. She had her turn, now it's yours. You have beers?" he asked Spike. "We'll take some beer."

I grunted. "We'll be so shit-faced I won't know which way to throw the water. The rod, I mean."

"The line," he corrected. "You cast the line."

"So what?"

"Curmudgeon." Spike laughed.

"Come on." He stood up and grabbed my hand. I grabbed it back.

"Okay. You don't have to pull me."

Spike became a mother hen, clucking here and there for towels, gloves, cold beers, and flip-flops. Mozzarella climbed into the canoe, spread the towel, and offered his hand.

"My lady," he said.

What is he, I thought, *a broken record?*

But when I turned to wave to Spike as he paddled us farther from the shore, the smile on her face was drawn. She looked as if she'd been duped.

Mozzarella pulled the canoe up to an abandoned dock—really a platform of jagged, broken planks. I climbed onto the dock; he secured the canoe, then began diving for his glasses. Once he gave up, he pulled himself up onto the dock where, by this time, I was snoozing, belly down, gently adrift on his expensive dope and the caress of the sun. He tickled his finger down my spine. "Hey," I warned him.

"Ready, babe?"

"Don't call me that either." I sat up.

He picked up the rod, which was now fixed with what he called a lure instead of bait, slid behind me, his crotch to my vertebrae, held the rod in my hand with his, and cast. He showed me how to open the bail, hook the line in the crook of my index finger, and let it go.

"Then reel it in," he said. "Sometimes you can tug it."

I made a few casts with his hand on my hand and his crotch to my vertebrae. Each time I slid farther along the dock to put some space between our bodies, he inched up, and pretty soon I was going to be in the water. "Come on," I said finally.

Without verbally acknowledging a thing, he stopped what he was doing and sat back on the dock, his legs thrust forward in a V. He pressed his hands flat on the planks and began to push, trying to lift his body.

"Nervous energy?" I said.

"I feel relaxed with you."

"Sure," I muttered under my breath. I cast, let the line drift, and reeled it back in, having absolutely no feel for what I was doing. This blankness bothered me. I didn't cast again, preferring to stare at the still water.

"Why don't you sing?" Mozzarella said. He was lying on his back, one arm behind his head.

"What's your favorite song?" I asked.

"'The End,'" he said.

"By the Doors?"

He moved his chin up and down in a nod.

I thought, *If he knows all the words to that ten-minute death march, he's been spending a lot of time alone in his bedroom.* "You know it?" I asked. "Why don't you sing it?"

Without hesitation, he shot up to a sitting position and, with no introduction, with no coyness at all, began to sing. "This is the end. Beautiful friend. This is the end. My only friend, the end . . ."

He recited the words on the barest melody, without looking at me. He stared at the water.

If I wanted, I could have mistaken his intensity for feelings, but instinct told me it was the intensity of a performance. The water lapped lazily against the reeds, and every once in a while, a striking turquoise dragonfly would hover near the dock.

He finished. The utter silence of the pond was all the applause.

"We should head back," I said. "I doubt I'm going to catch anything. Especially if I'm not casting."

It occurred to me as we stepped into the canoe that the day seemed cooler—a late afternoon cool—and the light was not as bright. The colors of the pond were sleepier than when we'd launched.

As we made our way back, the paddle cutting smoothly, almost inaudibly, in the water, the feeling grew that it was late, much later than I thought. Hours of stoned time may have passed. I remembered then that Spike had said she was leaving by three o'clock to beat the traffic back to the city. She'd probably left already! Why hadn't I remembered before? She'd probably be angry with the two of us for paddling off and forgetting to come back in time to say goodbye to the person who was the reason we were together at all.

The chaises and the cocktail table and the towels and the books and glasses were all still on the lawn. I could imagine her waiting and waiting and finally deciding the hell with it at the last minute when there was no time left to put anything away. Maybe, though, she was inside, and I ran into the cabin, expecting to crash right into her. I dashed to the basement, then around the side, then finally headed for the driveway, grasping that all I had to do was look to see that her car was gone.

"I found a note," Mozzarella called out. "Two notes. One for you. One for me."

Oh no. I had become increasingly aware that there was a right and wrong in Spike's kingdom; there were rules, silent ones, which I found out about when I stumbled on them.

"She says she hopes we caught a lot of fish and that she'll see me next weekend if I'm around." Mozzarella was reading from his note.

"Whirly," mine began. "Hope you had fun. Had to leave to beat the bridge traffic. Don't feel like you have to stick around with M if you don't want to. I didn't have time to take care of my fish, so could you at least get it out of the water and maybe freeze it till I get back? Or have M fillet it for you and have it for dinner."

That's all?

"Hey, are you hungry?" Mozzarella said then.

"What time is it?"

"A little after six."

"Six!" I said.

"Let's go, I'll take you to dinner."

Why not? I thought. *We both have to eat. And maybe I should try to have compassion for people I don't like. Plus, I'll get to ride in his car, which I don't care about.*

It gave me the giggles to see a low-to-the-ground, elegant, poised-to-roar, hot, coral-red car in our rutted dirt driveway. On the hood was a yellow shield with a rearing stallion. This was the Ferrari symbol, he explained, retrieving from the glove compartment a brochure that presented the history of Enzo Ferrari, with photographs of the early days and photographs of all the kinds of Ferraris a person could own.

"If you walk into a dealership and try to buy this," he said, flipping the pages, "it'll cost you sixty dollars. They're collector's items. People hold on to them and sell them for hundreds of dollars at auctions."

"Just the brochure?" I said.

The car—the technological animal—had a buttercream-hide interior, and Mozzarella slipped on matching buttercream-leather driving gloves as if a camera were moving in for a close-up.

He drove as fast as possible at that dinner hour, and when he braked, the car didn't stop. It suspended its speed. He grinned at me. That machine, that baby-smug face, and that speed—that was Mozzarella Klein.

About our quirky conversation at Monika's I remember this: I learned he was moving into his own apartment for the first time in his life and his head was filled with furnishing schemes. Black on black, he wanted, with gray tones in the ceiling. He told me his drug of choice was cocaine.

"Why cocaine?" I said. "You don't want to be any faster."

"If you want to know the truth," he said, his eyes fixed on the platter of pizza in front of us, "it's so I can get it up seven or eight times a night."

I tapped the table. "That's not how I heard it works."

"Let's dance," he said suddenly, and grabbed my hand. The jukebox was playing "I Only Have Eyes for You." The bar was empty except for three old men watching the sports news; Vince, the bartender, who was also watching the news; and a young father with a small boy in tow. He was the one who'd slipped a quarter into the jukebox.

Mozzarella moved me around our table with the greasy napkins crumbled on top and the slab of uneaten cold pizza congealing on its tippy aluminum platter. Both of us kept banging our heels into the table and chair legs. I remember how different it was to dance with him than to talk with him, and how different it was to dance with him period. We were slow dancing, but he was still all jitters and pulse beats. And just as suddenly he said, "Okay, that's enough for me," broke away, and sat down.

Was this still the same weekend?

The Ferrari delivered us back to the cabin.

"I forgot my towel," Mozzarella said, loping to the door. He followed me into the cabin, which was dark.

"In there?" I asked, immediately flicking on the living room light.

He bounced out of the bathroom on the balls of his feet to where I was standing in the kitchen. "Do you have anything to drink?"

Just as I was turning to look, he grabbed my shoulder, pulled me toward him, and kissed me lightly, with just his lips.

I backed out of the kitchen, found my voice, and asked, "Don't you find this confusing?" He opened the refrigerator door and reached for some orange juice.

It did not seem purposeful to press for any long-term truths here. I remember thinking that Spike's theory about mating fever did not appear to be entirely accurate—unless the foreplay to that fever was helping yourself to whatever drew you at the moment. Then, if one of the girls managed to make her presence known and shine a bit of herself past a boy's dark, skittish lust and actually hit into the very heart of his fantasy—then, then, you had my version of mating fever and maybe nothing else.

Instead of leaving, Mozzarella sank into the sofa, mumbling that he wanted to rest before he drove home. I turned in the other direction and walked outside to the pond.

It was nine thirty. Spike's fish had to be saturated with death by now. I went over to the bank to pull up the rope and couldn't find it. It had to be there! This was her one request. The bushes looked foreign to me in the dark, and I kept getting scratched every time I tried another spot. The water looked inky, and I began to imagine a snake uncoiling through the slime and the vines, slithering toward my legs.

"Tina!" Mozzarella called from the deck. "Telephone."

I untangled myself from the bushes and, fishless, tramped up the slope to the cabin. "It's S," he said when I got there. He went back to the couch where he curled up on his side and closed his eyes.

I leaned across the counter, my back to him. "Hey!" I said, happy to escape from the slime and vines. "What a nice surprise. What's up?"

"Hi." Her voice was clipped. "Did you find my note?"

"Yeah." Something was wrong. Had I misread her note?

"Why's he still there?"

"What? We went out to dinner."

"Tina . . ." A long exhale of smoke. "You and I have to talk."

Some more smoke. "I was a little disturbed to hear a male voice answering our phone."

"I was outside." My voice was unusually high and thin. "Trying to find your fish."

"Why don't you call me tomorrow when you're in the city. I can't talk now."

My stomach began to pucker, and though it was humiliating, I knew I was afraid. I stood over the sofa. "Mozzarella," I said, shaking his shoulder. "Wake up." Why did he have to answer the phone?

"Hmmmm." He rolled on his other side, facing away from me. "Mozzarella." I shook him again.

I turned off the lights, went into my own room, and crawled under the sheets with all my clothes on. At two or three in the morning, he knocked on one of the windows till I woke up.

"Hey, thanks for everything, babe," he said, and bounced out of sight.

CHAPTER FIFTEEN

"I THINK IT'S TIME FOR ME TO TELL you about a promise I make with every girlfriend, and I hope she'll make with me." Spike poked the olive in her martini and looked up at me as if I were the olive. We were outside at an Upper East Side café. The spirit here, except for ours, was festive. No one seemed to mind the plumes of bus exhaust, the car horns, the homeless man in a wool coat dragging by, turning his ash-gray face toward the pink shrimp curling on Spike's plate of lettuce. Ah, New York in the summer! Always a gallant effort, but today it seemed hellish.

"The promise"—Spike paused dramatically—"is that I don't even think, even *think* of their boyfriends in a sexual way. That's their property, period. And if one of their boyfriends says something to me in any kind of suggestive way, I put him straight and I let her know about it. No fucking around. You get it? And that's the way I hope she'll feel about my boyfriends. Because that's sacred, you know."

"Spike—"

"Mozzarella isn't my boyfriend. He tries to act like he is, and I don't like it. But he's a good example to bring up. I don't like being fucked with. By him. Or by you. I don't like calling my house and having him answer the phone like he owns the place. I especially don't like all the things that went through my head about him and you."

"Spike, I wasn't horning in on anything."

"I don't know if you know yourself what you were doing. You didn't like him. You hated him! I felt like I couldn't even bring him back to the house after you and Ohara got done with him. And then you go off fishing, and that's the last I see of you. *I thought she hated him*, I said to myself. I didn't know what kind of game you were playing. If you were just horny and wanted to fuck him, fine, he'd probably do that. But he's a kid—you don't want to fuck a kid like that."

"He wasn't as bad as I thought," I said. "I got to know him a little better. We had pizza at Monika's. To tell you the truth, I wanted to get a ride in his car. It's embarrassing. I'm not supposed to care about those things. At least you admit it."

She took a swallow of her drink to make it look as if she weren't remembering. "Fucking great, isn't it?"

I laughed, still nervous.

"And he probably tried to make a move on you, right?"

"Why do you say that?"

"Because I know him. I know a thousand Mozzarellas."

"Yeah."

She waited.

I told her. "He kissed me. And I told him to knock it off because of you."

"And what'd he say?"

"He said I was right," I lied. "Then he fell asleep on the couch."

"He did what?"

"Yeah. It was insulting. He fell asleep while I had to go and look for your fish because I felt real bad I'd forgotten about it up till then, and I couldn't find it anyway. That's where I was, I told you, when you called. You woke him up."

"Ha! I hope he was having the best dream of his life."

"I don't know. I was outside with your fish."

"Whirly, look," she said, "this is exactly what I'm afraid of. It's not so much if you fucked him, and I don't care if you did, that's all he's good for anyway, but a Mozzarella can come between us. He can make us lie to each other and compete with each other and, hell, just not trust each other. That shit always goes on when a man gets in the picture. The women just split; their brains fly off into space. I can't stand that shit. We've got too much to lose. We've got more communication going than I've ever had with a man. I don't want to lose that, Whirly."

She was leaning forward with her red hair falling over her arms down to where they folded on the table, and she looked so handsome and so sure of me, so sure of wanting to trust me.

And I wanted to please her. I wanted to be a good girl and make her believe in me, but part of me, I could feel, wasn't budging and couldn't be trusted. Still, I said, "I don't either."

"Fuck Mozzarella!" She saluted her triumphant speech with her raised glass. "On second thought, don't. He'd probably come too fast anyway."

I STAYED HOME EVERY NIGHT that week and worked. I waded through the batches of letters the *Courier* forwarded me from immigrants who had sent in money to help fix the Statue of Liberty, and I placed calls around dinnertime and copied down what was said.

"When I first saw the lady, I cried for joy. The lady looked beautiful. I'm so glad she will be able to get a new dress. America is the land of freedom."

One night, seconds after I hung up with a woman who had escaped the pogroms in Russia, the phone rang and it was Spike calling from a pay phone in a bar. Over the clatter in the back, I heard her say that she was crazed, that she felt like throwing herself on the floor right there in the bar and kicking her legs in the air, she was so excited.

"Can't talk now, Whirly! Are you going to be up later? I'll call you later, I'll fill you in later."

At one thirty in the morning, she called. "Is it too late?" The light in my living room looked bloodshot. "Five men came in today for a meeting," she gushed, "two-thirds of New York City real estate. Tisch was there, Macklowe, Schrager and Rubell. Carlos 'Los' Lamperti was one of them, I'm not sure which one—I think I know which one—and if I'm right, he's got thick, wavy, dark hair and the most perfect nose you can imagine. He owns half of Queens and flies his own helicopter and he called me tonight."

"Tonight? I thought you were out."

"I was. He called at twelve thirty. Told me he'd seen me bending over a file drawer and asked my boss about me and couldn't wait till the morning to hear what I sounded like, and I had two messages on my answering machine by the time I got home."

"Jesus."

"I'm telling you, these guys play hardball. They see something they want—boom!—they go after it!" She giggled. "And get this, he wants to fly up to the cabin this weekend to meet me."

"What?" Now I was alarmed. A real estate gangster spreading his silk-dressed haunches on our ugly nubby sofa?

"I told him absolutely not. The cabin is sacred, it's where I do my writing and that, I added, is sacred too. Besides, I didn't think you'd appreciate Lamperti landing a helicopter on our lawn."

She steamrolled on. "I gave him the number, though. I thought that would be okay."

"Is he married?"

"Separated, so he says."

"I see."

"Right. Well, we'll see . . . we'll see what happens . . . we'll just have to see."

One thing was sure: Mozzarella was piss water. Piss water of the past.

It was overcast when I pulled up to the cabin Thursday night. Spike had arrived that morning. This would be our pattern—she arriving early, I staying later. The air was heavy with the threat of rain, as if we hadn't had enough, and there was the sense that nothing had changed or moved much in our absence. The only large motion up here was the motion of people, if they were about. The tops of the beech trees swayed lightly in the breeze, and the pond looked slack in the weakening light. Driving toward our oak tree, I saw a bright-pink blur, then realized it was Spike in a leotard, her hair loose and flying, pumping up and down with her knees high. "Whirly! Whirly! Am I glad to see you."

"What?" I said. "What is it?"

"Here, let me help you." She yanked open the door to my car, loaded up with two bags in her arms, and hurried into the cabin. On the table was a rolled joint waiting in an ashtray, a plate of pastries, and a vase of pink-and-white mountain laurel. "Whirly, I can't stand myself, I'm going nuts. Los Lamperti keeps calling me. I can't get any sleep, look at me—what am I going to do?"

"You look good." She did, too, with her color so high.

"Light up that joint, go ahead, go ahead, hurry up, I waited for you, light it!" She began doing pliés, holding onto the countertop. Then she threw herself down on her back and kicked her legs in the air. "This is what I wanted to do in the office when my boss told me—they'd probably think I'm nuts, right?—but not you if I did this in front of you in your office, would you think I was nuts?"

"You'd be a little strange. But I guess it's understandable. He owns a chunk of Queens." She turned onto her side and began doing leg raises, her head propped up with one hand.

I was quietly toking and digging into a cinnamon and sugar donut.

"He called last night around eleven because I told him I usually go to sleep right after that." She switched sides so that her back was toward me and whipped her leg to the ceiling and down again. "He wanted to know what color my nipples were."

"What?"

"Yeah." She rolled onto her back and kept her knees bent as if she were about to try sit-ups but instead motioned for me to pass her the joint. "He wanted me to describe my body."

"I thought he knew what you looked like. Didn't he ask to meet you?"

"Yeah." She took a hit. "But he wanted me to describe it. He wanted me to tell him what I was wearing. What kind of nightgown I was wearing. How I was lying in the bed. If my panties were silk . . ." She drifted off and I stole a look at the pond, wondering if it was too late to take the raft out to where the water lilies were.

I said, "You haven't met this guy yet?"

"No."

"Spike, what do you think your date's going to be like?"

"I don't know."

"You don't?"

"He wants to fuck me." She shrugged. "Why wouldn't he? I like it when a guy's being honest."

"Then maybe you should've asked him what color his cock was."

"Ha! You know what bothered me?" she went on, switching to a philosophical tone. "I kept having the feeling that all the time he was talking to me he was jerking off."

I turned to look at her.

"His voice would get real low and he'd talk in waves, like up and down, up and down, then suddenly he was talking normally again."

"He probably was. Phone in one hand, cock in the other. So I guess you've had your first date."

She let out a shriek.

"Who paid?" I asked glibly.

"He did," she said, sure of herself. "That's fucking creepy." She considered this some more. "Probably he can't get it up in person."

"Or maybe he can get it up but he can't get it down. At least," I said, "if he can't get it down, you can impale yourself all night long and watch his face turn red."

"Why am I thinking of candy apples?"

"'Cause you're stoned!" I screamed.

"Ahhh!" She started pulling at her hair and stamping her feet. The phone rang.

It rang again.

"I can't answer that," she said, frozen in her chair. Her eyes were wide as cherry tomatoes.

"Don't," I said.

We sat still, neither of us breathing too loudly, until the ringing stopped. A chilly silence overtook the cabin. I licked my sugary teeth and glanced at the pastries on the plate. "Let's go to the Starlite," I said.

"I know. I can't stand it. I can't sit still."

The phone rang again. This time it stopped after only three tries.

We were too early for the Starlite, so Spike aimed her car toward another place we'd heard about from Jamie Ann. The Corkscrew Grill sat at the edge of a weedy field, and we would've missed it if it weren't for a neon Budweiser sign in the window. This was a ranch-style home painted white with black shutters. In front was a white picket fence and a small play area for children, set up with seesaws and a jungle gym. Whoever saw a bar like this?

"Well," Spike said, mastering the steering wheel with one hand, the other poised with a cigarette, "what've we got to lose?"

I've always hated the first moment of entering a bar. Typically, the door slams behind you and people look up. You're obviously a stranger, blinking back the strangeness of a room filled with smoke and lights and a cluster of people who all know each other and who are all drinking. Eyes look you over directly or sneak a peek in the mirror behind the bottles. Then you saunter—slide, scramble, hunch, shuffle—trying to look relaxed, while you find a decent seat and continue to affect a look of self-containment, at least until it's clear that you've come there to be with other people and to talk to someone, someone who's already turned back to his conversation since you sat down.

Spike and I chose stools toward the center of the bar, each of us separately enduring the scrutiny. To our right was a college girl we knew who was working that summer as a secretary at the real estate office, and our hellos were more boisterous than necessary. She was surrounded by three boys who were talking mostly to each other. Once in a while she glanced down demurely at her cigarette, flicked the ashes deliberately, then looked up again, as if she were very much involved.

To our left were early arrivals in the weekend race from New

York, New Jersey, and Pennsylvania. Four college boys—a lot of thigh slapping and giggles and "*aarghs*" and other syllables I couldn't make out. Next to Spike was a drink that looked like bourbon, and someone had thrown down a few dollar bills and a pack of Marlboros to keep it company. Spike ordered a martini, I, a draft beer, and as if on a cue of discomfort, we spun around on our stools and moseyed into the next room to escape the awkwardness of having no one to talk to but each other, now that we were after company.

"Hey, look at that," Spike said. It was some kind of bowling machine. We played a fast game, with her cheering me on as I tossed balls the size of Chinese apples up a pinball landscape of rings and tallied up points and bonuses. She had me challenge two local boys who were playing on the second machine. I did and won by five points and they called me a few names.

"One of them facho types," they half joked. Like a good manager, Spike steered me back to the bar, already talking about tournaments and taking on the whole town, when a voice behind us said, "I saw you two sneaking around back there. Looking for something special? Or just hiding?"

In one hand was the bourbon we'd seen abandoned at the bar and in the other a Marlboro. His shirt was red with brown palm trees.

"Come on," he urged, gesturing for us to come closer, a cigarette hanging out of one side of his mouth, one eye narrowed, the other eyebrow raised. "Come on, you can tell me. What were you doing back there?"

"Bowling," I said.

"You mean to tell me you came in here to bowl? Two foxy-looking chicks like you? Come over here, let me buy you a beer. One each. That's fair. Keep you from prowling around the back rooms."

The real estate secretary, whose name we didn't know, was laughing. Spike looked at her. "Is this guy for real?"

"Hey!" He jolted back, dipping his hand like a bro. "Don't I look real? Okay, don't drink with me. But at least know who you're turning down and why it's a mistake." He extended his hand. "Klaus Meinsk. What you girls call a local. I just say I live around here. And it's borrrrring. So when I saw you sneaking around back there, I said to myself, *Klaus, check this out. These two look interesting.*"

"You should only know." Spike's tease rang with menace.

"Whoa!" He ducked his head back. "Catch that heat! I have to tell you the truth, though. This isn't the first time I've seen you."

"No?" I said.

"You two were at the Starlite last Friday night, weren't you?"

"My God, this is a small town." I knew I sounded startled.

"Listen, when two chicks like you walk in and it's been the Sahara for nine months, you tend to take notice, you know what I mean?"

"I don't know," I said. "Sounds like crap to me." And I had the sudden urge to look in the mirror to see what I looked like.

"Friendly, isn't she?" he said to Spike.

"That's my Whirly." She smiled.

"Now there's an interesting name for you. Who are you—Moe?"

"Spike."

He tilted his head as if a fly just buzzed his ear. "Okay. Spike and Whirly. I can live with that. You girls must be from the city. You have that New York attitude, those names. Am I right?"

"Yep," Spike said.

"And you're renting over on the pond there, is that right?"

"How'd you know that?" I gulped some of my beer.

"I got connections."

"Come on."

He nodded toward the real estate secretary. "I asked her. So, you see much action over there or what?"

Spike told him about Bambi, the woman with the football chest, and there were snickers all around the bar. Suddenly, the three boys surrounding the real estate secretary were talking about Bambi, a local physical celebrity.

"You know Maurice?" Klaus asked us. "Maurice owns Le Chalet, the French restaurant near you. Maurice"—he nodded to a slight man at the end of the bar—"say hello to Whirly and Spike."

"Bonjour, mademoiselles. May I buy you a drink?"

"Tell you what," Klaus said. "I'll buy us drinks first, then Maurice can buy us drinks." He turned to the bartender. "Vince, you want to buy us drinks too?"

He rolled his eyes. And we began drinking.

At two thirty in the morning, Spike and I unfolded our lawn chairs and began basking under the light of a full moon. "He knew who we were," I kept saying. "He knew about us. Spike, I've never been a legend. I don't know if I can take all this attention. How come I'm not this pretty in New York? He knew who we were!" I grabbed my sunglasses. "The moon is too bright. Can you see me?" I started to howl at the moon. "Spike, there are bugs out here. Why can't I see them?"

"Whirly, you've been sitting with your sunglasses on for five minutes."

I couldn't stop laughing. Then Spike couldn't stop laughing. Then my chaise collapsed, and I laughed with my legs up in the air.

"Scotty," Spike pleaded at the moon, "beam us up! Please! Beam us up, Scotty!"

The sky was shaking with the sound of crickets, and I was shrieking, "No, not yet!"

CHAPTER SIXTEEN

"COME ON," I SAID, AND WE were in the car, Spike at the wheel, a bottle of wine in the back seat, a bag of croissants, a joint or two. Spike in her black shorts, white tank, peppermint-striped sunglasses, and me in my nylon running shorts and T-shirt. We were headed to the river to check out the ten-mile stretch from one of the canoe rental sites, and then we were headed anywhere. Anywhere that would take us in and around Warrenville.

I was higher than the sun. All the terror—the death-knell terror, house-key-clinging terror, phone-ringing terror—had broken like the passing of a storm, and all at once there was joy, sweet and gorgeous as honey. Whatever Spike looked at, I looked at too. And when I said, "Let's go there," we went. "Let's try that," and we did.

We got lost on the way to the canoe launch and found instead an old cemetery. The headstones were so tiny, they looked like crooked baby teeth that had just come through. A captain from the Revolutionary War was buried there, and the oldest date, 1693, was inscribed in a stone the size of a holy tablet and shaded by the leaves of a sumac tree. The baby who had died that year was three years old and the words of the mother, now dead too, were as bright and tearful as if she were standing there.

My joy of light has been extinguished. I know there is bliss in heaven.

Spike had become abruptly quiet and I turned to see her mouth working as if she were close to crying.

"We shouldn't have stopped," I said. I put my arm around her and petted her wild hair. It dawned on me that we were lost on some side road that could wind for miles with no familiar spot in sight. At about the same time, I noticed a man mowing the grass at the other end of the cemetery. He was using a power mower and wearing headphones to mute the buzz. No one else was around. His back was toward us. I considered our predicament.

"Did you ever sneak up on anyone in a cemetery?" I asked.

"Not while they were alive."

"Well, he's not going to be able to hear us until we're well on top of him. We'll scare the shit out of him."

This revived her. "We've got to do it, Whirly."

"You do it."

"We'll both do it."

She waited for me to take the first step. The grass was high enough to tickle our ankles except, of course, where he was mowing. Oblivious to the bees, I stopped near a clump of clover about ten feet from our prey. "Excuse me!

He didn't hear a word. He was young and his bare back was twitching with muscles that were too conspicuous. A bandanna was thrust in the back pocket of his chinos, and his boots were high-top leather construction boots. *This is what the boys in the city dream about*, I thought, *and here the guy's actually working.*

I crept a little closer. "Excuse me!" It sounded like a roar to me. He kept on mowing. I didn't want to have to tap him on his back.

"Hey!" Spike yelled, and he shot around, dropping to his knees.

"Don't shoot!" I actually had my hands up. He put one of his own over his heart and grinned while his neck turned scarlet. He shut off the motor.

"I'm sorry," I said. "We didn't mean to scare you; we knew it would be bad." He was still grinning, shaking his head as if to rid himself of a swarm of gnats. "We need directions," I said meekly.

He had a tight smile, big brown eyes, and a mass of curly brown hair. He told us how to get to the launch we were after.

"Sorry," I said again, and he told us to forget about it, but he was still waggling his head. When we got back in the car, I said to Spike, "Well that was fun."

"You think he'll have nightmares tonight, or what?"

"We should be flogged."

"Right," she said. "Light up that joint, will you?"

The launch was beside a snack bar that sold Genesee and hamburgers and deep-fried chicken in a basket, and the air spewing from the exhaust was laden with the smell of dead fat.

"How outdoorsy," I said.

Aluminum canoes were stacked to be hauled from one point on the river to another. A few picnic tables, some spotted with bird turds, had been arranged in an area bereft of grass, and industrial-size garbage drums had been stuck here and there among the ragged hemlocks, attracting yellow jackets that droned over syrupy cans of Pepsi.

"Well," I said, "I don't think I'd like to put in here."

Spike was smoking.

"I can tell you're thrilled about the whole idea."

"No, I want to do it," she said. "I'm just thinking about that cemetery."

I looked down at my feet and kicked some dirt around. "Want a hamburger?"

"I didn't say I wanted to kill myself." She glanced at me. "I was just thinking, that's all. It's going to take time. I've got a lot to work out there, you know. He left without answering a lot of questions."

"Your father?"

"Yep."

She looked puzzled and sad.

"Sometimes," I said, "I think we're all doomed to spend at least one decade of our lives thinking about what our parents did to us. If we're lucky, it only lasts ten years." She kept on smoking. "Then we find out that the answers lead to more questions." I stopped myself. "I think we're back at the debate about whether or not it helps to know why people do things."

"If I know why, I'll be able to forgive him."

"Maybe." A breeze swept the smell of French fries toward us, and I waited till it blew off and I could smell the river again. The light on the water was making the riffles sparkle, and where they weren't white like chiffon, they were clear like ice. "Maybe you could forgive him without reasoning it out. Just follow the urge."

"I do, sometimes. But I can't stick with it. I get angry again and then all the questions rise up and don't go away." She looked wistful.

"Let's get a beer," I suggested, "before we go home. See what Monika's like in the daytime."

"Yeah."

"Hey." I squeezed her hand. "It'll be all right." I added, "Maybe we shouldn't get high before three in the afternoon, huh?"

"Oh, who cares." She turned and headed back to the car.

I put three dollars on the bar and ordered two beers, and Vince, the bartender, looking forbidding, left me $2.30 in change.

"What?" I said. I had never paid before. "Spike, the beers are only thirty-five cents. Do you know what that means? We could drink here all day."

She grunted. She was sitting with her handbag on her lap and clutching it as if it were a bag of groceries. An elderly woman with a dachshund was sitting at the other end, and next to her was a man in a shiny, emerald-green shirt. They were trying to feed the dachshund some beer nuts. I ordered another round of beers for both of us and ended up drinking them both. I was feeling pretty giddy.

"Let's go home." Spike nudged me. "We've got to start the barbecue."

"Huh?"

"I want to eat dinner."

"We just got here."

She frowned at me, looking bored. "I was thinking about the hoedown," she said abstractedly. "The one they've got signs for on the trees. We should go to that. It might be fun."

"Okay." I was up for anything, but she didn't seem too buoyant. "Are you sure you want to go?"

"What am I going to do? Sit home and write in my diary? No, I think I'd like to get shit-faced and forget who I am for a while. After dinner, that is. Come on"—she tugged on my shirt—"I'm starving."

At the hoedown, we made the rounds of the dart games and picnic tables and listened to the amplified fiddle of Vern White. Vince, the bartender, was there, glowering at the sidelines, and Alma, our neighbor, was peering in from behind a gigantic speaker. We saw the cemetery-mower, too, slow dancing with a willowy girl and looking blissful. Somewhere among the dart games, I got stuck on the naked deltoids of a kid mobster who was throwing darts like they were loaded with rocket fuel. Under the orange lights, his skin looked like candy, and the night was warm, and Spike pulled me away to check out the hot dogs. We stuffed ourselves, then dragged ourselves home.

Almost as soon as we walked in the door, the phone rang. Spike answered it. I heard her say, "Would I do that?" in a voice that was climbing higher up the scale. She hugged the phone to her ear and drifted into her bedroom. When I walked past, she was lying on her bed, staring at the ceiling, her legs limply hanging over the side, and she was murmuring into the phone. I undressed, brushed my teeth, and went to read myself to sleep.

Half an hour later, I heard Spike cursing. "What's the matter?" I called out.

"Nothing. It's just fucked, that's all."

"What's fucked?"

No answer. "Spike?"

All I heard was the click of the light switch in her bedroom.

AT NINE O'CLOCK THE NEXT MORNING, Spike was standing over a power mower, in her bikini, studying the thing. I meant to sleep late, but something told me that I was alone in the cabin and I'd better get up. Peering out the deck windows, I saw Spike's chaise, her large men's shirt draped over the back, her mug of coffee, her papers, but no Spike. When I walked outside, I found her staring intently at the mower.

"Where'd you get that?" I asked.

"From Pullet's shed. Imogene gave me the key. Remember he said we'd have to pay to have the lawn mowed? So look at this. Sitting in his shed."

I considered the state of our lawn. "You're going to mow the dirt?"

"No," she shot back. "There's grass there. See? It's overgrown."

I turned to where she was pointing, to the islands of grass. I almost said, "Spike, we only rent the place, why bother?" but her look of determination stopped me. Instead, I asked, "Was that a bad call last night?"

"I don't want to talk about it. I want to mow the lawn." She marched away, past Imogene's trailer and into the shed, and came back carrying a can of gasoline and a spout. Just then, a door slammed and Imogene emerged. A door slammed again, and Alma slipped out.

"I don't believe you girls," Imogene said in her gravelly voice. "Why don't you let me call my son and have him do it for you? Cost you five, ten dollars."

"It's nothing," Spike said. "All I have to do is make sure I don't put the gas where the oil's supposed to go."

"Let me call him," she insisted. "He'll know." Imogene did not look her best in the mornings. Her face was heavily wrinkled and her curly hair was coarse with beauty-parlor color, a sort of egg-yolk yellow. She wore a long, sleeveless housedress, and her arms were jowly, though the rest of her was pretty trim for a woman in her sixties. Her best features were her large blue eyes, adept at showing amazement, and her habit of cupping her hand over her mouth like a child whenever she giggled, pretending to be shocked. She had come to Warrenville fifteen years ago, leaving a husband in the city (her sons were grown by then), and she made her living as a cashier in the Stop 'N Shop across the bridge in Lomatia Falls, where she thrived on gossip.

Alma, her sister, was the opposite. She had married her husband, twenty years her senior, soon after he left the critical care unit of the Trenton hospital where she worked as a nurse. He lived only four months longer, and Alma inherited enough money to buy a trailer with Imogene. She'd been coming up for ten, twelve summers now, and it was *her* canoe that was docked off our property and used with her consent by Spike and me. Imogene hardly ever went in the water. Alma, who was only a few years younger than Imogene, was fond of Chinese lanterns, stringing them everywhere through the trees so that they dangled, hung crooked, tipped over, and gave the grounds a bargain-basement look.

Alma was the writer Jamie Ann had mentioned, but I don't think she wrote much. When she wasn't in her trailer listening to religious programs on the radio, she was strolling along the banks practicing bird calls. Whenever we saw her, she was usually hurried and flustered, eager to make conversation and eager to go back inside. Her gray hair was shot with white, and she wore old brown polyester pants and shirts of gray and brown paisley, and on her feet she always wore Red Cross cushioned walking shoes. The one person she spoke with regularly, of course, was Imogene, and now she stood behind Imogene, in the shade of their apple tree, and *oohed* and *aahed* and *tsked* about the decision to mow the lawn.

"Don't let them do it," she warned Imogene. "Someone might get hurt."

"What did she say?" Spike turned to me.

"You heard her."

"For Christ's sake. Look, if men can do it, so can we. I don't think it takes any special brains. After all," she said, turning to me, "Pullet can do it."

Alma blinked her eyes nervously and tugged at the corners of her paisley shirt. "But do you know where to put the gas? What if you put it in the wrong place? Is that the right kind of gas?"

"We'll figure it out."

"Let me call my son," Imogene repeated.

Spike didn't bother to answer this time. She was squatting over the machine, pouring gasoline into its innards.

"That looks good," I said. "Especially with the bikini."

"You're a lot of help."

"Let me pull the cord," I offered.

"No."

"Why not?"

"I want to pull the cord. I'm dying to pull this fucking cord."

"So pull it!"

"I'm pulling it!" And she yanked as if she were tearing a limb or other body part from its roots. "Come on, you sucker. Work!"

The thing started up with a belch of bad, black smoke. "Whew!" Spike fanned the black cloud away from her. "When was the last time he oiled this pig? What's this? Oh, the choke." She moved the lever down and the machine coughed and died.

"Let me do it this time!" I shouted.

"Shit." She was shaking her head at it.

"Let me. Let me."

"Stop acting out."

"What's that mean?"

"It's a psychological term for jumping up and down like a baby."

"Oh, for Christ's sake, I'm entitled." Now, I could tell, I was really being obnoxious.

"Okay, so pull it."

I looked up at her, grinning, and confided, "I've never been able to do this, you know."

"Well, here's your chance."

I put my foot on the machine like I'd seen men do and like I just saw her do and I yanked the cord. Nothing. Again. Nothing.

"Don't be a pussy about it," she said. "Pull it. Hard!"

"Well, open up the choke some!" I shouted. Then I pulled it, hard, and it rumbled to life, belching and farting again.

"Okay. Now," she said, "I'm going to close the choke, but slowly." She did and we got it to a reasonable idle. Then she grabbed the handles and, with her body shaking like jelly, bulldozed the machine in a straight line down our skimpy lawn. She sheared off the tips of grass blades and pressed the pine needles deeper into the ground in a wide swath. Then I took over. I couldn't keep the thing in a straight line, and before I knew it I was headed directly for the ant hills.

"Hey!" I was mowing dirt. And ants. Billows of dirt multiplied and surrounded me, and the machine started grinding and retching as if it were under attack.

"Vietnam!" Spike started shouting and laughing. "Look at Whirly."

Imogene had her hand over her mouth, giggling. Alma, who had gone inside, now peered around her screen door to see what all the commotion was about.

"Get me out of here!"

"Push it."

"I can't see!"

The flying dirt was a regular dust storm, and Spike was laughing so hard she was holding her stomach. Suddenly I thought of the chopped ants falling between my toes, and I charged right out of there. I parked the machine on an island of moss and started sneezing. Spike strolled over.

"That was great. I wish I had a camera."

"Thanks a lot."

"Well, that's how you learn what to do and what not to do."

"You got all the good parts," I whined. "All the grassy parts." She looked at me with what I took to be some smugness. "Okay, you've reduced me to an eight-year-old," I said.

"I didn't do anything."

"I did it myself."

She nodded.

I shrugged. Meanwhile the machine was grinding away on its moss patch. She patted me on the back. "That's okay, Whirly, you're just not used to this kind of stuff."

She finished mowing our lawn and proceeded to take on Imogene and Alma's small plot.

"Oh my," Alma clucked. "Oh my, thank you. Here, let me give you something. Let me give you five dollars."

Spike mowed right on by, shaking her head no.

After she put the mower away, she came into the kitchen to fix herself coffee. I was, by that time, eating a late breakfast of fried eggs. Suddenly I heard her say, "Shit." She was standing over the stove with her back toward me. "Shit, shit, shit."

"What's the matter?"

"We've run out of gas."

"What? How can you tell?"

"Because the stove won't light. The tank probably ran out."

"What'll we do?" I was hopeless. Let's face it, if I were reincarnated as a cat, I'd sleep fourteen hours a day and show up when I heard the can opener.

"We have to switch over to the second tank. Shit. Why don't they tell you how long the tanks are good for?" She banged her fist against the sink. "Oh no. You know what this means? It means the hot water heater went out. We're going to have to light that fucker again."

Before I could say anything, she tore out the door to the tanks. I ambled over to the stove. Turned the knob. No flame. I went back to my eggs.

Spike marched into the room, the door slamming behind her. "Where're those pliers?"

"Over there, I think." I pointed to one of Pullet's cupboards. "What's the matter?"

"I can't get the valve open."

"Want me to try?"

"No." She grabbed the pliers and strode out of the room. Five minutes later, she was back. "Imogene's calling the gas man."

"What happened?"

"I can't figure it out. Nothing turns."

"Okay. So, we'll wait."

"Damn it."

"Spike, it's no big deal."

She flopped into the chair next to me and began tapping the table with her fingers. "I hate when I can't do something."

"You did something. You got Imogene to call the gas man. And you mowed the lawn." She grunted.

"Now me, I didn't even know the gas was out. And I killed eight thousand ants and missed all the grass."

She broke into a smile. "Whirly, what would I do without you to make me laugh?"

Softly I purred, "That's okay, I don't mind being a clown for your amusement. Makes me feel useful."

"Cheers." She saluted me with her cigarette. "Here's to usefulness." A broader smile now. "Women with a purpose."

With my fork, I lifted a piece of cold fried egg and toasted her. "Women with a purpose."

"Let's go for a swim," she said. "I'll go for a sun, you can swim." On the way out, she took the phone off the hook.

"Hey," I said, "what're you doing?"

"I just don't want to be bothered."

"Just don't answer it."

"I don't even want to hear it." And she walked ahead of me, out the door.

CHAPTER SEVENTEEN

SUDDENLY THERE WAS SILENCE. We were back in the city and there was no word from her. I left messages on her answering machine and waited, wondering what had happened, if it was good, if it was bad, if I'd said something or not said something. When she finally did call, it was seven o'clock in the evening—too normal, too early for her. "Where've you been?" I asked. "Are you all right?"

She sounded stiff. "I'm fine, thanks. I'm sorry I haven't called. I've been . . . out of it."

"Oh? Anything happen?"

Her laugh was bitter, as if I were a master of understatement. "Yeah, but I can't get into it now. I called to tell you something else."

"Other than what?"

"I probably should've told you a long time ago. I kept meaning to mention it, but then I kept forgetting."

I held still.

"I have an aunt and I promised her she could come and visit me at the cabin, and she wants to come this weekend because it's July Fourth."

I couldn't say anything at first. Then after a minute I finally managed, "Well, I'll try not to get in your way."

"Don't be ridiculous. It's your place too. If you don't want her to come, just say so."

"It's yours too."

She was quiet, waiting for the squirming to stop. "She just wants to get some sun and be with me for a while. I'm the only one in the family she has left, and you know, I try to take care of her."

"How old is she?"

"Sixty-four."

"Is this the same aunt who told you that story about scooping your business from the toilet?"

Spike laughed. "Yes, but it wasn't my business, it was someone else's." I heard her draw on her cigarette. "She's very important to me. She practically raised me, if you want to know the truth."

"What's her name?"

"Annabel. But everyone calls her Bertie."

"Well, will we still be able to go out?"

"Yes! Yes. We'll just do what we always do."

"Okay." I paused. "Listen, I'm sorry I wasn't more gracious."

"Look. As you would say, you're entitled."

"Okay. You okay?"

"Yeah," she said, but she didn't say goodbye.

"Is there something else?"

"No. Yes. Bertie's had some hard times. And she's under a doctor's care. She's on mood stabilizers. I thought you should know, not because you'd notice but you might think she acts differently from women her age."

"Really?"

"You might say she's . . ."—Spike giggled—"a little immature for a sixty-four-year-old."

"What does she do, throw temper tantrums?"

"No, nothing like that. She's just merry."

"TINA!" SHE CALLED OUT to me as I parked the car. "It's Tina!" she said. The voice was plump with girlishness and didn't seem to fit the thin woman in the doorway—impossibly thin, and dressed in matching sky-blue sweatpants and sweatshirt. "Oh, I'm sorry, I shouldn't rush you," she went on. "Collect your things, take your time. We'll be here all weekend. What a lovely place you have. Janet, look who's arrived."

Who was Janet? Were there two aunts?

Inside, the cabin smelled of baked apples and fabric softener. Did they change the days on me too? It smelled like a Sunday afternoon. On the table, the couch, and the counter were piles of folded laundry, and Spike was busy at the oven basting apples.

"We did all the laundry," Bertie hurried to explain. Her dark auburn hair was cropped feathery short and her large, myopic brown eyes were shielded by thick glasses, much too large for her tiny face, which showed the dents and swellings of a long-ago acne. Not an attractive woman to be sure, but a woman of instant warmth and cheerfulness.

"We didn't know what to do with your jeans, so we let them be. But look! Fresh towels. Fresh sheets."

"You did my laundry too?"

Bertie's bright smile faded for a moment. "We thought it would be okay."

"Sure. I'm just surprised, that's all."

"I hope you don't think I was intruding. I know you probably don't want me here anyway, so I thought I'd make myself useful, but if I've already invaded your privacy, I'm terribly sorry." She sat down on the nubby couch. "I can be such a dope sometimes."

"No, no." I was still holding my bag of groceries. "I'm not used to people being so . . . nice."

"Well, Janet told me that both of you took this place so you could concentrate on your writings, and I promise I won't say boo. When you want to work, just let me know and I'll go away. I don't cotton much to busybodies and I understand completely the way you two girls feel, the way you've created this place for yourselves, as Janet told me. Oh, she's very strict, you know. She always lays down the rules when I'm around, but I didn't think there'd be any harm in this." She jumped up from the couch and came back with a box of Russell Stover candies. "For you," she said, grinning.

"Thank you." I put down the groceries and took the box from her. Then because I didn't know what else to say, I asked, "Would you like some?"

"Oh, not now. Not before dinner. Janet's taking me out to dinner tonight."

"Janet?" I looked at Spike who hadn't said a word and who was standing with her back toward us, looking out the window at the yard. "Why do you call her Janet?"

"Because that's her name."

"I know her as Spike."

"Yes, I know." Bertie was petting the pile of soft towels and blinked at me from behind thick lenses. "She started using that name in college when she left home, and sometimes she insists that I call her that too, but I forget. To me she'll always be Janet."

This definitely blew a hole in the glamour. So here was Janet Smith baking apples in the kitchen.

"Is this true?" I said to Spike's back.

"Yep."

Spike said, "Bertie, why don't you take a nap now? You've been running around all day."

"That's okay, I'm not tired."

"Well Tina probably wants to get comfortable and unpack and maybe go with me to pick up a few things. You'll be here by yourself, is what I'm saying, so you might as well rest.

"You'll be sleeping in my room, and I'll be sleeping on the couch out here."

"When will you be back?"

"We'll be back for dinner, okay?"

Fifteen minutes later, Spike and I were having thirty-five-cent Gennies at Monika's. She did not want to talk about herself as Janet Smith. She wanted to talk about Los Lamperti, and men like him, men like Tommy Joe Johnson. Her voice was flat and her skin waxy, as if she'd been up all night inhaling nicotine, though she claimed this wasn't true.

"You know, Whirly, I never used to think I picked these people. I thought they picked me. But I realized after Lamperti that I pick them up. I set it up for myself."

Immediately, I thought, *Like you showed up on my porch?*

"It started with the obscene phone calls. The way it started, I had to know it wouldn't be good. Then I realized that there was something about the calls, something about his way with me that made me feel as if violence could burst out at any minute, and that . . ." She stopped talking and stared straight ahead at the twirling invitation to Have a Miller. "Oh God."

"What?"

"It's too awful."

"You were intrigued by that?"

She nodded. "I seek it out. It's all fucked up with sex. I realized that the sexual attention I seek, I seek for its potential violence. I had to know it was there with Tommy Joe. I had to. I don't think it's an accident anymore. I can't play the ingenue to myself."

There were no tears. Her monotone was so flat, I could've stood on it. How many times had she uttered these same words? I heard myself ask, "Have you ever said this to anyone else?"

"What?" She looked at me as if I'd thrown a bucket of cold water over her.

"It just sounds as if, maybe, you knew this once before, and you, maybe, talked about it, and you forgot about it until now, and now it's all coming back since your father died."

"What difference does it make? Are you so self-centered that all you care about is being the first to know?"

"No," I said weakly. "I just meant . . ." And for a second I couldn't remember what I'd meant, but then it came back to me. "If you've had these problems before, what have you done to help yourself?"

"Oh." She slumped on her stool. "I've gone to my share of shrinks. But I can't find one smarter than me, and I was sick and tired of indulging their neuroses, which they always use as a base point for describing mine. Besides, like I told you before, I don't think anyone's worth their salt until they have a nervous breakdown. None of my shrinks ever hit rock bottom like that."

"But you're still screwed up."

She grinned, taking this as a compliment. "As long as I'm with men, I am. I never have these problems with women. Sometimes I think it would be easier if I were gay; then I could get everything from women."

It felt, right then, as if my insides were caving in from some enormous pressure. *She's not going to say it, is she? I mean, we're here together feeling pretty peculiar, but this isn't what this is about.*

"Unfortunately," she continued, "I like men too much. I like that nice curve in their asses, you know, the one on the sides. Yeah." She grimaced to herself. "I like them so much I could kill them."

That night at dinner, Aunt Bertie regaled us with stories about Janet Smith. Over too-sweet duck with raspberry sauce at Maurice's restaurant, Bertie chattered happily about funny little Janet whose poor, dear parents were too childish themselves to know what to do with Janet and her brother, both of whom she said were precocious geniuses.

"You might think they traveled along with tiny light bulbs over their heads. Snobs, both of them, because they thought they were so smart," she said, pleased.

"Well, you know Janet's daddy was your typical New England farmer. Never said much. Never expressed his feelings. But he was crazy about my sister, any blind man could see that. She had Alex from another man when she was only sixteen, but Janet's daddy took him in, and then they had this one." She pointed her fork at Spike. "And she was the apple of her father's eye. My goodness, he couldn't get enough of her. Just like a little baby with a new toy. And my sister, she couldn't help herself, but she started to resent it, and then, well after that, well she's"—she pointed the fork at Spike again—"probably told you the rest of it."

I looked at Spike, who looked back at me dully, as if anesthetized. "No," I said, "she hasn't told me."

"Go ahead," Spike said to Bertie. "Let's hear your version."

Bertie blinked her large brown eyes behind her glasses. "I'll tell it for a cigarette."

"You know you're not supposed to smoke."

"Oh, pooh, I'm on vacation and that lousy doctor isn't here, so why can't I enjoy myself?"

Spike pushed the pack toward her aunt. "Be my guest. Tonight we'll celebrate indulgence. That's the same as independence, isn't it? July Fourth, Indulgence Day."

"What're you talking about, honey?" Aunt Bertie exhaled, obviously satisfied.

"Nothing. Go on with your story."

"Well, my sister and I were very much alike, in temperament that is. Our daddy spoiled us, I'm sure. She was much prettier of course, as my late husband was fond of repeating, but she was also more fragile. Anyway, she became awfully sad. You see once she had thrown lavish parties for her friends and family, and suddenly she wouldn't go anywhere, and she and Alex became inseparable. Sometimes I think she was more responsible than I like to acknowledge for the accident."

Bertie puffed contentedly on her cigarette, then held it away from her mouth and examined it from tip to filter. Of course it was my function to ask, "What accident?"

"You know, you *must* know. It's part of our history, like the Kennedys. Poor Alex was just trying to scare Janet's daddy, that's all he meant to do, but he got everybody involved, the whole family, and he didn't count on anybody moving. He certainly didn't count on my sister getting in his way. I don't really know what happened next. But my sister was dead, Janet's daddy took off, Alex disappeared, and the only one who knew anything was this one"—she nodded toward Spike—"and she was mute, so there wasn't enough evidence for a conviction. Anyway, my little Janet suddenly had no one but me."

"Are you saying her brother shot someone?"

"I'm not really sure who shot my sister." Bertie looked at me as if we were discussing recipes or dinner. She turned to Spike. "Why didn't you tell her?"

Spike shrugged. "Let's get the check."

In the parking lot, Spike grabbed my arm and whispered, "Remember what I told you about Bertie? She makes things up. It's not true what she said."

"What *is* true?"

"What I told you. My father was the one who tried to shoot us. My mother had a heart attack, and my brother and I went to Aunt Bertie and Uncle Frank's to live. My brother, though, was sent away."

"He never hurt anybody?"

She shook her head. "Not physically. He was like Bertie. She was sent away too." Just then, we heard an eruption of firecrackers. "Hey!" Spike shouted. "I almost forgot, it's July Fourth."

The Roman candles didn't look much like candles. I followed like a dumb puppy and stood quietly on our ragged piece of dirt lawn, inhaling the watery smell from the pond as if it were medicine. Spike gathered her fireworks at the bank, and Bertie stood behind me, puffing on a second—this time, stolen—cigarette.

"Okay, here goes!" Spike screamed, and a whizzy rocket of gold sparks shot out over the brambles and fizzled into the branches.

Bertie clapped her hands.

"Are the trees going to catch on fire?" I mumbled.

"Nah." And another rush of gold shot into the sky, this time farther over the pond, the flecks of light disappearing into the blackness.

"One more." Another rocket spattered the dark with pinpoints of light while a tremendous boom was heard in the distance. "Happy Fourth of July!"

Spike pulled my arm. "Come on, I think you need to see some of the Peels family. You've had enough of us." She turned to Bertie. "It's been a trying day for Whirly. She's heard too many stories today." Spike smiled at me and kissed me on the cheek. "That's what happens when you meet the family."

SPIKE HAD HER ARM AROUND Chuck Peels, who was grinning wildly. This was her gift to me. "I told you he'd be here."

"Hey!" I was more than overjoyed to see him. His clean blue jeans, crisply pressed shirt, and wide-awake eyes made for a picture of red-white-and-blue mental stability.

"And look who else is here," Spike said.

"Hey, babe, so, like what's happening?" First I hugged Chuck, then Klaus.

Chuck's eyes widened. "Heyyy. Let's do that again."

"Let's dance," I said, and took his hand.

On the dance floor, crowded with holiday people, it felt more as if I were flailing than dancing. I closed my eyes and I was alone on a bloody, noisy stage, keeping my space to myself, keeping it free of other bodies. When I opened them and saw Chuck, a little shock of reality invaded my dream, and while he wiped the sweat from his forehead with a gesture of mock exhaustion, he was nearing real exhaustion, but I didn't stop.

I remember Chuck Peels's glittering, stunned eyes from that night. I remember leaving him. Disappearing into the crowd, outside, to find Spike with Klaus getting high. Me thinking it wasn't true. She was okay now. Me getting high and thinking, *Poor Spike, what a life, what beginnings*, and wanting to put my arms around her: Spike the survivor, like I wanted to be; Spike, wild and battle-scarred and full of fright and letting me know all of it, wanting to trust simple, nonexotic me; Spike, one of the little geniuses.

I remember seeing her smile upon me as if there were no one else who knew her as well at that very moment, and I remember wanting to protect her from any more pain, to take care of the wild girl genius.

Then Chuck Peels appeared, waving like a flag from another country. Puzzled. Hurt. "Where'd you go?"

When I asked him for a drink, he asked twice, "You gonna be here when I get back?"

"Yes," I promised.

Klaus grabbed my arm and we tore off. Spike—there she was climbing over the trunk of Klaus's convertible and leaping into the back seat, her skirt flying up like a parachute. Klaus—jamming on the gas with some thin, sullen boy beside him. A sky full of stars and shrieks. The air whipping my hair, pushing my hair back.

Then, "How'd we get here? Oh my, Bertie! Is Bertie still here?" Spike and me giggling. "Shhh. Shhh."

"Janet?" From the dense black in the bedroom. "Janet, I broke a glass. Watch where you walk."

"That's okay, Bert." Spike tried not to giggle too much, looking at me like there was a beagle in the house. *Isn't she sweet?* Grinding ice and peaches and rum in the blender at four a.m., regardless of Bertie.

The boys reclining on chaises on the lawn, holding flashlights to see each other. Who was that? The ghost of waitresses past. Spike delivering the peach daiquiris. Me, tottering behind her, holding a bowl ever so graciously, as graciously as Audrey Hepburn might hold a bowl. The sullen kid slapping mosquitoes off his arms. Me, Audrey, asking, "Some grapes?"

Spike exploding. Falling down, crippled with laughs.

The only thing I said after that was "Excuse me," and I wobbled off to bed, but that was no good. The bed was swaying in choppy waters. I held onto the sides, groaning, begging forgiveness, and finally I fell asleep and had a horrible, horrible dream where pieces of my body fell from the sky like chunks of plaster and littered the dirt and grass that was our lawn.

CHAPTER EIGHTEEN

"THE TROUBLE WITH YOU IS THAT you can't accept the fact that you and I aren't that different," Spike said to me, slamming down a plate of eggs. I was barely functioning.

"Huh?" I said dully.

"Can you accept the fact that you can be bad?"

"Sure."

"Let me rephrase that. You know you can do bad things. But have you allowed the notion of your own, let's say, evil, to permeate your consciousness?"

"Huh?" I said again.

"Everybody's both bad and good. But the more you deny that you're capable of being a real shit, the guiltier you feel when you do something worthy of a shit, and the more you insist on the fact that you're a good girl."

"What're you trying to say?" This dialogue had been going on since I'd refused to admit how drunk I was the night before.

"Can you accept the fact that you were cruel to Chuck Peels?"

"Yes. No." I clutched my mug of morning coffee. "I didn't ask him to keep pursuing me. That's his choice."

"What about telling him flat out that you're not interested? Wouldn't that be kinder?"

"I've tried that before. It never works."

She smiled wryly at me.

"It doesn't," I protested. "Besides, I like Chuck. Not in the way he likes me, but I don't want to have to stop talking to him because of that."

She waved my words away. "Chuck is an example. What I was thinking of is the role you put me in."

"You?"

She nodded and stabbed her fork into a chunk of egg. "I'm the bad girl, the screwup, the crazy one, and you're the sane, good one. But the truth is, you're as bad as I am. No one would ever suspect you as long as I'm around."

I stared at her plate. It made my head hurt, but I couldn't take my eyes off the way she was chomping on those eggs. Nothing seemed to get in the way of her appetite.

Yes, I almost said. I thought of her as the crazy one. But hadn't she fed that image? Hadn't she said many times before that she considered her state of mind preferable to that of most mortals? My thoughts ground to a halt, and I reached for more coffee.

"Don't worry about it, Whirly." She patted my knee. "I just want you to think about it. It's okay that you're not a good girl. I always knew you weren't. But I'm smarter than the average schmuck. All I ask"—her voice turned softer—"is that you recognize that you and I aren't that different."

BERTIE'S DEPARTURE CAUSED A minor sensation. We found her trying to wangle a room at the motel next to Al & Nancy's Roadside Bar with Spike's Visa card.

"I'll stay here at night and sun with you during the day. I won't eat anything but fruit, I promise," she said.

Then when she was supposed to be packing, we discovered her rapping on the door of Alma and Imogene's trailer. After much discussion, she handed over the Visa card and Spike's Mastercard.

There was peace, of a kind.

Spike returned from driving Bertie to the station and began cleaning furiously. She rushed out to gather wildflowers and placed them in vases all around the cabin. Finally, she disappeared into her room and the cabin was still. At around three o'clock I heard hammering, then I heard nothing.

After she left for the city, I peeked into her room. The picture of Cody was nailed to the wall.

Oh no.

No.

The revelations she'd had in the bar were gone, forgotten. He was going to be next. And she'd want me to go through it with her. I couldn't. I couldn't pretend Cody was more promising than the others. It was futile. I knew what he was.

Then I did something I hadn't done in weeks. I picked up the phone and called my mother.

"The stranger from paradise," she said too brightly. "You know I was thinking about you—we haven't talked in so long—and I was going to give you a call tomorrow night, when you returned from your weekend. I've missed you, Miss Busyness."

"I've missed you too."

"Well, I'm glad. I don't want to be the only one. Are you there?"

"Yeah," I barely managed.

"Is everything all right?"

"Sure. I just called, as a matter of fact . . ."—I took a deep breath—"to invite you up."

"Oh!" She seemed pleased and surprised, as if she hadn't expected so easy a victory. "You know," she said pensively. "I was just saying to Phil, 'I wonder if Tina'll invite us to the cabin so we can get a look at it and meet Spike.' After all, how could I not want to meet a woman by that name?"

I gave out a small laugh, then said resignedly, "Her real name's Janet."

"Oh?" my mother said haughtily. "That doesn't surprise me."

"Her aunt was here. That's how I found out."

Another "Oh?" followed by "Well I guess if her aunt was there, then your old fart mother can come up."

"Come on, Ma. Don't be like that."

She went on anyway. "This cabin's been such a secret. Such an . . . experience for you, I just didn't want to intrude."

"Well I'm inviting you—you and Phil." I always had to be careful to give her husband specific acknowledgment. "Okay? Pick a weekend."

She did, and we hung up, and I immediately regretted the invitation. How could she help me if she was too busy competing? Before I could think more about it the phone rang and I jumped. *It's Spike! She heard me on the phone, and she knows I'm planning something.*

"So where'd you go? You promised me you wouldn't disappear." Chuck's voice seemed deeper than sleep.

"I thought you went back to Virginia."

"I am, in fifteen minutes, but first I thought I'd call you."

"Listen, I'm sorry about last night. I just got too high. I guess I was in a state of high anxiety."

"I noticed."

"You did?"

"Yup."

Poor Chuck, calling just when I was hot on the trail of a savior, looking for answers from, as usual, someone other than me. "How?" I asked, half joking. "Were my arms gummy?"

"What?" he asked, exasperated. "Gummy? Your head's gummy. That's what's wrong with you, girl."

I laughed. "So, really, how'd you know?"

I could almost see him fidgeting at the other end. "You couldn't stop jiggling. You were standing there tapping your foot, clicking your fingers." His voice got louder. "And you didn't wait for me! Shit, I never seen such a jittery girl."

"Well, that's why I wanted to get high. So that's where I went."

"With Klaus?"

"And Spike and somebody else I didn't know."

"Yeah, well, Klaus. He's trouble."

"What do you mean?"

"That's all I know about him. People'd say his name and the next thing they'd say is trouble."

"But you don't know anything else?" It was beginning to look as if even young Chuck knew better how to carry on than I did.

"No." He paused. "I didn't call to talk about Klaus."

"Sorry."

"Stop saying you're sorry."

"Okay. Sorry." I laughed. God, I felt fragile.

"Hey," he said.

"Okay."

"Now you ready to listen?"

"Yeah, go ahead."

"All right then. So you want to go to the Lomatia Falls firehouse picnic with me next weekend?"

"What's that?"

"The Lomatia Falls firehouse picnic. I just told you what it is!"

"Oh, you mean it's a picnic?"

Exasperated again. "What do I have to do, spell it for you?"

"I just meant . . ." What did I mean? I meant, *Give me some details, like what're they serving, why are you asking me? I'm supposed to be the responsible one here, who knows better, because I'm older, divorced, blah, blah, blah.* "Who goes to it?" I said.

"I go to it! That's enough. And Joey and Karl—all the Peels. Everybody from Lomatia Falls goes to it. It's the event of the year. Far as I'm concerned, anyways. My dad'll probably be there, he usually works the barbecue. So you want to go or not?"

"Well, yeah, sure, I guess so."

"'I guess so?' Let's have some enthusiasm."

"Yes. I'd like to go."

"You're not gonna stand me up now, are you?"

"No."

"I'll be going anyway."

"Okay."

"I'll pick you up at one. Sunday."

"Okay."

The Lomatia Falls firehouse picnic. What a long way from Park Avenue. Which reminded me that I'd forgotten to tell anyone that I'd gotten a promotion of sorts. I was going to write PR for the Ellis Island Museum, even have an office a few days a week. My immigrants had come through; the Statue of Liberty was unveiled. Spike and I had watched it on TV at Monika's the night of Bertie's arrival.

Spike was already on the phone by the time I pulled in the next weekend, and one look at her radiant face told me who she was talking to.

"You know what he said when I called him last week?" she bubbled to me after hanging up.

"What?" I said, with what I hoped was obvious indifference.

"He said, 'What took you so long?' That fucker. Like I believe he was just waiting for me to call."

"Hmmm."

"He told me that he's been reading this stuff on healing by laying hands on the body. Get this, the word 'disease'—break it in two and you've got 'dis' and 'ease.' Dis-ease of the spirit. There's also a chapter in the book about how to make love to a woman, not just her body but her spirit. Plus, we've talked three nights this week. Oh Whirly, I've never had a guy that looks like him. I mean you remember what he looks like, like one of these mountains."

"Right."

Peevishness crept into her voice. "You were the one who wanted me to see him." She eyed me. "Now you've got your wish."

"You're right, but that was before . . ." I stopped short. "Before I really thought about it," I finished.

"Liar."

"He's kind of creepy," I said tentatively.

"Oh, who knows." Her voice turned cold. "They're all creepy."

I tried to make amends. "Look, it's great. Maybe he'll turn out to be a surprise."

"Yeah, he'll probably hate me after the first date."

"Cut it out, Spike. He was obviously interested in you."

"He was probably drunk. Or desperate. Maybe I shouldn't have called him. I tried three times before I actually did it, you know. I'm sure he didn't know who I was when I said my name. I know he lied when he asked me what took so long."

"He knows who you are now, doesn't he?"

"Yeah," she said meekly.

"Well then, there you go."

"I love you, Whirly."

I smiled but I felt sick inside, bitter.

"Will you tell me how to act on my first date?" she asked.

"Oh, come on."

"I'm serious. I don't know how to act on a date. I'm always . . . inappropriate. I spill the popcorn. Or I don't know that I'm not the one who's supposed to get it."

"So now you know. He gets the popcorn. And don't spill it."

"Does he pick the movie?"

"You can pick it together." She clapped her hands.

Was she putting me on? Or was she putting us both on?

"I'm so nervous."

"About what?"

"About seeing him."

"Jesus, it hasn't even happened yet."

"But it will."

"So worry about it then."

"How do I stop worrying?"

"Get high. Here. Pacifier." And I stuck a joint in her mouth.

CHAPTER NINETEEN

THE NEXT DAY DRIFTED IN A SLOSH of date etiquette: "What if he gets boring? What if he doesn't show up? What if he really didn't remember me? At my wedding—I told you I was married—"

"No."

"It lasted two months," she said. "At my wedding, I ate everything in sight. I didn't make the rounds, I sat and ate. And when I cut the cake, I ate that too. I just don't know about these couple things."

"It's simple. He does something, then you do something. You take turns."

"Like what?"

"He says he likes the restaurant and you say you want to leave."

"Whirly!"

"I'm trying to be realistic."

By the time Chuck Peels arrived on Sunday, I felt as if I were crawling out of a cave into the first sunlight in days. There was Imogene's picnic table in front of me and a man—Was it Chuck?—with his back to me. Why hadn't I noticed those arms before? Or the thickness of his neck?

"Hi," I said to Imogene. "You two know each other?"

"Oh sure." She riffled her fingers through her short hair. "Me and his mother go way back."

"Yeah." Chuck smiled. "This is Aunt Imogene."

Great. And Aunt Imogene was probably wondering what I was doing with Nephew Chuckie.

“Well,” he said, swinging two pairs of muscles out from under the table, “we’ll be getting along then.”

I could feel someone watching me. I turned around. Spike was standing in the vestibule, peering at me through the window.

“Hey,” I called to her, and waved for her to come out.

“Is that your roommate?” Chuck asked.

“Somewhere in there.”

“Maybe she wants to come.”

“I doubt it, but I’ll ask her.”

“Hey.” I waved again. Then I went in.

“Your date looks charming,” she purred.

“He wants to know if you’d like to come.”

“What about you?”

I sighed. “I didn’t ask before since I assumed you wouldn’t be caught dead at anything in Lomatia Falls.”

“Well tell him for me thank you very much but I’m going to the Bavarian festival today.”

“You are?”

“Of course. I thought it would be a kick to take some pictures of the old Germans. You’re welcome to join me if you want.”

“I can’t. I’m going to the picnic.”

“Well, it was a thought. Maybe we’ll meet up later. Excuse me.” She went into the bathroom and closed the door.

“All set?” Chuck was leaning against the side of a two-door Colt. I nodded.

“She ain’t coming, is she?” He looked amused. “I coulda told you that.”

“Truck pulls aren’t her thing.”

“She was afraid there’d be truck pulls? This is the Lomatia Falls firehouse picnic! We only got one truck.”

He started up the car. “Mind if we take a little detour? I got to stop at my house and pick up a jacket for my dad.”

He steered his car over the one-truck-limit bridge across the river, then down the valley on a road cut between large oaks and hemlocks. He pulled into a driveway, bordered on one side by a roof-high load of wood, and on the other by the white clapboard of a three-story house listing to the left. The house had a wraparound porch, and it wasn't until I was up close that I could tell the place needed a new coat of paint. I walked onto the porch and promptly sat on the swinging chair, overlooking the valley. A cat crept from around the corner and tried to rub against my leg. "That's Grandma's chair," Chuck told me.

When I didn't get up, he sat down beside me. "I can't believe you like this," he said.

"You should see where I live."

"I been to Yankee Stadium."

I didn't feel like saying much. And while he talked about no one understanding why Grandma liked to sit on the porch like she did for hours, I sat, wanting to have her view from the gently unbalanced house and to have certain parts of my life over and done with. The air was so pure and warm, it was like being touched, just slightly, all over.

"Well," Chuck said, "I'm going inside. You can stay out here if you want."

"No, I want to see what's inside too."

He raised his eyebrows. "Don't expect much. It's just a beat-up old house."

When the door opened, I smelled baby formula. The hallway was long and dim, and as we made our way through, I spotted needlepoint samplers with declarations of pride: *Cozy and kind. With walls that hold love . . .*

"Ma!" Chuck shouted, tramping up the stairs to the larger rooms. The wallpaper was sooty, and the rug under our feet was littered with scraps of paper and clay chips from the cat's box. We walked out of the darkness into a room filled with light. A baby was lying on a blanket sprawled on the floor in the middle of the room, and next to the baby was a girl who looked no more than sixteen. The two of them were sleeping. On the couch was Chuck's mother, dressed in a pink bathrobe and holding a rattle. She smiled from underneath a head of soft blonde hair, and her fair skin seemed to capture the light in the room and hold it around her smile. Chuck introduced me, and embarrassed, she buttoned another button on her bathrobe, explaining that she was sick with the flu. The girl asleep on the floor was one of Chuck's sisters and the baby was hers.

"You all start young here," I said, picking up Chuck's Southernness for the occasion.

His mother chuckled. "We got nothin' much else to do," she said.

Chuck sat down in a rocker. I sat on a doily-covered sofa, the doilies long in need of being changed.

"So what are you up to?" his mother asked gamely.

"We're going to the picnic," Chuck said.

"And then you're driving to Virginia?"

"Yup."

"Then don't leave too late."

"We won't."

Silence.

I took up the ball. "I've never been to a Lomatia Falls picnic."

"Well, they're a lot of fun," she said. "I used to go all the time, but no more. Too much to do."

"Can't stand being around my dad too long," Chuck said.

She laughed. "Chuck and his dad. Like this," she said, making two fists and smashing them together at the knuckles.

"Yeah, well, he deserves it."

She shook her head at me, unwilling to say he was wrong.

I smiled back, then looked at the baby and the girl asleep on the blanket. All of the family's ties were spread out for me, for anyone, to see, and that struck me as generous. As if to show my appreciation, I tried not to notice the pile of clothes thrown into the hallway to be washed.

Finally, Chuck retrieved his father's jacket. "So long now."

"Bye-bye," she said.

We retraced our steps down the hall, down the stairs, and back outside to the car. I stopped, wanting to memorize each inch of the porch and the swing chair and the valley in case I never saw it again, but he tugged me along.

"Your mother looks like an angel," I said.

"Yeah. Wait'll you meet my dad."

His dad was stationed under a tent in front of an eight-foot-long rack of decapitated chickens. Dressed in a chef's apron and dark-green T-shirt, Woody Peels still managed to look covered with grime and grease from the barbecuing coals. His face had the shape of an elongated bean as if too much weight had been allowed to drop below his mouth, which he pursed so that it was small and round like the barrel end of a popgun. He thrust two paper platefuls of chicken at us. Then he flashed me a malicious smile, like he knew better than his son what to do with me. Immediately, I stepped on the tines of a rake and almost clobbered my forehead with the handle. Chuck slid his hands into his pocket and wagged his head.

"She's a great one," Woody said, as if I weren't there.

Chuck simply steered me away to the picnic tables. "Don't let him get to you," he said. "And don't step on no rakes no more."

At the table, Chuck and I sat for a long time saying nothing to each other, our plates heaped with chicken and corn and bread and coleslaw. Suddenly, I was too aware of Chuck sitting beside me. He had one leg on either side of the picnic bench with his hands in between near his crotch and he was rocking back and forth. It seemed as if every part of him were bulging, his arms under his short sleeves, his legs under his jeans, his cock under his jeans. The deep bass of his voice startled me.

"You want a beer?" he asked.

"Sure," I said, but I moved away.

Just then, Joey came by with some friends of Chuck's from Virginia. Joey's electric-blue eyes were gleaming with his private form of sanity. He introduced us to a handsome, tall boy named Charlie who was dressed in overalls, and despite his claim to being nothing more than a hick, he had a silken charm that propelled him to kiss my hand and grin. He winked and turned to leave with the others to play some wheels of fortune. Chuck and I eventually found our way to the ring throws and dart games and big-bowed stuffed animals. I put my quarters down at one of the booths, and Chuck watched me lose for fifteen minutes.

"I'm usually lucky," I said as I squeezed out from the stand. The crowd closed over the space where I'd been.

Charlie and the others wanted to have a last drink at the Lomatia Falls Lodge before taking off for Virginia, so we piled into two cars and drove to the edge of town.

"Everything here's old-fashioned," Molly announced from behind the bar, "except for me." She was busy squeezing four oranges in an upright press for screwdrivers that cost $1.75 apiece. I was actually sorry when Chuck said it was time to leave.

"Come back soon," Molly called, "with or without him."

Me and the boys—as I kept calling them in my mind—piled into the Colt and drove to the cabin. When we pulled up, Spike was in the yard by the large oak tree, bending over as if she were planting something. At the sound of our car, she stood up and turned to look at us, her expression slightly foggy. She wore a black shawl, one I hadn't seen before, and her bright-red hair fell in snaky clumps down her back.

"Yow!" Charlie said behind me. "Get back. Witchwoman."

"Hey," I said, "watch it."

"She's her roommate," Chuck explained.

Charlie made a sound like a fart. "*Shee-it*. That woman's scary."

"She's very friendly," I said, feeling right away as if I were talking about a pet dog and disgusted with each tiny betrayal. I got out of the car. "Hi."

"Hi," she said vaguely.

"What's the matter? You look lost."

"I lost my lighter somewhere and I can't find it." I heard the sounds of Chuck and his friends scrambling from the car. She looked down around her.

"Is that shawl new?" I asked.

"Do you like it? I got it at the festival. What a trip, two lesbians tried to pick me up. They followed me to the frankfurter stand, and I told them to fuck off."

"German lesbians? How demanding."

She grunted, and in a heartier voice than before said, "Right."

"Let me introduce you." She looked over my shoulder, warily, at the bedraggled crew I'd brought home with me. "Come on," I said, "they're nice." But her look told me I was out of my mind—what was I doing with these hillbilly children?

Charlie, with his unfailing confidence, broke through the stalemate. "How do you do?" he said, stepping forward with his hand outstretched.

"Charmed."

I wouldn't have been surprised if she'd curtsied. She shook hands politely with each of them, then excused herself and went into the cabin.

Charlie made a circular motion with his finger pointed at his head to let me know his opinion, and the others shifted their weight uncomfortably from foot to foot, wanting to be out of there. Chuck shooed them back into the car.

"So you gonna be here Labor Day?" he said finally.

"I should be. I'm thinking of taking my vacation here around that time."

"Well, I'll see you then. I'll be back up for that week."

"Oh." That was the week Ohara and Ben were getting married. There was no way I wouldn't be here.

"Oh," he mimicked me. "There's that enthusiasm again."

I broke my own train of thought. "I had a good time. I really did."

"Good. So did I."

He looked back at his buddies waiting in the car. "*Shee-it.* I gotta go."

"Okay."

He got in his car, one hand still in his pocket. He honked at the end of our driveway. I waved goodbye to the clouds of dust stirred up from his wheels. Then I went inside to Spike.

CHAPTER TWENTY

"IS SHE VERY DIFFERENT FROM YOU?" my mother asked as she hovered around the kitchen counter, watching me prepare a marinade for the chicken I planned to barbecue. Her eyes scurried to Spike's things.

"No," I said. "Yes. I don't know."

I watched her examine some elaborately wrapped chocolates Spike had bought for us, then she noticed the bottle of VSOP cognac, and finally she stared at the black shawl Spike had hung over the entrance to her room.

"How old is she?"

"Thirty-five." I was chopping onions with one of the blunt knives Pullet had left in the utensil drawer. My mother had already asked twice if she could help, not being used to me doing the cooking, and twice I had refused.

Now she said, "What are you fussing for? Come outside with us. You don't have to be so fancy."

"Mom, it's a simple marinade. I just have to do it now so the chicken can sit in it for a while."

"Well, what can I do?"

"Relax."

She stepped back from the counter and turned around, and around again, until she'd completed a circle. I understood the cabin probably seemed quite rough to her compared to her condominium.

"No, no," she protested. "This is fine." Then, "What does she look like?"

I sighed. "You mean Spike?"

She nodded vigorously.

"Well, she has long red hair." I stopped. Reducing Spike to a picture wasn't my choice. "You'll see."

"Is she pretty?"

"Ma!"

"All right, all right." She threw up her hands. "I'm just curious, that's all. You're obviously taken with this woman and I'm just . . . curious."

"Okay. Let's go outside. You take the wine. That should help."

"I think so," my mother said, and fretfully made her way out the door, holding the bottle like a guiding light, her curly hair bouncing as she moved along.

Phil was sitting in a lawn chair he'd brought with him. He smoked a cigarette and sipped on a beer, enjoying the peacefulness of the pond. My mother plopped into her chaise and poured herself a glass of rosé. "She's thirty-five," she announced to Phil.

"Who?"

"Spike, her roommate."

"What do I care? She's not my roommate."

My mother shrugged and pouted. "Nobody wants to talk to me about her."

"Oh for Christ's sake." Phil never really got angry at my mother, but he liked to carry on as if she were testing the limits of his patience. And when she wasn't being "silly," when she was being as sharp as she really was, he stepped back and let her be. She also let him be, the times when he drank too much and would rant. Sometimes I thought this way of relating to one another was commendable and sometimes I didn't.

Phil told my mother to drink her wine and not worry about Pike, Mike, Spike, whoever.

Then he asked me about the fish in the pond. My mother carried out a table from the living room and set it on the lawn.

She steamed the corn inside on the stove while I tended to the chicken on the grill. We drank more wine; I lit two or three citronella candles and brought out sweaters, though it was so warm no one needed them.

My mother sat on the end of her chaise lounge, balancing her dish in her lap and looking drunkenly out on the water. "I knew I should have brought my easel. I could've set it up right here in the morning and sketched."

"Why didn't you?" Phil asked. "You always say you should've brought your easel and you never do."

"Oh, I don't know," she said. "It just seemed like too much trouble. But it's so beautiful here."

"You see," I piped up. "That's what I'm doing here. This is what I wanted. And Spike got me here."

"What do you mean she got you here?" My mother sounded insulted.

"I couldn't have found this myself. I wanted to, but it took Spike to really get me moving."

"Why? Does she know so much more than you?"

"Well, she's moved a lot."

"So what?"

"They run her out of town?" Phil said, amused with himself.

My mother laughed loudly. "I wouldn't be surprised."

"All right. Enough," I said. "Help me carry this stuff inside."

My mother rose languidly from the chaise. "Oh, Phil," she said, "I think I'm drunk."

"No, you're not," he assured her.

She batted her eyes and looked around her in the dark, trying, it seemed, to understand what she was doing here. "Maybe I'm not," she said softly. "But I've sure drunk a lot already."

"I'll make some coffee," I offered.

"Tea for Phil," my mother said.

She followed me into the house. "I think Phil likes it here. I think he's enjoying himself."

"Good."

"Good," she repeated, setting the dishes down on the counter. She walked up to Spike's room and fingered the shawl that was hanging over the doorway. "Isn't she coming up this weekend?"

Spike had called earlier to say that at last she had a date with Cody and would try to make it up that night, but probably it would be very late. She also said she might not stay the entire weekend because she had work to do. Things kept coming up, and if she made it at all, it would be for the day.

I answered my mother, who was now seated at the table, her fingers drumming on the oilcloth. "She'll be here late. She has a date tonight."

"And she's driving up after the date? So late?"

"I guess so."

I turned around and she was staring at the geese in the dark mural above the couch. "It reminds me of something. Something awful."

"Ho, ho, ho." It was Phil, walking into the room as if his joints hadn't been oiled in years. He blinked his eyes. "It's very bright in here." He joined my mother at the table. "So where're we sleeping, in the basement?"

"On the deck," I said.

"Oh, wonderful. I haven't slept on the porch since I was twelve. Does this place have a latrine or do I go outside?"

"Funny."

"Spike has a date," my mother said.

He blinked at her. "Drink your wine."

I brought them fresh glasses and sank into the nubby couch just as I heard a car scraping over the pebbles of the driveway.

My mother was wide-eyed. "Is that her?"

I tried to remain calm. "I guess so."

Phil gestured to the ceiling. "The queen has arrived. Off with your head!" He laughed merrily. "You"—he pointed to me—"off with your head!"

"Try to be normal," I said.

"Me? Why should I try to be anything? I'm the elder here. You have to behave for me."

My mother put her hand on his arm, as she does whenever he steps on that particular soapbox, and Spike flew into the living room.

"Hi!" She was breathless. She was cradling a lamp in one arm and lugging her two bags with her other hand. Her hair was pinned up, and she wore a black, clingy ballerina dress that made her look stunning to me.

I was so glad to see her in the wake of my mother's endless, tiny questions that I couldn't take my eyes off her. *You see, you see!* I wanted to shout. *You see how magnetic she is. You see how illuminated.* And I almost laughed at the irony of the lamp cradled in her arms like an infant. *You see what she is, don't you!*

I smiled uncontrollably, enamored of Spike's cheekiness, her boldness, her hair, her body, her laugh as she talked nonstop about her evening with Cody, first only to me, then to my mother and me, but never to Phil, who smoked his cigarette quietly at the table.

"I finally had my first date with this gorgeous guy," she was saying. "Tina knows him, and I'm telling you he's the kind of guy you see in *Playgirl*. You know, where you wish you could pour water on the pictures, and they'd grow to life-size in your living room."

My mother's laugh sounded tinkly and weak.

"He's crazy," Spike went on. "Why do the ones who look like that have to be crazy? But he's fuckin' nuts."

A guttural sound from Phil.

"He met me at the car rental place, and get this, he was wearing a big straw hat and carrying a hoe. That's right, a hoe. And he came in and in front of everyone he said, 'Okay, darlin', you ready to harvest?' I nearly blew lunch. We rented a Jaguar convertible and we drove out to Long Island where his friend has a boat."

"Another boat?" I interrupted.

She looked at me quickly. "Yeah, all these guys have boats or friends who have boats. Just my luck." She laughed. "He said he knew I liked fishing, so he took me out to fish. It was incredible! I'd never been fishing at night off a boat. He had a bottle of champagne and some corned beef sandwiches from the deli, which I despise, since that's all we used to eat at the PR firm, working sixteen-hour days, so I went into the galley, found some hamburger meat in the refrigerator, a few onions, and made us a meal that he seemed ridiculously thankful for, and then he read to me, he read to me, of all things Edgar Allan Poe's 'The Raven.'"

"Quoth the Raven, 'Nevermore,'" said my mother.

Spike laughed coldly. "You think it was a message or what? Shit, I'm telling you." She looked at me. "Where do I find them?"

She turned in a flash and picked up the phone. "I promised I'd call," she said, and disappeared into her room.

"Well," Phil said, rising slowly, "I'm going to bed." My mother looked deflated, her lips closed tightly together as if she were bracing herself. I smiled placidly, careful to avoid her eyes, and helped them with towels and gave them instructions about the bedding.

They had washed their faces, brushed their teeth, burrowed under the covers, and switched off the light before Spike emerged again from the bedroom. I sat slightly loaded on the couch, the wine glass resting in my hands, the geese in the mural above me eternally landing in the mucky marsh.

Spike appeared like a ghost, her figure outlined by the light from her bedroom lamp. She put down the phone reverently. Her eyes in the dismal light looked calm and misted over, and when she saw me sitting there, she smiled and asked innocently into the darkness, "Have they gone to sleep already?" When I nodded that they had, a sweet, insincere pain crept into her voice. "I didn't get to say good night."

"No, you didn't," I said, my voice sounding heavy. "Let's go outside." What I intended to do then I didn't know; I just knew I wanted to be alone with her away from the deck. I wanted to talk with her, stand by her where we knew each other.

My mother and Phil slept, encircled by the glass windows of the deck. I listened to their breathing, then started out ahead of Spike. My legs were clumsy from the wine but my mind was alert, and I felt the distaste I always had when I was on the verge of knowing too much. I felt vain and mentally supple.

I walked outside over our lumpy lawn to the edge of the pond and she followed. When the water insisted that I stop, I stopped and raised my glass and drank my wine, lowering it to look out over the sheer blackness of the pond. Above, the ever-present, ever-ignorant stars shone brightly. I knew she had come up alongside me, that she was standing next to the gashed pine tree, its sap still bleeding down the length of the trunk. I smelled the dense musk of her perfume and smelled—imagined—her softness, and when I turned and saw her mass of upturned hair like a pillow against her face, I couldn't help myself, I smiled fatuously, but my eyes, I knew, were slivers, slivers of conceit. And I felt—like an idiot, like a poor stupid idiot who's tried not to know all along—a tingling from way down. She turned and smiled at me, a smile that slid across her lips as if she knew, and I heard myself telling myself, "Reach for her!" and I stared at her lips, then her hair; I squeezed my legs tighter, wanting the tingling to go away, but instead it spread through me, paralyzing my thighs, my stomach, and reaching like little fingers toward my nipples. I was sure that she knew and could see everything as if barium were lighting up my body in the dark.

We looked at each other, smarting as I was with this eerie longing, and finally she spoke. "We don't even have to speak, do we?"

I laughed lightly. "I know." And the spell was broken. The sound of our voices was too familiar.

"Your mother's suspicious," she said.

I slid my eyes toward her and saw a jeering smile on her lips. "You have the same eyes. They're beautiful."

"Thanks."

I did not want anything made clear. We stared out over the pond at nothing but darkness and smelled the thick, swamp-like smell of decay and felt its moisture on our faces. And after a full minute, she said, "You're welcome." Which brought us both to the edge of hysterical laughter.

"Shhh," I said. "You'll wake them up."

"Fuck them." She turned around, not to the house, but to her car.

"Where are you going?" I thought of that first, rainy night when she had left me alone in the cabin.

"The Starlite," she said, and after a moment that was too long, added, "do you want to come?"

I felt like a zombie, all of my cleverness drained in the face of the real hunter, as if that surge a second ago had just been another touch of her taken on, and my body had come back to me dull and fatigued. I closed my eyes and walked back to the house.

CHAPTER TWENTY-ONE

I ENTERTAINED MY MOTHER AND PHIL alone for most of the next day. Phil was content to sit upright in his lawn chair, smoking cigarette after cigarette and drinking tea. The day was overcast, but there was little chance of rain; the sun seemed trapped behind a muggy veil of gray, which every now and then lifted. During one of these spells of sunlight, I helped my mother into the three-man raft I'd bought, told her to settle back and drink her orange juice, and began rowing us out toward the middle of the pond and away from the cabin, Phil, and Spike.

My mother, I knew, felt quite pampered. "Where did you learn to row?" she asked.

"Here. On the pond," I said, where I seemed to be able to do things I'd never done before.

The pond was a murky green and I rowed us over cold springs too deep to see—loose threads from a waterfall, I liked to think—and around the bend, past the dock where Mozzarella had sung to me. The water was now shallow with tall grass rising up like feathers to touch our raft. On either side of the dock were coves, which held the water still, as if it were resting in their palms.

Soon we were in the narrow part of the pond that curved like an S and the water became deep again. I rowed us alongside the water lilies, two of them fanned side by side, and my mother reached over and broke off a length of stalk that held the white flower.

"How strange," she said, pinching the meaty flower. Its base was almost leathery, the snow-white beauty of its petals hardly suggesting their resiliency. "Weird," she said, and the troubled expression on her face told me we weren't discussing flowers.

"So," I said, "what're you thinking?"

"She's very different, your friend. She's not at all how I pictured her. She's shorter for one thing."

My mother shook her head suddenly as if shaking off flies. "She's . . . strange. Odd. When she came in last night, it was a whirlwind. I could see she could run that house like that," she said, snapping her fingers. "No trouble at all. But I have never felt so . . . so invisible in my life. And Phil, it was like she hated him on sight. She never looked at him once. She looked at me, at you, never at Phil. She felt very uncomfortable with us being there, that I know."

The raft was drifting slowly to the shore, and I dipped one oar into the water to straighten us out. "She's usually nervous when she meets people," I offered.

"It was more than that, Tina." Her voice was firm now. "It was like a show she put on for us. The laughter, the smiles, her story—it was artificial, like she wasn't even listening to what she was saying, just talking, talking for the sake of talking. And the way she looked at you."

I started rowing again, slowly, to diffuse my concentration on what she was saying.

"She has feelings for you, Tina, that . . ."—my mother stopped, her blue eyes that were my blue eyes watching me—"that make me uncomfortable," she finished. "She wants something from you. I'd be careful if I were you."

"You talk about her as if she were dangerous." I could see the beginnings of the dead, broken trunks reaching up through the water, signposts of the end of the pond.

"I think she is," my mother said with such an even tone that for a moment I forgot my theory that she might be jealous. "Look, I did not say a word of this to Phil, but this morning *he* said to *me*, 'That woman's violent. I felt like she wanted to hurt me, and I never even opened my mouth.' I felt it too," she said. "I think she's unstable," she went on, "and I think she could do you some harm."

"You talk as if she's a witch. A dragon lady."

"Exactly!" My mother leaned forward, and I could see she was trying to be careful so I would listen. "I don't know what she is. But she's not a woman, not a woman who would be attractive to a man. She's a . . ."—again she groped for words—"a creature."

I laughed softly. "Isn't that a bit extreme?"

My mother sat back against the rubber cushion of the raft. "No, I don't think so. She's not normal, not in the way that you and I are normal."

I stared at her, at her pretty blue eyes, her brown hair curling around her face, her slender shaved legs poised over the bubble edge of the raft, at the gold in her delicate bracelets and the shiny rose polish on her nails. No, Spike wasn't normal like that.

"Well," I said finally, "I'm not afraid of her. It's true, she's different from the other women I know, but I like that. It's . . ."—now I was groping for words—"challenging. And, of course, I've known her for longer than forty-five minutes."

"This is true," my mother said. "I'm only reacting from my first impression. Maybe it was the circumstances; we were all tired." She dropped her hand into the water. "Is she coming to dinner with us tonight?"

"I don't know. She was going to, but now she says she's too tired to do anything."

"Mm-hmm," she said, as if she suspected as much.

IT WAS FOUR O'CLOCK IN the afternoon when Spike finally stumbled onto the lawn, looking sheepish and pale from so much sleep. She was in her emerald-green bikini and her arms and legs moved plump and jellylike as she walked toward us. After some brief apologies for missing most of the day, she announced that she was going in the water and invited me to join her. She dragged both our black inner tubes from the basement and rolled them sloppily toward the pond.

She hadn't been sleeping the entire afternoon. Twice when I'd gone in, she'd been on the phone, cradling it close to her cheek in that way I'd seen her cling to it before. Now we faced each other on the water in our giant black donuts, the ladies of the house flapping like ducks to keep still in the current. I felt an urge to tell her I thought she was being rude, but heard my mother's voice in that admonishment and didn't broach the subject. Besides, I reasoned, she had no obligation other than manners to help me entertain Phil and my mother, and since she was not a lady of manners, she had no obligation. Of course, if I made it clear that it would please me . . . and then I became confused.

And while I was murdering my best instincts with all of this gobbledygook reasoning, she asked, "What are you doing tonight?"

"I told you before. We're going out to dinner. Phil would like to treat us all."

She looked away toward the narrow part of the pond and blew out a little cloud of smoke. The pack of cigarettes floated along on her dry, bare belly. "I don't think I'm going to go."

"All right."

"What're you going to do after that? Are you going to stay with them?"

I shrugged. "I hadn't thought about it."

"You probably don't want to go out while they're here, do you?"

"I don't know. I'll see how I feel."

"You'll see how you feel," she repeated.

"Yes." My hands under the water were closed, I realized, in fists.

"Are you always going to do what they say?"

I frowned at her. "They haven't said anything. If I want to go out, I will, but I just might want to spend time with them since it's been a while."

"I see. Well, I know I'm going to be shaking off some shit tonight. Klaus'll be there. He asked for you last night. In fact, a lot of people asked for you. 'Where's Tina?' they said. "I don't even know how they found out your name because I know you couldn't have talked to half of these guys."

I laughed, flattered.

"But I've got to go," she persisted. "I'm a mess."

I began paddling my black donut away from her back to shore. "I have to change the reservations," I called out, knowing full well that a table for four was the same as a table for three.

My mother was dozing in her chaise, her head fallen to her shoulder, and Phil also had his eyes closed, though he was still sitting in his upright chair. I was turning the pages of the phone book when I heard her come in.

"Where're you going?" she asked. Her soft, floppy shape emerged from the shadows of the vestibule.

I kept my attention on the alphabet. "The Inn of the Willows. Great name, huh? It's supposed to be very pretty inside and the food is supposed to be good." I offered this information as chatter, noise to keep me from hearing her breathing.

"Maybe I will go," she said finally.

I still didn't look up. "Whatever you want to do."

"I should get out," she explained. "I've been inside all day. It'll probably be better if I go."

"Whatever you want to do," I repeated. And put down the phone book and said, "Well, I'm taking a shower."

The shower was four feet square and seven feet high, but it was space, private space, and I stayed under the water until the skin on my fingertips was as ridged as the pit of a peach.

THE INN OF THE WILLOWS was forty minutes away. Spike suggested we take a shortcut. The back roads were fine for her Honda, but now we were gliding along in Phil's wide-bodied Lincoln, and he was trying to keep us from kissing a tree. He was sure we were lost.

"Have faith," I urged.

"I'll have faith when I see another car on these roads."

The inn came up so suddenly, Phil had to jerk the wheel, just missing a Ford pickup. "Christ, I need a drink," he said, his legs shaky as he stood locking the car from the controls on his door.

Phil was not supposed to drink anymore, and I looked at my mother but all she said was, "You did real good, Phil."

"You think it's easy to drive these roads?" he asked her, hitching up his pants.

"You did real good," she repeated, taking his arm.

In the bar, he ordered a bourbon for himself, rosé for my mother, scotch for me, and a martini for Spike, and paid for us all.

"Nice car," Spike said in a voice I recognized as her professional conversationalist's voice. She was probably preparing to tell him everything she knew about Lincoln Continentals.

"Thanks. I'm glad it's in one piece."

Too quickly, he ordered another bourbon. I looked at my mother. "Phil," she said, her hand on his wrist, "don't you think you better slow down?"

"Slow down? Hell. With her around?" He shoved his glass toward Spike's face. "What, do you think I want to get killed?"

Spike smiled broadly, showing her large, square teeth. "I knew he'd like me," she said, then broke into a coarse laugh.

"Like you?" Phil went on like a man storming into a fire. "I don't think 'like' has anything to do with the way you are."

Her eyebrows went up and I could see her mouth twitching.

"Okay, Phil," my mother said, just as we were called to dinner. "Let's try to enjoy ourselves."

We were seated in high-backed winged chairs plumped with cabbage rose cushions, and Phil ordered another bourbon. By the end of the salad, Spike was slouched low in her chair, her cigarette sending smoke past her ear and over her head.

Every now and then she'd say, "Right. Right. You're right, Phil, everybody's stupid. Nobody's as smart as you are," her voice mocking him with deadly boredom.

"You kids think you understand money? You spend it like water. You think a place like the one you got is worth anything? There's no heat," he pronounced triumphantly. "It probably leaks in the rain."

"You're right," Spike said. "It's awful."

"And I'm paying for her dinner?" He jabbed his finger through the air at my mother. "She can't even pick a decent place to rent. Why should I pay for her dinner?"

"I can pay for my own dinner."

"Sure you can." He drew his lips back, exposing his teeth, and actually said, "Tee-hee, tee-hee, tee-hee. You're a big shot."

She licked her lips as if she tasted blood there, and I excused myself from the table.

In the restroom, the first toke filled me with hope. I looked at the joint and laughed to myself about smoking in the girls' room, then the door opened, someone came in, and I froze.

"Whirly?"

"Spike?"

"You've gotta see this. Come on, come out of there."

I took another toke and walked out. She was standing by the sink with a joint in her fingers. "Great minds think alike." She smiled, and we both collapsed in laughter.

"God, how can your mother stand him? I feel sorry for her, I really do. And I'll tell you something else, if she weren't there, I'd let him have it right between the eyes. He's such a pathetic, abusive, threatened little man. Why doesn't your mother say something? At least to stand up for you? Me, fuck, I'm damned to hell, but you, you're her daughter. She shouldn't let him berate you like that."

"She can't do anything."

"Yes she can," Spike insisted. "He listens to her. She could tell him to shut the fuck up or she'll leave."

"She wouldn't do that."

"Why not? Is he just allowed to carry on like that all the time?"

"Yes."

"That's disgusting. Women are stupid."

Just then, I caught sight of us in the mirror hovering around the sink and I started to laugh. "What are we, chickenshits? Let's get out of here."

"Fuck, I'm too stoned," she said, and giggled.

"Me too. Shit."

We wound our way back to the table, looking a little too merry, I thought. "I see you found each other," Phil began.

"We're ready," my mother said abruptly. "Come on, honey, let's go."

"All right, all right, just let me pay the bill for this wonderful evening."

"Here, Phil," Spike said, and slapped a fifty-dollar bill on the table.

"Get that outta here."

"I insist."

"I don't want your money," he hissed.

"Well maybe someone else does." And she reached over and put the fifty on the table of a young couple dining next to us. "It's your lucky night," she said, and rose to leave.

We became lost on the way back because Spike and I were too stoned to navigate.

Almost as soon as we set foot in the cabin, my mother and Phil declared that they were going to sleep. Spike and I began gathering our things for the Starlite.

"Back in the den of iniquity," I heard Phil mumble as we left.

When we returned at four in the morning, they were fast asleep, and I awoke five hours later in the sofa bed in the living room to see my mother carrying her packed suitcase into the vestibule.

"You're leaving already?" I asked hoarsely. "It's only nine o'clock."

"Phil wants to get on the road early," she whispered.

"Weren't you going to say goodbye?"

"Of course, but I wanted to let you sleep."

"Oh. Don't you want to have breakfast?"

"We don't eat breakfast."

I sat up in bed. Phil came up next to her, hitching his pants over his skinny hips. "Take good care of yourself, babe," he said softly.

"Okay."

They were gone so swiftly, it was as if I'd dreamed we'd spoken.

When Spike padded out to the kitchen at noon, she fixed a pot of coffee before she realized they were gone.

"Hmmm," she said, trying not to smile. "I didn't even get to say goodbye."

I sat with her in the sun for most of the afternoon, feeling awful, agitated, and finally I went inside and made the call. "You got home all right?"

"No problem," my mother said.

"Did you have a good time?"

"Fine. We'll forget about dinner; it was fine up till then."

"About Spike . . ."

"Look, if we agree, we'll discuss it. If we don't agree, we won't discuss it."

I hung up, diminished by the effective punch at my heart and frightened, too, that I had been set adrift with no life preserver by the one woman who could have buoyed me. I shuffled outside to the chaise. Mercifully, I fell asleep again. Less than an hour later, I was awakened by the sound of Spike shouting. I turned to see her galloping down the lawn.

"He just called," she cried. "It's definite!"

"Wha—?"

"Cody's coming next weekend. And he's going to teach me how to shoot!"

CHAPTER TWENTY-TWO

MY WORLD WAS A BIG, BLACK inner tube. Floating on the pond. Cranberry juice and vodka in a plastic glass balanced on the inner tube. The sun was low, a lambent orange. It was eight o'clock and the air was still so warm, I hadn't bothered to change from my suit and leave the water.

Long ago, Spike had set off in the three-man raft in her flowing white sundress. Queen of the pond, her long hair draped over her bare shoulders.

Oh, the stage was set. The stage was so set for the human experiment. Floating sirens on the water. The pastel sun bathing the sky a citrus orange and the air like warm tea.

Spike and I had ceased speaking to one another at around four in the afternoon. She'd been trying to sit me down to *have a discussion* all morning, but I kept finding things to do away from the cabin. I did not want to talk about the human feast she had planned for the weekend. Finally, she tore out of the cabin and pushed off in the raft.

Even without my glasses, I could see that the male volunteer had arrived. A large beige van pulled into the driveway next door. I squinted to watch it back up and disappear, ostensibly to park under the white oak in front of our cabin.

I kept squinting and watching as he climbed into Alma's canoe as if he owned it. He paddled expertly and I spun around in my big black rubber bomb so my back was facing him. Just when I heard the paddle dip into the water close to my ear, I bobbed face front.

He made me catch my breath. What a corny, overworked phrase, but he did. He was spectacular. *This is a vision*, I thought. *This man isn't real.* And, as if he had come prepared to be a fantasy, he untwisted the lid of a thermos slung over his shoulder and poured into my glass exactly what I had already been drinking—cranberry juice and vodka. I felt like I was staring at a piece of Spike's mind. He was her invention. He had to be.

"I parked in the wrong driveway," Cody said. "Then I saw you floating out here. I thought you were the golden lady."

Mildly drunk, I snickered. "The golden lady went away." I pointed. "Out there. In a boat."

He turned to look behind him, but the pond flipped around its S curve and he couldn't see much beyond.

"A rubber boat," I added. "Why don't you go find her?"

"Is she coming back?"

Maybe she wasn't. Maybe she bullied her way through stumpville and the marsh grass and was now out on the river, headed toward Pennsylvania, quoting Oscar Wilde to the custom officials. "Nothing, gentlemen. I have nothing to declare except my genius."

"Maybe you should go find her," I said again.

"Aren't you gonna come with me?"

I stared at him, trying to penetrate his dark glasses. "I think you should go alone."

He seemed more intent on sipping his cranberry juice and vodka. "So what do you think of the saga of her and me? You've been following it, haven't you?" He touched my leg.

"I don't get you."

"Her and me. She's talked to you about me, hasn't she?"

I nodded.

"So you're in on it too. You were there when we met."

"I'm not in on it," I said with more scorn than I knew I felt. "I don't want to be in on it."

"But you already are."

I stopped the urge to begin an "I-am-not-you-are-so" battle and realized, with amazement, that this great big picture-perfect handsome man was frightened at the thought of being alone with Spike. Did he intend to sit here all night, paddling in the wading pool? I pointed the way again.

When, an hour or so later, I heard the dipping of the oar in the water—heard it before I saw anything in rapidly darkening cover—I was relieved to discover they'd found each other. Cody had tied the raft to the canoe and was paddling them both homeward. Spike's smile was beatific, and Cody looked enormously pleased with himself. Oarsman, cocksman, king of the pond, and the golden lady, seductress, witch of words, floating in tandem, now that they'd managed to say hello.

"I found her!" Cody called to me.

"I see."

"Oh, Whirly," Spike said, looking tamed. "It's good to see you." Cody immediately ran his finger down one of my legs.

"Great legs," he said loudly.

Now I know I'm not the kind of voluptuous woman who catches the eye of men like Cody. I glanced at Spike, sure she would realize that whatever he said to me was for her benefit, but she was trying hard to be part of the fun and her smile looked rubbery.

That night Cody built a fire for us. He had brought an axe to chop the wood. I almost asked him if he'd brought his rifle, but I let it remain unmentioned and hoped it would never appear. The fire burned slowly over the rocks he'd arranged on the lawn, and it made the night air even warmer and the shadows from the trees darker. We toasted marshmallows until they gobbed down the sticks and were sickeningly sweet. It was peaceful. Almost normal. After I left them, I could still hear their voices and smell the charred wood from the fire, and I slept soundly, feeling as if everything was for once happy.

CODY'S FACE WAS OVER ME. His hands were on either side of my shoulders, and he was descending. I turned my face away. He kissed me on the side of my forehead and I turned on my stomach and pulled the pillow over my head. "Go away," I mumbled. "I'm still sleeping."

He tickled my back.

"Cut it out."

"Come on now," he said softly. "I used to wake up all the girls."

"Fine. Go find them."

"Come on," he said, pulling at the pillow.

"All right, if you get out of here." It was stuffy under that pillow. "Where's Spike?"

"Taking a shower." He added, "It's just you and me."

"What a bonus." I tried to act tough to hide my puzzlement. "Okay, let me get dressed so I can come out civilized."

He didn't move from the edge of the bed. "We're going to take a trip down the river today. Spike said you wanted to do that."

I did. "Yeah!" I sat up. "You know how?"

He heard the water turn off in the bathroom and moved off the bed to the doorway. "We need somebody to make sandwiches. You're elected." Then he disappeared.

Even though there were plenty of canoe rentals, we decided to use Alma's canoe and our own cars. We were able to fit most of the canoe in Cody's van, and we all agreed that Spike would drop her car off at a designated point, and Cody and I, following in his van, would retrieve her. Then the three of us would travel to the launch site.

I made and packed the sandwiches, with Cody issuing orders about waterproofing. I helped him load the canoe, then we waited for Spike who was inside making drinks. When she didn't appear, we both went in. She was in a tight bathing suit, shaking the brew inside the thermos. Cody walked up behind her.

"Look at these tits," he said, squeezing each breast. "What great tits."

Spike looked up at me with a mixture of pleasure, pride, and shame. I walked out. Cody came out again, alone.

"Now what?" I said.

"She has to find something." He sounded annoyed.

When she finally emerged, he called out, "Ready, darlin'?" She tossed her hair and dumped herself into her car.

We followed, and as Cody rambled on about his days as the local whorehouse resident, I noticed that Spike drove past the drop-off point and kept on going, driving in a circle until we weren't far from where we'd started. "Honk for her to pull over," I said.

Cody jumped out of the van. "What the hell are you doing? You were supposed to stop three miles ago."

"Fuck, I don't know where you want to go."

They screamed back and forth at each other until I said, "Look, I'll drive Spike's car to the point. I know where it is. You two follow."

As she was getting her things out of the front seat, Spike whispered to me, "I just want to act like a dumb blonde. This is his idea. I don't want to have any responsibilities. If he wants to go down the river, let him figure out how to do it."

"Spike," I whined, but she was gone, a glass of her brew already in hand.

Our flotilla consisted of one canoe with a lawn chair set up in the middle for whoever wanted to be queen, and our two black inner tubes tied together to the canoe by a long rope.

The sun was high and the river was studded with canoes and rafts. We set off in a slow-moving current with Cody in the back, me in the front, and Spike being towed in an inner tube. And, naturally, because we were so loaded down with conveyances, we moved like sludge on water. It wasn't until we pulled into a faster current that Spike made her move. She put one leg in the canoe and tilted us toward her tube and the water.

"Wait a minute!" Cody yelled.

But before he could stop her, she quick-rolled over the side, and we shifted fast to the left then the right to keep from flipping.

"What the fuck's the matter with you?" he yelled.

"It didn't tip over, did it! Did it?"

"You're lucky."

"What do you think, you're the only one who knows how to get in and out of a canoe?"

The water became shallow and the canoe drifted to the banks where it was now nearly motionless. I stepped out, away from their screaming, and began swimming. Cody paddled up next to me.

"Hey, you're pretty good. Can you make it across?"

"I don't want to," I said, and swam away.

When the canoe caught up a second time, I pulled myself into one of the inner tubes. The banks rose steeply and I was able to look back and be towed down the river, relaxing finally, until Cody suddenly crawled into the tube next to me.

Spike quickly unknotted the rope that held us to the canoe and set us loose. "Fuck you!" she called out.

I was appalled.

"Sweetheart," Cody called to her. "Don't do this to us. Look . . ." He tried to crawl into my inner tube. "We're defenseless."

"Don't do that," I hissed. "Stay away from me. It only makes her worse."

"Fuck you!" she said again, and again, as she paddled in circles around us. "How does it feel to be helpless?"

"Not good," I answered. "Come on, Spike, don't play games on the river."

"Who the fuck is playing games here?" And she continued paddling around us like a hawk to its prey.

"Hey, baby. Be a sweet baby," Cody cooed. "We both love you. We wouldn't want to hurt you."

I glanced at him. Maybe he had experience I didn't know about.

"Fuck," she said, but it wasn't so ardent. "Sorry I'm ruining your fun on the river."

"It wouldn't be fun without you," I said, aware that we were floating farther from the rim of the circle she was inscribing.

"Just grab the rope, baby," Cody cooed. "Grab the rope and pull us in."

"What for?"

"Because we want to be in the canoe with you."

"You blew that," she said, but grabbed the rope anyway. I was astonished.

"Now pull us in," Cody said.

She dropped the rope. "I'm sick of you telling me what to do."

"Could you please pull us in, baby? It's a long walk back."

Maybe she was tired of her game, I don't know, but she pulled us back to safety. When we were all in the canoe, Cody retied the rope and kissed her on the forehead. "Now, please don't do that again, baby. It'd be awfully lonely without you."

I was too angry to say anything, and when Spike insisted on sitting in the lawn chair where I was, I sat down in front. After a few minutes, she decided she wanted to sit in front. Without saying a word, I gave up my seat for the lawn chair. And that's where I was when we went through our first set of rapids.

"Hold on!" Cody yelled from behind. My hands were glued to the arms of the chair. We hit riffles and the canoe shot forward with me sitting upright, waiting to drown. In a flash, we dropped a foot. "We made it!" I screamed, at the bottom of the riffles. "We made it!" How bad could we be?

But Spike was miserable. We steered the canoe toward the bank to stop for lunch, and on the way she slipped out and pulled down her suit so that her breasts bobbed in the sunlight.

Standing naked in the water, she asked him to throw her his T-shirt. He did, glancing casually at her. She came up wet, the shirt clinging to her breasts, which bobbed up and down in a Sophia Loren wet T-shirt mockery.

"Look at those luscious tits," Cody finally said, but he was more intent on steering the canoe safely to shore.

He and I pulled the canoe onto the beach that led upward to a meadow of goldenrod.

Spike went on ahead of us. By the time we reached the edge of the goldenrod, she had pulled off the T-shirt and stood with her back to us, her bare breasts to the sun, her long hair hanging down to the waistband of her shorts.

I saw a trail and took it, leaving Cody to deal with his golden lady. If he wanted to fondle her or fuck her, now was the time.

The trail led to an abandoned shack built into rock high above the river. It was cool and shaded with a tiny window propped open by a stick. As soon as I stepped inside, there was a sudden drop in aggravation. I felt content, but weary, as if the price to pay for such contentment would always entail a struggle through tangled jealousies until a small miracle of a trail was sighted.

There were footsteps behind me. I stood up and bumped my head. "What're you doing here?" I cried, alarmed all over again at the sight of him. His shoulders, his massive arms.

"I came to find you," Cody said. "We have to go back."

But he walked into the shack and came up beside me to look out the window at the water. "This is nice."

"Why don't you go back?" I said after a while. "I'll follow."

"How can I be sure you'll come?"

I reluctantly let go of the temporary peace and trudged after him. Spike was still in the meadow but her shirt was back on. "I found her," he called out, just as he had to me on the water when he was towing her back from the marsh.

"Whirly," she cried, changed again. "There was a beautiful green moth the size of my fist that landed right in front of me. You should've seen it. I sent Cody to find you, but it's already gone away."

"Let's have lunch," I said.

We had our picnic on the slope of the bank. I rested my back against the trunk of a hemlock, and Spike and Cody sat opposite me wedged against two rocks.

"My two wives," he said.

"What?" I asked.

"You wish," said Spike.

"Don't you feel it? Don't you feel how close we are?"

I looked at Spike, who was smirking. She leaned forward and kissed me on the cheek. "Whirly and I've been through a lot of shit together." She started laughing.

"I want to kiss Whirly too," Cody said.

I pressed my back harder into the tree. My knees were bent in front of me, and the steep incline made it impossible to scramble to the left or right. I could picture and feel their two mouths on me, smothering me, their hands all over me. I tried to turn my face into the tree.

"Come on," he said to Spike, moving in closer until I felt his breath on my cheek.

"Get away from her," she said finally from behind his shoulder.

He moved back. "I just want to treat my two wives equally."

"Knock it off with the two wives shit," she said.

I was halfway down the bank before either of them came after me.

It wasn't anything, I told myself. Just a minor crisis, not a major crisis. *We've got to get off this river. Keep it together.*

The wind was picking up and the light in the sky was now dimmed and growing dimmer. Storm clouds were blowing in. Only one other canoe was in sight, and it seemed to be having difficulties moving in a straight line. Before we could get started, Cody ran to the river to hail them.

"They might be disabled," he called back over his shoulder. We waited, shivering in the brisk wind, until he returned with a broad smile on his face. "I was right. Two of them have Down syndrome, and the third's never been in a canoe before. I used to teach disabled kids," he said, motioning for us to get in.

"You believe that shit?" Spike whispered to me.

I shrugged. "Maybe he did."

"Do you believe they rented canoes to them with no guides?" Cody asked.

"They rented to us," Spike said.

"Listen, honey, we may have problems, but that ain't one of them."

"Let's just go and get off this fucking river," Spike said. "It's going to storm."

We missed our drop-off point because under the darkening skies, I didn't recognize it and insisted it was farther on. As soon as we passed the point, we all realized I'd made a mistake. The banks began a steep rise seemingly never to descend again. We were the only canoe on the river. The water no longer looked friendly to me, but dark and cold and oily, running in slick currents over sharp rocks and dropping us deeper and deeper into the gorge between the mountains. Spike was in the lawn chair, I was up front, and Cody was in back yelling orders to me to set a line of navigation through one set of rapids after another.

"Set that rock as your point! Head straight for it. Paddle! Paddle!" Rain began to fall in heavy drops and the rain blew at the sides of the canoe. "Over there!" Cody shouted, and I aimed the canoe at the first clearing we'd seen since missing the drop-off point.

We hurried out and dragged the canoe up to shore, the rain pounding on our backs and the skies thundering and breaking open to jags of lightning. The leaves on the trees climbing up the bank broke the fall of the rain so that we had some protection, but all around us was junglelike foliage, before us the river, and behind us, the side of the mountain. There was a rudimentary trail worked into the side of the mountain that looked as if it might lead to the road. We remained quiet enough to hear the cars way above us, sounding as if they were whorls of wind gathering force as they approached, then jetting past.

"We'll never be able to drag the canoe up that bank," Spike said.

We sat on our inner tubes, Cody cursing me for missing the point and cursing himself for listening to me, Spike cursing Cody for everything.

Finally he said, "Look, I'll take the canoe and the tubes downriver to the next point. You make your way back to the car and come and get me."

"Out there?" I said.

"Can you think of anything else?"

I shook my head, numbed by the cold slashing of the wind and rain.

We watched him drag the canoe back onto the river, fold down the chair, and tie the tubes in closer. Then, with a big smile, he waved and pushed off.

"I hope he drowns," Spike mumbled as she charged ahead of me into the dense jungle.

"Wait, don't lose me."

She pounded through the brush. "I can't stand a man who takes charge like he's the big general. If I had to listen to one more minute of him telling me what to do, I was gonna punch him."

I was walking fast behind her and breathing hard. The trail was getting narrower and muddier and the vines were thickening, reaching for my hair, my face. She didn't seem to notice.

"What I don't get," she went on, "what I don't get is why they *all* do it. Why do they think that just because they're men they can take charge? I can get in and out of a canoe better than he can." Suddenly she stopped.

"What's the matter?"

"There's no trail."

In front of her was what looked like a canal filled with water. Her feet were deep in mud. "Let's go back and cut through the side."

"Fuck! I hate this fucking shit!" she screamed.

By the time we got to the road, I had slid twice down the bank and scraped my arm badly.

Spike had slipped and gone knee-deep into a hole of mud, and her feet were so caked with cold mud, she had to take off her shoes and walk barefoot down the highway.

"We should just leave him on the river," she muttered as we walked toward the car, not knowing how far away it was. "If he was such an expert, he should've just pulled the canoe in and checked before going on. Why didn't he do that?"

"I never thought of that."

"Because he knows as much as you or I. Either one of us could've gone down the river without him to guide us. Without him telling us every two minutes what an expert he is." The rain was soaking our clothes and hair. "I just want to act like a dumb blonde when men pull that shit. They want to be big-ass men, fine, then I'm gonna act like I don't even know how to breathe. They can take care of me up the ass, buy me sapphires, buy me a floor-length drop-shoulder mink, and I'm gonna be too dumb to even know how to say thank you. I'm gonna be so dumb, I'm not even gonna know how to tell them apart." The sky brightened, then went dark. "Maybe he'll get struck by lightning."

I never thought I'd be so happy to see our car. I ran to it. I pounded on it. I yanked on the door. "We made it!" I was hollering. "We made it." Spike was sanguine. "You have the keys, don't you?" I panicked.

Without answering, she unlocked the door. I was so glad to be in the warm car, so glad to be safe, that I forgave her striptease on the river. She was herself again to me, angry and confident, and I was sure that Spike would make everything right. We'd come to safety together, so now everything would be all right.

She backed out of the spot and started heading toward home. "Hey," I said, "aren't we going to get Cody?"

"I haven't decided yet."

CHAPTER TWENTY-THREE

I APPEALED TO HER SENSE of neighborliness. "He's got Alma's canoe."

She pulled into a driveway, backed out, and turned around. "If he's not there, we're leaving."

It took us forty minutes to find Cody. Everywhere we went, we met somebody, usually a scout for the rental companies, looking for their canoes, who said, "Yeah, a red canoe? Just left."

We checked the cocktail lounge of a resort on the water. "Yeah, he was here for a beer. Just left."

"What the fuck's he doing? Touring the country?" Spike slammed the car door for the sixth time.

By the time we caught up with him, the rain had stopped. We stood on the bank, twenty miles from where we'd come, and looked down on a cheerful Cody, piloting Alma's canoe and our two black rubber donuts through a set of rapids. "Hey, girls!"

We were far enough downriver that the banks were scalable and someone, probably the electrician across the road, had built a rough-hewn set of wooden steps into the weeds, which we used to climb down to Cody.

"Where were you?" he asked. "I kept shouting for you."

"Like hell you did," Spike growled.

"Sweetheart." He grinned at her. "I missed you."

We lugged the canoe and the tubes up through the weeds and over the metal guardrail at the highway. Cody helped Spike tie Alma's treasure to the roof of the car, and we shoved the two inner tubes into the back hatch.

"I hope you don't mind," Cody said, pulling off his jeans, "but I'm freezing my balls off in these things and I'm taking them off."

"Nobody gives a shit about your balls or the fact that you're freezing," Spike said.

"Thanks a lot. I could've left the canoe on the river, you know."

"Just get in."

He climbed in the front seat in his jockey shorts and motioned for me to sit on his lap.

This, unfortunately, was the only seat left.

"Ooh, that feels good," he said when I climbed in. Spike lurched the car forward.

She hit the gas hard.

"Watch it!" he shouted. "You've got a canoe on your roof. Brake! Brake, will you!" We were speeding downhill and the canoe suddenly shifted, its shadow spreading like a black lagoon over the windshield.

"Stop yelling at me!" she shouted back, but she slowed down.

We arrived with a cockeyed canoe and a half-dressed man who ran for the front door. "Open up, please! Whirly, do you have the keys?"

Spike took her own sweet time letting him in the house.

THE WINDOWS STEAMED WITH the heat of our showers. Even the garish yellow of the lamplight looked warm to me, healing. I opened a bottle of wine and poured three glasses. Drank one straight off and refilled it. "Cheers," I said to the geese for still being in the mural. "Cheers!" I drank to the Starlite, where we were going. The Starlite, the club that brought people of all classes, all harrowing experiences, together. I toasted the music from the radio; it was so good to have music singing from a radio. And just as "String of Pearls" came on, Cody ambled out of the bathroom, and I grabbed his hand and spun him into a few turns. A loud crash came from the deck; Spike had thrown something.

"I'm not going," Spike said when I looked in.

"Oh, for Christ's sake," I said aloud, realizing too late in my euphoria from the wine and the warmth that I'd forgotten the fragility of the shells underfoot. I glanced at the page of phone numbers tacked to the wall, grabbed the phone, and called Klaus. "Are you going to the Starlite tonight?

"Yeah, why not?" He couldn't hide his surprise at my call.

"Good. So am I. I'll need somebody to dance with. See you later."

I began to pace. Suddenly the warmth had changed to heat. I wanted to move, I didn't care where, I just wanted to get out of her way, to speed, the way she sped, in the opposite direction with little thought, little heart. *Let everything, everything, come to a head,* I thought, *every desperate passion, every cell of energy that ties us together.*

Cody was calming her down. When he left her to gather his things from the bathroom, she began a frantic search for her hairbrush. Tense like a headache, I waited.

"Now what?" he said to her bitching.

"She can't find her hairbrush," I explained from my seat on the couch.

"Jesus. H. Christ," he said. "Look in your car!"

"That hairbrush cost me fifty dollars," she cried. "It's a special hairbrush."

"Come on," he urged me. "We'll all look for her hairbrush."

In the back seat of Spike's car, I was quiet. And when we finally reached the Starlite, I bolted in ahead of them, scanning for Klaus.

The place felt really cool, I noticed. Chilled almost and quiet. It was Cody. The local boys were moving aside for him, looking at him, exchanging surly smiles. The breadth of his shoulders alone, the sculpted lines of his physique, rendered him glaringly out of place—a sexual monument of dubious origin and reality. He was wearing a white boatneck shirt with navy-blue horizontal stripes, tight jeans, and of course, dark glasses. He seemed straight off the highway billboards, ready to curl his handsome lips around a cigarette. I'd seen women frozen by the entrance of a beautiful woman but never men frozen by another man. For a minute, I thought they were going to jump him.

Cody grabbed my arm—he already had Spike's—and led us both onto the vacant dance floor.

"My two wives!" he shouted, as the canned music began to blare. His dancing was obscene. He grabbed Spike's ass, he raised his hands in front of my breasts and made squeezing gestures, he twirled one of us, then the other. I heard sniggering, and I was aware of being stared at, of boys in groups standing with their beers stomach-level, snickering and muttering and looking at us sideways.

The front door opened and closed, and more voices were added to the shrill of the music, and the groups of boys grew larger until there was an anonymous dark mass of spectators. A stream of darkness detached itself and flowed onto the dance floor next to us, and I was terrified until I saw it was two girls and two boys merely dancing. Then another clump of darkness and another and soon the dance floor was hot and crowded. The cloying heat of the bodies around me made my hair wet with sweat, and I pushed my way through the people to the bar. A deep voice funneled down to me.

"Can I buy you a drink?"

I opened my eyes wide. I knew what I looked like when I danced and sweat like that. Was I sending signals?

"Sure," I said.

I sipped the scotch he paid for, alternately biting into the edge of the plastic cup, while he chatted about another bar he liked to visit in a town I'd never heard of. When Klaus wandered by, I grabbed his arm. "Excuse me," I said to the deep voice, splashing my scotch down on the bar, and led Klaus onto the dance floor.

"Hey," he said, curling his spine like an oily snake, "whatever you're smoking, I want some."

"Nothing!"

"Then you got a fever. What'd the lady do, spike your prune juice? Stick her hand up your skivvies?"

"Nothing!"

"All raaight! Conversation! I like it."

When Klaus suddenly leaned forward and shoved his tongue in my mouth, it didn't dawn on me that he was kissing me. My body was too violent, shaking in another warp of speed—and I pushed him away and kept dancing and when he turned in a tight spin, I left him. I bullied my way through the dancers to the opposite end of the bar and collapsed into a seat. My mouth hung open; even my palms were wet with sweat. Then I felt him before I heard him.

"Would you like to dance?"

Were these all the boys who had been standing around gaping before?

Like a machine, I got up and walked back into the crowd. I hadn't even looked at him. His breathing was labored. My feet hurt and I kicked off my shoes. Then Mozzarella was there. Demon with a demon smile.

"They're calling your license plate!" he shouted in the man's ear.

"Huh?"

"They're calling you, Eddie."

Bewildered, Eddie stumbled off and Mozzarella stepped in, pool stick in hand. He grinned arrogantly at me, then sashayed over to the side, leaned his stick against the bar, and sashayed back. His sunglasses were tucked into the neck of his T-shirt. He wiggled his rubber knees and spun like a thief. He recognizes me, I thought. He recognizes the need to shake, shake her out, shake her out of me. He left me like I left Klaus; I spun and he was gone. I slithered to my seat and jumped into it, turned to sight a row of crooked tables—Spike and Cody. Like every other couple. She was on his lap, making small talk with three other couples. The sight made me cock my head like a spaniel.

"Can I buy you a drink?" It was Eddie.

"Sure."

"Are you gonna be here when I get back?" I looked up. No, it wasn't Chuck Peels saying that.

"Sure."

He left for the bar and Klaus strolled up to me. "What, I got BO or something?"

I laughed. "I got tired."

"Drink this, perk you right up." I took a hit of his bourbon. "This is my favorite song." He bowed and came up to face my navel. "Do me . . ."—he paused at length—"the honor."

I rose to my feet like an automaton and let him draw me back into the crowd.

My dancing was passionless now, mindless, bodiless rocking left to right. Klaus moved close to me so he could talk. "The lady seems to be having some trouble with her new boyfriend."

"Huh?"

"The dude."

"Oh, Cody." He was talking about Spike and Cody.

"Yeah?" I managed. "What'd she say?"

"She says he won't fuck her."

I was awake now. I let myself drop into the arms of Klaus's gossip. "Are you kidding me?" I said. "She told you that?"

He raised his right hand. "Swear to God."

"Why'd she tell you?"

"I think she wanted me to give him lessons."

"Directly or indirectly?"

"Oooh"—he knuckled my chin—"mean, mean, mean."

I leered at him. "It was too easy."

"What, am I a sucker with BO?"

"What else did she say?"

"She said, 'Is this a bitchin' body or what? What's wrong with the guy?' So I told her he had to be a fag. He looks like a fag. I also told her that I wasn't a fag. And I liked the idea of taking both of you girls on, you know, as in the holy trinity."

Suddenly I was scared. "Why'd you say that?"

He looked at me blankly. "Because I would."

"What made you think you had the right to even think of it?"

"Huh?" Klaus winced at me as if I were painful. "Unscrew yourself, girl. Wake up, smell the coffee."

But I persisted. "Isn't one of us enough? Do we have to come together? Do we seem like we're interchangeable? What is it?"

"I just thought it would be kinky, that's all." He'd stopped dancing and was speaking evenly. "Sometimes I like to get kinky. You seem like two very kinky girls. Does that answer the question?"

"No."

He looked up to the ceiling and faced his palms to heaven. "Women," he joked, but he'd lost his patience. "Buy you a drink?"

"No." We left the dance floor in opposite directions. I walked smack into Eddie.

He smiled sadly at me. "When I couldn't find you, I left your drink on the table, next to your chair."

"I'm sorry."

"Did you get your drink?"

"No. I had to talk to someone."

"Someone else must've drunk it then."

"Maybe. Listen. I've got to sit down."

"Can I buy you a fresh one?"

I looked at him. What was it he wanted from me? Punishment? "Sure," I said.

"Will you wait for me this time?"

"Sure."

As soon as I sat down, Mozzarella bounded over. "Dance?"

"No."

"You don't have him getting you a drink again, do you?"

"What do you care?"

"He's my friend."

"That's how you define friend?"

"Yeah. I don't like too many of my friends."

Eddie came back, this time approaching the table like a defensive lineman. He wedged his bulk between the table and Mozzarella and sat down in the chair so that Mozzarella couldn't see around him. After a few minutes of awkward conversation, he explained that Mozzarella brought him there. They worked together in the city.

"Kind of low-end," he said, looking guiltily around him. "I didn't expect it to be like this."

I couldn't concentrate on what he was saying. Besides, this was where I belonged tonight, at the bottom; making conversation was somewhere above me, in the province of careful people.

Either know me and talk fast or don't know me and don't talk. But don't try to know me, not tonight.

When Mozzarella jogged up and said it was time for them to go, Eddie looked abject. He slipped me a piece of paper with his number on it.

"Call me?" he said wistfully.

And, as usual, I said, "Sure."

I looked around. It was later than I thought, and the place was emptying out. The sweat was drying and I felt chilled, suddenly stiff. I went to the bar to get another drink; I must've had close to eight by now, but I wasn't feeling the effects of any of them.

A new voice said to me, "Buy you a drink? And then can we dance?"

We were one of four couples on the floor, and he said, "Man, I've been trying to dance with you all night. You've got quite an entourage."

"I do?"

"I couldn't even get close to you. And who's that guy? Your brother?"

He turned me around so I faced Cody sitting next to Spike at the bar. They waved to me and Cody mouthed, "We want to leave soon."

"No," I said, "he's my roommate's boyfriend. Quasi-boyfriend."

"He's pretty protective."

"He is?"

"Yeah!" He shook his head and I expected to hear next, "Wake up. Smell the coffee."

The boy I was dancing with was lanky and fair with an unused, good-looking face. He rolled his eyes over my body as if he were touching it and said, "I like the way you dance."

On cue, I answered, "I like the way *you* dance."

"You do?"

"Yeah."

Suddenly he said, "I'm a chef. Let me cook you dinner."

"Sure."

"When?"

"Call me." I gave him my number. He could call if he liked. Call away.

He glanced over my shoulder. "My friends are waving to me. They have the car. Unless"—his eyes scurried to my face—"you can give me a ride?"

"Better go with your friends. I've got to go with mine."

"Yeah, sure. Okay, I'll call you. Maybe for tomorrow night?"

"Sure."

And he hurried away.

Like a homing pigeon, I walked over to Spike and Cody. "Having a good time, darlin'?" asked Cody.

"How come you two are still here?"

"We're waiting for you," Cody said.

Spike laughed ruefully. "How's it feel to take advantage of your ratio, kid? Cleaning up tonight?"

I spied Joey Peels, with his blue headlight eyes, standing at the edge of the dance floor, his knees bending with the beat, and excused myself for a minute.

"I saw you out there before," he said.

"Are you going to stay a little longer?" I asked.

He nodded.

"Could you give me a ride home if I stayed?"

"Anytime."

"Thanks."

"Look," I said to Spike and Cody, "I'm going to get a ride home with one of the Peels. Why don't you two go home and take advantage of the cabin? I'll give you forty-five minutes. Is that enough time?"

"Takes me longer than that, darlin'," Cody drawled. "I got it shot off in the war." At that, Spike whacked the bar and slid to the floor.

"Tell me it's not true," she wailed, shaking her head. "Tell me he's lying."

"Honest. I got a button implant on my side. I got to push it to crane the thing up and sometimes it doesn't work."

"He's full of shit, Spike. Get off the floor."

"I'm not kidding."

"Spike, get off the floor."

She grabbed the barstool and dragged herself up. "You're kidding, aren't you?" she asked, half joking, half pleading.

He leered at her and didn't say a word.

"Well, good night," I said.

Joey Peels and I danced two dances, then we walked out to his car. He drove to the river and lit a joint, and while he talked about his dreams, his murmur settled over the water like mist. I pulled my legs up close to me and thought of a refrain from a poem I loved: "The cruel things I did I took to the river. I begged the current: make me better."

Joey Peels was talking about Chuck. How the family hadn't expected much of him, how he used to kid him about being lazy, but now look at him.

"It's only an hour till sunrise," I said.

He started up the car. "Yep, let's go home."

We drove silently, comfortably, to the cabin, as if because of Chuck we could relax; he could be Chuck's cousin and I was Chuck's friend and there wasn't any of this speedy edge stuff to Chuck—he was solid as cherrywood. Joey steered through the fuzzy end of the night to the cabin, and as soon as we made it to the driveway, it was clear that something was wrong. All the lights in the cabin were blazing and the door was unlocked. Clothes and socks and shoes were scattered over the sofa, the table, and the kitchen counter, but Spike and Cody were gone.

On my way back across the driveway, Joey said to me, "Look at this. Some dude took a headlight out of this van."

He pointed to the socket. I stared at it as if it were a bad omen. We crossed the lawn to the pond and Joey said, "Nice," as he surveyed the property. He looked behind him up at the cabin, the large windows of the deck filled with light, making it glow like a jack-o'-lantern. The bits of grass were still damp from the storm and the mud sucked at our shoes. Joey had one hand in his jeans pocket and was puffing on a cigarette with the other. He looked content, gazing out over the water, as if he were remembering something.

"I can't believe it," I said. "They're out there. I see a light."

"Probably the headlight," Joey said.

Then I said, more to myself than to him, "Jesus, you mean I could've been home all this time? They didn't even use it."

Joey laughed. "I bet I know what they're doing."

"What?"

"Catching frogs."

"She's out there with him, catching frogs?"

"That'd be my guess."

Their light shone like an eerie beacon on the water. "Boy, Joey, I'll tell you . . ." But I didn't tell him anything.

"You take care," he said, and moseyed back to his car, looking very much like a man who was pleased to have been of some help.

CHAPTER TWENTY-FOUR

THE PLASTIC PITCHER SHOOK. Was still. Shook again. The pitcher with the tight red plastic cap used to hold juice. It was set on the edge of our kitchen counter and shaking all by itself. How could that be?

It was only eight o'clock in the morning, but I caught the phone on the second ring. I'd been half awake anyway, tossing and turning with another hangover. The sun seared through the row of deck windows and cut into my eyes. I looked back at the pitcher just as I recognized the voice on the other end. "Klaus?" I said, warming to his sound then letting the words filter through. I asked him to repeat the words. He had to say them three times, and finally the contents of the pitcher came into view and I heard what he said.

"Joey Peels was in an accident."

The top frog stared at me, its cheeks pumping in and out. There were at least five of them, layered one on top of another, the top frog springing up to the lid and back down on the heap.

"Oh no. No."

"Someone said he left with you. I just wanted to make sure you were all right, you know, that they didn't overlook anything."

"He wasn't drunk," I stammered. "Do they want me to testify that he wasn't drunk?"

"No, they know that. The guy driving the pickup was drunk. Went through a stop sign and burned right into him." Klaus sighed.

"Man, I hate this shit. It would've been all right if he stopped at that sign."

The pitcher rattled on the counter. "He'll be okay, though, won't he?" I asked. "He's okay?"

"Yeah. They took him to Lourdes Hospital. One of his legs is broken. Some ribs. But they say he's stable. I heard it on the police band last night. When I can't sleep, I listen to that." He took a drag on a cigarette. "That's what happens around here. Too much drinking. I gotta get outta this place. Shit, it's good for a summer, but I seen enough."

He talked. The sun, my blown-up head, and the news—I tried to fend it off. "Klaus, I'm looking at a pitcher full of frogs. I think I better go back to sleep."

When I woke up three hours later, the frogs were gone. I walked past Spike who was fixing coffee at the stove while Cody was in the shower. My bathing suit felt sticky with soap, but the pond would rinse it.

The morning light tickled the water, and I rowed slowly out beyond the bend to the spot where my mother and I had picked the water lily. There was danger, she'd said. Things that weren't normal.

My eyes burned and I put my head down on my arm and fell asleep again—deeply, like I used to sleep after Edward had left. When I woke, I had the feeling that hours had passed. My thigh sprung back white from where I pressed with my thumb to see how burnt I was. A watery noise made me turn around. A man paddling a canoe was headed straight for me.

"Yo!"

Klaus slid Alma's canoe alongside my raft. "Got any beers in there?"

"Nah," I said.

"Spike told me you were out here, might want to talk." When I didn't say anything, he said, "I hate paddling a canoe. I'd much rather be stomping on the avenue with bad sneakers and a piña colada, my friend."

"Steely Dan."

"You got it." He looked around as if noticing the scenery for the first time. "You feeling all right?"

"All right."

The breeze picked up his cigarette smoke and sent it away from me. Klaus was dressed in the same Hawaiian shirt he'd worn last night, or maybe he had a dozen of them. He sat hunched in the canoe, looking as if he weren't quite sure what he meant to say now that he was here. The greenery threw him. His khaki shorts looked very clean, and I could see the outline of the pockets pulling against his thighs as if he'd gained weight since he last wore them. Finally, he thought of something to say to make himself feel comfortable. "The last time someone asked me if I was feeling all right I was in Vegas. I'd taken off for the weekend with this dude, Black John he was called because he had no color. What do you call those?"

"Albinos," I said.

"One of those. Right. Me and Black John took off courtesy of American Express and a dummy card I had made up. Anyway, in the morning I was standing in the road in front of Pauline's coffee shop and in the afternoon I was holding the arm of a slot machine and my mind went krypto. Nothing was happening. Like, total freeze-out. And Black John said, 'You feeling all right?' and all I could think was that I had to call my girlfriend and tell her I wouldn't be there at seven because I was in Vegas, and that even if I held the phone up to the slots, she wouldn't believe me. No one else knew where I was 'cause I didn't tell anybody, so she had no one to check with. It was weird, man, wanting to get back there by seven to keep her with me and not wanting to move from where I was."

He looked at me, unsure why he'd told me any of that. "Spike told me you used to be married."

"Mm-hmm."

"I thought you were one of those career women." I smiled at him.

"I can't picture you married."

"Why not?"

"You just seem too . . . It just doesn't seem like something you'd want."

I turned my face to the sky. The sun had ducked behind heavy clouds, and the sky was looking murky all of a sudden.

He lashed my raft to his canoe, and like Cody had done for Spike, he paddled us back together, his oar dipping into the black-green water with skill that he wouldn't admit to.

He wanted to ride back to the city with me, and I lied and said I was leaving in the morning. I didn't want to talk with him anymore.

"Well Joey's gonna be all right," he said. "He might even be out in a few days."

"Thanks. Thanks for telling me. I'm going to call a little later."

"No problem."

Almost as soon as he left, Spike came out of the house. She was wearing her huge white cotton shirt that came down to her knees. The shirt flapped in the breezes, and I noticed how luminescent she looked now that the sky had changed to a charcoal gray. I felt a drop of rain on my arm, and I looked up like a zombie to catch another on my face. Then Spike was on me.

"We've got to talk, pal."

Her fist was curled in at her waist, bunching the shirt, and her red hair fell loose and snaggle-toothed over her shoulders. I thought, *Oh no, not now*, and bent down to fold up the chaise lounge just as the rain crashed from the clouds.

"Hey!" she yelled, grabbing my arm. "You were too busy riding your bicycle before, running, and swimming—well you're gonna listen to me now."

I felt my mouth settle in a perfect, dry O, and my cheeks just hung. What was she talking about? What had I done that was so awful?

"Your attitude sucks."

"What?"

"If I have to walk by the garbage one more time as if I'm the only one who knows where the dump is, I'm going to puke. Did it ever occur to you that I'm not the housekeeper here? This entire weekend all I've done is clean up after you and him and make you and him every meal and I'm sick of it."

Meals. Garbage. Housekeeping. "What the fuck are you talking about?" I screamed.

The rain was soaking everything. Pouring down on my hair, her shirt, my suit. I started to shake.

"I'm tired of being responsible for you!" she screamed back. "I'm not a man! I'm not your husband."

"Oh, for Christ's sake." I picked up the chaise and sloshed my way across the lawn to the moldy basement. She picked up the second chaise and came after me.

"Nobody said you're responsible for me!" I shouted at her. "You cook because you want to cook. This is a summer rental. I don't intend to spend all my time cooking and cleaning and taking out the garbage."

"You don't even shop for any food. You wait for me to buy it."

"If you didn't buy it, I wouldn't eat it. I'd eat pizza and beer. What the hell is the big deal?"

I stormed outside to get the table.

"You have no consideration for anyone other than yourself!" she yelled at me, the rain pouring down.

"That's not true!"

"Eeoow!" It was Cody, wrenched from his nap on the deck. "Catfight!" he howled. "Look out!"

"Look, if that's what this is all about," I said, meaning Cody, "I'm sorry it didn't work out. Everything's crazy up here. Maybe you shouldn't have brought him up. Maybe you shouldn't have gone to the Starlite with him, I don't know. It's too strange—it was weird last night. I couldn't sit down, I couldn't stop dancing. Each time I stood still I wanted to leave."

"Well, why didn't you?"

"What?"

"Why didn't you just leave?"

"Spike, I stayed out late to give you time. I stayed out with—"

"Why'd you have to come along all day? Every time we did something you invited yourself along."

"Joey Peels is in the hospital!" I cried.

I turned away from her. "I tried to stay away," I muttered to myself. And I thought how the man whose picture was nailed to a wall was now crying like a cat. And how the only one I'd come with that I thought I knew well was Spike.

"Oh, honey," she said, and wrapped her wet arms around me and turned my face to her shoulder. All the lumps in her body pressed against mine through that cold wet shirt, and I felt the bone in her shoulder against my cheek and smelled her bitter odor of musky perfume and cigarette smoke. Then she was laughing. She pushed me away from her and held me there so she could look at me shivering and blinking in the rain. And then she pulled me back and held me again, whispering, "Oh, honey. Oh, Whirly, I love you, Whirly," and I clung to her, afraid if I didn't, I would wash away in the confusion without having anyone at all to pull me out.

I WAS ON THE FAR SIDE of the egg now where it was dark and the footing was treacherous—the egg where we slid down the one side and worked our way up through all we thought we knew but nothing looked familiar anymore. All that week when we were in the city and I was away from her I didn't dare call, thinking she needed time—I needed time—to put everything in its proper place, as if our psyches were houses full of furniture to be rearranged and dusted and plumped up again. My house was in shambles. My mind was wading through piles of junk and mishap and I was certain, so certain, that if I could knock on Spike's door when everything in her house was set in order, I would feel warm and comforted and decent again, able to peer back at myself and ask, "Whose mess is this? Let's get her straightened up."

I arrived at the cabin, grinning like a fool. It was going to be all right. I was so happy to see her car, I smiled at the tires. I looked down the length of chrome trim and followed the line across the lawn to the steps, remembering the different times she'd come out to greet me there, once in shocking pink tights, another time holding a bag of groceries, another a joint, held out as if it were a life preserver. I stepped into the cabin, oddly quiet this time instead of anxious with her stories and the stupidities and delights of her week.

The glass pitcher on the table was empty of flowers. Nothing had been done to replace the Queen Anne's lace from last weekend, and pieces of leaves stuck to the dry sides of the glass. But the kitchen was spotless, the dishes drying in the drainer, and the coffeepot sparkling and empty. Even the magazines that had been multiplying in three corners were tidied into one pile by the sofa. *Oh, Spike, you too felt the need for order, to begin again.* I planned to surprise her and say, "I stopped by that mysterious restaurant on the bend in the road and it looked pretty good. Let's try it tonight."

I unpacked, and after a while when she hadn't shown up, I looked for the third time out the deck windows and this time spotted her, floating home in the canoe, a wide-brimmed straw hat topping off her ever-astonishing red hair. Her fishing rod extended behind her, the line curling in the water, and she paddled slowly, sometimes waiting until the canoe turned ninety degrees to dip her paddle back in the water. I lost track of time waiting for her. When finally the front door opened, I was standing just at the point where the vestibule leads into the house.

"Hi!" I said too brightly, and I heard a low, dismal "hello" as she steered her fishing rod into the living room, her eyes fixed on the tip.

"How was it?"

"I didn't catch anything."

"Oh, sorry." Her back was to me since she was lifting the rod to rest on nails she'd hammered over the entrance to the deck.

"Say, how would you like to try that restaurant we've been wondering about? I passed it and it looks pretty good."

"No thanks."

"Why not?"

"I don't have any money."

"I'll pay. We haven't—"

"I don't want you to pay."

She took the rod down and began examining the reel.

"Well, how about pizza at Monika's? You can afford that, can't you? And if you can't, I can certainly afford pizza."

"No. I don't want to eat pizza."

"So what do you want to do for dinner then?"

"I haven't thought about it." She began swearing at the reel.

"You always think about it." She was on one knee, her hat still on and her fingers fluttering over the reel where, I saw now, it had snapped off the rod. Her voice, low and toneless, drifted forward and away from me, and I spoke to her mass of hair. "Why won't you look at me?"

Without turning, she said, "I'll look at you."

"So look at me."

She held the rod in one hand and turned with great annoyance. "Okay?"

"No, it's not okay. What's bothering you?"

"My reel snapped off, is that all right with you?"

"That's not why you won't look at me."

"I'm looking at you!" she shouted, turning again. "Not everything that goes on with me has to do with you. I'm tired of tailoring my behavior for you."

I shrank back. "Well maybe I can help you if we talk about it."

"I don't want to talk about it with you."

"Why not?"

"Tina . . ." she paused, "I can't afford you anymore."

"What? What does that mean?" She was fumbling with her reel, and I felt something unstick and I began shouting, spitting her words as if they were the punch line to the most absurd joke I'd ever heard. *Afford!* There wasn't enough room for me to thrash around. "Afford!" I repeated, rushing back and forth from the deck to the vestibule while she remained in the center of the room, her eyes on her fishing rod. I was talking to her. I was fed up. I'd had it. The mood swings. The unpredictability. The erratic behavior. The silence. The blame. *Now I know why men go to bars*, I thought, seething. *I don't think it's a good idea to be attracted to people who aren't quite formed.* And I banged out of there and into the car and didn't know I was headed toward Monika's until I got there. I'd never been to a bar like that just to drink by myself. Another benefit of being with Spike.

I got out my journal—not completely comfortable alone after all—and even before my thirty-five-cent draft was served, I'd lowered my head and begun scribbling.

> *Well, sweetheart, you chose wrong. You want to stay with the Codys and Johnsons and fuck-offs of the world, go right ahead, but I'm not coming with you. I go along thinking, "Well that's over," but it's never over for you. There's always unfinished business in your head. Deep bitterness. "Do you like me?" all the time in the beginning. "Do you like me?" and now the silence, the blame. I won't beg.*
>
> *I don't know if I can keep this going. I doubt it. And, yes, I said I keep it going. Keep it going by being other than who I am? I can't make it that way. No. What's the point?*

When I'd spent myself, I looked up and found a man staring at me. He was in his thirties and dressed well enough to tell me that he was from out of town, that he was maybe, even, rich.

I smiled at him. When he ambled over to the jukebox, I let him know I was still watching, and soon enough he slid onto the barstool next to me and offered to buy me a drink. *See that*, I told Spike in my mind. *Ha! I can do it without you. I've graduated.*

When I came home later that night, the cabin was dark—not even the outside light had been left on. I felt myself sinking into the ground with every step, walking slowly into a house weighted with spoilage. Without turning on any lights, I made my way to my room and lay down, surrendering to the darkness that pulled me under and felt like her darkness. Maybe I would be lucky and dream of Atlanta, the town of Jules McNamara, the man I'd met, who made his money—how perfect she'd find it—from managing his daddy's office buildings. Tall, New York–style buildings with lots of glass and steel. What the McNamaras wanted was everything gleaming and sunny, the sidewalks sparkling with mica chips. *Oh, yes, dream of Atlanta, Tina, with its clear glass exterior and a schedule of hustle and bustle that can be depended upon.*

I woke up late with a feeling of dryness. For a few moments I wondered if I'd been crying, then doubted it. A sadness crept over me softly as a kitten and I pushed it away. On the stove there was a pot of coffee that I reheated, and I filled a battered aluminum pot with water to boil an egg. When I sat down to eat, I discovered the egg was overdone and my toast tasted like cardboard. Flicking crumbs into the air, holding a magazine with one hand and looking not at it but over the edge to the window, I decided that I was back where Spike and I had met. Back at the pond in Pentacook, New Hampshire, where the trees and the water seemed less precious because I had no one to share them with. Oh, I would never learn. Never learn how to keep people with me. Always be tossed from influence to influence, then left with holes in my beliefs because they weren't mine to begin with. Somehow, I had to learn how to hold on to myself while loving another person.

I thought I could with Spike. Thing was, this had become more difficult than it had ever been with Edward. This. It. What was I talking about? Our relationship. I hated that word, but there it was, bringing with it rules and tactics and a certain illumination. I knew what I was going to do next. I piled the dishes in the sink, ran water over them, and pulled on my clothes.

When I found Spike on her chaise lounge in front of the pond, I asked her if she was feeling better this morning.

"What?" she asked, frowning.

"How are you feeling?"

"Fine."

"Would you like me to bring you some coffee?"

"No thank you."

She was reading Somerset Maugham.

At lunch, I asked if she wanted to talk about what was bothering her. She sighed. "Can you leave it alone?"

"I have come to the conclusion," I said, standing over her, "that if either you or I have a crisis, a major change, anything, it affects *us*. Not just me or you. We're in a relationship. And it affects both people."

Her lips curled into a wry grin. "Did you read that somewhere?"

My eyes filled and I couldn't hide it. "Don't condescend to me."

"I'm sorry."

I still stood there, nervous, and she looked up at me, her face a mask of politeness, her hands resting on the book she was eager to return to. "If it's true that you just want to be alone," I went on, "how do you explain the hostility? I'm not convinced this doesn't involve me. A relationship requires responsibility. Not in the sense of financially supporting one another but in realizing that one's behavior will affect the other's behavior. Shutting down is no good. For either of us. We both have to take responsibility for presenting our feelings to one another."

She swung her legs over the side of the chaise and stood up. "I can't take any more of this." All at once, it seemed she grabbed her book and her towel and began forcing her toes into her sandals. "Responsibility? You're lecturing *me* about responsibility? Excuse me, but I think we had a talk about that a long time ago. Maybe a few times."

"You mean about the house? Taking out the garbage?"

"Look, it's too late. I don't want to teach you anymore. I don't want to tell you how to act around me or tell you how to talk to me." And she walked off into the house, leaving me seething with impotent anger.

When I woke the next morning, her car was gone. I took my own to buy donuts at the Stop 'N Shop in Lomatia Falls and continued driving deeper into Pennsylvania. I followed the river through towns that began and ended quickly, their borders marked only by signs that said Speed Zone Ahead. At three in the afternoon, I rolled back into Warrenville and pulled up at the general store to buy beer. The screen door was tugged open and out came Jamie Ann, our realtor.

"Well," she said, "I haven't seen you in a dog's age. You having a good time?"

"Oh yes," I said, hoping it didn't sound as uninspired to her as it did to me. I smiled blandly.

"Good. I'll see you at ten next Friday."

"For what?"

"Oh. Maybe she forgot to mention it. Spike asked me to set up an appointment to look at some property to buy. I just assumed you two had talked it over."

"We did," I lied. "I just didn't realize she'd contacted you already."

"Yep. You know everybody that's rented that cabin has bought property in Warrenville."

"No kidding."

"See you Friday, then."

"Okay." I sped back to the cabin. Her car still wasn't there. And the first thing I noticed in the kitchen was that the toaster oven was gone. The teapot she'd brought from home was also missing, and the seven steak knives she'd brought to replace Pullet's dull-edged things were no longer sitting upright in their wooden block. The wooden block was gone. I went into her bedroom and found a list tacked to the wall, with various items crossed out, others checked, and others with question marks as if she wasn't quite sure who owned what.

It was only July! My God, what had I done?

CHAPTER TWENTY-FIVE

MY DESK WAS NO LONGER REAL to me, or the papers on top of it. A man with a whiny voice was badgering a secretary.

"Why didn't you tell me you were leaving for lunch at one? I wouldn't have promised this to him by one thirty."

I wished the door were shut, but I couldn't move. And though the phone receiver was hurting my jaw, I kept pressing into it. "You're leaving me," I whispered.

She took a long breath of air as if coming up from some great depth. Her voice cracked and rang oddly melodic. "That's ri-ight." We were riding a merry-go-round, down on the horse . . . ri . . . up on the horse . . . ight.

"Why?" Was that voice mine? High and contorted and nearly hysterical.

Again, the oceanic breath. "Because I can't take the way you hold me in your head."

"My head?"

"That's ri-ight. You don't see me anymore, Tina. I've become something else to you. A label. A crazy person. Some *thing* to be dealt with. That's not very good for me to be around."

"Well, I admit when I haven't understood you, I sometimes . . . use shorthand. I try to get a grip on you so I can talk with you."

"You don't have to get a grip on me. You just have to look at me. Listen to me. Accept me for what I am."

"I like who you are! You're the most . . . exciting person I know." Oh, I hated the way I sounded, trite, sputtering, stupid. Thrashing under a lid of dead words—no oxygen, no breathing space. "Spike, that's true."

Silence.

"I've never known anyone like you. Look at all I've done because of you. No one tells me how brave I am, or anything else."

"Tina, I don't want you to look up to me either."

I heard an invitation in her voice, suggesting that there was an answer. Maybe I didn't have to be ripped from my bearings if I could think—or stop thinking, stop relying on old, useless wit. I had to steady myself for a deep plunge through layers of glib and stone-cold responses, make the words rise out of their Jell-O slumber. "Spike, I want to look right at you. Not up at you, or down at you, but *at* you. Do you understand?"

Her voice was quieter. "Yes." She was waiting.

"Will you meet me for a drink so we can talk?" I asked.

"When?"

"How about tonight?"

"Okay. Where?"

She wanted me to be efficient at all these arrangements. If I were really going to come through, I had to start now, and I had to choose the right place, somewhere that was convenient *and* expensive, a bar that would make us feel wealthy rather than poverty-stricken by our problems.

I named a Midtown club where the drinks cost three times their value and the customers were usually over forty. Then I put my toe in the water.

"Spike, what would you have done if I hadn't called? Just moved out?"

"That's ri-ight."

THE CLUB WAS AT A BUSY Park Avenue intersection, but as soon as the cast-iron door closed behind me, daylight and traffic were blotted out and I was wrapped in the dusk of a late-afternoon lounge at happy hour. A towering bouquet of birds-of-paradise was set at one edge of a baby grand piano, and a middle-aged woman was tinkling at the keys. This was not a European or socialite crash joint, but it wasn't a sawdust, computer programmer bar either. It was a no-man's-land of advertising directors and vice presidents of small departments. There were three or four people scattered around—two hunched at the bar and a couple in the corner whispering furiously to each other. The men at the bar were staring glassily just above their drinks, and the gilt mirror behind the bartender returned their glassy stares back. The bartender in black spandex, suspendered pants was wiping a glass over and over again.

I slid onto a stool next to one of the blank-eyed men and, after ordering a scotch, took up the stare. I fixed my numbed vision just over the edge of my drink and just like the others, looked ahead, my hands around the glass. I'd never felt so tired and so agitated before. Pins and needles were pricking my legs, and I had a steady ache in my shoulders. Suddenly the man next to me was moved to speak.

"Are you in advertising?"

His question fell with a thud. I let it stay there for a while before figuring out how to kick it away.

"Veterinarian," I lied.

"I thought maybe you'd be in advertising." He had a dense mass of gray hair that was styled in well-cared-for waves, glass-blue, good-natured eyes, and puffy cheeks that defied the tight, straight lines of his beige suit. His tan was a shade more caramel than the suit. "If you have a practice, though, you understand about accounts." He turned talky. "Ever have to battle to hold on to an account you've had for, Christ, for eight years, for better or worse, till death do you a favor?"

When I didn't respond, he asked again. I'd been looking at the door, and I kept turning from him to the door to make sure I didn't miss her.

"No, I've never had that experience," I said finally.

"Let me tell you, you don't want to have it either." I agreed I probably wouldn't.

"Right now, I'm sitting here while the jury's out. That's what I'm doing here. Waiting to see if three daddy's boys let me keep their account. I don't want to lose that account. I've been sitting here telling myself if I lose the account, I can retire to my wife's father's farm in Vermont. I'll preside over vegetables."

"It's a tough business." The door swung open and two women whooshed in with shopping bags. "Isn't it?" I said, turning back.

"Well, all they want is kids under thirty. You know, something fast, something hot, a new idea that isn't middle America. Gimme a napkin, I'll give you an idea. How old are you?"

"Around that." I turned around for the umpteenth time.

"You don't look it. You look younger."

"A lot of people say that."

"Get pretty used to the same old compliments, huh?"

"Well, not really." I turned and this time she was standing there, holding a Saks bag and peering into the darkness to find me. How had I missed the second the door opened?

"Spike!"

The man next to me jerked and swirled some booze out of his glass. "Excuse me," I said over my shoulder, and swiveled off the stool to where she was standing.

Like a lollipop, that's how she looked to me—wearing a lime-green sweater and matching hair ribbon, waiting coyly with both hands close to each other on the handle of her Saks bag. I wanted to tell her how pretty she looked, but I was afraid of going too soft too soon. I had the feeling that I was already grinning too broadly and looking too relieved to see her.

"Let me settle up and we'll get a table," I said.

She walked ahead of me. We ordered fresh drinks and I listened to her talk, almost bashfully, lowering her eyes, then raising them again to show me how bright they were. I was pleating the linen tablecloth. I couldn't help it. She looked so sweet, and I was waiting for the bomb. If she left, I'd be alone again, back to my fractured apartment, full of ghosts.

She outlined what I had done wrong. I took out my notebook. If I were to do the shopping now and cook dinner, I had to make a list. I wrote down tissue, Brillo, coffee, half-and-half, milk, eggs, knives (to replace the ones she'd taken home with her), zucchini bread (which I promised to bake), and marinated shrimp (which I vowed to make for dinner). I wrote down laundry detergent, because, she said, she was tired of being the only one to worry about the laundry supplies and it was about time I did a wash not just for myself. And I wrote down a carton of Carlton 100's (box) and some vodka.

"God," I said. "I don't think I've written a list all summer."

"I know," she said, smiling demurely.

"It's just that a summerhouse to me means a place to crash, not a place to take care of like a regular house. It's a vacation for me."

She leaned forward and spoke slowly. "Tina, there are two of us living there. If I cook, you eat it. If there's trash, I take it out. I'd like a break too."

But you don't have to cook and clean, I wanted to say. I didn't, though, I knew better.

All she really wanted was for me to pay attention.

"Tina," she said, "I think you've got a good heart. And that's all I ask of you, that you speak to me with your heart."

"Me too." I clicked my glass to hers, relieved but strangely sad. And I repeated, "That I speak to you from my heart."

THE STARS WERE CROWDING the sky the night I barbecued my famous spicy shrimp, exactly as I'd done at the beginning of our time together. That was when we both discovered how the water swept quietly one way then another depending on the direction of the breeze, and when whole afternoons passed dreamily, mostly with our feet propped up.

Spike was happily boozy and I was exhausted from running errands all day. "Whirly," she said, "don't think I haven't noticed all you've done so far. I have. And I very much appreciate it. Believe me, we've needed a night like this for a long time. It's good, isn't it?"

I nodded. "More wine?"

After I filled her glass, we started talking about a new story she was writing, a piece about a Phi Beta Kappa girl who decides to become a prostitute for a few weeks to do research for a thesis. The girl finds she has no trouble "putting out," but she can't get herself to collect the fee.

"Talk about self-deprecation," I said.

"I don't know. I really want to get inside this girl and find out what's going on with her. You know, trespass while she's dreaming." I thought of her other stories.

I started remembering a lot of things as I reached for a towel to tuck around my legs. The nights were cooler. The silt-like heat of the summer had been steadily and gradually lifting, and now it seemed that it had risen completely, thinned out, and drifted away, leaving the trees and the lake to grow new skins for the cold weather.

I gathered the dishes and slogged my way up our hill of stiff grass into the house. The lights were burning a corrosive yellow. When I turned around, Spike was right behind me.

"Why do you think a smart woman would let herself be used like that?" she asked.

"Your Phi Beta Kappa girl?"

She leaned over the counter scummy with marinade drippings and watched me scrape our dishes into the trash.

"Well, let's see," I said, "either she has a hellish self-image or she feels sorry for her customer. Or both."

"She feels sorry for them."

"I figured."

"They're more pathetic than any whore because they're the buyers. The thing that must be had is the thing in control."

When I didn't respond, she said, "Whirly?"

"I don't see how giving it away for free helps anybody. Not when it's your self-respect you're giving away." I was standing,

I noticed then, with my feet hip-distance apart and my hands gripping the edge of the sink. *What an ugly sink*, I thought. *This sink could make me vomit.* If I thought for one second that it was emblematic of anything that had anything to do with me . . . if I looked up and the living room looked as worn out as this piece of—

I smiled at her. "Coffee?"

"You're stoned." Her mouth curled into a snide, broad U. She watched me plump up the trash bag and turn the water on to fill the kettle. I sank back against the drainboard and crossed my arms in front of my chest.

"This is what I need from you," she said. "There's no one right answer. No one could really ask for that. But affection . . . and laughter, that's always the right answer. That's what I look to you for."

Don't say those things to me, I thought. I turned around to watch the kettle hiss and steam and rattle on the burner. *Write them down or something*, I wanted to say, *it's easier to take.*

When I turned back, she was staring out the deck windows, which at that distance, showed only a solid scrim of black.

"C'mon, let's go outside and watch the temperature kill the ants," I said. "Bring an ice cube, we haven't tried that yet, ice cube bombs."

"They probably burrow in their little ant places."

"Predictable, isn't it?"

"Yo, angels!" Klaus came loping down our grizzled lawn and stopped at our chaises, towering above us. "Hey, what a familiar scene. Sacked out on your backs. What say we do some imbibing at the local sleaze joint? It's *Fri*-day night." He flicked his ashes toward the lake and jerked back around.

"I don't feel like it," I said.

"Me neither."

"Come on," he pleaded, bending at the knees then straightening again. "This is totally rad, man, I mean totally like dead. What's with you two lezzies?"

Spike gave him one of her challenging smiles. "Why go out when you've got the best thing at home?"

"Yeah, shit, well. Listen, you change your mind, I'll see you at the Starlite." He started off then turned around to wag his finger. "No monkey business."

"Christ, Spike," I said after he'd left.

"You loved it. It's a compliment. And anyway, he's a minnow. What do you care what the minnows think?"

That night I dreamt about meeting Jamie Ann at the store. She was walking through a gigantic doorway that made her seem minute. I looked down at her and said I'd come to enter my cat in a contest. She said she didn't know I had a cat. "Oh, yes, I have a little black cat." And I opened the plastic container I was carrying and out slithered a black worm. "What happened to my cat?" I shouted. Whatever it was crawled under a bush and I lost it.

Jamie Ann said, "That wasn't a cat anyway."

CHAPTER TWENTY-SIX

IN THE MORNING, I COULDN'T remember if Spike and I had talked about her appointment with Jamie Ann, and I really meant it when I asked, "Did I tell you I ran into Jamie Ann and she told me you were looking for a place to buy?"

"I forgot to tell you." She whisked around me, placing forks on napkins and plates full of eggs on the table. "I was hoping you'd be free to look at some property. Whirly, I've been having these fantasies about buying some property and building our own place and actually *owning* something."

"You have?"

"Yeah, I've been thinking how to swing it. Look at this book." She threw a copy of *Groundbreaking* across the table, its cover traversed by geometric shapes. "It has everything you need to know about designing your own house, being your own contractor, choosing materials, wiring, plumbing. Shit, the property here is going to go sky-high. We get in now, we'll do all right. Better than all right. We'll be fucking free."

"You want to do this with *me*?"

She stopped shoveling eggs into her mouth. "What, am I speaking English? Or is it coming out different and I'm not hearing it?"

"I'm just surprised, that's all. I mean I'd like to, I'd love to have my own house on my own land, but won't it take long? Isn't it expensive?" *Didn't you just nearly move out?*

"Before we talk about anything, we'll make a list. Here." She threw me a pen. "Get your notebook. This is how I see it. Our options."

Neatly, I wrote down "Land Purchase: Options" and underlined it. "First," she went on, "I've figured out a two-house plan."

"We're already building two!"

"Listen, these are the pros. Make a list."

She waved a finger at my notepad and obligingly I wrote "Pros" and underlined it. "First, we'll learn from our mistakes in building the first house. We'll get an exact idea of cost."

I wrote "(A) Cost. Labor, materials, and time."

"Second, we can live in the first one while building the second one. Third, we could buy more land with our combined incomes, have a lower mortgage, and put both houses on the same plot. Fourth, we would each have a home that would be our own."

"But we'd be near each other?"

She nodded. "Like Tillie's bungalow colony. We could even start our own artists' zoo if we had enough land. I'm sure the zoning laws can be bent around here, half an acre per plot the way things are being peddled."

I sniffed, reread what I'd written. "Who gets the first house?"

"Whoever wants it!" Her color was high. "It doesn't matter, either way there are trade-offs. The first house has flaws and the second one isn't built right away. If you want the first house, fine, we'll talk about it. The point is it's the cheapest way to get the most."

"Are you sure we can do this? Have you ever built a house before?"

"Look, thousands of people do it. Pullets do it. Most of the people around here have done it, and most of them haven't been to college."

"That's what I mean. College ruins your hands. You forget how to hold blowtorches."

"So, you find out again. Don't be such a worrier, Whirly. First read the book, then tell me what you think. If you think we can't do it by ourselves, we'll hire a contractor. We'll need to hire someone to do the wiring because that I don't want to touch. And I think I can get someone to do the plumbing. Oh!" She stopped, overcome by her own excitement. "I can see it. A log cabin, maybe even one of those ready-made jobs if we decide on that, no rent, no Pullets. Writing in the woods with no lease."

"What's that?" I said then.

"What?"

"Isn't that a car coming up our driveway?" We listened. A door squealed open and slammed shut. Spike was up in a flash and hurtling toward the door.

"Oh my God, it's Max!"

"Who?"

"He said he might come by, but I didn't expect him to drop by all the way from Albany. Max!" The door banged behind her and I heard the giggling and shrieking of her hello and the more subdued nasal greeting and shuffling of Max. "What a time to come," she was saying as she led him into our house. "We were just on our way to look at some land. Whirly," she said to me, "Max is a real estate lawyer."

"You're kidding."

How did she do it? How did she get these people to show up? It never failed.

"This is Whirly."

"Tina."

"I'm confused already," Max told her, laughing. "That's not to say I wasn't confused the last three hundred miles. Hey, man, it's good to see you." He embraced her as if he wanted to squeeze the life out of her into him.

In the meantime, I said, "What's that?"

They looked down at their feet where a large orange Persian was rubbing against Max's ankles.

"That's Roberta. Rowboat for short. My fellow traveler." Seeing the look on my face, he said to Spike, "Doesn't she like cats?" Then, "Don't you like cats?"

"It's just that I had a dream about one last night and it was sort of . . . prescient. And now here you are, just when we need you." I waved my hand in front of my face as if brushing aside gnats. "It's strange."

"Strange things always happen around this beauty." He winked at Spike. "She ever tell you about me? We grew up together, but

I knew better than to have a crush on her. Man, she was cutting down dudes before she was thirteen. Besides, I was too fat. I'm still too fat."

"Max has always been shy about himself," Spike chided.

"Listen, I've only got eight hours, then I have to go back to Albany." He grinned at me. "When you've got no slack, you tend not to dress up the message too much. Hey, you're cute. I could go for you myself if I weren't already in the mess I'm in, which is why I'm here. You got any soda, beauty?"

"Sure, take it with you. We've got an appointment."

"Aren't you going to listen to my troubles?" He sank his wide rump into one of our chairs and spread both hands on our dirty oilcloth, as if getting a grip on the place where he'd landed.

"In the car," Spike told him. "Or after, we'll have lunch. C'mon, get those flanks in gear."

"Still a bitch, isn't she?" He smiled confidentially at me. "You really are cute. Maybe I'll forget about my mess."

"Let's go, Max," Spike bellowed.

We jostled down the road in Spike's Honda with Max spread out in the back, babbling on about a new scheme to finance real estate that had me picturing a ladder with rungs and platforms on which were points and zigzags of further directions: Go back two rungs, closing delayed. But I liked his baby-soft face, the plumpness of his lips, which he wet constantly, the way his hair still fell in a shock over his forehead, though he had to be close to forty. Max was someone who probably frequently heard that he would be handsome if he weren't fat. And he let me know, as he veered in and out of his scheme, that he'd been much more blubbery than he was now—up to three hundred when he was really depressed and now maybe around two hundred and under six feet.

He struggled out of the back seat of the Honda and into the front of Jamie Ann's Jeep where he tried out "Max's National Formula."

"Take one-third of your gross monthly, subtract your primary house rent, what you have left over . . ." Jamie Ann kept her tiny foot to the pedal, said "Mm-hmm" a lot, and only once or twice turned to look at him.

When we were deposited at the border of the first land parcel for inspection, Max said hoarsely to me, "Well, your agent's pretty typical. Hustle you right into the toilet."

Spike breezed on ahead of us and came marching back two minutes later, her ponytail swinging rapidly. "Too close to the water. The land here is already swamped. I don't want to find out I'm going to have water in my basement."

"There's water under a lot of the land," Jamie Ann told her. "It just depends on the grade. Personally, I think it's great. You can practically dig up your own pond wherever you like."

Max grunted.

We piled back into the Jeep and drove to the parcel that Jamie Ann thought we'd *really* like. She'd shown us the waterfront lot first because it was closest, and Spike had mentioned something about being on the water. "Not thirty thousand for two acres, half under water," Spike had snarled at me before climbing in. "She can do better than that."

We arrived in front of fifteen acres for sale. *Fifteen acres*, I thought. *How do you look at it all?* Not to mention clear it all. I tried to tally up the acreage of my New York City apartment—.0102 acres—something way behind the decimal point. Jamie Ann produced a map showing us the borders and where a creek burbled back and forth across our property line and someone else's. We had water.

"Go ahead," she encouraged. "Walk around. I'll wait here."

"What do we do with all these trees?" I asked Spike, as the three of us traipsed through the woods single file.

"Clear them."

Behind me, Max was wheezing but keeping up with the military pace. "That's right," he huffed. "You have to bring in a company and get all the crap out of the way." He took a breath and I heard him stumble and swear. "If this was an old logging camp, they did a pretty lousy job of cleaning up after themselves." He kicked a pile of branches and tree remains I'd just passed.

"There's the creek!" Spike shouted. We bumbled our way down a slope of slippery tree roots.

"Déjà vu," I said to no one in particular. It reminded me of Spike yelling, "There's the cabin," and there it was, diarrhea yellow.

We stood reverently in front of the creek, our toes slanting forward. "Awfully small creek," I remarked. On various tree limbs, switching back and forth across the bank, were tiny orange surveyor bows. "I get it, this fourth is ours, that eighth is his. Who's stone is this?" I threw it in the air.

"We can dig it out," Spike told us fervently. "We can widen it. That's no problem. At least we have *some* water on our property." Max had sunk against a large maple and was playing with the coins in one of his pockets. He lifted his shoulders. "You got money, you can do anything."

She slogged onward, the two of us following due east, or what we thought was east.

Pretty soon we found ourselves back at the pile of branches and tree remains. "Wait a minute." Spike opened the map again. "This isn't right. We should be over here."

Max, wiping his face with a handkerchief, whimpered, "How much farther do we have to go?"

"I want to pace out the boundaries, that's all."

"I'll meet you at the Jeep."

But Spike was already off—without Max—and we trekked until we found another orange bow and then another and then the land started to rise. At the top of the hill, we looked down into a huge natural bin for trash wood, the leftovers of the logging operation.

"This is the site for the first house," Spike proclaimed.

And I flashed on a scene from a movie about a troop of explorers looking for El Dorado.

"Everything on this side of the river I claim for Spain," they pronounced. "Everything on *that* side of the river I claim for Spain."

"Down there," she went on, indicating the trash bin, "will be our pond." She looked above her at the cloudless sky. "It's a natural runoff; you see, the water runs down the hill to the pond." She drew her cigarettes from her pocket, put one in her mouth, and looked at it while she lit the end. Blowing out the smoke, she looked in my direction, past me. "Over there can be our second house. We'll keep these trees. And we'll lay down a path between the houses and down to the pond."

It sounded like utopia. Two golden houses in a big green forest with a big blue pond and maybe a floating chaise lounge in the pond and a striped beach umbrella attached to the arm of one of the chaise lounges and a few frogs—that we could catch—on lily pads. Yes, it sounded nice.

"Tina," she said softly. "It can be done. They're asking thirty thousand. That's only two thousand dollars an acre." She turned around slowly, squishing the soggy dead leaves at her feet. "It can really be done," she said again, "and it's time we moved on." She looked down at the future pond and began twisting her hair so that her arm hid her profile from me. "Renting the cabin was nice, but now we should go to the next phase. I like it here. I'd like to stay in Warrenville, and I think this is the way to do it. I really do."

"What if . . ."—I considered my phrasing—"what if something happens to one of us in the middle of the project? For instance, what if one of us, I don't know, leaves the country, or gets married?"

"Ha! We tried marriage once, remember? Well, I should speak only for myself. But you're right. We'll write some clauses into the contract. If so-and-so happens to you, then so-and-so will take place, that kind of thing."

"Oh. Will that do it?"

"If we write it to do it, it'll do it."

When we found the last orange bow, Spike was satisfied and we began hiking back to the highway over what I realized I was thinking of as *her* land.

Max was bending Jamie Ann's ear, who, polite as usual, smiled as she waved to us.

"What did *you think*?" she called out.

Spike's laugh was throaty and her voice deep and sensual. "I loved it."

"I thought you might."

"Let's go back to the office and look at the numbers," Spike told her.

"Already?" I said.

"Why not? I want to see how much of a down payment we need."

"That's my beauty," Max said, looking better, now that he wasn't exerting himself. "Whiz-bang."

Back in the office, Jamie Ann offered us coffee in Dixie cups and laid out the binder with all the paperwork. Taxes, I learned, were seven hundred a year until development. We'd need DEC approval for a pond permit eighteen months in advance, and they'd be looking at "downstream life" and "fish migration patterns," among other things. We'd need $10,000 down at a 10.5 percent mortgage on a fifteen-year term.

Fifteen years!

Then we'd take out another mortgage on the house.

Oh, this was just the mortgage for the land, I realized. Of course, we'd need two mortgages.

But on a five-year mortgage, we'd pay $429 a month. We'd have to pay $500 to make the offer, figure 10 percent of the costs for the closing, and then there were insurance costs.

Spike clucked at me. Yes—she was radiant—it was doable.

I could almost feel her heart fluttering, see all her other thoughts fly out the window. "How soon do you need the money?" she asked Jamie Ann.

"As soon as you're ready."

My stomach, I think, inverted. I felt like someone was frantically waving two last tickets in my face. "Fly with me now! This is the only way out!"

"All set?" Spike fixed me with a steady eye and smiled provocatively.

"Sure."

"Well thank you, ladies." Jamie Ann shook hands all around. "I'll look forward to hearing from you," she said, and we, the VIPs in the back room, tramped back into the reception area and out into the sun.

Max was waiting for us at Pauline's coffee shop. He had a milkshake planted in front of him and was making strenuous sucking noises. "Ah, my land barons." He motioned to our seats. "Do tell. A killing? A slaughter?"

"Order me a deluxe cheeseburger with onion rings and coleslaw, will you, Max? I've got stomach cramps." Spike rubbed her belly and excused herself for the bathroom.

"Puzzling," Max said. "But if she can't eat it, you know who will."

It didn't take long for Max to launch into the story about his mess, as soon as Spike came back. It seemed that someone wanted to marry him.

"She's wonderful," Spike cut in, looking a little less green.

"But I'm a cheat. A disaster," Max said. "A lot of women like fat men, you'd be surprised." He explained. "They find me homey. Anyway, I think I should do it. I know I should do it. I just can't bring myself to do it. But if I don't, she'll leave me."

He hung his head.

"Then once she's married to me, she'll find out what a pig I am. Closer or farther, I'm sunk."

"Try this," Spike offered. "Either way you're not bored."

Max smiled. "As I always say, be honest and you'll get all the action you want."

"I think this is normal," Spike told him. "This is the same as postpartum blues except it's, I don't know, pre-adjustment anxiety."

"Well, as long as it has a name, I'm all right."

"Good as captured," Spike fired back, smiling.

Max's agitation grew at the cabin. He couldn't stay in one chair for very long and Rowboat, his cat, imitated him, climbing from cushion to chair to floor to table. At dinnertime, we decided to go out to celebrate our land find, but Max preferred staying home. He said he didn't trust himself in a restaurant.

When we returned around nine o'clock, he was gone. Spike rustled around until she found a note under a pile of chewing gum foil. (Max had also been trying to quit smoking.)

"The heebie-jeebies got to me. Decided to leave and face the dirge. Thanks for your gracious hospitality."

"Poor Max," Spike said.

"That was the fastest meeting I ever had with anyone. This was the fastest day I ever had."

"What're you talking about, don't you remember our weekends when we first met?" The phone rang before I could answer. "Maybe it's Max," Spike said, jumping to it. I heard her say, "Oh. Hold on a minute."

She held out the receiver so whoever was on the other end could hear everything. "Who is it?" I mouthed.

"Chuck Peels," she said loudly.

When I'd finished with my call, I went into her bedroom. I sat on the side of the bed and faced her propped-up book. "He wants to see me the weekend of Ohara's wedding."

She looked confused. "I'd forgotten about their wedding. What did you say?"

"I said I'd be here because I was taking my vacation that week."

"Oh, you are?"

"Yeah, it seemed a good time because of the wedding. Anyway, he wanted to meet me at the Starlite that night; he's coming up from Virginia. I told him I'd *try* to meet him but I couldn't promise anything."

"So, why'd you say you'd try?"

"Because I'd like to see him. I like him. But I told him that I didn't want him to think of me as a girlfriend."

"Let's be friends," Spike mocked.

"Well, shit, I can't stop him if he wants to call me."

"Right," she said, then changed her tone to sound more agreeable. "You're right."

"Anyway. He called."

"I remember. I answered the phone."

The next morning, I found her at the oilclothed table, her spirits sunk in a mug of coffee. "I've been thinking," she said, without looking up. "Maybe that land isn't so great. Maybe we shouldn't jump on the first thing we see."

"Probably we should see more," I said, shuffling to the coffeepot.

"It's a great deal, though. I can't imagine finding a deal like that if we wait too long."

"One week, or two, isn't going to hurt us."

"I guess not," she said mournfully. "I was just thinking that it's going to be a pretty big job to clear that crap out of there. Whoever logged that land did a shit job of cleaning up after themselves."

"It looked pretty wrecked."

"I'm going to call Jamie Ann and ask her what else she has to show us—maybe next weekend."

"Next weekend's the wedding."

"Well maybe I'll come up during the week."

I watched her back as she dialed, her long hair hanging like rusty straw down to her waist. "Jamie Ann? This is Spike. Listen, I don't know what came over me, I saw that land and I just, I don't know, got too excited. I'd like to think about it a bit . . . take some time . . ." Her voice trailed off behind me as I left for the pond.

WHEN I CAME BACK, she had a new scheme. She had asked Jamie Ann if she knew of any rentals in the fall, so we could stay around and look for property. Pullet wanted us out, no extensions whatsoever, by Labor Day. Jamie Ann couldn't come up with anything, so we drove all afternoon, went to Monika's for a break, and met a man who put us on to some cabins a few miles away. Straightaway before dinner, we had them, reserved for the fall when our lease with Pullet was up. Cute log cabins with green trim. No heat, but I didn't think I'd be staying into the winter. There were two of them. A small one for her and a small one for me.

CHAPTER TWENTY-SEVEN

THE WEEK BEFORE THE WEDDING while I was vacationing at the cabin, Spike called me every day, sometimes three times a day. Things were not going well for her. Her voice on the phone was scratchy, distressed, full of aches and gripes, and she was haunted by an impending doom. I would be folding a fresh pillowcase that seemed full of sunshine from being dried on the line, or pushing my fork through a burst of breakfast egg yolk, or sipping my third cup of coffee with my feet up and a breeze wafting from window to window, and Spike would be talking to me about failed car batteries, bounced checks, and the way bad luck always came in threes.

One morning she called to tell me the distributor cap in her car had cracked but she'd continued to drive it on two cylinders and now the catalytic converter might be damaged—and if that were the case, well, she wouldn't be able to make it to the wedding. That same day, she called back to tell me the exhaust in her car might also be shot. Then later, just before dinner when I was getting ready to try my luck at fishing, the phone rang and Spike's jarring voice didn't even bother to say hello.

"Guess what, pal?"

"What?"

"I've got crabs."

"What?"

"Crabs. You've heard of them. Little white bugs that crawl into your pubes."

"How'd you get crabs?"

"That's what I'd like to know. You ever let Klaus sit on my bed?"

"No," I said, taken aback.

"How about any of those Peels?"

"Spike, none of them has been near the place in weeks."

"Well, I got it somewhere and since I've lived in this city for so long without getting them, I figure it had to come from our cabin, and *you* were the one having all the action. Cody never even took his pants off."

"But doesn't it happen right away? Don't they . . . jump?"

"Look, I don't know the answer. All I know is you better check yourself and wash everything. There's stuff you can get at the drugstore. Maybe if there's time, you can ride into town and get it."

"I'd have to go to a bigger town. They won't have that here."

"Tina, I can't help it if I don't feel so sorry for you right now, but I've got this shit crawling between my legs."

"Well, wouldn't I have it too?"

"Maybe you do."

Immediately I felt itchy. "I better get off and start throwing things in the wash."

Crabs! I was horrified! What kind of person gets crabs? It took me a good forty-five minutes to check through all of my hair follicles, using the bathroom light, a flashlight, and a few mirrors. When I found nothing, I began to wonder if they were still incubating so I checked all over again for any speck that might be an egg. Crabs!

I attacked the sheets. By this time, the sky had darkened but not just with evening. An end-of-the-summer storm was brewing, and the breeze in the cabin turned cool and moist. I plugged in the heater. Then I put on my nylon running suit, figuring it would be too slippery for crabs to cling to, pulled on some rubber gloves, and began stripping her bed. After her bed, I stripped my bed. The sheets would just have to hang to dry in the rain, that's all. I bustled them down to the basement, which looked ominous at that hour of the storm, and shoved them into the machine, turning the water temperature up to scalding.

Then I called Ohara to see if she knew anything about crabs. She told me she wasn't sure, but she did think they spread very quickly, as in the next day.

"Not two weeks?" I asked her.

"Sounds unlikely."

"Do you think she could have them and I wouldn't if they were in the house?"

"I'm no expert. I mean I've heard they can live in old mattresses, but then they jump to other furniture. They *infest* is the word. I'd guess you'd both be infected. Are you sure she got them from the cabin?"

"That's the only place she can figure."

"Maybe she got them from some guy in New York."

"I don't think she's slept with anyone."

"Maybe she doesn't have them at all."

"Oh, come on," I said. "Why would anybody pretend they have crabs?"

"Maybe she thinks she has them but she doesn't. Some of the things that happen to her are, sometimes, a little hard to believe."

"True, but I've been with her when some of these unbelievable things have happened. Like when we met Cody and, oh, other things."

"Maybe she got it from him."

"I don't think he's called since that weekend."

I hung up to vacuum. Except as soon as I plugged in the vacuum, all of the lights went out. I checked the electric heater. Dead.

Great.

The sheets were billowing in an ocean of stagnant water when I opened the lid of the machine. Another casualty. The fuse box was in the darkest corner of the basement, and with the help of the crabs flashlight, I was trying to read the crunched print on the inside of the little door that told me what each glass knob was responsible for. The instructions were divided into six boxes supposed to correspond to the layout of the fuses, but there was also a geometric sprawl of lines from fuse to fuse, telling me there were additional points to consider. I saw "Amps," "Volts," "Poles" and under "Circuit Directory," someone had scrawled in pencil, "Kitchen Appliances, Basement." Why divide things ten different ways when none of it works? I touched the fuses, wondering if that would tell me anything, and when my fingers hit a "Type S 15 Amp," I let out a cry. It was hot. All right! Science. I unscrewed it, expecting it to look like a blown light bulb and screwed in a "Type S 15 Amp" I'd found in Pullet's kitchen drawer. The washing machine glugged and started whirring.

All of the lights were blazing when I returned to the living room and I decided to open a beer. "I'm a homeowner," I said out loud to myself, turning on the water to wash my hands. "When I own fifteen acres of land, I will be able to deal with it. I'll solve things." Which is about when I noticed the water was cold.

I checked the stove. We had gas, but the pilot light from the hot water heater must have blown out when the electricity clicked off.

I went back down to the basement. The floor was frigid and seemed to be crawling with muck in that part where the heater stood, large, white, and cold. Scattered around me were boxes of old tools and cans of crusty nails and screws and picture hangers. There was a lamp with its wiring pulled out and an ugly maroon chest of drawers, each drawer wedged almost shut at a different angle. I had to kneel between a picnic table supporting two bags of gravel and a pile of old tires, with the chill from the concrete floor seeping through my jeans. I peered into the opening of the heater and saw the pilot for the flame doing nothing but sitting there. I used my crabs flashlight to read the directions on the sticker pasted to the side of the tank. They told me in step number one to release the valve for the gas, in step number two to light the pilot, and in step number three to hold open the gas valve for at least thirty seconds to make sure the pilot stayed lit.

Outside it began to rain—hard. The water sounded as if it were slapping the ground, and periodically a sheet would crackle in the doorway. Next to my knee was a long piece of coat hanger that had been shaped to hold a match far away from the person at the other end. Why so far? I loaded it. The match jerked around in its wire loop and I aimed the contraption into the gut and toward the pilot. I pressed the valve and a hideous rush of gas sounded. It hissed through the pipe and when it met the tiny jittery flame of my match, the pilot ignited. I counted as quickly as I could my thirty seconds, then jerked my finger from the gas button.

The pilot light went out.

A minute or two passed before I tried it again. The cold from the floor had spread all along my body, and my shoulders and neck were stiff. I pressed the gas button and the noxious rush began again. This time I held it for one full minute, never taking my eyes off my finger pressing the button.

The pilot light went out.

I did not want to blow up.

I did not know enough about contraptions with free-running gas to be sure I would not be vaporized. I sat back, took a breath. Walking out into the downpour and gazing at the stars to reacquaint myself with time and place seemed a possibility. But I sat there, my cheek pressed to my knee in the bowels of a house with crab sheets and blown fuses and a woman who kept calling about bad luck. When I closed my eyes, I smelled mildew and the rain. I tried to smell the beach. At times I have been able to do that—actually smell the suntan oil and the ocean and hear the high-pitched screams you always hear at the beach. But I couldn't do it this time. I was inextricably stuck where I was.

I set up my match, shoved it into the opening, and held the gas button for three year-long minutes. The pilot light stayed on.

I was alive!

Okay, maybe I could own fifteen acres. Then I went to check the laundry.

It was almost finished. The machine had broken down before the spin cycle, and the sheets were half drowned and bloated with water. I dragged them out of their swamp and figured there was nothing to do but carry them through the rain and lay them on the line so at least the machine could drain if it felt like it. This was a mess. The appliances were imploding all at once. I kicked a fat sheet up to my chest and staggered to get a hold on it, which is what I was doing when I spotted Klaus coming around from the driveway.

"No problem," he said, walking jauntily through the storm, "you're washing 'em this way."

"Everything's breaking!" I bullied another sheet onto the line and yanked one end to spread it out.

"Hey, you could be riding around in a convertible with the top stuck down."

"That sounds stupid," I said, before noticing his convertible had no roof.

He looked at my sopping sheets drying in the rain. "Well, I'm on vacation!" I screamed. "I'm having *fun*! I didn't plan it this way. I thought I'd be having a different kind of fun. Alone-fun, without ten thousand . . . oh, never mind."

"Your phone's ringing," he said.

"What did you want, anyway?"

"See if you were feeling in the mood."

"What do you think? Klaus, you don't have crabs, do you?" *When you've got no slack, you tend not to dress up the message too much.*

He stopped smiling. "Who . . . ?"

"Could you check? Maybe now? You could use the bathroom."

"Tina, I'm a freak about my body. A lot of people don't know that. They think Klaus is something else, but I am a freak about staying clean and healthy." He grabbed my crabs flashlight.

I was slipping into dry clothes when he emerged from the bathroom.

"No," he said, slamming the flashlight on the kitchen counter. "Great seeing you. If you change your mind, I'll be at the 'Screw." I heard the sloshing of water when he opened his car door. He cursed, slammed the door, and drove off in his four-wheel boat with the top stuck down.

The phone rang again. "Tina, did you find any?"

"No."

"Well, I've sure got 'em. I got my doctor to write a prescription."

"Good."

"I hope this gets rid of them before the weekend. I don't think I could go to the wedding like this."

"I see."

"Don't sound so glum," Spike said.

"I'm tired."

"Good news, though. My car may be all right. Maybe it didn't get to the converter."

"I see."

"What's the matter with you?"

"Nothing. Bad day at Black Rock."

"Yeah, it's been pretty shitty here." I knew that.

"Well, I'll let you know what happens." I knew that too.

I didn't answer the phone again. I slept.

I slept again the next day. Stayed in bed fourteen hours. When the ache in the back of my teeth started, I knew I was sick. I held the mirror to my throat and saw white polka dots. Imogene brought me some penicillin from her trailer. And I fell into a deep well of sleep and had long-playing dreams of shimmery images, with waves in the pictures like Mylar bending and I couldn't rise.

CHAPTER TWENTY-EIGHT

SPIKE APPEARED IN A PASTEL DRESS. She fed me thick, gooey pieces of chocolate cake. I was giggling with fever, and she listened to me talk. Oh, I had lots to say. All about the people who were going to be at Ohara's wedding, most I hadn't seen since the Edward Era. "And this guy Lewis will be there who was always great-looking, but he used to be obnoxious and have a drinking problem. He wrote a book, fell in love with his agent, but she had a drinking problem too. The last I'd heard, he'd split up with his agent and was living in Palm Springs, writing music and scores for an independent filmmaker.

"Then there's Daniel. Daniel's a landscaper-turned-sculptor. A great shy bear. He finally got engaged to a woman he's been living with for a couple of years, and she walked out on him a few months ago. Ohara said Daniel's been drinking a lot of rum and trying to decide whether to go after her."

"Get some sleep," Spike whispered.

"I'm going. I don't care if I pass out, I'm going."

In the morning, the fever lifted. The battle must've been going on all night because there wasn't a trace of the milky white spots on my throat.

Now we were in a rush. We showered, shampooed. I slipped on the dress I'd saved for the wedding—a sundress with a bright abstract print, low in the front, with a T-strap in the back and a dropped waist. Then we set sail in the canoe to dry our hair. Spike blew up balloons to attach to our wedding gift and she tied them together with ribbon. Red and green and blue and yellow bubbles floated high above the water.

"Look who's spying on us," she said.

It was Alma peering from behind the ravaged pine. "She thinks we're nuts," I said.

"We are," Spike gloated.

Spike floored it as soon as we hit the open road. She shot over the empty hills of Route 72 and into the next county. We parked in a jam of cars across the way from Ohara's garden and slipped through the trees that edged the driveway. And there it was. The house with the uneven stone floors and inconvenient barbecue pit. The house full of uncomfortable furniture with the violent art curling on the wall. Except the rawness was gone. Baskets of wildflowers studded the lawn and the stone floors: black-eyed Susans, blue vervain, purple loosestrife.

Then, Pow! He was right in front of me. Blocking the baskets of black-eyed Susans.

Lewis. Smiling. Sober. With his arm around me and a kiss.

"You look great!" Another smile. Then, as he moved away, in his favorite silky, come-hither voice, "Great dress."

"Which one was that?" Spike stared at me.

I didn't move. I was waiting for the pressure to drop so I could unstick my legs from where I'd been pinned. Meanwhile, I was nodding and winking my way around the crowd and then I spotted him. Looking extremely handsome in a pewter suit and suede shoes.

"That one's Daniel."

A guttural sound. Spike smiled at me. "I'd fuck Daniel in a minute."

Lewis's fingers began grazing over an acoustic guitar. We were standing in a small circle, all twenty of us, listening to Lewis close in the afternoon on the two people in the center. Ohara and Ben were holding hands and looking fidgety, as if they were thinking, *Aren't you all used to seeing us together? Doesn't it seem like we're married already?*

Lewis had written them a wedding song, and he stood in the clearing of trees, strumming about love and time.

Now that he was performing, I felt free to stare at him. And I took a while over his light-brown hair pulled back into a short ponytail and his eyes, which I knew were hazel and changed color.

Ohara looked as if she were having trouble concentrating. Ben stuck his chin out trying not to cry or laugh. What was he doing in that showy white suit? It fit like a room around him. Maybe he needed the extra space to hold in his amazement. *Why do we do such private things in public?* Ohara was grinning off and on and shifting from foot to foot.

Ohara's uncle, a minister, performed the service. Lanky Hank, a friend of Ben's from college, snapped photos and another friend from Hollywood moved a videocam around.

Ohara and Ben kissed and behind us Ohara's three brothers popped three bottles of champagne.

"All right!" somebody said.

The tension collapsed. The circle began to fall apart. Most of the guests were from California and Oregon and they coasted, turned around, and talked to whoever was closest, moseying over to the cluster of chairs. There was no music, no "big band," no "pictures for the book," just this moseying and the baskets of wildflowers and a few chairs.

Roger, a friend of Ohara and Ben's, turned up in front of me. I knew him from their parties. Almost every time he'd come to New York, there'd been a party, and each time he seemed to forget what had happened to him since the last visit. He began introducing himself.

"Roger," I interrupted, "don't you remember the first time I met you at Ohara's? You'd just broken up with your girlfriend because of an incident in a hot tub."

"That's right." He looked dumbfounded.

"She had the same name as another girl you'd broken up with six months earlier."

"Barbara."

"You'd just lost all your sound equipment from your truck."

"My van. That's right." Now he looked stunned—and uncomfortable. "You must've met me when I came to New York the first time."

"And lost your luggage."

"That's right."

"I was married then," I said.

He grabbed my hand and looked for a ring.

"Then. We divorced."

"Oh."

"I think I'll see if that's lemonade there."

I strolled across the front yard to Lewis, who was sitting in a beach chair across from Daniel. As soon as I sat down, Lewis told Daniel, "I want to talk to Tina for a while."

Without a word, Daniel slipped away.

"You didn't have to do that."

"I see him all the time. I haven't seen you since I moved back." And then he talked, straight, without any undertow.

He was living in New Haven, he told me, writing music. He was finished with screenwriting, or the screen was finished with him. Once in a while, he wrote music for videos.

Interesting, interesting, but . . . "How's your romantic life?"

"There's a woman," he said laconically. "At first it was platonic, but it's developed into something more. For her—I'm not as passionate about it."

I suddenly remembered the way Lewis was. Those alluring eyes and the barriers. The bullshit that sometimes got worse when he was drunk. Okay, I'd be polite and flatten everything.

I took up the stare. A different stare from the bar on Park Avenue where I'd been waiting for Spike in a faraway world from here. We watched Ben joke with his father-in-law. We watched Ohara. Time to move along. Roll on in that vaporous West Coast spaciness, and I left Lewis brooding about something—and collided with Kyle. There could be no mistake about Kyle. Everything about him screamed *New York actor!* He'd shaved his head, and a scar on his scalp made him look like a gangster. He claimed not to remember me, but I was used to that from the actors Ben knew. They had a way of looking at me just above eye level, waiting for me to remember *them*; then they became animated. I told him I remembered him from a reading Ben had recently given.

"That's right," he said, becoming animated. "I was with someone."

I remembered her too, but who was I to be doing all the remembering? Kyle told me that he and Ben had never acted together, but he'd like to. His eyes changed, and I saw the light that came into the eyes of lesser actors who really want to work with somebody, man. *Yeah, he'd like to. Yeah, yeah,* I could hear him thinking, *his life was about to change as soon as . . . as soon as . . .* It was Edward I was thinking of, anyway, watching Kyle down three drinks.

"So you see! You see what I mean!" Spike's voice cut through the drowsy afternoon. I'd lost her when I'd gone to see Lewis, and now she was leaning into Daniel, talking and swaying. Daniel had his chin tucked into his throat, bracing himself.

"What're you drinking?" I broke in, squinting at the sun.

"Vodka on the rocks."

"After champagne? You'd better slow down." I took her glass and emptied half and poured in soda water.

"Hey," she said.

"Hmmm," Daniel said. "A mother-daughter thing."

She'd turned back to him and was already talking again, loudly. I walked off.

Near the garden were more baskets of flowers—wild irises and mullein. Someone had brought an orchid as a gift and the perfume was strong and lazy. Food appeared, delicious food that Ohara had made herself. Pâté, marinated olives, marinated crab legs. The day softened.

Lewis took up his guitar and started serenading Ben's parents. Roger and Hank brought out their guitars and started singing. Dinner appeared. Lemon chicken, cold poached salmon, tortellini.

The sun set. The horizon glowed pink. A group gathered around Lewis and he began crooning a 1940s love song. Ohara's aunt Eileen let her head sink to her shoulder.

"I love that kid. Anything he sings I love. He reminds me of Gary Cooper. Doesn't he remind you of Gary Cooper?"

Lewis sang his wedding song again to Ohara, and she started to cry.

It grew dusky, gray enough to see shadows in the lights from the house. I thought I saw Spike pressed up against someone, but as I made my way toward the kitchen, the bodies disappeared.

Moira, fifteen, and Kevin, thirteen—Ohara's cousins—were at the coffee counter eating crackers from some open boxes.

"Did you see Aunt Eileen?" Moira said. She blushed and giggled at Lewis, who came over to sit down next to the counter.

He took up the stare, aiming it somewhere above the cream I was pouring into my coffee. "Whatever floats your boat," Kevin said, smirking and reaching for the olives.

I drank my coffee and smiled at Moira, who kept glancing at Lewis, checking him out.

Suddenly Lewis came to life. He turned to gaze at me. "Tina," he said solemnly, "would you like to take a walk?"

Moira froze. She started chewing on her necklace. "Sure," I said.

Lewis nodded at this.

"What're you going to do?" Moira asked me. She almost sounded breathless. I turned to Lewis. "What're we going to do?"

"Well," he said, "he's going to ask her for a walk."

"And she's going to say yes," I said.

"Then he's going to take her to his home," Lewis said.

"And she's going to ask for some wine," I said.

"Then he's going to pick out some music. What music does he pick out, Moira?"

She looked at me. Frozen again. "I don't know. Kevin, what music does he pick out?"

"I don't know," her brother mumbled.

"Think of something!" she shrieked.

Out in the garden, Lewis turned to me. "Would you like to smoke a joint?"

"Of course." I thought that was the whole point.

"Do you have a match?"

"No."

"Wait, I'll get one." He turned around and *Pow!* Spike! Straight into those vodka eyes he looked. "Do you have a match?" he asked in his deliberately mellow style.

"Whoa, is that a joint?" Her eyes were swimming, trying to focus. "Hey, if I'm lighting it, I'm smoking it! Use my cigarette."

Spike followed us out of the garden and onto the road. "Where's everybody going?"

"We were going for a walk," I said.

"Oh, am I interrupting something?"

We were on the road and groups of people were straggling about, just arrived back from a drive. Daniel was there, and Hank and Ben. Lewis was walking ahead of me.

"No," I said to Spike.

Ben's white suit nearly glowed; in the dusk, he was his own spotlight. He was holding a video camera and wanted someone to shoot him walking down the blacktop road in front of his house, down the hill, until it looked like he'd disappeared with the road into the mountains at the horizon.

He said, "I need somebody to stand over there where I'm gonna start walking so I can focus this."

Spike ran over.

"Not you, clown."

She didn't hear him. Lewis moved her over, but she grabbed the camera. "Lemme have it! Lemme have it! Here, I'm good at this. Okay. Turn around. Now run. *Run!* Run, look at the camera."

I walked away.

I leaned against a car in the driveway until the filming was through. Spike walked right by me, talking at Ben's neck as he trooped back to the house. Lewis swung by the car. He put his foot on the car panel by my dress.

"All through?" I said.

"I'd like to sing one of my songs for you." His voice had turned to silk again. "It's called 'Certain Men, Certain Women.'" He took a long hit off the joint. "It's about, let's see, it's about a man obsessed with a woman but she isn't around. And about a woman who thinks she loves a certain man but she's with someone else."

He lifted his head slightly and began to sing a cappella. It wasn't at all like Mozzarella's singing at the broken dock on the pond. Lewis sounded like he was teasing when he sang, as if he were pretending to make an invitation, then he dipped his head and began singing in a very solemn tone, until he felt rain.

"My guitar!" He took off.

I walked back alone along the stone path, and Moira came running out to meet me. "So?" she said, her eyes glinting.

"So what?"

"So what happened?"

"Nothing," I said.

She steadied me with a look, *Are you crazy?*

Lewis was on the porch, showing Kevin how he packed up his guitar. "Go ahead," I said.

She put her necklace in her mouth and daringly approached the porch, her question practically tripping out of her mouth.

Lewis looked up from his guitar and said, slowly, "I made a move but she turned me down."

Moira whirled around. "Do you have a boyfriend or something? Are you married?" I heard Lewis laughing as he went into the house.

"No."

"So, what gives?"

"You see, Lewis, he's . . ." I tried. "There's this wall . . . and . . . you can't believe . . . I've known him a long time."

She stared at me, wide-eyed, moony. "You're right. I can't explain anything."

Now it was dark. The porch was lit only by the light shining through the kitchen window. I pushed up onto the wobbly porch railing and looked inside the window. The brilliance was almost surreal. Such a sharp, white square of light against the pitch-black on the porch. I felt someone tilt the railing. Lewis pulled himself up carefully so that we didn't rock backward and fall into the moss.

"Where are you staying tonight?"

"At my cabin on the pond," I said.

"Where's that?"

"Two and a half hours away."

"That's a long drive."

"Not too long."

"I've got to drive to New Haven."

"Tonight?"

"Maybe not." He paused. "Is anybody else there at the cabin?"

"I share it with Spike."

"Is there a man at the cabin?"

"No, there's no man."

He let his feet swing a while. "It's a small cabin," I said.

"Mm-hmm."

"There's no man."

"You told me that. Twice." I slid down off the railing. "Do I bother you, Tina?"

"No, you don't bother me."

"Do I scare you?"

"No, you don't scare me."

"Good." He thought a minute. "Then what is it?"

"I don't know." I waited to see if something would surface to give him a better answer, but it didn't. "I don't know," I said again. "Maybe that's it. You're unknown."

He laughed. "Well, don't you think it's worth an investigation?"

I could feel wit leaving me. "Unknown," I said again, and giving up on making a complete sentence, uttered, "Trust."

He stared at me. "I've always liked you. I liked you when you were with Edward." I didn't say anything.

He continued to stare at me. "Don't stop to think about it," he said finally. He slid off the railing and laughed. "Don't stop to think about it." And he walked out of the brilliance from the kitchen and disappeared in the darkness on the lawn.

Moira came out of the house. She was about to quiz me but suddenly turned. "Look!" she said. "There she is! Look! Look!"

It was Spike stumbling across the lawn, her long red hair streaming around her shoulders. Moira started giggling. "You know what she did? She walked into a tree and started talking to it. Look out, here she comes!" And Moira fled back into the kitchen.

Spike swayed in front of me. "Fireworks. They're going to light fireworks. I'm so drunk."

"I know. I hear you're talking to trees."

"It jumped out at me!" She pouted with glassy, little-girl eyes.

"Why don't you have some coffee?"

"Where're my shoes? I was looking for my shoes." She propelled herself into the house.

Lewis reappeared at the porch railing just as Spike came out of the house with her shoes. "Are you leaving?" he asked. "Where're you going?"

"No." Spike couldn't stand still. "But *she* has a date tonight."

"A date!" he said.

"I don't have a date," I said.

"Yes, she does."

"I don't have a date."

"Jesus, a date!" Lewis walked off.

I called after him, "I don't have a date," then stopped. What was I doing?

Spike lurched back into the house. She meant Chuck Peels; she knew Chuck wanted to meet me that night at the Starlite.

"Spike!" I called, but she had disappeared.

Two candle torches created pockets of light on the lawn. An actor from Hollywood was standing behind one of the torches, thoughtfulness carefully displayed on his face. His hand was against a tree. Another actor with a videocam was down on his knees, slowly guiding the camera upward. Someone came around to my right. It was Daniel. The torch threw a light on his profile, and I could tell he'd had a lot of rum. He talked about sculpting and about LA. Then he wanted to talk about the first time we met at Ben and Ohara's. He leaned his back against a tree.

"I fell in love with you the first time I saw you," he said. "But you were married."

I stood stunned. All I could think to say was, "But you never showed it."

Two people to our left suddenly stopped mid-conversation and looked at us. It was Lewis and Roger.

Roger stepped up to Daniel. "But you're engaged."

"Damn." Daniel blew out his breath and sank back into the dark.

The fireworks were announced. I took a place up front, next to Daniel. He turned to look at me and he looked at me for a very long time—until Kyle came up and pulled him away. I saw Daniel with his head bent listening to Kyle. Then Daniel walked over to Lewis and started going on and on about something.

"What's the matter?" I asked Lewis, after Daniel walked away.

"Daniel doesn't say anything he wants to say until it builds up and then he gets himself into a corner. He wants to know where we're staying tonight. Kyle's bugging him for a ride."

It was raining again. Lewis had pulled on a down vest. His hair was wet and his face was lit by a candle torch.

"You can stay at the cabin," I said.

"Thank you."

"There're only three beds." I looked at him.

"Don't stop to think about it,"he said.

The first rocket *zzz'td* into the rain. I heard Spike's laughter from behind the screen of sparks on the lawn. She sounded electrified and her screams and screeches crowded around the explosions in the black sky. Pink and gold sparks flew into the rain.

Spike came running up to me. "Wasn't that wonderful?" Her eyes were unfocused and her body couldn't stop its own motion. "Are you going somewhere?" she said to Lewis, maybe because of his vest or maybe, being Spike, she just knew.

"To your house," he said.

"What!"

"I invited them," I said.

"To our cabin?"

I nodded. She looked dazed as if slowly remembering she'd been doing something and weaved her way back toward the fireworks.

"Are you ready?" Lewis said.

"Soon."

Ohara was sitting on a bench in her living room and she waved me over. "By the way, what happened to those crabs?"

"They never appeared." She shook her head.

"Well, I'm learning things about my own behavior."

"That's an odd person to learn with."

"Maybe."

She started to ask a question just as Lewis pulled up to the bench. "Will you be ready to leave soon?" he asked.

"Soon. I have to find Spike. And I'm afraid to look."

"Kyle asked her to go into the sauna," Lewis said, heading outside.

I looked across the room and there was Daniel, sitting on a hassock, staring at me. I mouthed, "You shocked me," but just then Kyle swung in without his shirt, in a funk of sweat from the sauna. A near-empty half gallon of whiskey hung from his fingers.

"I love the golden liquid. I love it! Love it. Ow!"

"Get him out of here!" Ohara yelled from the sofa.

I ducked out to find Spike and ran into Lewis in the doorway, moving his guitar out. "I'm leaving," he said.

"All right. All right. Where's Spike?"

"Right there on the lawn."

"Okay, get Daniel."

In the vestibule, someone tapped me on the shoulder. It was Moira, waiting to give me a hug goodbye. She giggled, then opened her big, wide eyes at something behind me. I turned around and found Spike wearing shorts and a cotton undershirt that looked as if it should've been under something. Her dress was in a roll under her arm.

"Let's go," she said, and when I turned back to finish my hug, Moira had slipped away, leaving behind a faint scent of sweat and acne lotion and airy perfume.

CHAPTER TWENTY-NINE

LEWIS WAS STANDING BY HIS CAR, SCOWLING. "You're driving with me. Daniel can drive with her."

"No," I said. "Spike doesn't like people she doesn't know driving her car, and she can't drive. You and Daniel follow me."

"Okay. But don't lose us or we're fucked."

I scavenged in the back seat of Spike's car and produced a map. "This is where we're going."

"That's out of my way."

"Yes. It's west."

A moment of truth for Lewis. "Okay, just don't lose us." He walked with Daniel to his car, but Spike had disappeared again.

I found her on the porch where Roger and one of Ohara's brothers were playing chess. "Spike, we have to go," I said.

She grabbed both men's arms. "Can we take these?"

"Come on."

"Tina," Ohara said, drawing me aside. "Daniel asked me for your number."

Spike snatched the car keys from me. "Let's go."

"Don't let her drive," Ohara called after us.

By the time I got to the car, Spike had turned over the motor and was sitting in the driver's seat.

"You're not driving."

"Get out of here. I am too."

"Move over. Relax."

"I'm not drunk. I can drive."

"Move over! Enjoy the ride! You're *not* driving!"

"Oh, all right."

"Tina," I heard from Lewis's car, "are you leading us or what?"

"I don't have any cigarettes," Spike said.

"Relax."

"Do you have any more of that gum?"

"No."

"Gimme some of yours."

"I can't. I probably still have tonsillitis."

"I don't have any tonsils anymore. Gimme some gum."

"No."

I turned onto the road and noticed then how bad the driving conditions were. Black night, intermittent streetlights, and a steady rain mixed with fog. Plus a car following me that was depending on my taillights to get through the back roads that had nothing but reflectors on telephone poles.

"Turn on the light," Spike demanded as soon as we hit our first pocket of blackness. "Why?"

"I dropped a lit cigarette. Stop the car."

"I'm not stopping the car. I thought you didn't have any cigarettes."

"I found a butt. We're gonna catch fire."

I saw the red ash glowing between her seat and the hump and reached for it, trying to keep us straight on the road. "Here."

"Oh, Whirly, great. You're amazing. I thought we were dead—bacon crisps. Let me drive."

"No."

"You can go faster."

"What's the point of going faster? I don't want to lose them."

"They'll be okay."

"Spike, there's no reason to go faster."

"Gimme some of your gum."

"No. What're you doing?"

She was half across me, reaching under the steering wheel, but I didn't want to take my eyes off the road. The interior light went on.

"What is that for?" I asked.

"I'm looking for a cigarette." She had the ashtray pulled out and was scavenging for another butt. "Why're these two following us?" she asked abruptly. "Why're they coming back to the house? I have to hand it to you, Whirly—*two* of them. Two of them!"

"I invited them. Turn off the light. I can't see."

The rain began to pelt us. The wipers were banging left to right but still the rain blurred what I could see, and it sounded as if the roof of the car were being pummeled by thousands of tiny fists. I was nosing the car through a war zone, pushing back shafts of rain only to have them close in on us as we slid through. The rain was pressing against the door, pounding on the roof, zinging off the lights. What was she saying?

"Why're they coming to our house?" Spike persisted. "Two of them?"

"Spike, look, you're under no obligation. Daniel will sleep on the sofa." To make sure she heard me and understood, I yelled, "You do not have to sleep with Daniel!"

"Oh," she said meekly.

"They're my guests. You don't have to sleep with anybody. Understand?"

I turned into what I thought was the beginning of the road home and discovered I was in a parking lot—barely missed a rubbish can—and made it back onto the road.

"Thank you," Spike said, not even noticing. "Thank you for saying that. He's a confused boy. He's one confused boy. I don't need any more of those in my life."

"What're you doing?" Her head was nearly in my lap and her hand thrust somewhere under the dash again.

"Turning on the light. I'm putting my dress back on. I changed because I thought I was going to drive."

"I can't see."

"Please give me some gum."

"Turn off the light! Is that the road?"

"Yes. Can't I have some gum?"

"Here." I tore half of what I was chewing and gave it to her.

"Great. Tonsillitis gum."

"You asked for it."

"Go faster."

"No. Watch the signs for me."

"Can I drive yet?"

"You're not driving."

"But look where we are. We're only twenty miles from where we left."

"So what? We'll get there. The point is to get there."

"I had a good time at the wedding."

We hit a small flood and I inched the car through."I liked Roger best," she said. "I'd like to fuck Roger."

Now we were riding smoothly again. "Yeah? The thing about these guys is that I've known them when they were all going through their first romances. Anybody meeting them now would see attractive, confident men who seem to have a lot of experience, but they don't."

"That's why people move."

"Right."

Abruptly she fell silent. I waited. Finally, after all that badgering, she was quiet. Too quiet.

"Don't fall asleep!" I cried. "I need you to keep watching for the signs."

The storm became worse, and we had started to wind through the empty hills of Route 72 where there were no houses, no gas stations for miles. Lewis and Daniel were falling behind.

"Whirly? Can you see?"

I was down to twenty-five miles an hour in a fifty-five zone. The rain was a solid sheet in front of me, and there were no streetlights.

"I can't see shit," Spike said. "I've never driven in a storm this bad."

"I can see," I told her.

Right before we hit our county line, the rain slackened and in its place came the fog, snaking in off the river. I started switching from high to low beams to keep from being hypnotized. With the high beams, the road was a sliver of yellow line and black under a canopy of gauze. With the low beams, the road stopped fifteen feet ahead.

"Let's go to a bar," Spike said. "I need a drink. Let's go to Monika's before we stop at the house."

The yellow light at the four corners of Warrenville flashed in the fog. Spike started shouting. "We made it! Go, Whirly! All right!" It was only five hundred feet to Monika's parking lot.

DANIEL'S COLLAR WAS UP, his hair was pushed off his forehead like his fingers had been through it a few times, and he looked as if he'd gotten shock therapy through the eyes. Vince, the bartender who never smiled, took one look at him and laughed. Daniel ordered two beers, a shot of rum, and a package of beer nuts. Vince poured him his shot and Daniel threw it back. Since the bottle was almost finished, Vince poured the remainder into Daniel's shot glass.

"You're a gentleman," Daniel said, and threw that one back. Then he turned to me. "Three hours!" he screamed.

"She showed me what we were getting into," Lewis said mildly. He shook his head. "But that was one hell of a drive." A nasty smile. "And you drove like shit."

"I did not!"

"We had to stay back because of the spray from your car."

"We tried to get your attention," Daniel said, "to tell you to pull over at the next bar. Jesus Christ, I was scared."

"Vodka and tonic," Spike ordered.

"Scared?" I said.

"You're wide awake," Lewis said to Spike. "Your energy doesn't quit, does it?"

"Nope."

"Scared?" I repeated. Of what? The rain? The dark? I looked at Spike. *There are scarier things to be scared of.*

"Tell me," Lewis began, touching three red welts on my arm, "these mosquito bites here . . . do you have bites all over your body?"

One of the waitresses appeared just then and said, "He'd like to find out," and started giggling. She flushed when she looked at Lewis.

"Do you have any quarters?" I said. "I want to play pinball."

"I want to go to bed," Lewis said. "I've got a long drive tomorrow."

"Let's go to the Starlite." Spike pulled a lemon rind from between her teeth. "Let's go dancing."

"No, Chuck Peels is there," I said. "My date," I told Lewis. "I don't want to do that to him. I seem to crap on him all the time."

"Oh, come on," she said. "They've got to see the Starlite."

All at once, Lewis leaned forward and struck me full force in the eyes with his eyes.

Direct hit. It was the less sweet version of "our eyes met."

"Maybe he's gone home by now." Spike's voice came back to me, small and distant.

"Maybe," I said, feeling flushed.

"I'd like to show it to them."

"Where're we going now?" Lewis asked.

"Dancing. I'm driving," Spike said, and hurried out to her car.

Lewis grabbed my wrist and steered me toward his.

Daniel stood between the two doors of the two cars. Lewis pointed, and Daniel climbed into Spike's.

Lewis's car was neat and had a Christmas tree air freshener hanging from the radio knob.

He backed carefully out of the lot. "Daniel's scared shitless Spike's going to make a move on him."

"He shouldn't worry," I said. "She's scared he's going to make a move on her."

THE STARLITE WAS PACKED as usual. Spike and Daniel had sped way ahead of us and arrived first. As soon as I walked in, I heard her call my name.

"Tina!" she shouted, beaming. "Look who's here!" Her arm was around Chuck Peels's shoulder.

"Is that your date?" Lewis asked me.

I introduced everyone. I told Chuck I had just come from a wedding and that these were my friends whom I hadn't seen in years. I knew I would say something like that from the minute I'd decided to come to the Starlite. He looked at me as if I were speaking another language.

I ran to the dance floor. Spike grabbed Lewis, and Daniel was left for me. Lewis shouted, "All right. A fuck beat!" just as the band dived into "Shout" and a herd of boys started to scream and pound their way onto the dance floor. Boys started jumping off the tables; a few threw themselves on the floor, kicked their feet in the air, rolled on their backs. They held hands, twirled each other around, jiggled their arms and legs and bodies like Holy Rollers in a frenzy.

Daniel and I were shaking and stomping, squatting and twisting on our heels, untwisting upward, screaming, "Everybody shout, shout, shout, shout, shout!"

We were soaked with sweat. Daniel helped me find a spot to lean against at the bar. "Did you ever notice we always end up talking to each other?" I asked. He looked at me, as if to say, *I've been noticing for a long time.* Then Lewis was back, and Spike was standing beside Chuck Peels. I began putting one word after another again, not really listening to what I was saying. Chuck went away. Lewis looked pleased with himself.

"He *loves* you," he cooed.

"Knock it off."

"He really loves you," he said again.

"I've never done anything with him," I said. "I've never even kissed him. In fact, I've never kissed anybody in this bar."

"You've never kissed any of these guys?" Daniel asked.

"No."

"None?"

"No."

"Come on," Lewis taunted. "You've fucked these guys."

"I've never touched one of these guys."

Lewis asked me to dance though the band was taking a break. The piped-in music was bubblegum bop, sung by a girl with a pinched voice. I started to bounce up and down on the balls of my feet and Lewis said, "No, not like that. I want to hold you real close and do dirty things and grab you in front of your boyfriend."

I pushed him away.

"I like you," he said. He still held me, but this time to dance.

"I didn't think you ever liked anybody."

"You didn't?" His eyes grew foggy, looking at me from some distance.

"You never let anybody in."

The fog lifted slightly; his eyebrows peaked.

"When I see all these men here," I told him, "I remember how you hated to be in a room with a lot of men you didn't know. You would be rude or ignore them."

"I did?"

"You used to go off by yourself. I remember once a group of us rode the subway downtown and you sat all by yourself."

He nodded. "I used to do that on subways."

"Do you remember Glassport?" Glassport was a town Lewis and I drove to one summer weekend to see a show of Ben's. It was the first time we'd ever spent any time together, and I always felt as if he'd discovered me on that trip.

"Discovered?" he said now.

"Yes. Noticed."

"I had a good time in Glassport," he said. "Why did we have separate rooms? You must have been married."

I didn't say anything. After a beat I said, "The last time I saw you was at Ben's show at HU Gallery. That was two years ago."

"Was it?" Lewis laughed. "So let's make up for lost time."

We found Spike and Daniel who said again to me, "I can't believe you never kissed one of these guys."

When we got to the cabin, I ducked into the bathroom to change quickly from my afternoon dress, but Spike was already talking in a high voice, speeding into fifth gear. She banged on the bathroom door. "Hurry up, hurry up, hurry up!"

"What for?"

"I want to smoke this, I want to go to bed, I want to get high. Hurry up, come on."

When I opened the door, Lewis and Daniel were seated at our oilclothed table, stuffed with chocolate cake.

"Good," she said when I came out. "I bet I know how to get you all outside." She lit the joint and walked out the door. We followed in a single-file shuffle.

There was mist on the pond and it began to drizzle, softly like a shower spray. Daniel and Spike headed back toward the cabin. Lewis started to follow and when I didn't said, "Guess I'm not," and walked back to me.

"I'm the girl who doesn't know enough to come in out of the rain."

He shook his head no and put his arms around me from behind. I turned around and he lifted me up into the air. "You look different at your cabin," he said to my fluttering hair.

DANIEL WAS HOLDING ONTO the pages of a story Spike had written. He was slumped on the sofa, with Spike sitting at the table, smoking a cigarette and watching him read. Daniel was mumbling to himself, and when I got closer I realized it wasn't about the story at all but about Spike.

"She has a great sense of humor," he said, then he went back to reading, saying the words just under his breath so he could follow them.

Spike said, "This is horrible watching someone read your stuff."

Lewis said, "I always leave the room."

Spike turned her back to him and walked into her room. I remained by the sofa where Daniel was clinging to the story pages. His lips were moving rapidly, his eyes fixed on the page, and without moving them, he'd stop his reading to himself and talk to me.

"Wow, this is strange," he said, and again I didn't think he was talking about the story.

He said, "I like this cabin. This is a great place to write." He looked frantic.

Finally I said, "The couch pulls out to a bed."

"Thanks." He dropped the pages. "Thank you."

Lewis was standing by the deck windows pulling the Afghan over his shoulders. He began to edge toward my bed, then Daniel piped up.

"Tina, do you have a blanket?" He asked. He was on the other side of the wall from us, just around the corner from my open doorway; there was no door, just a metal bar across the top over which I'd slung a cotton quilt held back by a rope.

I delivered his blanket and went back to Lewis. "How does that close?" he asked.

I released the rope.

"That's it?"

"I told you, it's a small cabin."

He put his arm around my waist. His face was in my neck, and he fell backward with me onto the bed. For the first time, he kissed me. He turned off the light and whispered, "We have to be quiet because of Daniel."

We kissed and stripped and stripped and kissed and he kissed my back and ran his hands along my back, and while he was running his hand along my hip, Daniel said from his couch around the corner, "I better get to sleep fast." Even Spike, who was supposed to be asleep, started laughing, then Lewis, then Daniel and me. We were a dark cabin full of laughing, nervous disorders.

Lewis kissed me. He moved on top of me so he could kiss me head-on. "I like to kiss," he whispered. "Do you like to kiss?"

"I like to be safe."

"Don't you have anything?" he asked.

"Of course, but that's not what I mean by safe."

"Oh, all right," he sighed, and reached for his wallet.

He kissed slowly and he moved slowly and he entered me one quarter inch at a time, until I was breathing so loudly it felt like the air was rushing out of my ears, nose, mouth, eyes. All at once, he put his hand on my shoulder, stopped moving his hips, and whispered, "Calm down." We stayed still.

We rolled onto our sides; he ran his hand along my hip, and we started again. I whispered, "I haven't made love like this in a while."

"I make love like this a lot."

I said, "I would've liked to have seen more of you first."

I meant seen more of his body before he turned out the light, but he answered, "I have this involvement." It was tough not to hurt him. He'd forgotten which Lewis he was supposed to be, knowing and complicated or foolish and transparent.

"We should spend a weekend together," he whispered. And he kissed me. I didn't say anything. It was better to be kissing. Moving.

"When did you decide to fuck me?" he asked.

I didn't answer.

"When you fucked me?"

Now he was on his back, playing with my breasts. "I like that," he whispered when I moved over him.

"I like that too," he whispered when I moved him inside. "When did you decide to fuck me?"

"At Monika's," I said.

"I don't believe that."

"You?"

"When you walked in the door."

"At the wedding?" I asked.

"Yes."

Suddenly I was taken by surprise. My pelvis gripped like it was girdled and I felt like I could lift my entire body off of his in one long muscle.

"What was that?" he said.

"What do you think?"

"What?"

"I thought you made love like this a lot." He kept kissing me.

"Can I come now?"

I didn't answer.

"I've got to come now." And he kissed me harder and ran his fingers around me. My head sank into the pillow by his ear.

"Do you like to talk after sex?" he asked.

"No."

"I like to talk after sex."

"Go ahead." I rolled onto my side so that I fit next to him, my back against his stomach. "Let's snuggle," he said, and pulled me closer.

At quarter to nine the next morning he woke up. "I want to make love again," he said, but we could hear Daniel fidgeting on the other side of the wall. It was too sunny, too open.

"Daniel, do you want to take a shower?" Lewis called out.

"No."

"I want to be inside you," he whispered, but it wasn't going to happen. He lay back, propped on one elbow. "Having to be quiet added another dimension to last night."

He pushed himself out of bed and stumbled into the bathroom.

I made coffee and helped Daniel put the sofa bed back together. Lewis, showered and wrapped in a towel, walked past us and stopped at Spike's room. He was staring at the floor. A puddle of water was seeping from her closet, running under her shoes.

"I'm sorry," he said, looking lost.

"What happened?"

"I guess it's the shower."

"Did you put the liner inside?"

"I guess not. I'm sorry."

Daniel had disappeared. I figured he was out by the pond and I took two cups of coffee, one for me and one for him. He was standing by the pine tree with the gash. It seemed too much like autumn with a cold, brisk wind blowing over the water, making it impossible to steer a canoe if we'd wanted to.

I handed him his mug of hot coffee.

"Thanks," he said. "I've never lived in solitude like this. It's nice." He bent his face to the mug.

Down by the pond, the water was a deep blue, taking on the ruddier colors of fall. The things I didn't say were, *Daniel, I know you're scared about going to LA. I know what it's like to be scared.*

The things he didn't say to me were, *God, I wish my life were different. How do other people get what they want?*

We headed back.

Lewis was in the kitchen making a fresh pot of coffee. I asked if they wanted breakfast, but they didn't.

We started talking about books. *The Kandy-Kolored Tangerine-Flake Streamline Baby* that Lewis had just finished. *The Good Soldier* that Daniel was reading.

Then Spike woke up. The three of us—Lewis, Daniel, and I—were huddled around the kitchen counter, holding our coffee mugs as if the stove were a campfire. Spike stumbled into the living room, lit a cigarette, and shuffled up to the stove.

Lewis said, "I can see you're not a morning person."

"See this fist?"

He laughed.

But she didn't have the energy to keep it up. She disappeared into the bathroom.

Lewis said, "Thanks for letting us stay, Tina. I'm really glad you did. I really mean that."

"Me too," I said, but I was feeling the imminence of their departure and it made me reluctant to say much, so I repeated what he said. "Yes, I'm glad we did this."

Lewis began packing his things. I asked if anyone wanted provisions for the road.

They refused, but I gave them plums anyway. Daniel started eating his immediately. "Daniel," Lewis said, "you're eating your provision."

I showed Daniel on the map where he was traveling to. Then they were packed and in the car.

Lewis said, "Come up to see the band."

"Sure."

"I mean it. Come on up."

"Okay."

He carefully backed the car around and drove down the dirt driveway.

CHAPTER THIRTY

WAS I IN A MEMORY SO SOON? My body was dazed, massaged from within. I floated from the kitchen to my bedroom to the bathroom to my bedroom and I lay there on my quilt, my face turned up to the late afternoon breezes, the trees shimmying their late summer leaves, all of my senses open and at the same time stuffed somewhat with cotton.

I lay still, with the trees sweeping their green scent across my cheeks and the light dancing on my arms and legs and the fluid pulse of the pond slapping against the banks. The phone rang and I didn't answer. The night came and I lay there, not wanting to move to lock the door or close the windows. I touched my neck, half believing I would feel a puncture that would explain why I felt so drained and woozy, conscious but unconscious of real time.

I knew no matter how it seemed, or how I tried to trick myself, that it wasn't Lewis that unglued me like this. I remembered wheeling from person to person over a wedding lawn lit by torches and catching the lights in the eyes of the nonjudgmental faces, and how full it felt, how it felt like freedom, as if I had dipped back to another soul, still living, still breathing inside—far below where the black worm slithered in its container—and it had been waiting. Yes, I'd come close enough to the edge to step back and away—and I knew what would happen now. I would not be what Spike wanted. And she would not be what I wanted.

I WAS WELL INTO THE THIRD day of drifting when the phone rang, and this time I answered it. The voice sounded dense and heavy. It made suggestions and I agreed. It waited for an argument and I said nothing, and it asked me if I were all right. While I talked, the kitchen came into view, or rather the images in front of me coalesced into a kitchen and I saw the plates still caked with chocolate, the crumbs so hard they looked like tiny brown pebbles, and there was a vibrant green stain on the side of the sink where the faucet had been dripping steadily. The puddle in the closet had evaporated, but Spike's shoes were still jumbled in a pile next to the door. And there was the blanket I'd taken out for Daniel, folded and pressed into a smaller shape like a flannel sausage. Yes, we'd had guests. And now we'd have more guests. I asked Chuck Peels, the dense voice on the other end, to come over later and we would go out. Then I left everything exactly where it was, walked down to the pond, and set sail in the raft.

It was chilly. To stay out longer I'd need a jacket, so I turned back, docked the raft, and climbed back up the hill to the cabin. The door was locked. But I hadn't locked it. I twisted the knob six or seven times. Then I started kicking the door. Nothing.

"Spike?" I yelled. "Are you in there? Spike?" Nothing.

The only accessible window was over the toilet in the bathroom, and it would have to do.

I hauled myself up and crawled through on my belly until I could touch the toilet seat, my legs still dangling outside in the air. Then I pulled through and clattered to the floor, a little bruised on the hip bones but otherwise all right. I marched to the front door. I turned the knob. Nothing budged.

What the hell was this?

I yanked, kicked, turned. Nothing.

By the time Chuck Peels showed up, I'd cleaned up the kitchen and read halfway into a new Anne Rice novel. I waved to him through the kitchen window. "The door won't open. Something's wrong with the knob. I was stuck outside. Now I'm stuck inside. I wish I didn't see truth in everything." I laughed.

"How'd you get in?"

"Bathroom."

Chuck, who looked glaringly cleaned and scrubbed, disappeared from my view from the kitchen. I went and stood by the door to the bathroom. "Careful. Careful." First his head and shoulders, then his torso, then his legs, flipped over the sink. His face was beet red.

"You sure don't make it easy for a guy."

"I knew you'd say something like that. It's not me. It's the door. I'm not being cute."

"Don't be so serious. I like coming to the rescue. Okay," he said, grabbing the doorknob. "You go like this." Nothing moved.

"Then you go like this." He did it again.

"Then you go like this." He kicked the door. The wreath with the rotted oak leaves plopped at his feet. "Get me a knife."

He tried springing the catch, but it wouldn't give.

"Well, the lock's broke. You're gonna have to bust it out. I can do that for you. But I may ruin your door." He put his hand on his hip and studied the floor. "I can do it. I don't know what else you're gonna do. But you may lose some of your door."

"Okay, do it. Pullet'll just have to pay for it, that's all. I can't crawl back and forth through the window. Do it. Bust it out!"

With a roar, he threw himself against the door and wrenched the lock from the frame. "Jesus!" I said.

A huge splinter of wood stuck up from the hole where the lock had been. "Could've been worse. See? See what happened?" He showed me the lock and all its rusting parts clutching to one another in a dead freeze. "Let me just nail this piece of wood down. You can use some rope to keep the door closed."

"This place is really going to hell. Rope on the door. Blown fuses. Bugs in the sheets." I gave him the hammer. "What next?"

The phone rang. Chuck began whacking nails into the wood and I said, "Hello? Can you speak up? Spike?"

"Yeah, who else? How's it going? Get laid again already?"

"No, I just woke up. It's good to hear from you. Where are you?"

"At work, where else would I be?"

"I don't know."

"I just called to tell you I met somebody."

"That's great." Chuck was rummaging through one of the drawers in the kitchen and I pointed to another where the nails were. "So what's his name?"

"Are you ready? Irv. And he owns two appliance shops on the Lower East Side. That's how he makes his money."

"Irv? How old is he?"

"I'm telling you, he's gorgeous. He's gonna take me fishing on his boat next Thursday. He wanted to go for the weekend, but I told him about the cabin, then he wanted to come up to the cabin, but I said no." She paused.

"Yeah, well." Did *she* know this was her third boat?

"You should've seen me the other night. I was on all fours, sprawled across the floor by myself so at least I could get a rug burn. And I started screaming, 'I haven't gotten laid all summer!' But I'm happy for you. I'm happy for you that you're getting laid. What're you going to do now? Call him?"

"Nothing."

"Shit, I would call him. If he was good, call him. Go ahead. Call him."

"Spike," I whispered. "We had a problem here."

"We? Who's we?"

"It's okay. Chuck Peels came over and helped fix it."

"Chuck is there? I thought you weren't . . . What's he doing there after you showed up with your boys?"

"Well, let me tell you what happened. The lock got stuck and he busted it out."

"What!"

"We had to break the door a little. I couldn't get in or out." Suddenly she wasn't there anymore.

"Spike?"

Her breathing came back, slow, controlled, and after a good, long time, she began speaking in a deep, dead bass. "I wish you hadn't done that."

"We had no choice."

"You should've called me. I can't talk about this now."

"Spike, it's no big deal."

"I'll call you later."

I held the receiver limply in my hand. "She hung up."

"What was that all about?" Chuck wanted to know.

"She's pissed off."

"Man, I never seen you like that."

"Like what?"

"Like you were being—I don't know. Nobody should have that kind of power over anybody."

"She was upset."

"Hell, you should see your face. And you two are gonna build a house together? C'mon. Let's go."

Chuck took me to the Lomatia Falls Lodge. Woody, his father, was there, standing at the point of a pyramid of beer buddies anchored at the bar. He was wearing the same green T-shirt he'd worn at the barbecue pit, his belly stretched over his belt, his face stretched oddly like his belly so that his cheeks bulged and fell. Chuck steered me past Woody but my arm was caught, pulled, and Chuck was reeled back with me.

"Ain't you gonna make her say hello?"

"She can say whatever she wants to."

"What you gonna say?" His beamy eyes danced over my face.

"Hello," I said dully.

"You datin' my boy?"

"We came here to bowl."

He howled. "Bowl? You say bowl?"

"C'mon." Chuck grabbed my arm back and steered me toward the stairs. "You watch how you bowl, now!" Woody shrieked after us.

"He's always like that," Chuck said, shaking his head, but he looked uncomfortable. "Don't let him bother you."

The smell of fried steak followed us, heavy as the dingy carpet under our feet. Upstairs, the wallpaper was so yellow in spots it looked burnt.

Chuck switched on the lights for the bowling lanes and a hum set in. The lights came on in shadows because some of the bulbs were missing, but I could see well enough. The lanes were wooden and scratched like old school desks. The ball felt smaller in my hand than a regular bowling ball, and it didn't have any bubblegum-pink dizzy swirls on it either. I shot it down the lane and it rumbled like a grumpy old man. When the ball hit, the glory exploded and echoed through the empty room and left behind four unconscious pins. Chuck sauntered to a spot behind the pins, picked up my ball, and rolled it back to me in the gutter lane.

"What're you doing?"

"This ain't automatic."

I stared at him.

"Look, we got electricity."

I fired the ball down the lane again and picked off two more pins.

Chuck was solicitous. I was the date. "Look," I said, "I could just keep throwing until I've knocked them all down."

"We're on the honor system here. Two balls, that's it."

"Well maybe we should move on to something else."

"Sure." He shrugged, and just for fun threw a strike. I waited till he put all the pins back in place.

He led me downstairs and I excused myself for the restroom.

"Isn't this place a kick?" The girl was combing her cottony-blonde hair in front of the mirror. I answered her reflection.

"Huh?"

"I never been here before; it's such a kick. My boyfriend wanted to play pool." She smoothed down the front of her tight, starched jeans and wiggled her pointy boots.

"You should go upstairs. They have a bowling alley that doesn't return the ball to you."

"Oooh!" she shrieked, covering her cheeks with her hands and giggling. "Isn't this a kick?"

Molly was behind the bar, leaning on her elbows.

"Hey!" she said, her dimples crinkling. "Chuck ordered you a screwdriver."

"You did?"

"Yup." His hands were hugging his thighs. He'd opened his shirt because he was sweating but before I could begin to stare, I felt a flank of heat at my side. Woody was there glowering at my neck, and I made a move as if to unpin my hair and let it down to cover myself.

"No," he said, catching my wrist. "Leave it up." His smile slid across his face as he leered first at me, then Chuck. "I'll tell you, there's nothin' like takin' down a woman's long hair and seeing it fall over the shoulders of a white negligee. Long hair," he half whispered, "and a white negligee."

"Jesus," Chuck said. "Get over there, they're waiting for you."

"Long white negligee," Woody hissed, moving off to the table. I shivered, full of the creeps.

"Now you see why my mom can't stand to be with him too long." I nodded, preferring to be silent.

"He don't even remember sometimes he got a son. People come up to me and they say, 'I didn't know Woody had a son.'"

"Well . . ." I looked around and said, "What're they doing?"

"Sing-along."

Woody stood like a cowboy with one boot on a chair, his butt on the back edge of another. He was waving to us to come over.

"Should we?"

"Up to you."

Chuck drew his legs around and put his hand on my back. "Go ahead. I'm coming."

"See these?" Woody said to me. "This is called playing the spoons. You ever play the spoons, sexy?"

I shook my head. More people had started to circle around Woody and the organ. A large woman squeezed behind the keyboard and propped up her card. "Granna."

"Listen up, learn something," Woody said.

He wedged two tablespoons between his thumb and finger and clicked them together like castanets. He flipped them upside down and clicked, then right side up and clicked them against his wrist. He clicked them against the table. He clicked them against his thigh. He held them in the air and clicked them in front of my eyes. Heavy, church-like chords suddenly vibrated through the room. Almost as quickly, they were transformed into a fast, folksy gallop, and Woody waggled his balloon cheeks and began to sing.

Granna tore into the organ, her sausage arms pumping up and down and her shoulders heaving. She whipped her head left and right, her face clear and shiny as a china plate.

"Oh when the saints . . ."

"When the saints!" someone shouted. "Go marching in . . ."

"Go marching in!"

A man with a beer mug began leading a curl around the tables. Molly, the bartender, grabbed on to the last waist in line, then snagged Chuck. He started singing, "Lord, I want to be in that number . . ."

"When the saints go marching in!"

Granna belted it out, her flat fingers pounding on the keys. A bar menu on the wall was her backdrop.

HAMBURGER: $2.75. FRENCH FRIES: 75¢.

There was a round of applause and banging on the piano.

Then somberly, like guests at a funeral, a woman and her small daughter wormed their way to the edge of the organ.

"Mrs. Leider and Greta!" Woody shouted, like a half-crazed Lawrence Welk.

They were dressed in identical purple outfits. Greta took her place in front of her mother.

Mrs. Leider handed her her instrument. Then she produced her own: a hat-rack stand with bells—or was it a pogo stick with cymbals?—a banjo and bellows rolled into one. Mrs. Leider cast a sullen look down the spine of the hat rack, then nodded to Greta. The cymbals clashed up and down. The bells tinkled and Mrs. Leider fingered the banjo at the bottom.

Granna sang, "Swanee, how I love you, how I love you . . ." and Woody clicked the spoons.

"What is that thing?" I yelled to Chuck.

"Oompah."

"Oompah?!"

Woody clicked the spoons on my thigh. *Pay attention!* Granna's fingers churned the keyboard. Someone handed me a washboard. I passed it to Chuck. Someone else handed me a tambourine.

"My dear old Swanee!"

Behind us the menu reminded me where we were.

LEMONADE: 45¢. TUNA FISH SALAD: $1.25.
SCREWDRIVERS: $1.75.

We ordered three, four, five screwdrivers.

"Give her the mic."

Woody's meaty hand was under my chin, the bulb of the mic at my mouth. "Climb ev'ry mountain. Ford ev'ry stream. Follow ev'ry rainbow."

CHILI: CUP 45¢.

"Till you find your dream!"

AT THREE O'CLOCK IN the morning, I started typing. "This is great. This is r-e-a-l. I found it—what I came here for. Greta and Mrs. Leider playing the oompah." My typewriter broke and I moved to Spike's. "They wear flat hats with violets. They sing together every Friday night. This is what I wanted. Real people. Real life. A washboard. No dictionaries." I had to get it down. The orange band of the correcting ribbon interrupted. *Uh-oh,* I thought, *near the end, better leave some.* But I kept on typing.

CHAPTER THIRTY-ONE

I WAS STILL TYPING WHEN SPIKE ARRIVED. "I hope you don't mind," I said, "but something happened and I had to get it down and yours is the only machine working here." She appeared not to hear me but went immediately to the couch and pulled out the sofa bed. "Wait," I said, "I'm moving." I pushed back the heavy floral chair and looked fleetingly at the lush blueberry bushes outside her window.

Spike was already under the sheets on the sofa bed. "Wait," I said again.

She buried her face into a pillow. Her hair was ratty. When she finally turned to stare at the ceiling, her face wore a glaze of space and paste. "I want to sleep. I've been up all night in a motel room."

"Why don't you sleep in your room?"

"Too late." She pulled the sheets up to her chin and rolled them into a bulge. "I didn't want to go back to my apartment because I didn't want him to know where I lived. So we went to a motel. You know what it's like to be punched hard in the arm twenty times. And I kept drying up. Then he woke me up in the middle of the night and started banging me again. I wasn't even awake."

"Christ."

"It felt like I was being split open."

"This is Irv?"

She nodded.

"I'm sorry."

"Yeah, well, so much for getting laid this summer." She turned her face into the nubby arm of the couch so that all I could see was her tangled red hair bleeding over the sheets.

I went into my room and sat down at my spastic typewriter. It jammed every twenty minutes or so, the motor grinding itself into a protest. I shut it off and stared out the window at the pond. The view was much more earthy here. It was absolutely quiet. After a while, I turned the machine back on and began picking away at the keys.

At around two o'clock, Spike woke up and stumbled into her room. I heard her curse.

Then I heard her pick up what sounded like a mound of clothing and toss it into the living room. A bag dropped into the hallway. Her voice whispered and simmered and rose to a boil. "Fucking . . . irresponsible . . . selfish . . ."

"Spike?"

The boiling went on. "Fucking insensitive . . ."

I tiptoed to the edge of my door and peeked out at her back. She was bending over a pile, kicking it, her hair a mass of bedraggled snakes. Before I could slink back to my room, she spun around.

"Did it ever occur to you that when you use something that belongs to somebody else you should ask? And if you use up the ribbon, you should replace it."

"I was going to go this afternoon," I whined, knowing I was wrong. "I forgot."

"You didn't even say anything. It didn't even occur to you that I might want to type something. That I came all the way up here to type the last chapter of my novel."

"Novel? What novel?"

"The one I've been working on all summer. And now I can't do it. Now you've ruined it!"

"It's only the correcting ribbon," I said weakly. "You can type without that."

"Why couldn't you!" Her hands whisked through her hair and

she kicked a pile of clothes in front of her, rolling them toward the front door. "You've ruined it!" she screamed again.

"I'll get you another one!" I shouted, trying to make myself heard.

She stepped on the sofa bed and tramped over it to her room. I heard her thrashing around and another bag was thrown into the living room. "All you do is think of yourself," she cried, crashing out of her room. Her arms were dripping with sheets.

"Look what you're doing with poor Chuck Peels. I don't have a chance!"

She grabbed a garbage bag and started stuffing it with clothes and all I could do was smile like an idiot and try not to, because it was a sick, arrogant smile. The unassailable self-proclaimed, self-created fuck-you queen thought she didn't have a chance with me?

The car revved. Her wheels threw up a storm of dust and she was gone. I looked at the pile of sheets outside her bedroom door. A suitcase was next to the sheets. "It's only a damn typewriter ribbon," I said out loud. "A damn *correcting* ribbon."

I took off down Blind Pond Road, running at a good pace in the dirt until I reached the trout stream where I'd tried to drown my jealousies about Mozzarella with his Ferrari and his fishing pole. God, that seemed like a long time ago.

Spike had her car trunk full of bags by the time I returned. She was shoving another into place when I walked past her. "While you were gone, Alma's canoe nearly floated out to the middle of the pond. Next time try tying it up."

"I didn't use her canoe."

"No, it just lowered itself into the water." I kept walking.

"It never occurred to you to hose it down, did it?" she screeched, slamming the trunk. "No, that would be too much like taking care of other people's things."

I let the front door click behind me, the new door lock already installed.

I walked to my room, engulfed by a strange calm. She couldn't touch me anymore. Something had been growing around me all summer, like a second skin, and she'd helped. *Please,* I wanted to say, *it doesn't have to end like this. Change with me.*

But as soon as she came back, slamming into the house, I stiffened. No, I wouldn't plead for her forgiveness and attest to how horrible I was, how many meals I didn't cook and pounds of garbage I didn't move. That's not what this was about. I curled up on my bed, trying to read what I'd written the night before but listening instead, straining to pinpoint each sound and figure out what was being taken. When she went out to her car, I skittered into the kitchen and grabbed a bag of corn chips and a big bottle of club soda and ran back to my bed. The chips were salty and I sucked on them to minimize the noise of crunching so I could hear better. She seemed to have calmed down because all I could detect was a swishing sound as if surfaces were being wiped. Then the phone rang. I stopped moving altogether.

"Hello?" Her voice was cheery as roses. "Just a minute." *Clunk.* "It's for you." Deadly again.

"Hey." It was Chuck.

"Hi." The phone was tucked into my neck and I slunk into the bathroom.

"What're you whispering for?"

"Nothing." Barely a squeak.

"Well, you gonna get your voice back by tonight?"

"Yes." Another squeak.

"Do me a favor. I forgot to tell Spike I'd pay her for the tickets. She got me five Yankee tickets and I forgot to tell her I'd bring her the money. Plus, I want to find out where I go to pick them up."

"You better ask her yourself. Maybe tonight. Or you might find her over at the new cabins."

"Can't you?"

"No," I whispered.

Silence. Then, "I'll pick you up at seven. We'll have dinner at that French place. You said you wanted to eat something fancy, so I figured we'd go there."

"You don't have to do that."

"I know I don't have to. I want to."

"Okay."

"You excited?"

"Sure."

"That's what I like."

"Yes, I'm excited. I just can't talk too loud."

"Why?"

"Because it doesn't feel right."

I could see him shaking his mystified head, maybe sitting at the kitchen table in his mother's house, engulfed by the vanilla smell of baby formula.

When I hung up, I heard clothes hangers crash to the floor. Then the silverware drawer scudded open to the tinkling sounds of cutlery being picked over and stacked in a pile. The plug for the electric blender was ripped from the wall. Towels were flicked and balled. And the refrigerator opened. *Go ahead*, I thought. *Leave me with no food. Take the mustard. Take the pickles. Take, take, take.*

Her footfalls were giant thuds across the floor, a kick to the door, then silence. Her car motored off again.

My shoulders sagged. Even my stomach. All of me sagged deep into the bed with relief.

I swam out of the bedroom, moving my arms in wide arcs to get rid of the tension in the air. Of course I could leave, go home to the city, but as soon as I considered that, I dismissed it. I wasn't about to be driven out. I crept around and surveyed the damage. Hadn't I done this before? Wasn't that when I'd come back from Ohara's and found the knives gone? Oh, this was ridiculous.

She was gone a good two hours, and I figured she was setting up house in the new cabin.

If she planned on sleeping there, she'd be awfully cold.

I smelled her before I saw her. Her musk was unmistakable. "Your buddy Chuck found me at the cabin."

She was standing with her hand on her hip, half in shadow. "He brought his other friends with him too. That Karl. They were all drunk and drinking beer."

I brushed my hair.

"That's just great sending them over there. Makes a great impression on Konrad." Our new landlord.

"I didn't send them anywhere."

"How'd he find me, then?"

"I'm sure he wasn't drunk."

"He was drunk and they were all crushing beer cans!" she screamed, coming out of the shadows. "I was embarrassed!"

"Okay."

"Next time why don't you think before you send your trash over? We promise that we'll be quiet and the first thing Konrad sees is a truckload of boys drinking beer."

Nothing.

"And one of them pissed in the road!"

"Spike, I'm not going to play."

"It made me feel like a liar. And I don't even know them!"

"I told you I'm not going to play. Say what you want. I'm not going to fight with you."

"You think the world revolves around you. You never think, never consider how other people feel, how *I* might feel."

She vanished to her bedroom.

In my drawer, I found a joint. Grabbed it and decided to smoke it outside. At the last minute, I took my keys.

The lawn was soggy beneath my sneakers. The moon was almost full and lit the fallen maple on the water. The chill from the grass hustled me along, and I took the path behind the shed that led to a sandy clearing. Tonight the inky water lapped at the sand and the frogs trilled like birds. The moon seemed to be preparing the earth to harden, and the leaves rustled with hurried life before the change.

Damn.

The door was locked. How sad and absurd and rotten that I could predict it. I used my key and entered as if nothing were unusual. And she did not look up. She was sitting at the oilclothed table, papers scattered, a bottle of wine next to her. I went to my room. The bottle of club soda was gone. I opened the drawer where my writing was stored and also $200 as a deposit for my new cabin. Both were still there, and I immediately felt foolish. Then I flopped on the bed and began reading my notes about the oompah and laughed and I heard, "Why don't you just shut up? Can't you see I'm writing?"

I closed my eyes, wondering if she could hear that.

I NEARLY POUNCED ON CHUCK. "Hi, hi, hi, hi!"

"Hi, Chuck," Spike called in a sunny voice. "Come on in. Now, did you get everything you need to know about the tickets? Good. I think you'll have a really great time." My toes itched and I kept shifting from foot to foot. "I love the Yankees," she cooed, and I went back to my bedroom. I opened the drawer, took out my money and my papers, and walked nonchalantly out to my car. I shoved them both under the front seat.

Chuck was straddling a chair in front of her, tipping it back and forth.

"Whirly and I tried to see a game this summer."

Spike's voice sweetened the room. Did she say Whirly? Did she forget she was disgusted with me?

"It's really fabulous if you sit behind third base," she went on.

I sauntered outside and retrieved my things from my car. I stood there, alone. *This is ridiculous.*

I didn't want to be right about her locking me out. I didn't want to be right about her tampering with my things. *Give her the benefit of the doubt.*

I shoved my belongings back in my drawer and returned to the living room to listen to more Yankee stories. Chuck looked up, curious to see what I was doing walking back and forth, in and out.

"Ready?" he said.

"Bye-bye," Spike called from the table, her voice timid as buttercups.

"Tell me," I said to Chuck once inside the safety of his small car, "did you show up drunk at the cabin?"

"No."

"Are you sure?"

"Yeah. We had some beers, but none of us were drunk. Why? Did we cause some trouble?"

"I was just wondering . . . I heard . . ."

"We weren't drunk."

I looked out at the dark bumping past on the dirt road and sank down into the seat. "Spike's in a bad mood."

CHAPTER THIRTY-TWO

I CAN'T QUITE REMEMBER WHAT I expected to find that night when I returned to the cabin. Maybe that's because I was more intent on bracing myself for the next day, believing she'd be asleep when I got home. Even when I saw that the lights were still on, it didn't occur to me that anything was wrong. It was one in the morning; she must've fallen asleep at the table, I thought, knocked out by the wine. I've wondered since if she'd planned everything somehow—from the first day I saw her on Tillie Skokel's porch to that night. And I've even wondered if we both planned it, without knowing it, which doesn't make sense—but I can only say that finding her on Tillie Skokel's porch and finding her in the cabin that night, in the state I did, was like the beginning and ending of the same nightmare.

At first, I didn't even see her there on the couch beneath the awful geese. Then I knew she'd been waiting for me. Her legs were crossed at the knee. Her cigarette was pointing straight up. And her hair was flaming over her bare arms. I was prepared for her to tell me how selfish I was for staying out so late with Chuck, for leading him on; I was prepared for her to tell me that she had moved out and stayed awake to say goodbye. I started to ask, "Why?" but I felt myself go suddenly limp.

"How does it feel to be raped, pal?"

"Huh?"

"You heard me." The lights seemed to be on fire—more brilliant than I could ever recall.

I didn't move. "How does it feel to be raped?"

"I don't know what you're talking about."

"Nooooo. Well think again, pal." She began kicking the couch with the heel of her shoe, banging it back and forth like a metronome. I stayed back, standing at the kitchen counter, barely past the vestibule.

"Think of what?"

"Of my manuscript you stole."

"What manuscript?"

"The one you stole, the one I've been working on all summer and now it's gone. There's only one other person here besides me, pal. Don't fucking lie to me."

"What manuscript? I don't have any manuscript. I didn't even know you were working on a manuscript until yesterday. I've never even seen one!"

"Liar. Just tell me where it is and you'll get your typewriter back."

"What?" I let go of the counter and spun into my room. The typing stand was empty. I knew before I opened the drawer. Still, I thought, *She didn't, she couldn't.* I kept flapping my hand in the drawer, trying to feel the money, not ready to concede it was empty . . . because if it was, I wouldn't be able to stop what was happening—the grip that had taken hold of my fist and kept banging it into the dresser and banging it into the wall, I couldn't stop it, I couldn't stop screaming, "What did you do with my things? What did you do with my things? What did you do with my things?"

"How does it feel to be raped, pal?" she said, standing at the door with a rifle.

I was blinking my eyes and shaking my head, trying to make room for this madness. Was this a joke? Was she serious? Was it loaded?

"Maybe if you spent a night at home, you'd remember where you put my manuscript."

"I didn't know anything about a fucking manuscript! What did you do with my things?" My face felt like it was on fire. I thought if I could tell somebody, reach Chuck, get help. I stalked past her and grabbed the phone.

"Just try it, pal!" She turned the rifle on me. "I'm ready for it. I'd love it. Just try it."

I looked down at my hand, shaking as if I had blurred vision, and swam my eyes around the room. It suddenly looked so yellow in all that lamplight and so shabby.

"Go outside," she said. She nudged me with the rifle and I didn't move. My mind needed to be held in. It was exploding. "Go on, liar," she said.

Outside the night seemed frigid and dangerous. "There are your goddamned things," she snarled. "In your car." She poked the rifle in my back while I stumbled across the driveway, trying to make sense of her muttering. "Stop," she said, when I got to the car. "Open the door." I heard a sound that made me sick in my stomach. I turned my head and saw she had raised the rifle to her shoulder. It was shaking wildly and she was cursing. One side of her face was against the rifle and the other looked contorted as if she were grinning or in pain. I saw her finger move up toward the trigger. I saw the trigger moving. I dove into the car, smashing my head on the frame. For a moment I was dazed. Then I heard the shots.

When the upholstery came into view, I realized that I must have fainted. I was lying face down on the car seat, but there was no blood. My typewriter and files sat undisturbed on the floor. Slowly, I crawled out, dropping to my knees behind the open car door. I noticed an odd smell and turned to find that my back tire had been shot out. The front tire was flat too.

Trapped. She had me trapped. I scanned the driveway from behind the shield of the door. Her car was gone.

Alma's lights were blazing, and she came to the window almost as soon as I started banging on the door. "Something's happened!" I shouted. "I can't go outside. I can't go to the cabin."

She edged the door open and peered at me, too alarmed to ask a question. "Imogene's not here," she finally managed.

"It'll be all right," I said, barging into her living room. "I'll sit right here, on your sofa. You go back to sleep."

When she was still standing in the same spot next to the door, I said, "I appreciate this, Alma. It'll be all right. I promise. This is temporary." She locked the door and scurried into her room, and I lay down on her couch with my knees scrunched up to my chest.

I woke in my clothes. The lights were still on and Alma was snoring from behind the wall that separated us. I looked out the dirt-streaked window that faced the pond. Spike was pacing, more like drifting, back and forth across the same straight line, her head down, a black shawl wrapped around her shoulders. Her hair fell in dark coils down her back, and I watched her move a cigarette to her lips and take it away again.

I scuttled back to the couch and sat hugging my knees.

About half an hour later, I heard the trunk of a car slam closed. Then came the familiar sound of Spike's car motor and the crunch of her tires as she drove down the rutted driveway.

I waited another half hour before leaving the trailer. I crept outside and began to move toward the cabin, keeping my eyes wide open as if that would heighten my hearing. Once inside, the density of the air shifted and shifted again, and I knew, without looking, that the cabin was empty of all of her things. I stood still, breathing in the emptiness. Suddenly the phone rang.

Before I had the receiver to my ear, I could hear her crying. "Tina," she said, "are you there? I think I'm going crazy. Oh, Tina, I'm so sorry. I looked all over for that manuscript. Konrad's going to think I'm nuts. I kept going through the trash cans at the cabins, thinking maybe I threw it out by mistake. Tina, I'm scared, maybe I dreamed it up. Maybe I left it at home and I imagined I saw it on the bed. Maybe I didn't write it at all. What's happening to me?"

Oh how I wanted to hang up, to shout, "You almost killed me!" but I didn't. I needed to hear what she had to say. I heard her light a cigarette and I could almost see her sweeping her hair back.

"I was all set to mail that manuscript to Eric Blauner," she said. "Do you know who he is?"

"No."

"He's the editor who got Raymond Carver published. Irv knows him." I was quiet.

"If Blauner likes it, I'm in. I had it all ready to send to him. I had the envelope made out, I bought tons of stamps. Now I can't even find the damn thing."

She waited for me to comfort her. I felt like a piece of cold steel being asked to float. "Is the Sunny Lee story part of it?" I asked finally.

"Yeah. Sunny Lee grows up and finds out nothing ever happened that she thought happened to her. It's the best work I've done so far. I want to show it to one person. Blauner's it. He's going to make me famous. You don't know what power is. You haven't worked with it like I have. He can do it."

"I'm sure."

"As usual, whatever you haven't experienced isn't true."

I didn't argue. The sudden stillness of the moment seemed to corner us both. "Spike," I said finally, "I've had enough. Really. I've had enough for ten years. No more. Please."

I walked down to the creek to watch the clear water swirl through the rocks. When I finally went back inside the cabin, it felt as if a cold wind were blowing through, loaded with her musk. I swept the floor, unplugged the refrigerator, then went outside and hosed down the canoe for the last time.

The men from the garage had come and put two new cheap tires on my car. No one asked a question, and I didn't volunteer any answers. With the trunk full of worn clothes and boxes of books, I put the car in gear to make the long trip back to the city. All the way home, I kept talking to myself about ending things and starting things. If I'd come through this intact, I figured, I would be all right from now on. Really. I'd made it.

I arrived home by six. Before unpacking, I immediately went out and celebrated my survival by buying an aquamarine dress. It was the color that drew me. The bluish-green clarity of buoyant wave upon wave. I laid it on the couch so it could infuse the room with aquamarine light. I fixed a drink. That's when I noticed the blinking light on the answering machine. I punched the button to hear my messages.

"I'm calling from the cabin." The acid in her voice made my face hot, and I looked wildly around the room as if she would be emerging any minute. "It's midnight. You're out with Chuck Peels. I'm sitting here reading and drinking champagne. And I just wanted you to know—no matter what happens—I think you're a dangerous person."

SO MAYBE I DID steal her manuscript.

And this is it. When and if I have the courage to publish it, I hope she's far away. I hope she's living on one of those boats she always talked about, cresting the waves at their peaks and grasping the stars in her fists.

She never did return to claim her cabin at Konrad's. He and I went in there finally and felt the same cold wind that blew through from end to end in our other cabin. A picture of Eric Blauner, the famous editor, was nailed to the wall in the center of the room, a picture cut from a magazine. She'd left us behind, and I could almost hear her she-wolf laugh on the wind. And I see now what was obvious all along—that I was not so interested in the truth. No. She was such a good storyteller, she made the truth irrelevant.

This is what it comes to, a year later, in my mind.

Chuck, I hear, has returned to Virginia and become involved with a nurse. Klaus is living in the Bahamas, selling real estate. Mozzarella was written up in the papers for insider trading.

Ben and Ohara are still making pretty pictures from nature inside and outside their house. And every Friday night there's a sing-along at the Lomatia Falls Lodge and a live band at the Starlite. I know because I continue to rent Konrad's cabin and drive up from the city on the weekends. I took a job with an independent press and there is an editor here who cares for me, brings me gifts, and lets me leave him for the weekends and come back to him during the week. He's like a level raft that I float on.

But I haven't let go of Warrenville. It resonates, still, and the temptation to take my trips has weakened, but I would be a liar if I said I were clean of it. Instead, I can tell you that it takes just as much searching to find our own dark devils as it does to seek out someone else's, and that once you do, you won't have to dive as deeply into the shadows again and you'll know you can survive.

I dream of Spike often, without a face, only her hair and her scent and her big, bold laugh. And sometimes I spook myself and think I see her on the street, and other times I'm sure that I'll turn around and see her there, cigarette tilting upward, eyebrow raised, waiting for me, ready to ask, "Why did you steal my story?"

And I know what I would do. I would turn away, frightened. Then I would come back, curious to see what had happened to her and to measure what had happened to me, if I could think straight, because by that time the thrill would be creeping back into my heart. I know it, because every journey leaves some yearning. So I would smile. Yes, even after everything, I would grin like a conspirator and say, "Okay. Is there anything else you had to tell me? Load your rifle. Shoot."

PLAYLIST IN THE BOOK . . .

"Mad Love," The Pretty Reckless, 2016
"Shout," The Isley Brothers, 1959
"Half as Much," Patsy Cline, 1962
"The End," The Doors, 1967
"Bad Sneakers," Steely Dan, 1975
"I Only Have Eyes for You," The Flamingos, 1959
"When The Saints Go Marching In," Louis Armstrong, 1938
"Swanee," Al Jolson, 1920
"Climb Ev'ry Mountain," Oscar Hammerstein II and Richard Rodgers, 1959

BEYOND THE BOOK . . .

"You Wreck Me," Tom Petty and the Heartbreakers, 1994
"Maneater," Daryl Hall & John Oates, 1982
"New York," U2, 2000
"The Boys of Summer," Don Henley, 1984
"Love Shack," The B-52's, 1989
"I Wanna Dance with Somebody," Whitney Houston, 1987
"Get the Party Started," Pink, 2001
"Dance the Night," Dua Lipa, 2023
"I Love It," Icona Pop featuring Charli XCX, 2012
"Why?" Bronski Beat, 1984

"Everybody Wants to Rule the World," Tears for Fears, 1985
"It's the End of the World as We Know It (And I Feel Fine)," R.E.M., 1987
"Don't You (Forget About Me)," Simple Minds, 1985
"Waiting on a Friend," The Rolling Stones, 1981
"Every Breath You Take," The Police, 1983
"Summer Madness," Kool & The Gang, 1974

A DANGEROUS FRIENDSHIP CREDIT LINES

Half As Much

Words and Music by Curley Williams

The End

Words and Music by John Densmore, Robby Krieger, Ray Manzarek and Jim Morrison

Bad Sneakers

Words and Music by Walter Becker and Donald Fagen

Climb Ev'ry Mountain

from THE SOUND OF MUSIC
Lyrics by Oscar Hammerstein II
Music by Richard Rodgers

The lines of poetry on page 211 are from Richard Hugo's "The Towns We Know and Leave Behind, the Rivers We Carry with Us," which appears in *White Center: Poems* (W. W. Norton, 1980).

ACKNOWLEDGMENTS

THANK YOU TO Brooke Warner and the incredible She Writes Press community. To my family—Laura and Jon—and to my friends, who have supported me through a ridiculous number of years, you have my deep, deep gratitude and love. And to my husband, Douglas, who wouldn't let this manuscript sit on the shelf any longer, thank you with all my heart.

ABOUT THE AUTHOR

ROBIN MERLE is the author of *Involuntary Exit: A Woman's Guide to Thriving After Being Fired*. She has published short fiction in *The Chouteau Review*, *South Carolina Review*, *Kalliope*, and *Real Fiction*. She holds a master's degree from The Johns Hopkins Writing Seminars, where she earned a fellowship. In her other professional life, as a nonprofit executive, she has raised over a half-billion dollars in philanthropic support to improve individuals' quality of life and access to opportunities. A longtime New Yorker, Robin now lives in Maine with her family.

All About Headshots by Alissa Randall

Looking for your next great read?

We can help!

Visit www.shewritespress.com/next-read or scan the QR code below for a list of our recommended titles.